Raven's
WINGS

Lenise,
He will lift
you up because
He loves you.

Love,
Maxine
Johnson
I Kings 17: 4-6

Raven's WINGS

Maxine Johnson

TATE PUBLISHING
AND ENTERPRISES, LLC

Published by Tate Publishing & Enterprises, LLC
127 E. Trade Center Terrace | Mustang, Oklahoma 73064 USA
1.888.361.9473 | www.tatepublishing.com

Tate Publishing is committed to excellence in the publishing industry. The company reflects the philosophy established by the founders, based on Psalm 68:11,
"The Lord gave the word and great was the company of those who published it."

Book design copyright © 2015 by Tate Publishing, LLC. All rights reserved.
Cover design by Joana Quilantang
Interior design by Caypeeline Casas

Published in the United States of America

ISBN: 978-1-68097-983-1
Fiction / Christian / General
15.09.29

I would be remiss if I didn't honor our Creator God by giving Him the glory for all the work of my hands and heart. He has bestowed upon all of us the ability of create something. We are created in His image and have that gift. So, Father in Heaven, this book, inspired by the wonderful accounts of the lives of men and women in your Holy Bible, I dedicate to You.

I also want to dedicate this book to my dear friend Linda Simcox, who has been an inspiration to so many hurting hearts over the years. She has felt the sorrows of so many and comforted them as well as encouraged them. You are precious in His sight, dear friend.

Acknowledgments

I want to thank my wonderful husband, Bob, without whom this work of love never would have happened. He has been my encourager and as patient as Job with my peaks and valleys. I love you!

In addition to him and his support, I want to thank our daughters: Lorien Smith, for her much needed editorial skills and delightful insights, and Eowyn Lasecki, for her "tech support." I also want to thank all those who have read the first book and have cried out for more. You have truly been an inspiration. Thanks to all of you for your love, encouragement, and prayers. Here's "our" second-born!

1

Baltimore, Maryland, July 1880

The sweat poured off her brow. She could only hope the moisture didn't take off the charcoal and ash stains she had carefully placed on her face and in her hair to give it a graying look. She had to get away without being recognized. She just had to escape! Desperation ate at her heart like a canker and drove her to leave during the daylight hours.

"It will work out better this way, won't it, Lord?" She clutched at her bag, pulling it to her chest. *No one will miss me until later in the day. Morning is the best time with everyone else sleeping in, except for the cleaning girls and the cook. They won't start working until a little later, and they don't pay attention to us.*

She prayed they wouldn't see her leave if they were up. She didn't see anyone when she snuck out the back way. She had prodded and poked around in the back alley so she would look like a beggar woman looking through all the garbage lying around in the muck. She had found that old hat and scarf there. How providential! In her heart, she knew she would have to keep "small," not rush, and appear old and feeble when in reality, she is tall and only twenty-four.

"Only twenty-four?" she asked herself as she hobbled along toward the docks. "I feel older than dirt! Thank you, God, for giving me the insight to prepare for this day."

All she had was an old carpet bag that held just one dress, a small tin of ash, a piece of charcoal, and her brush. In addition to those, she had the clothes on her back. She had been saving for

9

this day for years. Had it been eight years? Yes, eight years next month since she had been taken—kidnapped, really. *I felt so angry with you, God, for my heartache upon heartache until I remembered Joseph had been sold into slavery by his own brothers, and your hand was in that for a greater good. Maybe that is what's happening in my life,* she prayed so.

"Hey, ya ole crone! Watch wher' yer goin'!"

"Oh, I'm so very sorry," she croaked to the man who stumbled toward the saloon a bit too early in the day.

Just a few more blocks and she would be within sight of her goal—freedom! She could feel the air coming off the ocean now. She also could feel some of her padding slipping from its place. She hobbled over to an alley and stepped just inside out of the way of the others hurrying here and there. *It seems Baltimore bustles with activity on every street. They look like so many June bugs buzzing around trying to decide what to sample next.*

She made it look like she was just in the alley to catch her breath as she shoved and tucked the rolls of old clothing and rags she had wrapped around her slim figure to make herself look more matronly. Dare she say fat? *No, I don't look quite that rotund, just plump.* As she looked down at her feet just beside her in the puddle of who knows what that added to the foulness of the air, she saw a cane. *How wonderful!* Now, she could really give the impression of being elderly. She had managed to keep slumped over, but with the cane that would be easier. *Funny, how appearances give people a variety of impressions about others.* As she squatted down to pick up the cane, she heard a man's voice right next to her.

"Here, now, let me get that."

She looked up to see a very large man looking right at her. His bearing and manner made him look like the captain of a ship with his feet spread and his fists firmly planted on his hips. *He's used to giving orders,* she thought as she slowly rose, holding on to the brick wall at her side her fingers grasping tightly between the bricks feeling the rough surface of the mortar and sharp edges of the bricks.

The cane may have been lost by some passenger of his, and he came back to find it for them. She could not find her voice.

Using the toe of his boot, he pulled the cane from the puddle, then wiped it off with a handkerchief, and handed it to her. "Here ya go, and where are you headed this beautiful mornin', little lady?"

Taken aback at his pleasant manner, her mind raced with a whole new series of thoughts. *Little lady? He knows! He gave me the cane. Speak to him, you simpleton!*

"Oh, are you talking to me? I am amazed you think I'm a little lady. I was once...I suppose."

He laughed a hearty laugh, looked, at her, and put on his best Scottish brogue. "Well, ye are a lady and ye are a wee bit smaller than me own self. Ye know, don't ye, now?"

"Well, yes, I suppose I do, kind sir."

"Where were you headed before you dropped your cane? That way goes to the docks, and a not-so-pleasant group of men might give you a hard time. How about I walk with you, if that's where you're going?" He had resumed his normal speech.

"Oh, that would be ever so kind! I was going there to find a ship to take me at least to Charleston. I want to go to New Orleans and then on farther West."

She appeared to be nervous or desperate since she was traveling alone, and she looked so much like his dear departed grandmother; his heart broke. *Dear Lord, help me to do the right thing,* he prayed.

"Well, I'm Captain McBride at your service, ma'am. My ship sails this afternoon for New Orleans, and we will be making a stop in Charleston, briefly. If you would like to sail with me, I'd be most delighted." He winked and slipped into his Scottish brogue, "Ye remind me of me own grandmater now, ye do. I was a wee lad when I last saw her." He smiled the brightest, most genuine smile she had seen since before her mother became ill.

Dear Lord, help me do the right thing, she prayed and then looked up into his bright, clear eyes.

"I am afraid I can't pay much. I will have to stay below in some sort of hole, I guess. But I am very grateful for your help, even if you use me for the anchor!" She half-giggled.

With that, he laughed again. "No, that will not do. I am so very sorry, but we have no 'steerage' on board my ship. I will give you the only cabin left, if you are willing to stay in it."

"Whatever you think is best. I insist that I must pay." Captain McBride began to shake his head. Raven quickly added, "Oh yes, that would be only right." Raven's voice dropped to a whisper, "I just don't have much."

"Well, tell me how much you can afford to pay, and we will see what can be done."

"I think I could pay…" With that, she grabbed his arm, pulled him down toward her, and whispered her offer in his ear. It was more than she had planned on paying for her passage, but she was afraid to offend him.

He looked at her and wrinkled his brow. "Now, I don't know who you think I am, but that is way too much for this little cabin I have available. Oh no, way too much. I will take only a third of that amount, and that will include your meals."

She looked at him in disbelief. She was sure passage by ship would have been much more even without the meals. "What kind of ship do you have?" Raven was a bit suspicious of his generous offer.

"It is a cargo ship, we don't usually carry passengers. But I will in your case."

"Oh, not a passenger ship;" Her heart took flight as she thought this was the best plan yet. *Who would look for me on a cargo ship? They would look on all the passenger ships, trains, and stagecoaches before thinking of cargo ships if they thought of them at all. I go before you, God had told His people. He must be going before me. This must be how a bird feels when she is let out of a cage.*

"All right, Captain McBride, we have a deal." They shook hands, her gloves covering her very smooth delicate skin. He offered her his arm, and they walked slowly toward the docks with her leaning slightly on her cane while he measured his steps to match hers.

Suddenly, it seemed the sun had come out from behind a Cloud, and the wind felt fresh and clean on her very dirty face. *Yes, God is in this adventure. Please, continue to go with me, Abba Father. Blind the eyes of Pharaoh, and keep his ears from hearing. I won't ask for his destruction. That is in your hands; you are the judge.*

2

A clipper ship? Captain McBride!" Raven stood next to him, looking at the most beautiful ship she had ever seen.

"Yes, ma'am. She's the fastest ship in this port, maybe in the whole Eastern Seaboard. I sail to Europe some, but mostly, I make runs to the islands in the Caribbean and along the coast of the Gulf of Mexico. I have been thinking of trying to get into some ports in Mexico and South America. I don't know yet. Maybe, if the good Lord will allow it. By the way, I don't think I heard you say your name."

"Oh my goodness, how very rude of me. I am so sorry. My name is Kerr, Mrs. Raven Kerr. I lost my husband some years ago and just don't even say my name to many people. No one seems to care anyway." Her voice sounded like an old crow cawing so the name fit her very well.

"They don't care? Why would they not care to learn your name?"

"People don't have much 'delight' in the elderly, Captain, especially when we are slow and need help. Most people are looking for the young and strong in this world."

"That is truly a sad thing to say. I hope it is not as true as you seem to have experienced. Perhaps in a new place, you will find new attitudes toward the elderly."

With that, he led her up the gangway and onto his ship, making sure she had a firm grip on his arm. "Shall I give you the grand tour?" he asked as he looked at the sun beginning to rise higher in the sky.

"Oh yes, please. I would love to see your ship."

"If you will excuse me for just one moment, I need to talk with my first mate." As she nodded and turned to reply, he had already covered a good distance with those very long legs. She noticed the man he spoke with was not dressed nearly as neatly as the captain, but he was not at all scruffy either. *He could use a haircut. Too bad he hadn't taken advantage of that while in port. I could offer to mend that hole in his shirt. Maybe it's the only one he has.*

She turned away and looked at the other ships docked nearby and wondered where each would be sailing. *Have they just docked? Are they getting ready to sail? Are the sailors happy to be in port finally? Are they anxious to set sail?* She thought of her father and the mood swings he would have, joy at being home after being away for weeks, sometimes months. Then restlessness would settle over him like a heavy blanket, and he would become more like those crazy little ants that scurry here and there without any apparent purpose. Suddenly, he would be gone again. He would sail off to some new destination or revisit some old one. He was so happy at sea.

"This way, my lady." She jumped at the sound of his voice. She hadn't even heard him come up to her.

"I'm sorry. Did I startle you?"

She smiled. "Only a little. I was trying to figure out if the ships had just come in or were on their way out. I was just lost in thought, pretending to know where they had come from and where they were going, and so I didn't hear you come back."

With that, he led her in the direction of the bow. "We will begin here and end at the stern."

"I can't wait." Her heart was beating so fast she again clutched her carpetbag to her chest hoping to cover any noise her heart might have been making.

"Oh, I am so thoughtless. Here, let me have that." He reached for the carpetbag.

"Whatever for?" She clutched the bag tighter.

"I'm going to have Sven take it to your cabin. Sven! Come over here, you landlubber!"

Sven's blond hair caught in a ponytail stuck to the sweat beading on at the nape of his neck. His blue eyes sparkled in the late-morning sun. His broad shoulders and large hands testified to his seafaring Swedish heritage.

"Now, Cap. Ya know I have been ta sea since I was just a little boy. Ja, I'm more a sailor than a landlubber any day."

"Sven, this is Mrs. Kerr. She will be traveling with us. Will you please take her things to her cabin?"

"Which one is her cabin, sir?" he asked, reaching for her bag.

Why, he looks for all the world like what I picture Vikings would look like! Raven thought as she reluctantly gave her bag to him.

"You know very well which one is her cabin! Now, get gone."

"But, Cap." Sven saw the stern look in McBride's eyes. "Aye, sir."

"Now, Mrs. Kerr, shall we?"

Confusion registered on Raven's face. *Sven is not the first mate he had been talking to, so how would he know which cabin was mine?* she wondered. Raven was not at all sure what just happened, but she was sure there were some hidden meanings in that exchange. However, she was not going to let it bother her. She was going to enjoy the journey. She couldn't wait to see what happened next in God's plan to help her escape. As dirty as she was, she felt cleaner already. The sea air blew gently against her skin. She wished she could take off all of her burdensome clothes and wear a light summer dress so she could be at least a little cooler. She was beginning to ripen beyond the point of endurance. Body odor in a man was one thing; in a woman, unheard of!

She saw the galley, crew's quarters, a small room that declared "McBride" on its door, and the hold filled with the most amazing things, stacks and stacks of crates, and barrels holding food, fabric, furniture, and even medical supplies. All headed south. The last place McBride took her was to her cabin. When he opened the door, she could not believe her eyes.

"Why, this is like a mansion! I cannot possibly afford this! Plus meals?"

"I told you the price, and we made a deal. Why are you backing out of the deal now? You can't anyway. We have set sail. Unless you want to swim back to shore, that is."

For the first time since meeting Captain McBride, fear gripped at her heart.

"We have set sail? When did we do that? I didn't even feel the ship move!"

Her voice was getting worse and worse. She was going to lose it if she continued to talk. She shoved past him, a bit too robustly for an old woman, and then caught herself. "Oh! Now I have done it! I have twisted my back again. I do that every time I get a little agitated and move too quickly. Sometimes, I think I'm still eighteen," she said as she gave a soft sigh, holding her hand to the small of her back.

McBride looked at her suspiciously and then let it go. She needed help to find a place to sit, the bed perhaps. "Here, let me take you to the bed."

"Oh no, no, just a chair will be fine. I don't need to lie down."

"Very well, come here. Let me help you to this chair by the windows next to this table. You really need to rest. You look exhausted. I'll have someone bring you some hot water. Maybe a good soak in a hot tub will help that back."

"Oh no, no, don't bother. I think I will sit for just a little bit, and then maybe some tea will make me relax. My throat is rather sore. I hope I'm not getting sick." *That's always a good excuse,* she thought.

"Very good, I'll have Jasper—you remember the cook down in the galley? He'll bring you the things you need for tea, a little something to eat, and some water for a sponge bath, if you don't want a tub bath."

"What are you hinting at, young man?"

"Remember, I think of you as my grandmother. Isn't that so?"

"Yes, that's quite correct as you've said."

Slipping into his Scottish brogue, he winked at her and said,

"Well, Grandmater, you've had quite a day, and you'd benefit greatly from taking a bath and maybe washin' those clothes."

"Well, I never!" She lowered her eyes and tried not to giggle. "Very well, I will try to make myself more presentable, but I can't promise I'll smell like a rose. It just can't happen overnight, you know."

McBride left the cabin, smiling to himself. *There is something just not quite right about that woman. Is she crazy?* "No. I think it goes deeper than that."

"What does, Captain?"

"Oh, nothing, Walter. Will you go and tell Jasper I need to see him right away? Above…by the wheel. Thanks."

"Right away, sir."

Something just isn't quite right. What is it, Lord? Show me. "I have such peace about it all. I know it isn't bad, just not quite right," he muttered as he went up to the wheel, looking at the blue, blue sky and smiled.

Raven looked out the windows in the very spacious cabin. It was in the stern of the ship with a bank of three windows. Each one covered with small diamond-shaped panes framed by wood and metal, pewter, perhaps. She opened the windows to smell the fresh sea air and look at the vast expanse of the ocean. She watched as the last of the land seemed to be flying away. She could hear the sea gulls crying their farewells to the ship. Soon, she would be completely embraced by the sea. She would truly be trapped, with all these men. What was she to do? *Who can I trust?* She had no idea how long it would take for them to get to

Charleston. *As fast as this ship is going, it could be tomorrow morning! Well, maybe not that soon.*

"Lord, I ask your forgiveness again, just as I have every night and day since I was forced into a house I never even imagined existed. I, to this day, do not understand, but, Lord, I take comfort knowing you loved Rahab and saved her out of her life of harlotry. Mine was not of my choosing. What am I to do? Should I tell McBride who and what I am? I just want to be safe. I want to break these chains of bondage I constantly feel. I know my life was in danger and more so with each passing day. Please, help me." Her whispered prayer caused her fears to subside.

"Mrs. Kerr, you in there?"

"Why, yes. Who is it?"

"Jasper, the cook."

"Oh yes." She hobbled over to the door, getting in character. As she opened the door, she suddenly had a really bad feeling about something. She just didn't know what.

Jasper, almost covered with the dirty residue from the galley, stood there in the passageway holding a tray of tea and sandwiches. Behind him, a man with a scar on his forehead stood with two large pails of steaming water and behind him another, more scruffy than the others, stood scowling holding a large tub and some towels. Neither of those men looked kindly at her. Being used to being polite to even the worst of men, she pulled open the door.

"Come in, gentlemen."

Jasper stepped over the threshold and ducked to make it through the door. He sauntered over put the tray on the table near the chair by the window, just like he had done that a thousand times before. His lean form decried his being a cook.

The other men looked around like they had no idea what to do next.

Jasper spoke gruffly to them, "Roger, just put the tub over there and pour the hot water into it. That's right. Now, get back to work, you two!"

He turned to her, nodded, and left just behind the other two men, closing the door behind him.

Quietly, she ran over to the door and waited half a second, then opened it stuck her head out, and looked for Jasper. "Jasper?" she called none too loudly. She doubted anyone heard her. Her voice would never be loud again. Just then, a head popped up the ladder/stairway at the other end of the passageway.

"Yes?"

"If you see Captain McBride, please, would you tell him I would like to talk with him in the morning? I think I will eat and take my bath, then retire for the night. I do feel rather exhausted. He thought I might need the rest, but I do need to talk with him as soon as may be. I know he is busy, so maybe the morning will be best, if nothing urgent is happening like weather of some sort. I mean bad weather, of course. Nice weather usually doesn't require a captain's attention. And weather happens all the time, doesn't it. Oh dear, I need to hush, don't I?"

"Yes, ma'am. And yes, ma'am. I will do both. And yes, ma'am, you do."

"Oh! Jasper, what do you want me to do with my dirty dishes? Should I just keep them until morning or put them out in the passageway, but then someone might trip over them and get hurt, and then I would feel just awful about that."

"Just leave them be," he interrupted her, fearing she would talk on and on. "I'll get them when I bring your breakfast things," Jasper replied, looking heavenward and sighing.

"That will be just dandy. Thank you ever so. Good night, then."

Jasper turned to go back down, but Raven could have sworn she heard him say, "Women! Don't need 'em on a ship!"

"Well, I guess, maybe he, I don't know, doesn't want me here?" she muttered as she closed the door.

What a wonderful thought. Imagine the entire rest of the afternoon and all night without interruption. How glorious!

She then looked at the door to her cabin and realized it had a lock. Better and better! This was the best day she had had in the last eight years, and maybe even before that.

"Darling, your father will not be coming back from the sea."

"What are you saying, Mama? Papa isn't coming back? Did he run away?"

"No, darling Erin. God took him home to be with Him. We will see him again, but it will be or could be many years from now.

"I am so sorry to tell you this, but I am going to have to teach you how to sew really well, and you will have to help me with my work so we can keep up the payments on the house and all the other expenses.

We do not have time for school or even to grieve. It doesn't even seem real to me. Not yet, anyway. He was gone so much of the time, but I really missed my loving Corvus, even when I knew he was coming home soon."

How old was I then? Twelve, maybe. I hated leaving school and going to work, but so many children were going to work in the textile mills about that time. I wasn't the only one who had to work. I didn't have those horrid conditions either. Working at home with mother learning to be a seamstress really was delightful. At least we had books to read, and I could always go to the new lending library in town and borrow a book. I loved to read those stories!

Raven's thoughts took her back to happier days, even if they were sad ones for a time.

Raven's mind wandered as she sat to eat her sandwich and drink her tea. Amazingly, her throat felt much better after drinking that tea.

"I wonder what kind it is. I'll have to ask Jasper the next time I see him."

She checked the door to make sure it was locked. The westering sun sparkled off the waves rolling toward land and the ripples created by the jumping fish. They looked like they were playing chase with the boat. She had never seen any fish like them before.

"Where are we, I wonder."

Right in the palm of My hand where you are supposed to be.

She smiled. It wasn't the first time she had heard that heart voice speak to her. She knew it was true. She was here, wasn't she?

The other girls were getting ready for their first customers, if the men hadn't started arriving already. There were some men who came early because they had to get home to their families. From what she had heard the men say, their poor wives, if they knew or suspected, didn't seem to care for fear of losing their place in society. Raven just knew she was free from all of that and would never go back.

"Please, God, keep me safe and free from all the misery and abuse of that world. Keep the girls safe. None of them would listen to me when I told them of your love, forgiveness, and protection. They just laughed and went back to their rooms."

As she prayed, Raven slowly undressed and slipped down into the still-hot water. It felt heavenly. There was even a bar of soap.

She washed her skin but thought a long time before she washed her face. She had decided she had to tell Captain McBride the truth. After all, he had given up his cabin for her, just like Jesus had given up his life for her, sacrificially. She owed Captain McBride the truth. She prayed and prayed for him to have understanding, forgiveness, and continued protection just like Jesus would.

She awoke from her nap and looked out the window. The most gorgeous sunset was painting the sky, looking like God's fingers stretching out to touch her and to show his love to her and to all who saw his handwork painted on the sky.

3

Daylight streamed through the windows. Raven had not drawn the drapes over them the night before. Instead, for a long time, she had sat and looked at the myriad of stars and watched the moonlight dance on the white caps of the waves. *What a marvelous sight! Even out in the middle of this huge body of water, God had planned to provide beauty for anyone with the opportunity to see it.* She felt like he had done it solely for her pleasure. It was the first night in eight years she had been able to sleep undisturbed. For so very long, she had not slept at night but caught some sleep in the very early-morning hours and then later into the day. Her work kept her up most of the evening and into the night. She rarely saw any money. She managed to keep secret the few coins her customers gave her as a tip and any change that fell out of their pants' pockets when they threw their pants over the chair beside the bed.

She had been planning from the earliest days to get away somehow. Then the first coin fell. The man left without so much as looking at it. Immediately, her plan took shape. She had no idea how long it would take her, but she was going to save every penny until she felt she had enough to get away. She had some regular customers who started leaving her a coin or two when they left and told her it was their own little secret. She hadn't argued. She just thanked them very kindly.

How would she ever get the horror for those eight years out of her mind? Compared to some of the girls, she really had not had a bad time until that drunken brute had come through her doorway. How could William allow him in? He had been so careful to keep his girls safe. That man would have killed her and almost did. Had not the bouncer heard the slaps and punches, the muffled scream, and the furniture being knocked around, she would have been killed. That was the only time Raven was glad the doors didn't have locks. His beefy hands were choking the life out of her when Jimmy came through the door like a bull after a red flag. He pulled the man off her bruised and nearly broken body and then proceeded to beat him to a bloody pulp. She passed out and didn't remember anything after that for some time. She prayed Jimmy had killed him. She had never seen him again, so it really didn't matter. She just didn't want some other girl to suffer the same or worse fate.

The knocking on the door brought her out of her mental wanderings into the past. She wasn't even dressed yet.

"Who's there?" she barely got out. Her voice was extremely hoarse.

"It's Jasper. I have your breakfast."

"Oh, Jasper. Well, I'm not dressed. If you will leave it by the door, I'll get it. Thank you."

"I was goin' ta pick up the things from yesterday."

"Oh yes. Well, how about if I bring them down to the galley?"

"Naw, I don't want you doing that. You'll kill yourself on the stairs. Just set them outside the door, and I'll send someone after them."

She heard the sound of a tray being put down right outside the door and heard footsteps leaving the passageway. He wasn't going back to the galley. She needed to decide how she was going to do this.

Quickly, she put on the oversized day dress one of the bigger girls had torn and had discarded. Raven had managed to retrieve it from the rag bag and mend the tear so that it was not so bad.

All of that fit into her plan. She carefully hid the dress and waited.

Now, it was proving to be very useful. She put the scarf over her head and carefully opened the door. She pulled the tray inside the cabin without really sticking her head out the door. If anyone had been out there looking, they would have only seen her hands. "Oh dear! I forgot to put on my gloves." Maybe no one was out there. She listened and heard nothing. "I will have to be more careful," she muttered to herself. She shut the door and picked up the tray.

Breakfast was wonderful. She enjoyed it so much. She never had such a variety and a delightful quantity as well. It had been a long time since she had eaten. She had had tea and sandwiches yesterday sometime after noon. She had not eaten since then.

She gathered the dirty dishes and arranged the things from the day before with them and put all of it outside the door. She still did not hear or see anyone. She would wait in her cabin until Captain McBride came to see her. She needed to set the record straight with him and clear her conscience. She would not continue to deceive this very generous man. He was truly a godsend.

She found a Bible on the bookshelf on one side of the windows.

She sat down in the chair behind the desk and began reading in the Psalms. Before long, she found her heart worshiping God.

She had not had a quiet time or any time for worship since her mother died. *The same day William's henchmen kidnapped me.*

She had to get control of her feelings and her fears. If she didn't, she might as well just die right now because her fear would just consume her, and she would go insane, perhaps even kill herself. She had thought of it before. *God is my refuge and strength. I must remember that! Please, God, take my fears and dark thoughts away.*

4

ell, Captain, she said she wasn't dressed yet. And it was late."

"She was very weary yesterday, and perhaps she didn't sleep well at first, out at sea, new surrounding, you know."

"Yes, sir, I know," Jasper replied. "I feel that way when we're on land. I can't sleep for the life of me. Maybe you're right."

"Don't worry. I'll check on her this morning sometime."

"Oh, that's right. She said yesterday that she wanted to talk with you as soon as you could make time for her. I forgot to tell you."

"Well, that makes it easier. Go see if her dishes are out in the passageway. If they are, take them on down. If they aren't, come back and tell me. Got it?"

"Yes, sir. I'll go right now."

"We've had a good, steady wind, and the skies are still clear. It doesn't look like any heavy weather ahead. Depending on what kind of weather we run into in the Gulf, we should get to New Orleans by early to mid-August at this rate. I'll decide what we'll do after that. I'm not sure yet if I want to go on down to Tampico or head back home."

"Yes, sir. Well, wherever you go, that is where I'm goin'. This is the best ship I've been on, and you are the best captain I have had the privilege to serve under."

"Thanks, Jasper. You far surpass my former cooks, with the exception of my late wife. God rest her soul."

Feeling uncomfortable and not knowing what to say, Jasper quickly said, "I'll go check those dishes."

Since Jasper didn't come back, McBride decided to go for a little visit. He had a few things he needed to find out from "Mrs. Kerr."

"Sven, take the helm!"

"Aye, sir."

The knock on the door startled her at first. Then she decided it must be McBride. She quickly put the scarf over her head and turned her back to the door as she looked out over the sea through the windows.

"Come in."

The door opened, and the sound of his heavy boots gave away his presence.

"Mrs. Kerr, you wanted to see me?" he asked as he closed the door.

"Yes, Captain McBride. I wanted to thank you for giving me your quarters. I never would have taken you up on your offer if I had known you were going to do such a thing. I am truly humbled."

"It is my pleasure to provide a little comfort to one who seems so weary. It is the least I can do for my Lord. I do it in His name."

"That makes it even better. I will strive to pass on to others what you have taught me."

She still looked out the windows. She had not turned or given any hint of doing so.

"Captain, this view is captivating. The ocean is so wide. Perhaps, wild and free would be a good way to describe it. I am envious. Now I understand why my father was so drawn to it."

"Your father, ma'am?"

"Yes. My father was the captain of a ship that went down in a hurricane about ten years ago, now. His name was Corvus Kerr."

"Why, that's impossible! I knew Corvus, and yes, he did go down with his ship and crew right off the coast of Florida in '71, but you are too old to be his daughter."

At that, she turned, revealing her true self. She removed the scarf and shook out her now clean raven-black hair. Gone were the charcoal lines and the ash graying her complexion. She looked like the beautiful young woman she was.

"My real name is Erin Raven Kerr. I ask your forgiveness for deceiving you. I had to get away from Baltimore, and I couldn't let anyone know I was leaving. I was so afraid. I needed help, and God sent you to me...or perhaps vice versa. My story is very sad, and it is long. I don't want to burden you with it, but I did want you to know the truth. I am not an old widow. I have never been married. I do apologize for giving you false information, but I didn't know who to trust and, in truth, still don't. I am afraid to leave this cabin."

McBride stared with his mouth hanging open. He had suspected there was something not quite right about her, but this was incredible. He had placed his hand on a chair when he entered and had intended to offer it to her, but now he practically fell into it himself.

"Corvus Kerr's daughter?"

"Yes, sir. And my mother was Cora."

"Was?"

"Yes. She died eight years ago. She became very ill and died suddenly. After father died and she taught me more about her seamstress business, we worked together to be able to pay the bills. She didn't want to lose the house."

"I went by there once, and no one was home. A couple of years later after my own wife died, I went back by to check on her, and the house was all boarded up. I didn't know what had happened...I felt terrible."

With that, Raven moved to the chair beside the table nearby.

"I don't want to keep you from your work, but I will tell you at least part of my story, if you want to hear it. I just don't want any of the crew to know who I am or that I am young and not old. They might let something slip when they get back to Baltimore, and I just can't be found. I just can't. However, I feel I can trust you."

"What have you done that would cause you not to go back or want anyone to know you have left?" he asked suspiciously.

"I have not murdered anyone if that is what you are thinking. No, I have just run away from a terrible situation. I am trying to get free. The day my mother died, I ran to her dear friend's house to let her know. She was extremely sorry and said she would come right away. Instead of waiting for her and going together, I wanted to go back as soon as possible. I left her house and started crying. I wasn't looking where I was going, really, and I turned down an alley instead of at the corner to our street. The next thing I knew, someone pulled a gunnysack over my head, and someone else wrapped their arms around me and covered my mouth with his big hand. I started to wiggle and fight but was hit on the head. When I woke up, I was on a bed in a room about seven by eight feet. All that was in it was a three-quarter rope bed, a chair, and a small, one-drawer table with a mirror over it."

Captain McBride let out a groan and covered his face with his hands. "My dear child, dear God, how could this happen?"

It was obvious to Raven that McBride did not need any other explanation. He understood immediately.

"Captain McBride, I was sixteen years old at the time. I am now twenty-four. I have been through hell and have escaped. Please, don't send me back. I think I would die. I still might."

"No, you will not. Not on my watch. We will figure something out. I agree with you. There are men on this ship who just might recognize you if they saw you as you are now. You came on board an old woman, and you must remain an old woman."

"Oh, thank you. I am forever in your debt. I fear William, the man who owns the house, will be furious someone has escaped from his control. He may even have people out looking for me beyond Baltimore."

"I will be more careful about who I ask to do things concerning you. In the meantime, I think it's best if you get very seasick.

You will have to stay in your cabin the entire trip. Thankfully, you have these windows and can even open them if there isn't a storm.

Consider this your time to rest. Who knows what the remainder of your journey will be like. You will need to gather your strength for what lies ahead...I fear. I think it will be best if you do not get off in Charleston. We are not staying there long. I just have some cargo to unload there and a few things to take on. We will sail with the next tide so we won't even stay twenty-four hours. Yes, New Orleans will be a much better place for you to start the next leg of your journey."

"How long will it take us to get to New Orleans?"

"It won't be much more than a couple of weeks. We should be there by the first week in August."

"That is close to when my father died at sea. Will we be safe?"

"That, my dear, is in the Lord God's hands. He is the one who controls the weather...and all else.

5

Riley! Get Up! You are going to be late the first day of school, and you're the teacher!"

The banging on his door would not stop, but he didn't want to lose the dream. He had to hang on to it.

"Riley! It's Michael, get up! Do you hear me? I'm going to come in there and get you up if I don't hear something in the next two seconds!"

"Stop! Come in, Michael. Just stop yelling. I am conscious but don't want to be."

The door flew open, and the biggest man anyone had seen in those parts entered the newly built home of J. R. Riley, Esq., new headmaster of Crystal Springs Academy. He had built the school with the money he had received from the reward on two cattle rustlers who had tried to kill him. Michael Israel and Josh Schmitt had saved him from being murdered while they had been rounding up cattle for Katie Kurtz, now Josh's wife. He had not recuperated enough to go on the cattle drive with them, and truth be told, he didn't want to go after his harrowing experience. So, when Katie offered him the reward money and said she thought he deserved it and that God wanted him to have it, he knew what he must do. He had always wanted to have a school of his own. He didn't want to be the teacher at someone else's school; he wanted his own academy. He even wanted to offer room and board for those who lived too far away and had no other way to obtain an education.

Now, his dream had come true. He had his academy and a home of his own. If only his other dream would come true. "Let it be so, Lord."

"Riley, what were you thinking sleeping so late? I came in early in case you needed help with any last-minute details. Now, I see what a good thing that was. God's hand was in it for sure and for certain."

"Oh, Michael, you wouldn't want to wake up either if you had been having my dream."

"Okay, what was so wonderful about this dream?" As they talked, Michael fixed Riley some breakfast while Riley shaved and dressed.

"Michael, you recall the accounting of Elijah living by the stream and the ravens coming and feeding him in a time of drought?"

"Yes, very well, that was quite a time for Elijah, but not as bad as when he outran Ahab's chariot and beat him to Samaria. And that was just the beginning of that little journey. What a time he had! Yet he was very obedient. Praise God for his example."

Michael had a faraway look about him and a smile like as if he had just seen an old friend.

Riley cocked his head and then continued. "Well, shall we continue with the recitation of my dream?"

"Certainly, Riley, I most humbly apologize for my interruption."

"Michael, you are mocking me!"

"I am not!"

"Then why did you just sound exactly like me?"

"Did I? I apologize for that as well. Why would I want to do that?"

"Oh, anyway, in my dream, I was resting beside a creek. It looked like a smaller part of Crystal Springs River, you know outside of town, farther west? Anyway, I was slipping in and out of sleep when a raven flew down and gave me something to eat and drink. I looked at the raven. There weren't a bunch of ravens like Elijah had feeding him, just one. This raven was at first old, and then it flew away and returned with more to eat and drink. I knew it was the same raven, but now it was younger. Isn't that backward, Michael?"

"Yes, in man's reckoning, it is. With God, all things are possible." "She kept feeding me, but then she came back and had orange blossoms in her beak."

"How do you know it was a she?"

"I just knew. When she came back with those orange blossoms, I wondered where she had been to get them. She wouldn't even speak. She just perched on a rock and then the most amazing thing of all happened. She changed, but I can't remember how. She was just different. I couldn't stop looking at her. You know what happened next?"

"You ate your breakfast! C'mon, Riley! The children, remember?"

"Yes, but Michael, you have to hear this. She was wounded!"

"What?"

"Not on the outside. She was wounded on the inside. She had multitudinous scars all over her insides. I could see right into her.

She looked like Jesus must have after they scourged him, only she didn't have a mark on her wings, feathers, or skin, but she was all scarred up on the inside. I have to find this raven and help her.

I just have to. Do you think that is what God was showing me?"

Michael sat down and began to eat Riley's breakfast.

"Hey, stop! That is my repast."

"Then eat it and listen to me." Michael shoved the plate toward Riley. "You cannot rush God. Right now, his plan for you is to teach the ABCs and 1-2-3s to these children who have scars of their own. But most importantly, you are to teach them about God's love for them and how they need to 'study to show thyself approved unto God, workmen who needeth not to be ashamed, rightly dividing the Word of Truth' just like he told Timothy. We need these children to grow up and become the leaders of tomorrow, or this town will die, as will its legacy. Be obedient just like Elijah, even when you don't understand why you have to wait or why you have to do something you don't want to do. Obey!"

Riley had finished eating and was ready to go. Michael breathed a little easier but still stayed by his side. They entered the school and opened the windows. Riley wrote lessons on the board, while Michael went out and rang the bell. Shortly after the bell had pealed its announcement of the beginning of school, Tad showed up, and Michael got onto Solomon and rode back to the ranch. "Almighty God, getting him going on the first day was harder than I thought it would be. It's a good thing You sent me to him. He never would have made it. He will be fine now."

6

ad, you come back here this minute!" Esther yelled as she saw her youngest son dart for the front door of the hotel.

"Aw, Ma, do I hafta? The bell is ringing!"

"Young man, that is 'have to' not 'hafta,' and the answer is yes! You have not combed your hair, and your reader is sitting right where you left it. Now, Mr. Riley did not give that to you last week for you to lose it the first day of school."

"Oh, I guess that would be kinda sorta bad." Tad hung his head. He wanted to be in school so much he could taste it. He even helped build the school and house for Mr. Riley.

"Tad, sweetheart, you are a very bright young man. Why, you are already eleven. Look how much you have grown this summer. You will be leaving home before you know it. Now is the time to learn obedience to your parents, teachers, and anyone in authority over you so you will be a good leader yourself keeping God as your guide and following his leading and certainly obeying Him."

She gave him a hug and handed him his things. "I'll see you at lunch. Just come to the back door, and Rose will have everything ready for you. I'll come out and eat with you."

"Love you, Ma!" With that, he darted out the door, once more just as the bell quit ringing.

Esther stepped out and stood watching him run, shaking her head slightly at the quickly diminishing form of her son running down the street past the last building and on toward the refurbished school building and new headmaster's home. She wasn't sure where he would run, but, to be sure, he would be the first student there. She turned and walked back into the hotel and was headed toward the dining room when movement on the stairs caught her attention. Glancing that way, she stopped and smiled. Willow fairly floated down the stairs.

"My goodness, Willow, why are you so dressed up this morning?" Esther couldn't believe this was the same girl who just almost six months ago had been saved along with the twins, Wade and Cade, by Josh and Riley when there was a flash flood.

Indians had captured Willow when she was a young girl of seven. Her family had been killed, and she had been raised by the tribe until she ran away from them at age fourteen to avoid being given as wife to an abusive brave whose first wife had died.

Willow knew how she had died and did not want to face the same fate. She had taken her horse and ridden long and hard for several days until she found some caves to hide in.

She managed to stay in the caves for three years. *She certainly is a resourceful young woman,* Esther thought as she hugged Willow firmly. Willow decided to move to another place to hide and live when she found another cave high on a promontory beside a stream in the big arroyo. God's hand was at work in that as well.

Josh and Riley might never have found her, otherwise.

Katie Kurtz took in Willow and considered her a younger sister. Esther loved both girls as if they were her baby daughters who had died. *It seems like yesterday Katie married our Josh, certainly not four months ago. That is when Willow came to live with us. Our hotel and restaurant have not been the same since.* Esther smiled and gave Willow an extratight squeeze.

"Mom, do you think I could ride out and see Katie this morning?"

"In that dress? On a horse?"

"Well, ah, I guess that is kind of out of the question. I just love this dress! I could change into my buckskin dress. Would that be better?"

"I have a better idea. Why don't we go see Marta? I think you will find a little something in her shop that may do a little better than that."

"Wouldn't she have to make something?"

"Oh, occasionally, she has some things made up ahead of time in case someone comes in and needs something quickly.

"Well, this should prove to be interesting," Willow said doubtfully.

"Let's eat breakfast and see to the morning crowd, and then we will run over there and see what we can come up with."

"Sounds like fun to me. What do you want me to do first? I could check the tables and be sure they have what they need on them and that they are all washed. That new girl, Daisy, seems a bit lax about her work."

"I know, but she is young. I need to spend some more time training her. She says she's an orphan. I think she is telling the truth although she looks younger than she claims to be, and I doubt she should be out on her own."

"Since I am closer to her age, I might be able to find out from her. She may be afraid you will fire her if she is too young. Where is she staying?"

"I think with the widow Mrs. Beunerkemper. I'll have to ask Rose. She said she would take care of it."

With that, the two women walked into the dining room and began their work for the morning. The aromas from Rose's kitchen made the whole room smell of homemade delights and hot coffee.

As the first guests arrived, there was still no sign of Daisy, so Willow took over the duties of taking orders and serving customers, as Esther managed filling the orders in the back and Rose did the cooking. Willow fairly danced around the room, filling cups with coffee and making pleasant conversation with the growing crowd of customers, most of whom gave her more than one admiring look.

As Willow wiped up the last table and replaced napkins in the canning jar arranged with salt and pepper in the center of each table, Esther tapped her on the shoulder.

"Let's get out of here! We only have a few minutes, and the lunch crowd will begin to arrive! My goodness, I've never seen so many people coming to eat so late. What was going on?"

"They said the stage was late, and they had not stopped for breakfast because the way station where they usually eat breakfast was burned to the ground, and there was no sign of anyone there. They came all the way on the same team, so they wanted to take it slower but kept a sharp eye out for anything or anyone suspicious.

Everyone's nerves were on edge. They were so glad to get a hot meal and feel relatively safe that they all wanted to talk about it. I felt like I was some sort of huge shoulder everyone wanted to cry on. I'm already exhausted. I don't know if I can go out to Katie's.

Has Daisy shown up yet?"

"No, and that is a puzzle as well. Rose said she saw her this morning, and she was on her way over."

"That sure is a puzzle. What do you think happened to her?"

"I have no idea. I'm beginning to think I should mention it to Brian. Maybe we should go there to tell him first, then on to Marta's. We need to hurry in any case."

"Let's go see Brian first. That is more important."

They crossed the street and went over to the sheriff's office.

As they opened the door, they heard Brian talking with someone about the way station fire. He had just said he would wire the Rangers in Fredericksburg when the women opened the door.

The man pushed by them and left.

"Mornin', ladies." Brian's eyes lingered on Willow. He couldn't seem to get them to go anywhere else.

"Good morning, Brian. I know you are busy with these strange happenings with the stage and the way station, but we thought perhaps you would want to know about another strange thing right here in town."

Suddenly, his eyes obeyed him, and he looked straight at Esther. He had learned she was never overly concerned but had a sense about things and wouldn't report something she didn't truly feel needed looking into.

"Esther, what's bothering you?"

"Well, Daisy, the new girl I hired a couple of weeks ago, has... well, I can't say disappeared because I haven't really looked for her yet. Rose said she saw her when Daisy was on her way to work, but, Brian, she never showed up. We had a mess there this morning with the stage crew and passengers with what they had been through. Well, you know all about that, so I won't reiterate. I just thought you might want to look into the Daisy disappearance."

"Let me send this telegram to the Rangers since they are closer to the way station than I am. After that, I'll check with Rose then go look for Daisy. Have you checked with Doc to see if she maybe got hurt and is over there?"

"No, I think Doc would have sent me word if that was the case, but I can go and see. We are on our way to see Marta."

"No, don't bother. I'll see him after I stop by the restaurant in a little bit."

"I'll...we'll see you later, Brian." Willow smiled as she looked over her shoulder just before closing the door.

"That girl is going to drive me insane. I must get over this!

I can't get involved with a woman. I'm a lawman and could die today. How could I do that to the woman I love?" Brian seemed to be talking to the top of his desk. Both hands were firmly planted flat on the top, and he faced the top with his eyes staring right between his hands.

Suddenly, he slapped the top of the desk.

"Let's get to work! That is the only cure." With that, he headed up to the telegraph office to send a wire to the Texas Rangers stationed in Fredericksburg.

The bell over the door jingled as the women opened the door to Marta's seamstress shop. They didn't see anyone there, but the cutest gingham dress, nearly finished, hung on a dress form near her cutting table.

"Marta, are you here? It's Esther and Willow," Esther said loud enough to be heard in the back room used for storage.

There seemed to be a muffled sound from the back, and then Marta came out of the back room. She looked a bit haggard and a bit frightened. What looked like bruises could be seen on her arms just before she lowered her rolled-up sleeves.

"Good morning, ladies. What can I do for you?"

"Marta, I was wondering if you had something suitable for a young lady to wear when she goes riding," Esther said pointedly.

Marta looked at Esther at first as if she was confused. Then suddenly, she jerked around and went into the back room.

Esther looked at Willow and shrugged. "I guess this is going to be an unusual day. Everything seems to be a bit odd today."

"Very odd."

"I do have this," Marta said as she backed out of the room, dragging a box with her.

Esther looked at Willow again and whispered, "Yes, indeed, very strange!"

"Here, let me help you with that." Esther stepped up next to Marta and reached down to help with the box.

"No, I can do it!" screamed Marta.

Esther jumped back. "Okay, Marta. I'm sorry. I didn't mean to imply you couldn't. It's just so cumbersome. I thought maybe I could make it a bit easier for you. I'm sorry, I won't interfere again."

Tears welled in Marta's eyes. She sat down heavily on the chair next to her cutting table. "I'm sorry I screamed. I am so on edge.

I don't know what to do. Nothing I do seems to be right. I can't make him happy, and he just gets worse every day."

"Marta, who are you talking about? Oscar?" Esther ventured to ask about Marta's husband, the blacksmith in town.

"Who else would I be talkin' about? There ain't a man in this town who would look at me a second time, even if Oscar thinks I have men stacked behind the boxes in the back room. He's the one. He's the one. He's the one who goes down to that saloon, and you can't tell me those *females* down there don't catch his eye."

The way she said "females" with such vehemence and hatred made Esther and Willow believe she had said a dirty word. "Now, Marta, I don't think Oscar would do that. He loves you."

"No, he doesn't! Just ask him. He tells me often enough that he can't stand the sight of me."

"Oh, Marta. I'm so sorry. You are such a beautiful woman. You have a heart of gold, and your work as a seamstress is of the highest quality. What would we do here without you? You add so much to our community. I wish you would go with us to church one Sunday, and you would see how loving everyone outside of this store is. This must be the only place you see anyone. I never see you anywhere else."

"The only way I could leave the house on Sunday would be if Oscar was so stone-cold drunk he would sleep through the entire morning. I can't take that chance. Do you know what he would do to me if he woke up and I wasn't there?"

"Is it that bad, Marta?"

"You better believe it."

"Would he let me come and visit you?"

"Maybe. If I ask him, he'd say no. So the best thing to do would be to just drop by sometime. Don't make an appointment."

By this time, Marta had calmed down somewhat. Esther gave her a hug. "All right, I'll do just that. Now, about that other item of business?"

"Oh, oh yes! Let's see what I have here."

She opened the box and revealed a lovely leather riding skirt and jacket, complete with a hat to match.

"Willow, try it on. Let's see if it fits." Marta looked expectantly at the young woman.

"Willow?" Esther said, turning to look at the unresponsive girl.

Stunned, Willow looked at Esther. "Why, that is the most beautiful riding skirt I have ever seen. It has a jacket and hat to match? I don't care if they don't fit. I'll make it fit. I may have to gain some weight or lose some. Whatever it takes, that is going to fit!"

They all laughed at that as Willow picked up the articles of clothing and slipped into the curtained changing area. A few minutes later, she came out with the outfit on. The jacket was buttoned up since she didn't have a blouse to try on with it, but it still fit nicely, and there was room for the blouse.

Marta beamed! "I've never tried to do leather before. It was fun! I'll have to keep doing that."

"You made this?" Willow all but whispered. "I sure did, missy."

"Oh, Marta. You are so gifted by God. I don't have words to express my feelings. I will wear this with such honor. I'm happy to display your talents."

"How you do go on. Now, run along, I have things to do. I need to finish that dress over there, and there are more on order."

"But I need to pay you," Willow said.

"No, that's okay. It's been taken care of."

Willow looked at Esther. "Happy birthday, Willow."

"But I don't think it *is* my birthday."

"Since I've missed so many, what difference does it make?"

The two women hugged as Willow softly told Esther, "Thank you, oh, thank you so much." Then Willow went back into the curtained space to change back into her other dress. When she came out, Marta had the box ready for the clothes and packed them away tenderly, like a loving mother tucking her little ones in bed.

By the time they left, they could see the noon crowd beginning to make their way toward the hotel and its restaurant.

"We'd better hurry. I told Tad I'd eat lunch with him out back."

"That is a handy table and benches Dad made for our little picnics when we get a minute to eat during a rush."

"Yes, it is nice to get out of the kitchen heat anyway, and away from all the noise." Esther smiled as she said that and then mock fanned herself. "Well, it is a different heat outside!"

The women laughed.

"I wonder what happened to Daisy. She loved sitting out there, maybe a little too much or too often. When is Liz coming back? Do you know?" Willow asked, wrinkling her brow.

"She said in her last letter that her mother was doing much better. She hoped to be home shortly after the first of September.

With business picking up, we really need her back to do the register and help wait on the tables. Even with Daisy helping out with the tables, I wouldn't want Daisy handling the money. The first of September won't come soon enough for me. You know, I still don't know why Riley wanted the children to start school in August. I think I'll ask him."

7

Ma, I'm going to change my clothes and ride out to Katie's. I'll be back before dark. If I lose track of time and it will be dark when I get ready to leave, I'll just spend the night with her and come back in the morning unless you need me tonight for the dinner guests," Willow said loudly enough to be heard in the kitchen. The last of the lunch crowd had left and the tables had been cleaned and set for dinner. "You will not ride out there alone," a familiar voice said almost too gruffly from behind her.

Willow turned and saw a firm, determined look on Brian's face just daring her to defy him. She was about to tell him he didn't run her life when she saw something almost pained in his eyes.

"What has happened?" Willow asked urgently.

"Where is Esther?" he asked.

"I'm right here. I heard you. What has happened, Brian? Tell me!"

"I found Daisy. She had been misused, beaten, and left for dead. She's at Doc's. He may need you."

Esther was already taking off her apron and heading toward the door, throwing the apron on a chair in the lobby of the hotel.

Brian turned toward Willow. "She was taken against her will.

She has skin and blood under her nails, so she gave a good fight, but there was more than one, Willow. I think you know what I'm talking about. You have seen the results in your own tribe. That's why you ran away, wasn't it? Now, I'm not saying it was Indians.

Don't get that look on your face. In fact, I know it wasn't Indians.

The horses were shod, and the men wore boots with spurs. There had to be eight, maybe nine, of them. She didn't have a chance." "How can that many come in town, grab a girl, and leave with her against her will, and nobody notice it? It just can't be, Brian."

"It doesn't take that many to grab someone. One can do that, maybe two. If that was their intent when they came into town, they weren't looking for anyone in particular, just someone... convenient."

"Daisy was coming to work real early so she was 'convenient'?" Willow asked almost sarcastically.

"I know this is hard to take. Willow, she is in a real serious condition. She may not make it. If I had not followed some tracks I happened to see leaving town from where her tracks stopped, I wouldn't have found her, and she would have died. She may anyway. I hope not. She's so young."

"How young do you think she is, Brian?"

"Oh, probably fifteen, no older than that."

"I knew she wasn't as old as she said. I wonder what her story is. How did she get here? I don't even remember. It seems one day she was just here."

"I know you want to go out to Katie's. I need to talk with Josh and Michael. If you want to go and it's all right with Esther, I'll ride with you, if you promise to come back before dinner. I know Esther will need your help. You *must* have someone ride with you.

You understand there is *no way* you should be out there alone, don't you?"

Willow looked as if she was going to sass him, but then lowered her eyes and nodded her head.

"I need to go and see Daisy. I want to talk with her," Willow whispered.

"No. She is in no condition to talk. You don't need to add to her misery or get in the way over there. I'm going to talk with Rose while you change clothes. Then, we can leave when you're ready."

"Oh, Brian, thank you. I have this sense of urgency to see Katie that I can't explain, yet I am torn as to what to do. I'll hurry and change."

With that, she ran up the stairs to her room. Brian turned and grabbed the apron off the chair and then headed toward the kitchen.

Rose was making bread for the evening meal. Pies were ready to go into the oven to cook while the bread rose. She looked up, the white flour a stark contrast to her much-darker skin. She smiled at Brian, but her eyes told of a deep concern and worry.

"Rose, Daisy has been hurt. She is bad off over at Doc's. Tell me exactly what you saw and said to her this morning. Every little detail may help me find out who did this to her."

"Oh, Sheriff, I's been goin' over and over in ma head about dis mornin'. It was early. De sky was just pinkin' up when I saw her singin' and swingin' her skirts. She's almost skippin' until she saw me. I was on ma porch finishin' up a cup a coffee. My Julius was headin' out to da saw mill in a little bit, and I needed to fix his lunch. So, as I gots up ta go back in da house, she hollers, 'I'll see you in a bit, Miss Rose. I'm gonna be early dis mornin'.' I was surprised when I gots to da hotel kitchen and she was nowhere to be seen. I figured she had forgotten somethin' and went back to gets it. I didn't hear narry screams nor other noise. What has happened to da chile?"

"More meanness than I would want you to imagine, my dear lady."

"I don' hav ta magin' meanness. I's lived thru't." Rose lifted her apron to catch the water spilling over the bottom of her eye.

Brian jerked his head in a swift nod then turned to go.

As Brian left Rose, he heard the beginnings of her prayer for Daisy, a heartfelt, mournful prayer. He silently looked up to heaven and said, "Yes, Father, hear the prayer of your servant. She is one of your loved ones. She deserves a special crown of love in glory."

Willow was waiting for him when he entered the lobby. She had sent one of the maids from upstairs to the livery to have Oscar saddle her horse so it would be ready when she was. Brian stopped to stare at Willow.

"Wow! Is that new?"

"Yes, Marta made it. But, Brian, the maid just returned and said that Oscar said he would have my horse ready. She also made a comment about Oscar's condition. He is a bit more liquored up this morning than usual. I'm not sure my horse will be ready."

"If it isn't, I'll saddle it. That man needs help. I believe he is getting worse every day."

"Well, let's walk down there. I'm just very thankful you're with me. I believe, Brian, you are my best friend. We can talk about anything and everything. I'm so glad I told you my story. You have told me some of yours. Someday, will you tell me the rest?"

Brian grabbed the reins of his horse, and they began to walk down the street to the livery.

"There's not much to tell. If you want to hear it, someday we will have some free time and I'll tell you. I have to get someone to help me first."

"You know that new hand Todd who Josh and Katie hired when Riley was shot? He really wants to be a lawman. He would probably be glad to work with you."

Brian's shoulders became stiff, and his demeanor cooled.

"Todd? That tall dark-haired kid who can't keep his eyes off you?"

"Brian! I haven't seen him in a month at least. And then it was only a brief 'how do you do?' I'm sure you are mistaken. I've only had one conversation with him, and that was at Josh and Katie's wedding reception. He was asking me about you! Brian Daniels, you just better get your thoughts straight before you start *accusing* people, especially when they aren't here to defend themselves."

"It looks like he doesn't need to be here. You're doing a pretty good job of defending him without his help."

"Listen, if you are going to be like this, I don't have to have you escort me out to Katie's. I'm perfectly capable of riding alone. I've been on my own for many years, and nothing ever happened to me. I just enjoy your company when you are civil. I had no idea you had a jealous bone in your body. That isn't what true friendship is about. I would rather not have your company. So, good day, Sheriff Daniels."

Brian was about to tip his hat and say "Good day" right back, get on his horse, and ride when he thought about Daisy and the condition she was in. He would not be able to sleep tonight if he let Willow ride out to the ranch by herself unprotected. What had gotten into him? Who was this other man he was becoming? He didn't like him much, and he had better have a talk with Pastor Mueller when Mueller came back through on his next circuit. Hadn't Josh mentioned he was being sinful at the reception? Maybe there was something to this. Why was he acting so possessive about Willow? He wanted to deny the only answer that came to mind. If he didn't think about it, it wouldn't happen.

"I'm sorry, Willow. You're right. I was being so...so...I don't know what I was being, but it wasn't the right way to act. I'll talk with Todd if he's around when I get there. I really need to talk with Josh and Michael, though. So let's get riding." They walked on, a tense silence surrounding them, making their footsteps sound loud in their ears.

"I don't see or hear Oscar. Let's see if my horse is saddled."

Brian walked into the darkened smithy. He saw no one and headed into the stable area. Still, no one and no sound could be heard. Willow's horse was saddled, but the cinches were not tight enough. She could have lost her seat with the saddle that loose.

"Pretty careless for the blacksmith and liveryman," Brian mumbled as he tightened the cinches on her saddle.

"Here ya go, pretty lady." He helped her up and mounted his own horse. They turned the horses' heads in unison and rode out of town toward the K & J Ranch as it was now called.

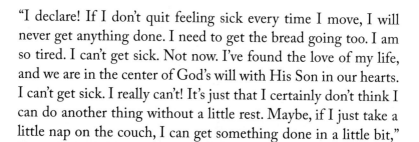

"Michael, the back of my neck is itching." Josh turned in his saddle and looked all around him at the hills surrounding the ranch. "Do you feel anything?"

"No, nothing like that. I just keep thinking that I need to get back to the barn or the corral, somewhere close to Katie. Maybe we are getting a prompting from God and had better listen to that prompting."

"Let's go."

They both turned their horses and headed back to the main buildings of the ranch.

"I declare! If I don't quit feeling sick every time I move, I will never get anything done. I need to get the bread going too. I am so tired. I can't get sick. Not now. I've found the love of my life, and we are in the center of God's will with His Son in our hearts. I can't get sick. I really can't! It's just that I certainly don't think I can do another thing without a little rest. Maybe, if I just take a little nap on the couch, I can get something done in a little bit," Katie said, talking to herself again.

She sunk down onto the leather couch that faced the now-clean fireplace. Both the front and back doors were open. The newfangled screen doors Josh put on in July were allowing the breeze to come through the house but keeping the bugs out. It was heavenly. Who would have ever thought life could be made so much better with such a simple invention? When they made a little money on selling the goat hair to the mohair operation in Kerrville, she would ask him to get some for a window in front and in back, for downstairs, and upstairs. That way, they could leave the windows open at night and close the doors. It would be so nice for both upstairs and down.

Katie had been missing Willow and was praying she would move back in with them soon. They had had plenty of "alone" time, as Willow had called it. Now she felt she needed Willow's help, especially if she was getting sick.

Her heart prayed for Willow, Esther, Adam, Tad, and Brian as she sank into a deep sleep almost before her head came to a full rest on the little pillow Mrs. Gruber had made for them as a wedding gift.

Michael and Josh rode cautiously into the barnyard, looking around as they headed toward the corral.

"Let's leave the horses saddled in case there's an urgent need for them," Josh said, looking around expecting to see something amiss.

"Hey, what's happened?" Todd asked as he came out of the barn. It was his day to stay close to the house and keep an eye out for Katie's safety. Whenever the men went out on the range, one man always stayed behind to "protect the family" as everyone called it.

Josh had explained that Katie still had the occasional nightmare of Red, an infamous outlaw who tried to kill her earlier in the year when the outlaw had heard there was hidden "treasure" on the ranch.

"We just had a feeling we were needed and had to come and check it out. Anything amiss here?" Michael asked.

"No, nothing that I'm aware of. It's been really quiet. In fact, I haven't heard a noise from the kitchen or anything else. Maybe we should check on Katie. She is usually singing or banging something around in the kitchen by now. I don't hear anything, do you?"

"Oh look, there are Brian and Willow. I wonder what brings them out here," Josh said as he had turned to look toward the house. "Katie will be thrilled!"

The horses were turned over to Todd to take care of. Michael and Josh walked toward Brian and Willow.

"What brings you two out here this time of day?" Josh asked.

"I wanted to see Katie. I've missed her so much. Where is she?" Willow asked, looking around.

"We just got here. She's probably in the house. I'll go and check for you," Josh said.

"No, that's okay. I'll go in. You boys have a good man-to-man talk, and I'll have a little hen party with Katie. See ya!" With that, Willow walked up the front steps and toward the front door.

"Hey, Josh, I love the door! This is great!" she yelled back down to him.

"Thanks! There are two. They have really been a big help!" he hollered back to her.

"Hey, you two could wake the dead. I'm amazed Katie didn't come running out," Brian commented.

"You know, you're right. Maybe she's in the privy. Willow will find her," Josh said.

"Josh, Michael, while there are no womenfolk around, I need to talk with you. Something happened today I think you need to be aware of. You know who I mean when I talk about Daisy?"

Both men nodded. "She disappeared. Esther told me about it between breakfast and lunch. You know your mother, Josh, when she has a feeling, we better not ignore it. She has a gift like that.

So when she came in and told me, I decided I'd better get right on it. Well, I found the girl, and I mean girl. She had been captured, taken, kidnapped—call it whatever you want—but she had been seriously abused and raped numerous times, then left for dead. If I hadn't found her out in the middle of nowhere, she would have died." Brian squeezed the bridge of his nose. "I'm not sure she will make it even now. She had no clothes on and was bleeding quite a bit. I managed to get her wrapped in my blanket, and I found bits and pieces of cloth scattered about the area, probably pieces of her dress and underthings they had ripped off her, maybe with the help of a whip. It was pretty ugly. I don't think she's more than fifteen. This will not be easy for her to overcome. She's at Doc's place, and Esther's with her. If anyone can help her outside of God, it will be those two.

"What I want you two to know is that eight or nine men are riding around doing harm to anyone they find vulnerable. I need to get the word out to the other ranchers and can use some help.

We also need to see if we can't find these men. They need to be taken care of and soon.

"Michael, you have insight into God's plan, it seems. Josh, you have the military experience behind you. I could use both at this point and need it quickly."

"Well, now I know why we needed to get back," Josh said, looking at Michael. Looking back at Brian, he shook his head.

"I would start where you found Daisy. Try to see which direction they went from there. If there is too much confusion in the immediate area to get a clear reading, then ride in a circle around the area, extending the circle each time to come back to where you began. Eventually, you'll reach the limit of the confusion, and there will be no more tracks until the place where they left. Then you will get the clear direction. You know, Willow is probably the best tracker we have here. She has an extremely keen eye. I have seen her track a fox over rocks! If anyone can track them, she can."

Michael interrupted, "Josh, I know Willow could do it, but I think there is a more immediate need for her here. Let Brian or Todd track them. I'm not saying they're better than her, but they do have quite a bit of experience in that as well. For that matter, so does Wulf, but I think Wulf is needed here as well. I think it would be very beneficial for Todd to ride along with Brian. I'll watch the town and jail. Anyone in it, Brian?"

Brian shook his head.

"Josh, you need to stay here with Katie. She doesn't need to be alone with this kind of thing going on."

Josh's face turned visibly pale. "You are right as always, Michael. I will stay here. I'll send some of the men out to warn the other ranchers. Todd can go with you. What needs to be done around here can be managed with me and the other four. The twins are really holding their own. They are becoming men right before my very eyes. Being away from their dad has helped them tremendously. They have become very hard workers and are making plans for their future, a really big change from almost six months ago."

Josh called to Todd to come over. When he got there, they filled him in on what was going on. He nodded and headed toward the barn, disappeared inside, and later came out riding his horse. When he approached the group, Michael had gotten his horse, and Brian was ready to go.

Willow stepped out on the porch. "Hey, Brian, tell Mom I'm going to spend the night, please?"

"Will do." Brian nodded, and Willow turned and went back indoors.

The three men rode out. Josh moved toward the corral to get his horse and go tell the men what they needed to do.

Willow watched from the window. She couldn't decide if she should've gone out to talk with Josh or just wait. She turned and looked at the still sleeping form on the couch. She decided to make bread and do all the things that obviously Katie couldn't or hadn't done yet today. Katie didn't have a fever, and that was a good sign.

She went into the kitchen and started the bread.

8

aven was content. The seasick story explained her absence from the deck, which suited the men. She felt they had, for the most part, forgotten she was even on board.

Jasper was content also. He happily let Captain McBride take the food trays to Mrs. Kerr. He couldn't abide weaklings, and that's what people who became seasick were—weaklings. "They would be better off staying onshore," he had told Captain McBride.

"Why didn't ye put her off in Charleston?" he had asked McBride.

"She doesn't need to be in Charleston, Jasper. She needs to be in New Orleans, and that is where we are taking her. I'll take care of her. No one else needs to bother," was the captain's reply.

With that, their routine had been established, and not another word had been spoken. "She was his aunt from his mother's side," everyone said. "So, that's why he treats her the way he does."

For the most part, McBride left her alone. He tended to her meals, and they spent the evenings together visiting over supper. He left her at an early hour and didn't disturb her again until after everyone had had breakfast. Then he took her a tray. She always had tea and fruit for lunch, so he had a bowl of fresh fruit he had picked up in Charleston in her room for her to fend for herself at noon. He also had a pot of water and little portable stove he had picked up at the market in Charleston and placed in her cabin. On that, Raven heated her tea water and the water with which to take a sponge bath when she felt she needed it. He

54

had also gotten her a light cotton dress, which she could wear while cooped up in her cabin. She would don her old things when they made port.

"Lord, I thank you for all your blessings! How beautiful are your provisions, creation, and love." Her voice was getting a little better with the tea, fresh air, rest, and silence. She had not had the luxury of not having to talk since she had been taken. The customers liked having the girls tell them how handsome, strong, and "good" they were. They had to comment on everything just to make the customer feel "special." Yet, in return, the girls were made to feel like trash, something to be used and forgotten or thrown away.

There was a knock at the door. It wasn't the right time for Captain McBride, so she was a bit nervous.

"Who is it?" she asked.

"Captain McBride, Mrs. Kerr. How are you feeling?"

"Oh, Captain, I am feeling better, but I still feel queasy. I guess I'm not meant to sail. Is there something you need?" She was hesitant to open the door. What if this was a trick by one of the crew.

"No, Mrs. Kerr, I have brought something for you. I thought you might need it."

"Can you give me a moment to get dressed? I'm still in my dressing gown. I have been just resting today."

"Certainly, take all the time you need."

Now, that sounded more like him. She still wasn't sure. She quickly slipped on her Mrs. Kerr dress and put the scarf over her head and then turned her back.

"Come in, sir," she said a short time later.

The door opened slowly. She heard it close and then thought she heard the lock turn. She could see a man's reflection in the window as she looked out toward the sea. Her heart started to beat a little faster. *Dear, Lord, please protect me as I flee the hands of the evil men of this world. Help me to be strong in Your strength and Your strength alone, for it is in You only I trust. Send me angels to protect me rom all that Satan will throw at me. In Jesus' name, amen.* Her heart calmed. It had only taken a few seconds for her to shoot that "arrow" prayer, as she called them, to her Heavenly Father.

"Mrs. Kerr, we will be in New Orleans tomorrow. I have brought you some charcoal and some ashes, if you need them.

I trust you will be able to disguise yourself as well as you did before," McBride said in a whispered voice but loud enough for her to hear him.

She could see him better in the window now that he had moved further into the room.

"Thank you," she said out loud to him and to her Father God in heaven. Her thoughts were on both of them. "I had saved a little in case I had to fix up my disguise. This will be very helpful. You are very kind…and thoughtful, Captain. I trust God will guide you and keep you safe as you look to Him for the paths you should take."

"I didn't want anyone to hear what we said in case they were listening through the door. I have been giving your situation a great deal of thought. There is a hotel in New Orleans that is about as busy as any place can be. I recommend you stay there.

Check in as Mrs. Kerr. Leave as Catherine McBride. That is my late wife's name. You should buy a stage ticket to Houston. Stay the night in this hotel. I have written the name down for you. It will also be busy. When you leave, you can be yourself, Raven or Erin, whichever you want. You decide if you want to go to San Antonio or Austin. If I need to find you, I will recognize either name. I want to keep track of you, perhaps come and see you at some time in the future if you will accept my friendship. I feel I need to take the place of your parents…if you will let me."

"I will go by Erin Raven Kerr. I don't want to forget what I have been through, or deny it happened yet. I want to be who I really am as well. I will be so glad to see you if you do find me.

I am inclined to think San Antonio. I really would like to find a small town where, perhaps, my former profession is not even an option. I hope to use my seamstress skills to find employment, but I could work at a restaurant or even be a maid. I know I will be able to at least earn my keep. God has shown me that much. That's what gave me the courage to run. I knew He would take care of me."

"If you will, write to me in care of general delivery at the New Orleans post office. Use the name Catherine McBride, and I will know who sent it. She would be proud for you to use her name."

He smiled and wiped a little at his eye.

"I will do that as soon as I am settled in a town I feel God has called me to live in."

"I want you to do me a favor. I have a package with some instructions with it. I don't want you to open it until you get to Houston. Then, promise me, you will follow my instructions. Please do this for me?"

"It is a bit unorthodox, but you have been so kind and such a trusted person in a time of great need. As you have asked to be a stand-in 'daddy' for me, I will do as you ask. I have no reason to doubt you mean me anything but good."

"Here is the package. Just before you enter the hotel, I want you to open it and then follow the instructions written in it.

There is a small park directly across the street from this hotel. Go there to open it, and no one will think anything of it. You will still be a nonperson. You might want to downplay your beauty, if there is any way to do so. You be careful, young lady. There are some really bad men out there who...well, I know... I know, you already know. And that, my dear, dear Erin Raven Kerr, makes my heart break."

"Dear Captain McBride, God sent you to me when I needed you the most. He will keep me and guard me under his mighty wings."

He reached for her hands and held them. "I am concerned about Raven's wings. I don't want you to be wounded any more."

He bowed his head and began to pray for her protection and for God's guidance in all that they both would do. He asked for their safety and for angels to be with them along their separate paths. When he finished, she fell against him and gave him a tight hug, resting her head against his chest and hearing the steady, strong beat of his heart and began to cry. She had the utmost respect for this man of God and hated to see their paths diverge.

9

Michael stayed in town serving as deputy while Brian was out hunting for outlaws. Everyone respected this gentle giant of a man. They knew they could not, or dare not, cause trouble while Brian was gone. Michael was more than able to take care of it. He bid the men good-bye as they left to go on the search for the men who so cruelly attacked Daisy.

After they had found the trail left by the outlaws, they rode with a determination to catch up with them, and then, without even realizing the change in the weather, they heard thunder roll and saw lightning in the distance. The clouds began turning a very ugly dark gray, almost black. It seemed they had turned a bit green where one still could see color in them. The horses began to sidestep in a jittery motion. Brian pulled his horse to a stop. The few men around him did the same.

"Keep your eyes peeled for a good place of refuge, men. I don't like the look of this at all." Brian scanned the sky and then the hills and cliffs surrounding them.

Mr. Gruber, the barber in town, looked down at the tracks then back at the sky. "These tracks are headed straight for that old cave with those funny-lookin' rocks in them. My son said they call them stalactites or som'thun'. Those men may be ther' or maybe moved on past ther'. Anyways, we could get in ther' for shelter from this comin' storm. We may not get that far before the rain breaks on us," he said nervously.

"Good thinking, Mr. Gruber. I know where you're talking about. We could find shelter for us and the horses in there, but we need to follow these tracks while we can. It doesn't look like they have been trying to hide their trail at all." Brian had wondered why Gruber had even volunteered to come on this mission. He had never pictured him as anything but a homebody. He seemed like a very meek man.

Mr. Ruger, the telegraph operator, shook his head. "These must be a reckless band of marauders. They don't care who they hurt or what they do. They're just out ridin' and bent on doin' bad deeds. Maybe they don't realize they will have to stand before

Almighty God and be held accountable for what they have done.

Then there will be no turnin' back."

Mr. Gruber looked at him. "I'd really like to tie them in my barber chair and put the fear of death in them with my razor knife, maybe—hey, what's that up ther'?"

Brian turned to look in the same direction Gruber was looking and saw a glint of something high up, probably from one of the last rays to break through the ever-growing cloud bank. The trouble was there shouldn't be anything on that cliff to reflect sunlight even in the brightest day.

"We are being watched, men. Someone's up there with binoculars or a spyglass. We best look very casual. Don't look down at the tracks. Let's point at the sky and look around like we are surveying for some shelter. In fact, let's ride over toward that glint like we see something that might give us some cover."

With that, the group of five men turned and headed toward the cliffs. Todd rode up beside Brian.

"Sir, perhaps Jakes and I can ride a little apart from the group and gather some firewood so it looks like we are fixin' to make camp. I can see the top of a dead tree just over there in what looks like a ravine." Todd pointed off to the southeast.

"I don't want you to get too far off. I'm feeling real uneasy about this, and I don't think it's the storm."

"I know what you mean. I'm feeling an itch. I hate it when that happens." Todd stood up in his stirrups and scanned the very rocky and mostly barren surroundings. Suddenly, he started feeling like spiders were crawling all over him.

"Brian, ride! Ride fast. Serpentine! We're in danger!" He spurred his horse and began riding toward the cliffs turning his horse to the right then to the left. Brian spurred his horse and followed. The other men began to ride as well. Jakes was the last one to realize what was happening. As he began to gallop, a shot rang out. He slumped to the right side but held on to the saddle horn. Blood oozed out on his shirt and began to run down his right arm. He tried to pull himself more upright but was struggling to keep his seat.

He knew then he was a dead man. He felt a rope tighten around his arms and torso. His body began to be pulled to the left. His right arm felt like it was on fire! That rope seemed to be right over the bullet wound. Slowly, he was righted in the saddle.

He turned his head and saw Todd riding alongside. "You can do it, Jakes! Hang on. Stay with me!"

Another shot rang out. Dirt flew up just to the left of them as they turned right at a sharp angle.

Brian, who had taken cover behind a large boulder, saw where the shot had come from. He had his gun trained on the site and waited. Todd and Jakes were coming closer. They turned a sharp left and then a sharp right again. A head popped up from behind a fallen tree about halfway up the cliff. Brian fired; the person fell backward, just as he fired another shot. Fortunately, the shot went high, very high.

"It looked like he was shootin' at the sky!" Gruber yelled.

Kaboom!

"Well, I don't think God liked that much. I think He is firing back," Brian yelled.

"I don't like where we are settin'," Mr. Ruger grumbled. "We aren't safe here, from them or the weather. We need better cover."

"Todd, how is Jakes?" Brian hollered to be heard over the cacophony of thunder. Todd had taken Jakes under a mesquite tree surrounded by some pretty big rocks.

"He has a bullet hole through the outside of his right arm. No bone broken, but he is bleeding pretty bad. I'm going to see if I can stop the bleeding. Did you kill that one fella?"

"Don't know. Looked like it, but ya never know."

"Brian, I can see a cave from here. It's about thirty feet up the side, halfway between us. As soon as I get Jakes bandaged up here, you want me to sneak up there and see what I can see?"

Todd asked with a little more eagerness than he intended.

Brian was about to answer back when rain started pouring down on them. Without another word, Brian started up the side of the ridge toward the cliff. He moved slowly and cautiously, going up and toward the right. When he was about halfway to the opening, he could see it. He ducked just as another shot passed right above his head.

"Jakes, can you reach my rifle?" Todd asked with a sense of urgency.

"I can."

"Pass it to me but do it slowly. Try not to make it obvious what you are doing. They may not be able to see what we are doing, but I can see the cave, so chances are they can see us even through this downpour."

"Okay, I have it. You want me to slide it over the ground?

With it raining this hard, we are not going to stay even close to dry under this mesquite. Water is streaming down here already."

"Just pick it up and move it over your chest. I can get it from there. Brian is pinned down and can't move; otherwise, they will be able to shoot him. They can now if they move out of the cave.

I'm counting on that, but I need to be ready."

"Here ya are."

"Thanks."

Brian looked down and saw Todd with the gun aimed at the cave. Todd watched as Brian reached out his hand and picked up a stone. He slung it sideways to a small pile of loose rock. When the stone hit it, the rocks started to slide down the hill. He pulled his gun and waited.

Todd waited. He saw one head come a little farther out of the cave, then another. They were talking to one another. Brian couldn't see them yet. He reached for another stone. He slung it over to just a little above where the other rock had landed. The men turned their heads and began to move in that direction.

With a precision associated with one mind, a shot rang out, but it was really two. Brian and Todd had fired at the exact same time. The two men crumbled to the ledge side and rolled down the ridge past Brian and almost straight for Todd.

Three more heads, then bodies came out of the cave, shooting in every direction. Brian and Todd fired again. Two more men fell. Then there were two more shots. Gruber and Ruger had surreptitiously moved over to where Todd and Jakes were so they too could see the cave. With their shots, the third man in the second group fell.

Todd scrambled up the side to where the first two lay. One had hit his head on a rock on the way down and was clearly past help. The other was moaning. Todd grabbed his feet, turned him around, and pulled him the rest of the way down the side. Shortly, Brian came down to the tree. By then, the other men had gathered the horses and had tried to find what shelter they could for them.

"There is room in that cave for us and the horses. I just don't know if there are any more 'surprises' up there for us," Brian said sardonically.

"Well, there is no way around it. We need to get some shelter. Jakes needs it bad. We all need it. I wonder if this will count for my weekly bath!" Todd said, trying to lighten the mood.

"That often?" Brian questioned.

Todd wasn't sure if Brian was joking. He decided he'd let it go. He crouched beside the surviving marauder. "You're shot pretty bad, but not beyond savin'. You want help?"

The man nodded his head.

"I'll tell you what. I'll help you if you help me. You tell me how many more are in the cave and how many altogether. If you do that and I'm satisfied with your answer, I'll see about patching you up. Keep in mind the more time you take thinking about it, the worse off you're going to get."

"Help me," the man choked out.

"Not until you help me. I have time to wait; you don't. Keep that in mind," Todd said.

Brian looked at Todd. He had a very casual way about him.

He seemed to have all the time in the world, as if they weren't even in a Texas toad-strangler. He was fascinated to see how this would turn out. At the same time, he kept his eyes on the mouth of that cave.

"How many men are there in your gang?"

"Eight."

"How many are there up in that cave now?"

"None."

Brian thought he answered a bit too quickly.

Todd nodded. He looked the man straight in the eyes. "You know you could be facing God in a few minutes to answer for what you have been doing. I wouldn't be surprised if you aren't part of the group who burned the way station. I know you raped that young girl. So if you want me to help you, I better come back alive from looking in that cave. You know why? These other men, they aren't going to help you, just me. I'm it. So I'll see you in a few minutes, after I go up there and have a look-see inside that cave. If something happens to me, well, I'm ready to meet my Maker. I've made peace with Him. If I don't come back, then I'll see you shortly up there, and we can face God together. If I do come back, I'll see you shortly right here. Then we can see about getting everyone comfortable and out of this torrent."

With that, Todd began to move in the direction of the slope. "Wait!"

"Yes, you have something you want to tell me?" "Shorty's up there."

"Really? What does Shorty like to shoot?"

"He has a scatter gun. His aim ain't too good."

"I see. I guess I'll have to be real careful then."

"Help me before you leave."

"I can't do that. You have already proven you're a liar. The only way you will get help is if I come back. By the way, that is only six of you. Where are the other two?"

"We got off our horses and walked over here through that gully. Then they rode on with all the horses so anyone following us would think we were all up ahead and pass us by. But you weren't fooled."

"You better start prayin' I come back."

"Wait! There's another man up on the ledge behind a dead tree. He might not be able to see you in this rain."

Todd looked at Brian and then said to the varmint on the ground, "That better be the last lie. You better start praying I come back."

Todd turned and started climbing the side of the ridge. He felt a presence with him. He turned to his right, and there was Brian.

"Sheriff, I really don't want anything to happen to you. I am expendable; you are not."

"Everybody is expendable, Todd. God is in control of how many days we have on this earth. If mine are up, they're up whether I'm here or down there. This is a two-man job. I have a feeling our outlaw wasn't telling you everything."

"I had that very feeling myself. Brian, thanks for letting me be a part of this. I've always wanted to be a lawman. I can't think of anything I would rather be doing right now, even in this downpour. Thanks again."

"Yeah, getting soaked, shot at, and climbing up and down slippery rocks in a torrential storm are just where I want to be right now too," Brian said with a smirk.

They were about to the top of the rise at the edge of the ledge where the cave was when they saw a man come stumbling down the side and turn to enter the cave. Just as he did, a shotgun blast blew him away. They very gingerly looked over the edge. They saw a man lying faceup with rain pouring down on his unmoving form. They were about to roll over the edge when another man came out to the mouth of the cave, clearly Shorty. There was a good reason he had gotten that name.

He let out a whole string of profanities as he looked down at the man he had just shot.

"Hold it right there, Shorty." Brian had his rifle aimed right at Shorty.

Shorty's head jerked up at the same time his shotgun did.

Todd fired his handgun, and they ducked. The shotgun blast scattered rock and other debris over their heads. They looked over the edge again and saw Shorty, leaning against the edge of the cave opening holding his right shoulder, his shotgun lying in the water. He eyed Brian and Todd as they scrambled over the edge, by now soaked to the skin and covered with mud and clay and appearing more like demons rising out of the earth than rain-soaked, muddy lawmen.

"I killed my own brother! I don't deserve to live!" Shorty yelled at them. He pointed his derringer into the base of his head right under his chin and pulled the trigger.

Brian and Todd fell to their knees. There had been so much violence. Why did this have to happen? Five bodies up on that ledge, one part of the way down, and one man still taking in breath as far as they knew.

"Seven, not six. I wonder how much more he lied about. Let's take a look inside. I can't imagine anyone not coming out to look when Shorty did. We need to be careful just the same," Brian warned.

They had been vulnerable in the last few minutes, and nothing had happened. Still, they very carefully looked inside the cave before entering it. When they did, they noticed a fire was barely glowing behind a short makeshift stone wall. They found some dry wood and put some on it to keep it going while they got the others up there. They discovered the cave had just the one chamber, so no surprises would come creeping out from the back. It had a narrow opening then widened out into a fairly large cave with enough room for them and their horses. The storm was worsening; they needed to move quickly.

When they turned to go back down, their men were just entering the cave.

"We heard th' shotgun and heard th' pistol at th' same time as th' shotgun, en' nothing for quite a while, en' a smaller caliber shot. We know'd 'at wasn't Shorty, so we figgered 'twas time to c'mon up," Gruber explained.

"The smaller caliber *was* Shorty. He shot himself with a derringer."

"Well, the truth is, we were miserable down there, and this couldn't be any worse. I've never seen a storm like this." Ruger shook his head as he spoke.

Shortly after getting all the horses and gear along with the people inside the cave, the men began to warm themselves in the fire, thankful for the stack of dry wood they found in the back.

"Maybe we can have some hot food to eat," Jakes said. "Or just coffee! Coffee right now would be such a blessing." As the owner of the hardware store, Jakes had a perpetual coffeepot on the potbellied stove in the center of his establishment. The stove provided a boys' club of sorts, circled with chairs and plenty of cups available for those who liked to jaw about what their newest horse looked like or how well their crops were doing, the weather, the latest political news when they had it, and any number of other things. Men told tales and listened with rapt attention to the tales of the others. They laughed, coughed, chewed, and spat. No matter what, that coffeepot was never allowed to run dry.

"I need to see about this feller first," Todd said. He looked at the man who had survived so far. He had a bullet wound in his chest, near a lung. He was all cut up from the fall off the ledge.

"I don't know about that bullet wound. He will need to see Doc, I'm thinking," Todd said sadly. I don't think I can do much for him now that I see his wound more clearly.

"Hey, what's that noise?" Jakes asked.

"Hail...in August?" Brian was mystified.

"Uh, 't can onliest mean un thang...twister," Gruber said solemnly and matter-of-factly.

10

aptain McBride, I can't believe how smooth our sailing has been. All except that one storm we had, we had great seas, didn't we?" Raven asked as she finished packing. She had her disguise completely finished. She whispered to him, "I didn't get sick once. I think I must take after my father."

He chuckled, gave her waist a little squeeze, and then whispered back, "Yes, you must. He was the best seaman I have ever known. But remember, you were 'sick' for the whole trip!"

Her laugh rolled out of her like the waves on the beach. She would miss the sea but wanted to go on to Texas to see what God had for her there. "Maybe sometime, I can go sailing with you as your 'niece'? Then I could go on deck and see the wonders from a new height. Oh yes, I wanted to ask you something. When we were leaving our port of origin, I saw some large gray jumping fish. They seemed to be playing games with the ship. Then I saw them again occasionally when we were in the Gulf of Mexico and more when we were closer to land. What are they? I just loved them."

"Those are called dolphins. They aren't technically fish. They are like whales. They give birth to their young and nurse them like humans. In fact, they really enjoy being around humans. I think that is why they stay close to ships. I have heard tales of them saving men who have fallen overboard or survived shipwrecks.

They push them in toward shore. Yes, they are fun to watch. They always look like they are smiling to me."

"I am so glad I had the blessing of seeing them."

Raven took Captain McBride's arm to "help" steady her as she walked down to the dock using her cane in her other hand.

She looked around as they left the area trying to get her bearings.

"Where to from here? It feels really funny walking on land again."

"I am taking you to the hotel and getting you settled in. I'm going to go to the stage office and check the schedule so we will know better how to prepare from here. I want you to stay in your room and rest, at least until I get back. The hotel is not far from here. We will be there in a few minutes."

"What an interesting place. It would be nice to explore, but I don't think I'll have time and shouldn't wander."

"Absolutely not. You need to take care of yourself and keep safe. You need to be as invisible as you can be. You'll never know who might be here on business. Perhaps, no one you know, and then again, you could run into someone who does know you. I wouldn't want you to take the chance of being…uh, shall we say reunited with an unwelcome acquaintance?"

"Thank you. No, I would not want to see any of my former acquaintances. They are not of the 'quality' I desire."

"They are not of the quality I desire for you. Here it is. Let's get you settled, shall we?"

They slowly walked up the steps to enter the hotel with Captain McBride assisting the elderly lady on his arm. No one who saw them would ever imagine the elderly woman was anything but elderly. She would make her transformation in Houston.

Not long after escorting his "aunt" to her room in the hotel, Captain McBride left and hurried off to the stage office just a block away. He bought the ticket for Catherine McBride to Houston. I trust you, Lord, to keep her safe. Show her the path she should take and keep your angels watching over her and befriending her as she travels. In Jesus' precious name, the name above all names, I ask this. Thank you for your answers according to your will. Amen.

He made his way back to the hotel and quietly knocked at "Catherine's" door. He heard her ask, "Who is it?"

"It's me, Catherine. I have your ticket ready for you. Do you want me to just slip it under the door?"

"No." The door opened, and there stood elderly Catherine.

"Please come in, and we can have a chat before I get settled in for the evening."

Their visit wasn't long. They talked about the trip behind them and the possibilities ahead. They prayed together. And then, just as Captain McBride started out the door, he caught a glimpse of a man who looked very much like one of his hands from the ship.

He turned and looked at Catherine.

"Truly, Catherine, you look so tired. I think I will order you a tray of food from downstairs and bring it back up here. Is there anything special you want to eat?"

"No, no. I don't think so." She looked at him, questioningly wrinkling her brow. He leaned a bit closer.

"What's that? I didn't quite hear you."

Then he whispered, "I think someone was watching us. You'd better stay in your room."

Looking at him with fear in her eyes, she then replied, "I think you are very right. I am tired. Just bring up anything you think will be suitable for my condition."

He nodded and left after she closed the door, and he heard her lock the door. *Good girl!* he thought.

"Now, why'd he call 'er Catherine? 'Er they be closer than we think? 'Er's somethin' a bit fishy goin' on 'ere."

The man left when he heard McBride's steps in the hall and headed in his direction. He hopped on the banister and slid down part of the way, then hopped off again, and walked down the stairs. He did not want to be seen close enough to appear to be able to overhear a conversation. When he came into the lobby, the hotel manager was headed his way.

"Hey, you." "Who? Me?"

"Yes, you. You are not allowed upstairs unless you have a room up there. Now, I will thank you to leave this hotel immediately!

I just don't believe you are interested in taking accommodations for the night."

"Well, what if I am?"

"I am sorry, sir, but we are full, and we have no room." As he said that, he mentally added, *For the likes of you.*

"You can't treat me like that."

"I can, sir, and I just did. Do I need to send for the law?" The manager looked around for someone to send for the sheriff.

"Well, what about him?" the sailor asked when he saw McBride come down and enter the room.

"Captain McBride has a standing room here. Not that that is any of your business."

"Good evening, Jacob. Are you having some trouble here?"

McBride looked at the manager. "I believe that is one of my men."

"No trouble, sir. Is he here at your request?"

"No," McBride replied to the manager. "Why are you here, Roger? You are supposed to stay with the ship and keep watch."

"I...uh...I...just...uh."

"You just want to keep your job, and so you will go back to the ship and won't leave it again tonight. Isn't that right, Roger?"

"Yes, Captain, yes, sir."

With that, Roger turned and almost ran out the door.

"Thank you, Jacob. You have always kept your eyes open for me. I appreciate it very much. I was wondering. Do you have another room available?"

"Why, uh, is your room not ready? Is there something wrong?"

"No, Jacob, nothing like that. I just have my aunt with me. I let her have my room. She was very tired. I was going to just stay on the ship tonight. She leaves for Houston on tomorrow's stage. I decided to come down and get her a tray for supper tonight, and when I saw Roger here, I decided, perhaps, I should stay closer to her. Some of the men were not real happy having a woman on board."

"Of course! In fact, the room right next to yours is available. Would you like it?"

"Yes, that will be fine." McBride looked around the lobby to see if he saw any of the other crew members there.

"I'll go and order some food now, and we will just eat upstairs, if that is acceptable to you!"

"Absolutely, Captain. In fact, let me get someone to help you with the trays. I'll also take care of checking you into your new room. Would you like me to keep your aunt's presence confidential in case any other ne'er-do-wells come calling?"

"Yes, Jacob, that would be most helpful. Thank you!"

"You are most welcome, sir. We are delighted you have chosen our modest hostel in which to abide when you are in town."

"I wouldn't go anywhere else, Jacob. You are most accommodating."

Not long after that, McBride was on his way up the stairs, key in hand and two helpers carrying trays up to his rooms.

He knocked on the door.

"Aunt Catherine, it's me Patrick. I have brought your supper."

He heard the lock on the door click and waited. The door cracked a bit, and then it swung open.

"I thought we might eat together, so I brought two trays. We can sit at the table by the window." McBride turned to his helpers.

"Come in, gentlemen, and just put the trays on that table over there." He indicated the table.

The two young men carrying the trays did as they were told.

When they passed him on their way out, he handed them a generous tip. The two left the room with very wide grins radiating on their faces.

The door closed with a soft click. Raven looked at Captain McBride. "What happened, uh…Patrick?"

"Well, I did see one of the men from the ship in the hall. He had no business here, and when I reached the lobby, the manager looked like he was about to have him arrested. I sent him back to the ship to stand watch and made sure he understood he was not to leave the ship all night. I will do a little surprise visit later. I decided I should spend the night here and accompany you to the stage in the morning."

"Oh, I am so relieved!" The color of her cheeks suddenly looked so much better despite the ash and charcoal makeup. "I have felt very uneasy, fearful. Actually, 'terrified' comes closer to expressing my feelings."

"I was considering sailing to Houston and taking you that far.

But with these recent developments, I think it is best you take the stage. It will be a longer, harder journey. There is no direct path.

There will be much swampy territory to go through and, I fear, many, many bugs. I trust it will not be too uncomfortable for you, but I feel it will be best for you to go that way. It will probably take three days since they have to travel north and then west-southwest to get there."

"Oh, I had not thought of the bugs. Ugh!"

"Also, let me warn you of the heat and humidity. This is early August, and we are very blessed we haven't had any tropical weather come in on us yet. I pray it won't. You will have some way stations where the coach will stop to change horses about every twenty miles and at times for the night and give everyone a rest although a brief one, probably. At least you will get a hot meal and a bed or cot on which to rest your weary bones. You may have to sleep in the stage. Not a happy thought, I'll warrant."

"I had not thought of all that. I guess it is best to be prepared. I don't even have an umbrella. Do you think I'll need one?"

"You can pick one up when you get to Houston. You probably won't need it before then. After all, you will be in the stage or at a way station for the next three days. When you get to Houston, follow the directions to the hotel that I wrote for you and go to the park across the street from the hotel to open the package I gave you. That hotel was one of my Catherine's favorite places, so I know you will like it."

"Patrick, is that your real first name?"

"Yes, it is."

"I like it. Patrick McBride. I am so proud to know you. It has certainly been a blessing from God for you to come into my life.

You knew my father and mother. That is truly amazing! I will pray for you and thank God for sending you into my life just when I needed someone the most."

11

Crystal Springs, August 16

hank you, Lord, for the safety of this cave. We are blessed to have this refuge. Keep our families and friends safe. Please watch over the whole town and direct this twister in a direction that will put no one in harm's way." As Brian finished praying, all the men, with the exception of one, said, "Amen."

"Hey, what's your name, fella? Where do ya think the others went in this storm?" Ruger asked.

"I don't think he is going to be able to answer that. He is barely breathing, and I can't do a thing for him," Todd replied.

Looking at him with compassion, Todd asked, "What's your name? I want to be able to pray for you by using your name. Will you tell me?"

The man just stared at Todd. Todd wasn't sure the man could even see him. Suddenly, he said loudly, "Pete," and closed his eyes again.

Todd began praying for Pete. He prayed that God would speak to Pete's heart and give him the willingness to believe in the saving grace of Jesus. "You know, with this twister, there is no way we can get you to the doctor. You may not last much longer.

Why don't you start asking God to forgive you of your sins and by accepting what Jesus did on the cross for all your sins and those of all men? He is waiting to hear from you."

"Watch out!" Gruber yelled as he dove for the floor of the cave with a canteen in each hand. A tree that looked like it had been snapped in two hit the side of the cliff right above the opening to the cave. "I thought 'at thang was comin' in to see us!'At was too close. I've never seen a twister before, and I don't thank I want to ever see another one. Hit's is just too much!" He stayed on the floor of the cave but rolled and crawled over to be near Jakes who was faring much better than Pete.

"Hey, Jakes, how're ya doin'?" he asked him.

"I'm going to make it. It will be some time before I can use my arm much, but at least, I'm breathing. Thanks for that coffee earlier. That helped!"

"Did you see 'at tree?'At scared the pants off me! I thought I was gonna lose my head!"

"Yeah, that was a bit too close. It sounds real quiet out there now. Is it still raining?"

"I don't know, but I don't want ta get near that openin'."

"Ask Brian, will you? I'd really like to know when we can get out of here."

Gruber, again, rolled and crawled his way over to Brian.

"Hey, Brian," he said from his position on the floor of the cave, "Is th' storm over?"

"It's quiet. Don't know. I'll see."

With that, Brian walked over to the mouth of the cave. The remains of a tree littered the ledge in front of the cave. It was barely raining, and the wind had all but stopped. He could see the sky was barely lightening up to the west, getting ready for sundown. *It's downright eerie, looking out over all this destruction. It doesn't look like it did before. Shorty and his brother are gone. The men who were on the rocks below are probably gone too.* The trees Brian and his men had been under were completely gone. *Thank you for this shelter in the time of storm, dear Father. How merciful you have been.* Brian wept one single tear as he looked out and realized what could have been. He turned to call to Todd and saw him leaning over Pete with his ear to Pete's chest. Brian looked back out and whispered, "I'm sorry."

Father, was I wrong about Todd? Help me to be more willing to see the truth as you see it not as I think it is.

"Storm's over, Gruber. You can get off the floor now." Brian chuckled as he looked back at Gruber. *Lord, keep everyone in the path of that storm safe. It may be over for us, but it's just beginning for others.*

"Wow, would you look at that! I wonder what happened to the other men and the horses we were chasing." Todd's voice right beside him made Brian jump a little.

"Sorry, you startled me. I was just looking out at the devastation all around and thanking God for His protection. I guess I was totally immersed in my thoughts."

"You have been around Riley too much. You have started using all those big words he uses." Todd smiled as he spoke.

"You may be right. I have been working closely with him all summer getting the school—oops…I mean academy and his house ready. That man really does know some words. He is full of wisdom as well. He has promised to give a dinner soon and tell all of us his story. I really can't wait to hear it. I guess it really isn't that important, but it would be nice to know where he came from and where he learned all that *stuppare*." Todd's befuddled look made Brian add, "Latin for *stuff*. I tell you the words that come out of that man's mouth. I remember my mom saying, 'Oh, stuff and nonsense!' I knew she was meaning any useless thing we could use to 'stuff' a pillow or throw out as trash. But Riley, he has to go into all the root words and where the words come from. What did he call that…et…e…m, etem. I remember it ends with *logy* or *ology* or something. I was going to remember that! I'll have to ask him again. I don't really need it. I don't guess. I might someday. It certainly wouldn't have helped in this storm. Look at this mess. I wonder if we can even get out of here."

"That has to be the most I've heard you say since I've known you. I didn't know you were so interested in words."

"I don't think a man can ever stop learning. And he shouldn't. I would really like to learn a new word every day. Maybe I can if I ever have a normal life." Brian looked off into the distance like he was trying to see into the future.

"I can go and check." "What?"

"I said, I can go and check."

"Check what? What are you talking about?" Brian looked completely lost.

"I can go and check if there is a way we can get out of here. It will be dark soon, and I would like to know what we are up against and prepare my mind for it before we bed down for the night."

"Oh yeah, right. Sure, but I would rather you take someone with you. If you fall or get into trouble, you need someone there to help or come get help."

"All right, Mr. Ruger, you can come with me. We are going to do some scouting."

"I sure could stretch my legs with a bit of climbing or sliding, whichever the case may be," Ruger replied, looking toward the roof of the cave. "Oh, and, Todd, just call me Horst."

"Whatever you say, Mr. Ruger."

Horst rolled his eyes and laughed. Brian shook his head. Todd walked over to his saddle and grabbed a coil of rope. "Let's get on with it while there is still some daylight."

He and Horst left the cave. As Brian turned, he heard Horst exclaim, "Dear Lord, you saved us! This doesn't even look like the same place."

"Yes, He did," Brian said to himself.

Gruber was tending the fire.

At least he is in a sitting position now. Brian thought the man would have to crawl back to town.

"Jakes, how are you feeling?" Brian asked.

"I'm doing better than I thought I would be. I am so grateful for Todd. If it weren't for him, I wouldn't be here. And he fixed me up so I didn't bleed to death or get trampled. He's a good man." "As soon as we get out of here, we'll head back to town and see what needs to be done there." Brian turned and looked at Gruber. "We'll need every man in control of himself in order to help the others who may need it. I pray the town was spared."

Gruber looked up at him and nodded. He knew without a doubt he had not been "a man" the last few hours. He stood up and went to get some things out of the saddlebags he had had strapped to his horse. It looked like he was pulling a whole pantry out of them.

As he squatted back down next to the fire, he looked up at Brian. "A man should nev'r be without food. I'll fix us all sompin'. We need ar' strength."

Brian raised his eyebrows and looked around at their "shelter in the time of storm." *Lord, you are our refuge and strength. What would we do without you?*

12

In the stagecoach to Houston, August 12

"Oh my," Raven croaked as the stage tipped yet again. "Hang on there, ma'am. We don't want you fallin' and breakin' something." The man sitting across from her had dark black hair, a black suit, complete with white shirt and tie. His collar had come unfastened and was sticking up a bit. Raven didn't think he noticed.

She smiled at him. "Thank you for your concern, sir. Perhaps you will be kind enough to catch me if I come flying your way. I feel so sticky that I believe if I did just go flying, I just might stick right to you."

The three men in the stage laughed at that and said they would take turns sitting across from her so each could have their turn at the game. Even though it was all said in jest, Raven wondered if what she had said could be called flirting? Would they think the old woman sitting with them would flirt with them?

"Oh, that won't be necessary. I promise I will sit here as tight as I can and hold on for all my life." She raised her hand to dab at the sweat beginning to form on her forehead but stilled her hand at her lips and just covered her mouth and coughed. It would not do to wipe the ash makeup and charcoal lines from her face. She needed to be very careful. She could not wait to get to Houston, take a bath, and change into…what? The dress she had with her was the most modest she had, but far from proper. *I could use this scarf I have to drape over the front of the dress, but the whole look of the dress suggests something I don't want to convey. I have the sum-*

mer dress Captain McBride bought, but it is too small for me to stuff and that would change my whole matronly appearance. I don't want to look too young, not yet."

"Now, what is bothering you to cause those wrinkles in your brow?" the man sitting diagonally from her asked.

"Oh, I was just wondering if we will have any trouble from Indians. Do you think we will be attacked?"

Again, the men laughed. "Oh no, ma'am. We don't have to worry about Indians here. Our biggest concern will be stayin' dry and lookin' out for outlaws." The young man next to her smiled and seemed to think that should make her feel much better.

The man across from him, an older man but not old enough to be his father, hit him with his hat. "Billy, you had no call to say that. Now, the lady will be worried about outlaws!"

"I'm sorry, Sam. I thought the worst would be havin' the stage leave the road and we end up in the swamp with the gators and snakes."

"Oh my!" Raven couldn't help herself. She truly did not like snakes at all. She nervously looked out the window and saw how the swamp came right up to the road in places, and the road was not that wide, more like a trail.

"Billy, now you've done it. Jest keep your mouth shut 'til we get to Houston." Sam hit him again with his hat.

"Quit it out, Sam. I didn't do nothin' wrong. Ain't it better to know the dangers so's you can get ready for them than to be su'pized by 'em?"

"It's all right. Gentlemen, we don't need an argument on my account. I'm fine, a little surprised, but fine. Sam, you may find me standing on your shoulders or head if we end up in the swamp.

Do you think you can handle that?" Raven asked, looking at the man directly in front of Billy.

"Why, yes, ma'am," Sam replied as he looked at her and was mentally considering her girth and height.

"Are you men brothers?" Raven felt she was being bold, but curiosity got the better of her.

"How'd you know?" Billy asked.

"Oh, I don't know…perhaps the way you talk to one another and the fact that Sam can hit you with his hat and you don't even seem to notice? That is not something strangers would do."

The "gambler," she had tagged him, burst out with a guffaw that almost shook the stage. It might have, but who could tell with the ruts in the road competing for the honor of dislodging them. If she let herself think about it, this was a miserable trip, and laughter is good for the soul. *So we must laugh and not allow ourselves to cry.* Raven looked at the gambler and laughed with him.

"I fear you men are at a disadvantage here. We know your names, but you don't know ours. Let me introduce myself. I am Garrett LeFleur, esquire. I'm pleased to make your acquaintance.

And this is…I'm sorry, I didn't get your name earlier, ma'am."

"That's quite all right. I'm Mrs. McBride. I'm very happy to meet you, gentlemen. I just hope my back survives this trip," she added as they hit another bump or hole in the road.

"Can anyone tell me what that wonderful yet spooky plant is that is hanging from the trees?"

Mr. LeFleur looked out the window. "That silvery gray plant is called Spanish moss. I've seen it in small clumps, like prickly balls or dry sea urchins. I've also seen it hanging long like an old man's beard. When the wind blows it, it takes on the appearance of ghosts moving through the woods."

"Fascinating!" Raven replied.

"Where are you from? Certainly, not from the South." LeFleur looked directly at her.

"No, no, not from the South. Northeast."

"What brings you here?"

"Well, Mr. LeFleur, after I lost my dear Corvus and Cora, I stayed inside most of the time. I finally realized I had to get out. Perhaps an adventure would be the best medicine. So, that is what I am doing, taking an adventure. Who knows, I just might like what I find out West."

"I'm sorry for your loss. It must be hard to lose a husband and a daughter at the same time. You are some woman taking an 'adventure,' as you call it, all by yourself."

Raven just smiled. She turned her head and looked out the window. The sights were so new; they were wonderful. It did occur to her that they were the same thing over and over. With the heat and mugginess of the air, she would not want to stay here. No, she needed to get out of here and the sooner the better.

"How long do you think it will take us to get to Houston?" she asked no one in particular.

"Depends on the weather," LeFleur answered her.

"Oh." Raven turned her head and looked at the scenery hoping to see something new. *Clearly, he is the more experienced passenger.*

"We're goin' to our ranch in Seguin," Billy piped up wanting his share of the conversation.

"Oh, you own a ranch?" LeFleur asked, a bit surprised.

Sam growled, like a watch dog.

"Naw, we jest work on one." Billy hung his head as he answered and then took Raven's cue and looked out the window.

13

Cave near Crystal Springs, August 16

All right, men. We can move out of here now if you want to, or we can spend the night in this cave." Todd looked at each one, trying to judge how anxious they were to get home and see if their families were safe.

Gruber looked up. "Now? Not fifteen minutes from now?"

"If we want to get down while there is still light, we need to move out quickly. There is a way, but I wouldn't try to go down it when it gets as dark as it will be say in twenty minutes, too dangerous."

"I've cooked some food. Everybody, 'cept you and Ruger there, have eaten. S'up to you."

Todd looked at Ruger who nodded and said, "I'm ready to ride. I want to see if my wife and kids are fine. I can eat some hard tack while I ride. We'll have to go a little slower so Jakes doesn't fall off. What 'er we gonna do with that dead feller?" Ruger reached for a cup of coffee and handed it to Todd and then reached for one for himself.

"Todd, did you find any other bodies out there?"

"Not a one is left, Brian. The trees are gone, but you saw that. The landscape is completely changed. We are going to have to move fast if we go tonight. No telling how much of the land has changed with that twister."

"Hmm." Brian rubbed the back of his neck and looked at the men. "As much as I want to ride out, I don't want to lose anyone else. We wait until first light. We will be rested. The horses will be rested. We will have plenty of sunlight and can move at a more cautious pace. I'm not saying we will be slow and leisurely, just cautious," he added when he caught Ruger's look.

"Well then, fellas, grab yourself a rock and eat a hot meal.

No sense in wastin' it now, is ther'?" As Gruber filled a couple of plates, he smiled at the two men.

Brian walked outside and looked up at the now-clear sky.

"Father, I need your guidance. I feel we should wait, but I'm anxious in my heart as well. What do I need to be doing? I don't feel confident. Give me peace and lead me in the right way."

"Brian?"

Brian didn't finish his prayer. He turned and faced Todd as if to say, *Yes, what is it now?* He didn't say it, just thought it. He had grown to respect this young man and see how wrong he was to be jealous of him.

"I'm sorry for disturbing you, but I just wanted to say it's okay.

I think you're wise in waiting. There's no telling what's up ahead, and we do need to do something with Pete's body. If we can take it in, it would be wonderful, but if we need to bury him out here, I'll go start that chore now. It's easier for a man to get down these rocks than it will be for our horses. "

"No, I think we'll take him back with us. We may need to show him to Daisy and see if she can identify him as one of her attackers. It might help her to see he's dead…if she isn't."

"I don't know if I'll sleep tonight, but maybe I will. I really am worn out. It has been quite the day. I'm going in and finish eating. I just wanted you to know whatever you decide is okay. I trust you. I also trust God to guide you."

With that, Todd turned and went inside.

Brian walked over to the side and fell to his knees. "Oh, dear God, how can they trust me so when I don't even trust myself? I have to lean on You and You alone. Point me in the right way. In Jesus' name, amen."

He sat on his heels there even though rock shards bit into his knees while he watched the sunset. Its fingers of red, pink, orange, gold, and purple streaked the sky. As he watched, the rays became the hand of God pointing toward town. He blinked, yet they still looked like a hand pointing in a direction. He looked back east and traced the straight line with his eyes. The line went right through that ravine and on toward town.

"Hey, Todd! Come here a minute."

Almost immediately, Todd popped his head out of the cave, and then the rest of him followed. "What's happening?"

"Look at that sunset. What do you see?" Brian never took his eyes off the sunset.

"Well, it looks like a hand pointing. I don't think I've ever seen anything like that before, and I love to watch the sunset."

"Yep! That's what I was thinkin'."

"What were you thinking?" Todd looked at Brian with a concerned look.

"Well, I was thinkin' you didn't go into that ravine over there, did you?"

"No, sir. We just found a way down and looked around for the bodies and to see if we could get through all the rubble. It looked like dynamite hit the side of the cliff. Rocks are strewn everywhere."

"Okay, then. Tomorrow morning we will have coffee and whatever Gruber has in his saddlebags and then set out for that ravine.

I clearly see God pointing in that direction. Once we find what He wants us to find there, we will head on east toward town."

"Whatever you say, boss."

"Right, will you let the others know? And, Todd, I'm not your boss."

"Yes, you are, if you want to be"

"The town can't afford to pay a deputy. You'll just have to keep ranching, at least for now."

"That's fine. But listen, Brian, if you ever need a deputy, you just call on me. I'll do whatever you need me to do. If the town can ever pay for the two of us, I'll be there. I love it here, and I couldn't learn the law and how to enforce it from anyone I admire more. Just holler, I'll be there." Todd turned on his heel and left, not even waiting for Brian to respond.

By the time Brian reentered the cave, the men were bedding down and letting the fire die down. The way Gruber had it banked, it wouldn't go out completely. Pete was totally covered by a blanket. Todd was bedded down close to him. Jakes was resting comfortably, and Brian was ready to do the same. The horses seemed calm and content. God's peace covered them all.

14

Houston, Texas, August 15

Thank you, Mr. LeFleur! I am so glad that trip is over. I feel like every bone in my body is out of place. I need to go to my hotel as soon as possible and get a nice hot bath!" She laughed with him as he agreed, wishing he would excuse himself and leave.

I'm just so very glad we didn't have any rain along the way. It was a pleasure to make your acquaintance, Mrs. McBride. I hope we cross paths again in the future. I feel like I have known you for years! There is something about you that reminds me of someone I knew in Baltimore."

"Oh, Mr. LeFleur, I'm sure I would remember if we had met before anywhere. Sometimes, people just feel a connection when they meet someone they can get along with. I'm sure you have felt that many times in the past. Perhaps our paths will cross again.

Until then, good-bye."

Raven looked around and began walking in the direction Captain McBride had instructed.

"May I see you to your hotel?" LeFleur asked.

"Oh look, there is a park over there! How lovely, I think I will just sit there for a short period of time and watch the children and that fountain! My, I haven't seen one of those in forever!

Thank you, Mr. LeFleur, but you need to go on and get rested. I'm sure you are planning some activity for tonight. I'm just going to take a bath and sleep. It has been a pleasure. Good-bye."

With that, she began walking away. She was beginning to wonder if she would be able to get rid of him. She found a bench in the park, and as she sat down, she saw her hotel just across the way. She began to take the package from Captain McBride out of her reticule, but when she felt someone sit down beside her, she took out the fan a kind woman at a way station had given her and began to fan herself.

"Mrs. McBride, I can't abide you sitting here by yourself. You never know who might sit down and just grab your bag from you. I want to protect you from such people."

"Mr. LeFleur, as much as I appreciate your concern, I don't have anything of value in my bag. I have paid for my room at the hotel ahead of time through a friend who was coming before me. Actually, they paid for it. There is supposed to be a stage ticket for me, and if there isn't, well then, I will just have to make do here. It will be an adventure. I may have to take in sewing to eat, but I will make it. I must! I can't go back. There are just too many bad memories for me. I am a poor woman. I just want to rest and *be alone* for a while and pray." She was beginning to feel very uncomfortable with Mr. LeFleur sitting beside her. His comment about her looking familiar and someone taking her reticule made her very nervous. She wound the string of it around her fingers.

"Oh look! There're Sam and Billy! Sam, Billy! Over here," she said, waving for them to come over. "It will be like old times on the stage." She laughed.

As they approached, Garrett LeFleur made his apologies.

"Forgive me, Mrs. McBride. As you have other defenders, I need to go and meet someone in a few minutes. Perhaps, I shall see you soon."

Not if I can help it, Raven thought as she watched him leave and the other two men approach.

"I thought you two were leaving immediately for Seguin," Raven said as she patted the bench, inviting them to sit beside her.

"Aw, we got to the livery, and our horses weren't ready. Since it's getting late and we are so sore from that blasted ride in that stagecoach, we decided to stay the night and leave in the morning," Sam said.

"How lovely! Where are you staying?"

"Well, we hadn't decided. We were thinking about that hotel over there. It's near to everything, and we just want to get some rest," Sam went on. "I need a hot bath to soothe these muscles of mine."

"I know what you mean. I'm staying there and had decided to get a bath as well. I have an idea." Raven glanced over her shoulder but didn't see Mr. LeFleur anywhere around. "Why don't we get something to eat? Then you two can check in and take your bath. I have a few errands to do, so I'll be a little later getting in than you will be. Or you can go ahead and check in. I'll be there in a minute, and we can eat in the hotel."

"We would like that. We won't likely see you in the mornin',
Mrs. McBride. We plan to ride out as early as we can, about daybreak." Sam was definitely in charge here.

"Oh my, yes, I plan to sleep in tomorrow. Well, let this be our farewell party. I have enjoyed your company on our grueling journey. I trust the rest of your trip will be uneventful." She smiled as they stood. She planned to sit on the bench directly across from the hotel until after they got there.

"We will see you in a few minutes, Mrs. McBride."

"Ma'am," they both said as they walked toward the hotel.

Raven looked around. No one seemed to be paying her any attention. She opened up her reticule again and, this time, was able to pull out the package without any interruption. She looked inside the envelope.

What is this? No, Captain, you shouldn't have! She found money, lots of it so it appeared to her. There was a note with explicit instructions on what to do before checking into the hotel. *Now how am I going to manage this? I'll just have to eat with the boys as Mrs. McBride. I'll make my transformation after they go upstairs.*

She got up and made her way to the hotel.

"That was the best grub I've had in a long time. I feel like a tick about to pop!" Sam said as he pushed back from the table in the dining room. A little grease glistened around his mouth. Raven fought the urge to reach over with her napkin and wipe his mouth. "I cain't keep my eyes open." Billy yawned. "I think I'll get me a hot bath and hit th' hay. We gonna start early in th' mornin'." Raven looked at him and sighed with contentment, "That meal was delightful! I feel like I'm about to explode as well. It's still early. I think I need to take a little stroll and let this food settle a bit. So I'll bid you men good night, and may God give you safe travels. I hope to see you sometime this side of glory."

"Good night. Same to you." The two turned and started walking away.

She heard Billy say to Sam, "What'd she mean 'this side of glory'?"

Sam gave a huff. "I need to get you to church more. Glory is heaven! She meant before she dies, I reckon, since she will likely see it before we will."

Raven smiled to herself. *So far, so good.*

She turned and walked away from the dining room and out through the front doors. She turned left and walked the block to the dress shop, which was very nice indeed. As she opened the door, the tinkling of a little bell announced her entrance. A woman in her late thirties bustled out of a side door, closing it as she came through. Raven smiled. *Such a happy face on one who had a thriving business.* She didn't appear to have a care in the world.

"Good afternoon!" she chirped. "What can I help you find?"

Raven had not really spoken with another woman since she left the house. She was suddenly painfully aware of how very hoarse her voice sounded.

"Oh, how kind. Yes, I need to buy some traveling clothes and some new essentials. Captain McBride sent me to you."

"Ooh, 'Mrs. McBride'?" the woman asked with her head cocked a bit.

"Why, yes…"

"Don't worry. Captain McBride came by to see me and explained that you would need a bath and everything from the… um, shall we say, the skin out? I am sworn to secrecy and did not ask any questions. He left it up to you how much you want to share. My name is Sarah Smith. He did say there would be a transformation. I can't wait to see it. He is an amazing man, a real godsend to people in need."

"Yes, he is. He is my angel."

"Mine too. I wouldn't have this wonderful business and the home I have if it weren't for him."

"Really?"

"Let's get the bathwater ready, and I'll tell you about it."

They went into the room Mrs. Smith had exited, and Raven found a tub waiting and water on the stove heating.

"The water should be ready soon. Now, let's see. I judge your size to be about—"

"You will have to wait until I take this dress and the padding off to be able to tell. You see, I am in disguise."

"He did say you were not who you appeared to be. Let's get these things off so I can get you the proper underthings."

"I have to tell you, it will be a relief to be able to be myself.

These extra things have made traveling very hot, especially through the swamp. I don't know what smelled worse—me or it.

I still smell like I brought it with me."

"I have some lavender soap and some rose water that will take care of that problem."

Raven let the dress and padding drop to the floor.

"My dear, you have lost considerable weight in such a short period of time! I wish I could lose it that quickly! My, my, I never would have guessed that that body was under all that padding. I certainly was fooled."

"I think I have sweat off some extra weight as well. I think I need to gain a little. I need my strength. We can allow for some weight gain. If I don't gain any, I can take everything in. I'm a seamstress."

"How wonderful! Then I may have even more you can choose from. Oh look! The water is ready. I'll let you take your bath while I fix some tea. I just love tea! A good cup of tea just settles the nerves. I don't think I will have any more customers this late in the day, so we should be undisturbed. We can have a little chat and a fun time with dress up and see what you want."

As Raven was taking her bath, Sarah came in with new undergarments. She brought out a screen, put it up next to the tub, and then brought a chair over with warm towels stacked on it. She pretended not to notice the transformation that had taken place in Raven as she washed her hair and her face. She just smiled and said, "Enjoy!" She bustled out again, quietly shutting the door behind her.

Raven closed her eyes. "Lord, again, I thank you for your provision. You are beyond my imagination." With that, she began to cry. She felt so unworthy of all the love God was pouring out on her through others. *How can I ever pass this on? I just don't feel like anyone will want anything good from me.*

"That was heavenly! Thank you so much for the bath, tea, and this great selection of clothing. Amazing. How did you have all this?" "Oh, I have quite the clientele. I know them and know what they like. So I keep making things in their sizes, which I think they might like. Sometimes, they do; sometimes, they don't.

Sometimes, they just don't really need anything yet; and, when they do, the style isn't what they want anymore. I can always sell them to someone else." She winked when she said that. "Someone who appreciates quality rather than the latest style being worn in the East."

"Tell me about you and Captain McBride. That is, if you don't mind."

"Well, I was married to a sailor. Captain McBride was interviewing for his crew just outside a local tavern near the docks. That is where most of that business is done. Most of the time, they would talk inside the tavern while taking part in the services offered in the place. McBride isn't like that. He knows that's where sailors go, but he gets them before they get beyond reason and talks to them."

"You mean drunk?"

"Yes, dear. My Charlie wasn't like that. He saw the big sea captain sitting outside talking to men and decided that's the kind of captain he would like to have. He went over to talk with him and signed up. He came home so happy to have a job. We hadn't been married long, and I didn't like the idea of him going to sea, but that is what he was, a sailor. So, I kept my mouth shut and was happy for him."

"What happened? I don't remember a Charlie Smith on board."

"They sailed, and Charlie loved working under McBride. When they came into Houston, we had him over for dinner. He was a wonderful guest. I will never forget those nights. He still drops in when he comes to port. That's why he was here the other day, and I found out about you. We even had dinner together just like the ole days."

"That scallywag, he came here after I left his ship. I don't think that had been planned. How long ago did Charlie sail with McBride?"

"His last voyage was twelve years ago."

"Twelve years? Where is he?"

"They were on their way back when they stopped in New Orleans. Some men jumped them, and McBride had one on his back trying to hold him with another trying to stab him with a knife. McBride didn't see the knife. Charlie did. Charlie had just knocked the man out who had jumped him. He lunged to grab the knife. That man stabbed him instead, right in the chest.

McBride somehow flipped the man off his back and really beat the other man to a pulp. The man who had been holding him ran like a scared rabbit. There was no hope for my Charlie. McBride knelt down beside him. Charlie looked at him and said, 'I only did what Jesus did. I gave my life for yours. Go see my Sarah for me. I'll see her again...someday. I'll be waiting for her.' At first, I wanted to die. Now, I see God had a plan for me I didn't expect. I'll see my Charlie again. In the meantime, I have an opportunity to serve others like Dorcas did. I feel honored to be in that position."

"So...McBride set you up with your own shop. He took care of you."

"Yes, that's what happened. He's my encourager. I couldn't have made it without him. We have remained dear friends. If he tells me someone needs help, I do what I can. I'm just passing on what God has done for me through McBride and others like him.

God weaves them through my life. Some I may never see again and others have become friends as well."

"I'd like to be your friend. I'm traveling on, but, perhaps, I'll make it to Houston sometime in the future. I must travel farther west. I need to find the place where God will use me."

"I have just the traveling dress. It is navy blue with a white collar. It will look stunning on you, and I don't think you will have to make any alteration to it. There is a cute, little gingham dress that will be perfect for hot weather. I have some other things along with bonnets, a shawl, gloves...oh yes, he brought over a carpetbag to pack your things in. Let me get it."

What next? Will his gifts never end? How do I even comprehend this? Raven sat in wonder.

"Here we are. I even found a parasol to help keep that hot sun off your beautiful skin. More tea?"

"No, thank you. I really need to pay you and get checked in at the hotel."

"If you think so, dear. That will be one dollar."

"One dollar! Why, all this costs more than that. You cannot possibly make a living with that kind of income. I sew. I know what goes into making an ensemble. Really, Sarah!" Raven's face turned a little red. *I never have spoken like that in all my days. What has gotten into me?*

"Well, McBride explicitly said, 'Now, Sarah, charge her a dollar for the bath, but I'm paying for everything else. She can't return the bath once she has taken it, and I am not returning the clothes.' He gave me some money that more than covers these things. So either you have a credit, or you can pick out some more things. Suit yourself, but it is yours."

"Well…I did have my eye on the pink and the yellow dresses. I was thinking I might need a coat for winter and maybe some heavier clothing, if you have anything? And would there be another set of underthings? I would truly love to have a soft nightgown." Raven enthusiastically looked around. "How much do I have left? Have I overspent already? I feel like it is Christmas in the middle of summer."

"Now, that is more like it. Yes, no, and yes, you can afford all of that and more. Let me get you some things. Let's fill up this carpetbag. When we are finished, you just might need a trunk! I think I have one of those in the back. It is a bit dusty, but you've been traveling, right?" She smiled the most beautiful smile Raven had ever seen. This woman's hair was going in every direction by now, and her bun had begun to come down, yet she didn't seem to even notice. The mousy brown color did nothing to detract from her loveliness. Her petite build and height gave her an elfin quality. Raven adored her. *We must write to each other,* she thought.

"Do you have any calling cards with your address on them?" Raven asked.

"No. My goodness! I had not even thought of adding an address to a calling card. I could do that and give them to my customers to share with their friends."

"I'd like to write to you when I get settled," Raven said tentatively.

"Oh, please do! Here, I'll write down the address for you. Of course, you could just write to general delivery. I just go in and ask for my mail."

"Okay, that will be fine." Raven had forgotten for a minute she was no longer in Baltimore where they had started postal delivery recently especially in the business district. She felt a bit silly for even asking.

"I would love to hear from you. Let's do keep in touch. Perhaps, I can come for a visit once you get settled."

"I'd love that, Sarah."

"You just go on to the hotel and check in. I'll have your things delivered. Oh dear. That reticule will not do. Oh no, not do at all. Let's see. Oh, here is one. This will be perfect. Go ahead and change your belongings to this one, and let's just discard all your old things. You don't want them, do you?" Sarah looked at Raven with a bit of concern.

"No, I certainly do not want anything that will remind me of anything I'm leaving behind, except my cane. That is how I met Captain McBride. I guess I'll have to leave it. A young woman wouldn't be using or carrying a cane. Thank you so much, Sarah. You are truly a precious pearl, beyond price. God bless you!"

Raven gave Sarah a huge hug and held on for many minutes.

"You know it's been a very long time since I've had a genuine girl-to-girl hug. There's just something about a friend hug that can't be replaced by anything else. It's the same with a mother's hug. Thank you for that as well." Raven began to tear up. "Now, where's that handkerchief?"

"Here. Now get on with you. I'll send your belongings right along. I'll also keep your cane. It will be here for you, or, if I can, I'll send it with Captain McBride when he comes to visit you after you are settled." Sarah discreetly dabbed at her own eyes with her handkerchief.

Raven hated to leave. She felt so secure in Sarah's place. She knew she needed to check in and get her sleep. She had a trip to make in the morning.

As Raven reached for the front-door handle, Sarah said,

"Wait, McBride left this for you. I can't believe I almost forgot!"

Sarah handed Raven an envelope. In it, she found a note and the stage ticket to San Antonio in the name of Erin Kerr. "He thinks of everything, doesn't he?"

"Indeed, he does. Good-bye, child, our prayers are going with you."

15

Heads turned as she entered the hotel. She walked straight up to the desk and checked in. She used her first name, Erin, and her last name, Kerr. She was given a key. The desk clerk looked at her. "Did you bring any bags?"

"Why, yes, they should be here momentarily. I couldn't possibly have carried them. I'll wait for them if you would like," she whispered since she didn't want her voice to be noticed by anyone.

"Why is madam whispering?"

"Sore throat. Do you have any tea?"

"No, ma'am."

"Oh, I see. A glass of water would help."

"I'll get you some when your luggage arrives." He smirked.

"I'll just sit over here." She started to cross the lobby when two young men came through the door carrying her bag and trunk.

She turned and walked back to the desk. "My bags are here. My water, please." She still whispered.

"I'll bring it to your room." That same smirk crossed his face, this time, with deeper meaning. His eyes skittered up and down her. She had seen that look before. She began to feel like spiders were crawling all over her. *I hate spiders!* She shivered as she thought that thought.

No longer whispering, she said, "No, you won't. Perhaps, I should go somewhere else. I would like to see the manager, now."

She straightened her back and waited. The young men came up to the desk. She turned to them. "If you will just give me a minute, there seems to be a problem with my room." They smiled and stood quietly next to her, waiting. The desk clerk stared at her. "The manager, please," she repeated. This time, the desk clerk glared at her, but he left the desk and entered an office.

Shortly, a tall, very handsome man, obviously of Spanish descent, she assumed from Mexico, came through the same door. He was impeccably dressed in a tailored black suit. She had seen many of those in the past.

"Yes, señor...ita? How may I help you?"

"Sir, I checked into your hotel expecting hospitality. My throat is sore. I asked for a cup of tea and was told no. So, I asked for some water, and again, I was told I could have no water until my luggage arrived. When I asked for the water after my luggage came, I was told by the desk clerk that he would bring it to my room. Now, sir, it wasn't so much what he said as how he said it and what was meant by it. I am very close to feeling I should find accommodations somewhere else. I'm leaving on the stage tomorrow morning and wanted to stay fairly close to the stage, uh, depot? I will go somewhere else if my accommodations and the hospitality of this establishment are not more satisfactory."

The manager turned to look at the desk clerk, who wasn't there.

The manager turned back to Erin. "May I see your key, señorita?"

Erin handed it to him. He looked at it. "I am so sorry. He has made a mistake and given you someone else's key. Let me make the adjustment." He stepped behind the desk and looked at the registration book. "Miss Erin Kerr?"

"Yes, sir. That is correct."

"Yes, he did give you the wrong key. Here is the key. And this is your luggage?" He nodded toward the two young men.

"It is indeed. And can you direct me to my room? It can't be too difficult; but, if you do not mind, I would feel more comfortable with your assistance."

"Certainly. If you can wait just a moment, I will get someone to cover the desk since John seems to have disappeared."

He walked into the dining area where earlier Raven had eaten with Sam and Billy. Shortly thereafter, he reentered the lobby and proceeded to show them the way to the room he had assigned to Raven. Raven looked back, and a young woman was removing her apron and moving quickly behind the front desk. Her coal-black hair accentuated her beauty. *She could not be more than just a year or two younger than myself.* The two boys Sarah had sent were following Raven up the stairs, sharing the load of the trunk, and the older boy had the carpetbag in his other hand.

It seems effortless to them. I could never manage all that. I will have to have someone bring them down in the morning and carry them to the stage depot. She decided to call it that since he had not corrected her.

"Here is your room, señorita. I trust your stay will be a pleasant one. If there is anything else I can do for you, just let me know."

Erin turned and looked at the two boys. "I will need help with my luggage tomorrow morning. It needs to go to the stage depot."

"What time do you want us to be here? We'll take care of that for you. Mrs. Smith said we should do whatever you ask."

"Oh, all right then, uh, thank you, boys…excuse me, Mr.….?" Raven waited for the manager to give his name.

He suddenly realized she was speaking to him. "Forgive me. Señor Martinez, at your service, Señorita Kerr."

"When should these young men be here in order to get my luggage to the stage on time? It leaves at seven in the morning."

"Then, they should get here by six thirty and take your luggage down to be loaded on the stage. You will not need to be there quite that early."

"Thank you, Mr. Martinez. You are very kind and helpful." She turned, smiling toward the boys. "Boys, be here at six thirty in the morning. I will have everything ready. Now, let's put those things in here." With that, Raven unlocked the door and opened it for the boys to go in. She followed them in as Mr. Martinez turned and walked down the hall. Raven gasped. This was the biggest room she had ever seen. "Can this be right?" she asked.

"Guess so, this is where he brought us, and the key worked," the older boy said, scratching his head.

"You are quite right. Well then, put the trunk over there. And the carpetbag, let's see, just put it on the bed. Thank you so much. Here, this is for your help. I appreciate it very much." She handed them each a $1 coin. In his note, McBride had told her the proper tip for people who did a service for you; she increased it a bit. The boys' faces beamed. "Now, be here on time and get my luggage to the stage in plenty of time, and when I come down there, I'll give you another one."

"We'll be here!" They almost fell over their own feet as they left the room.

She giggled as she closed the door. Just as she was going to lock it, a knock sounded on it. *Now, who can that be? What did the boys leave?* She glanced around the room. Nothing.

"Who is it?"

"Your tea, miss."

A sigh escaped from Raven. *How wonderful! Now the day was perfect.*

She opened the door, and the same young woman who had manned the front desk brought the tray inside the room and set it on the table.

Raven reached into her reticule to give the woman a tip.

"Oh no, miss. Señor Martinez is my brother. It is my pleasure to serve you." She turned and hurried out the door, closing it softly as she left.

Now, I will lock the door and enjoy the quiet solitude of this heavenly room.

It wasn't long, and Raven was sitting drinking the tea. She placed the cup on the table near the front window of the corner room. Looking out on the street, she saw the last light of day color everything with a golden hue making the park look like a fairyland. People were moving quickly as if to beat the last ray of the sun home. *Who will win?* she wondered. Then she saw Mr. LeFleur standing beside the park bench, looking at the hotel. She quickly moved back from the window. *I don't know if he would recognize me or not. I just don't need to take that chance.* She looked through the lace curtain and saw him talking with another man. He looked familiar as well. *Oh, it's the desk clerk, John! He is pointing at something at the other end of the hotel, the window of my 'old' room, perhaps? Who are they? Could they be agents working for William? Oh God, save me from my enemies!"* She turned down the oil lamp and proceeded to get ready for bed. She would go to bed early and leave early. If they were from William, they would not think a woman of her history would go to bed early and then get up early. When she had opened her little bag to make sure she had her "valuables" out before Sarah threw everything away, she found the Bible she had used on the ship. She would get it out now and read the Psalms. *Oh, how right David was when he referred to You as his refuge and strength.*

The knock on the door startled Raven. She opened her eyes; it was still dark.

"I am sorry to disturb you, miss. My brother asked me to bring you breakfast and to make sure you are up so you will be ready for your trip."

"Oh, how nice." She was talking in her normal voice, which fortunately sounded like she really did have a sore throat although not nearly as bad as it had when she started the trip. "Just a minute. I'll open the door."

She quickly wrapped the robe about her lovely nightgown and quickly took the key to the door to open it. She placed her foot so it blocked the door being fully opened and peeked out. The only person in the hall was the young woman from last night. Raven opened the door to let her in and closed it quickly locking it.

The young woman glanced her way as she set up the tray on the table beside the window. She picked up the tea things from the night before and looked at Raven.

"Excuse me, but what should I call you?" Raven asked.

"My name is Maria."

"Maria, how lovely. Maria, thank you so much for being so kind. You must have gotten up quite early since it is still dark out."

"I am used to it. It is this way when you own a hotel. Do you need anything else?"

"I don't know whether to mention it or not."

"Please, my brother and I are here to serve our guests."

"The desk clerk John. I saw him last night after I finished my tea. He was out by the park bench across the street talking with another man who had been quite rude to me earlier in the day. John was pointing at an upstairs window at the other end of the hotel. I didn't stand and watch them. I had finished my tea and wanted to go to bed. I don't know what else they did."

"Oh, this is not good. Thank you for telling me. I will tell my brother. A room at that end of the hotel was broken into last night, but it was an empty room."

"I am so sorry. I hope this isn't on my account. Perhaps, I shouldn't have been so upset with John last night."

"Believe me, Miss Kerr, we do not allow our employees to treat our guests rudely, and he had done that. Truly, it is our pleasure to serve you in any way we can. I need to go back downstairs now.

If I can, I will come back to check and see if you need anything."

"Thank you so much, Maria."

Raven walked to the door, opened it a crack, and looked out.

No one was in the hall. She then opened the door for Maria who was carrying the tea tray.

"Thank you. I will be back if I can."

Raven closed and locked the door. She turned and quickly ate her breakfast and dressed in her dark-blue traveling dress.

She had made things like this for other people when she had worked with her mother but had never worn one herself. She was surprised at how comfortable it was and how well it fit. She decided to wear the bonnet and carry the parasol and her reticule of course. The rest would be packed and carried to the stage depot by the boys.

Again, a knock sounded at the door. "Who's there?" "Maria and Jesus Martinez, Miss Kerr."

Raven carefully opened the door and saw they were alone. She let them in. She realized her hands were shaking.

"Good morning, Mr. Martinez. Maria has been a jewel. I would ask her to travel with me, but I know you need her here. She must be indispensable." Raven smiled a big smile at Maria.

"*Gracias*, señorita. She is my baby sister, and I have had to be her parent for the last eight years. Our parents died in an accident, and our other sisters did not want to take her in. I love my sister and would do anything for her. So, here we are."

"Thank you so much for your hospitality. I am sorry I was so upset last night. I just did not like what John was implying with his remarks, and it made me feel quite uncomfortable."

"*Sí*, yes, I think you had good reason to be, Miss Kerr. I have a suggestion. I hope you will heed my advice."

"Please, Miss Kerr, he has never given me bad advice. Please, listen to him." Maria's eyes were wide and dark with intent sincerity. By now, Raven was very curious as to what had them so insistent about this.

"Please, tell me what you have on your mind."

"Last night or early this morning, a room at the other end of the hotel was broken into. Since it was empty, no harm was done except I will have to repair the door and lock on that room.

Señorita Kerr, it was the room John had given you."

Raven sat down heavily on the chair next to the window. Her hands were trembling. Maria rushed to her, leaned down, and put her arm around her.

"There is more, señorita. You told Maria that last night you saw John with another man in the park across the way."

"Yes, that is correct. I did see him."

"There is a stranger sitting in the lobby. He came in very early this morning and is pretending to read a newspaper. He may be the other man. What did he look like?"

"He was tall and had dark hair. He looked like a gambler or something. His black suit looked travel worn but was tailored to fit."

"You could see all that from your window?"

"No, I recognized him from earlier. He spoke to me in the park. He introduced himself as Mr. LeFleur. I was not comfortable with him. Two other acquaintances of mine happened to come by; and, with them there, Mr. LeFleur left. Then I went to visit a friend. She sews, and I bought some things from her and ended up having more than would fit in my one bag, so I also bought a trunk from her. She said she would have my luggage delivered, and I could go on to the hotel and check in. That's when I met John. Of course, I only knew him as the desk clerk until you said his name."

"Yes, your description does fit the man in the lobby. Señorita, here is what I suggest. When you are ready to go to the stage depot, let Maria and my wife go with you. Three women together will not look out of place, very normal. I see you have a bonnet.

It would be wise to wear it. You will be less noticeable that way. Maria, you and Consuela should wear them as well."

"Sí!"

"Leave by the back stairs and take the alley to the other street.

Make your way to the stage depot. I will have Pedro y Jorge take the luggage. That way, it will look like you are seeing one of our visitors off. Do you have a ticket yet?"

"Yes, I do."

"That is even better. The three of you can sit in that little shop across the street and down a little from the stage depot. Drink some coffee and have a pastry while you wait. It is better than being in the open waiting on the stage. The two men will deliver your luggage. When it is closer to the time when the two men are supposed to be coming to take your luggage, I believe I will take a walk…in which direction, señorita?"

"Oh, that way." Raven pointed in the direction she had walked from Sarah's shop.

"I will recognize the two men; and, I hope, they will recognize me. I will give them an envelope from you with what you promised them in it and send them back home. Should I explain why they are not needed?"

"Oh, I don't think that will be necessary. If they ask, just tell them I changed my plans." Raven sat, wringing her hands and praying without ceasing in her heart.

"*Sí*, I'll do that. Mr. LeFleur will still be waiting for you to come downstairs until after the stage leaves. I will invite him to have breakfast while he waits for his party to come down. Perhaps, he will take me up on it. If not, I'll offer him at least some coffee to drink while he waits. It matters not if he waits for you in the lobby or the dining room. He will not see you."

"Mr. Martinez, how can I ever thank you, Maria, and your wife? You are so kind. I hope I can pass on that kindness to others someday. If I ever come back to Houston, I will be sure and stay here."

"Señorita, your throat is not very much better. Perhaps we should get a doctor to look at you?"

"No, no, I think I will wait until I get away from Mr. LeFleur and his friends. I don't want anyone else knowing I'm here."

"*Sí*, that is a good idea. We have some lemons that have just arrived. I will have Maria make you a lemon drink that should help soothe your throat."

"Thank you. That sounds delightful."

Raven could not refuse although all she had ever heard of lemons was that they were sour. She dreaded having to drink it.

As they left the room, Maria turned. "I'll be right back with your *lemonada*."

"Thank you," Raven said weakly.

Raven began praying and fell to her knees beside the beautiful four-poster bed she slept so well in. "Father God, God of all comfort, please give me peace and comfort now. I am so frightened. I don't know where to turn, and yet You keep sending me these angels to guide and protect me. Thank you! I know you have a plan for my life, just like Joseph when you led him into captivity and just like David who was chased by his enemies. Lord, I am not worthy of your notice or your aid, but you are giving it anyway. Keep my heart grateful and keep me obedient to you." Raven prayed and prayed, but it did not seem that long. The knock at the door surprised her.

"Who is it?"

"Maria, Miss Kerr. I have your drink."

Raven opened the door with caution. She saw Maria, again, was alone in the hall.

"Come in. Maria, I haven't seen anyone else in this hall. Am I the only guest?"

"*Sí*, yes, these are the more expensive rooms and also larger, so the guests who stay in these rooms usually come on special weekends to attend some of the society socials but want privacy.

The rest of the guests are up the other stairway in the other side. We will have this wing full this next weekend. There will be a big wedding in town and many other visitors too."

"I'm sorry, but I have lost track of time. What day is it?"

"It is Monday. Wednesday and Thursday are days with few guests. Businessmen come in on Mondays for business and leave on Wednesday and Thursdays. I don't know why."

"My, I had no idea."

Maria stood watching Raven hold the glass of lemon drink.

Raven knew she would have to try it in front of the girl and do her best not to make a face of dislike. She lifted the glass to her lips and slowly tilted it.

"Maria, this is not what I expected!" Raven took another taste. She could not believe how sweet and tart at the same time the beverage tasted. She found it to be very refreshing.

"I think this will help my throat very much. Would you please share with me how you make it? I will want to continue to drink this when I get to my destination."

"Oh, *sí*, yes, I will write it down for you. I will give it to you when we leave for the stage. We will leave in about ten minutes.

Will that be convenient for you?"

"I am in your hands."

"Mr. LeFleur is still sitting in the lobby. He doesn't even seem anxious."

"Where are the stairs to the back?"

"When you leave your room, we will turn right. Then we will go into the alcove at the end of the hall, practically at your doorstep." Maria smiled. "We will go left in the alcove where there is a door to the outside stairs. After just a short walk down the stairs and across the backyard, we will go down the alley to the street. Consuela will meet us in the backyard. This is exciting, no?"

Raven was drinking the last of the lemon drink and almost choked on it when she said that. Raven was not having fun. "Yes, my pulse is racing," she replied as she handed Maria the glass.

"Thank you, Maria. I will listen for your knock in about ten minutes?"

"*Sí*, yes, I will be here."

Now that the three women were sitting in the little shop drinking tea and coffee, Raven could see how busy the town was already with many people moving about. She hoped she would see "trouble" if either John or Mr. LeFleur showed up. So far, she had not seen either one. She did see her luggage delivered. "Well, that part went well." The three women chatted. Maria translated her sister-in-law's Spanish into English for Erin and vice versa for her sister-in-law. They were having a very good time. Suddenly, Maria got up and said, "Time to go. You do not want to miss your stage. It has been a pleasure having you as a guest. I will not forget your visit. It has made my life much more interesting. Thank you."

"No, no, it is I who should be thanking you."

"For what?"

"For just about everything, I think. Thank you for the room, your hospitality, the lemon-drink recipe, every time I make it, I will think of you, your friendship, your companionship, and your safety."

By then, they were out the door and almost to the stage. Maria hugged Raven, and then so did Consuela. Each time the bonnets bumped into each other, the women giggled. With a feeling of urgency, Raven turned, handed the man her ticket, and got into the stagecoach. About a minute later, the stage driver and his sidekick had the stage headed out of Houston.

As Maria and Consuela were walking back to the hotel with their heads down, just before they turned onto the street that would take them to the alley behind the hotel, a tall dark-haired man came running past them, swearing and yelling for them to stop the stage even though it was blocks away. Maria and Consuela picked up their pace and practically ran down the alley to the hotel.

Jesus met them at the back door. "What's the matter?"

"A man came running for the stage. He missed it. Was it him?"

"Yes, I held him as long as I could; and when he looked at his pocket watch, he jumped up, swore, and took off running. He missed the stage, didn't he?"

"Yes, yes, but will he hire a horse and chase after it?" Maria asked.

"No, I sent word to Hidalgo not to rent any horses to a man who looks like him and to pass the word to the others. He will not RAVEN'S WINGS find a horse anytime soon...not from our relatives and friends. The man is stuck here for at least a couple of days."

The three laughed and gave each other hugs.

16

Katie opened her eyes with the aroma of baking bread and coffee filling her head. *Delicious! What am I doing on the couch? Who cooked?* She sat up and immediately felt like she was going to throw up. She ran out the front door and over to the pecan tree. Willow heard the door slam as she came up from the cellar and went after her. When she stepped on the porch, she heard the retching sound and saw Katie bent over with one hand holding on to the tree as if it were her lifeline.

Willow reached Katie and put her arm around her to help steady her. "Are you all right? Here, let me help you. I know this is a hard time."

"What is wrong with me, Willow? I can't seem to stay awake, and I feel so sick every morning, well, most of the time. I'm so afraid to tell Joshua. Oh, Willow, I don't want to die now. I did before, but not now. What is happening? Why would God do this?"

Willow looked at Katie, trying hard not to laugh. "Here, let's get you inside. I'll fix you a nice wet towel to rinse your face and get some tea on for you. Then we will talk about this."

The two women walked into the house, Katie leaning on Willow for support.

Katie sat at the kitchen table sipping her tea. "Will it come back up? I hate throwing up!"

"No, I don't think so although some women do throw up more often."

"What do you mean? What is this disease? Were the women in your tribe afflicted with this?"

"Women in every tribe, nation, country, the world around are afflicted with *this*." Willow pulled a chair over, sat down right next to Katie, and put her arm around her once again. "Katie, do you not know or even suspect that you are pregnant?"

"Pregnant! That can't be! Can it? I mean we haven't been married that long. Doesn't it take longer than a few months to get pregnant?"

"Katie, it only takes once. I'm sure it has been more than once for you and Josh. Have you not watched the animals on this ranch? Surely, you understand how God intended all his creation to multiply. You are not going to die. This is a gift from God! He has blessed you with a child. You will have to wait to see that precious one, but you have nine months to get to know him, and he will get to know you. That child will be comforted by the sound of your heartbeat from now until he is too old to sit on your lap. Love every minute of it, even the tiredness and the sickness."

Tears were running down Katie's cheeks. She could not remember being in such awe and feeling such happiness. "This compares with the moment I asked Jesus into my heart and the day I married Josh, all of these within months of each other. It seems my life began six months ago when Michael arrived at the ranch. He saved my life that day, and he has been saving it over and over ever since he took over the ranch, and then he saved me from Red's clutches. That still gives me goose bumps all over.

He has also been teaching Josh not only about ranching but also more about God."

"Yes, you are surrounded by special men. Katie, God has blessed you abundantly. You will have to find a special time to tell Josh he is going to be a father."

"Are you sure that's what's wrong with me?"

"Okay, let's look at the facts. When was your last monthly?"

"Oh, Willow. I don't even remember. Let me see…July…no, it wasn't July. It must have been June. Let's see we had our first month anniversary the end of May, and about a week after that, I think. I don't remember one since then."

"So, about the first week in June and none since then, and this is the middle of August. So, we can figure we will see this baby about the ides of March. Just don't name him Julius! Riley will have a fit. I think that must be one of his favorite Shakespearean plays. He quotes lines from it all the time, especially when he is talking about the day he was shot."

The girls laughed and talked. "Are you feeling better? Willow asked.

"Yes, I believe I am." Katie smiled.

"Well then, enough of this loafing. You better get to work and help out a little. Josh will want supper when he comes in."

Willow got up and checked the bread. She turned and looked at Katie, who was still sitting at the table. "Well, are you going to get to work?" She laughed.

"I can't believe it, Willow! I'm going to be a mother? Are you sure?"

"I saw this same thing many times in the Indian village. I lived there long enough to pick up on the signs. Yes, I'm sure.

But if you need more reassurance, you can always go and see Doc McConnell. By the way, I've helped deliver many babies."

"Willow, I'm so glad you're here. I'm so glad we became sisters."

For the first time that day, Katie really looked at Willow.

"Willow! Where did you get that riding skirt and jacket? Wow!

You look stunning."

"Thanks, Mom gave it to me today. She said it was a birthday present. I told her I didn't think it was my birthday. She said it didn't matter; she'd missed so many. It made me think how very special she is. I can't call her Esther anymore. I call her Mom just like you do. I am blessed to be a part of this family."

"We all love you, Willow. Where did she get that skirt?"

"Marta made it."

"Are you saying that Marta, our Marta, the wife of the Oscar the blacksmith/livery man, Marta made this skirt?"

Katie felt the soft leather and examined the fine stitching.

"Yes, that Marta! She's the only one I know."

"Oh my, I didn't know she could do leather."

"She's teaching herself how to do it. She's so good. What a precious woman and so mistreated by her husband."

Katie's brow wrinkled. "I've wondered. I've listened to the twins talk and watched the way they act when they have an opportunity to go to town. They don't want to. I think they would love to see their mother, but they are afraid of seeing their dad."

"Katie, you know Josh has talked about building a line shack out where we set up the chuck wagon, remember? Why don't we suggest that he build it a little bigger than the usual small shack, especially with the baby and all, and then sometime, we could sneak Marta out there to spend some time with her boys, and they wouldn't have to worry about Oscar."

"You know, Willow, I had thought of asking him to build it bigger, just because...I don't know, I wanted it bigger. I don't think he would mind, especially now with a little one coming.

Oh, Willow, I'm so happy! How can anyone be this happy?"

"God truly is blessing you, Katie. You need to think of ways to pass that blessing on."

"How do I do that?"

"God will open doors for you. You have to be obedient and walk through them."

"Willow, you've been spending quality time with Esther. I can tell. She has that way about her. You're very much like her."

"Read Proverbs, Katie. We are to seek wisdom. She embodies wisdom. We can't go wrong following her example and listening to her counsel. Two motherless girls have been given a beautiful gift in the form of a new mother, Esther. Can anyone else be as blessed as we are?"

"I don't think so. We are blessed even in the bad things that happen in our lives."

Just then, feet pounded on the porch, and the screen door slammed shut, making the girls jerk their heads in that direction. "Good, you are both right here. The sky to the southwest is really angry looking, black as night. We're in for a really bad storm, it would appear. You girls may want to make sure all the windows are closed. That wash out on the line needs to be brought in and anything else you might need to do," Josh said, agitatedly, running his fingers through his hair. "Willow, you probably want to put out the fire in the stove."

"What on earth are you so anxious about? I've never seen you like this, Josh." Katie looked at him with concern.

"I don't want to upset you, but we have to be prepared for the worst. I have things to do outside with the stock. We need to be praying for protection. The last time I saw skies like this, a twister came with it. I just want you to be safe. So if it starts really blowing and you see any hail, get in the root cellar. We can replace all the rest of this, but we cannot replace you, so be very aware of the weather. I have to go."

With that, he was out the door and on his way to the corral.

"Willow, I'll go and shut the windows. You get the bread out and put out the fire." Katie turned and practically ran upstairs.

"What's a twister?" Willow asked to no one. She turned and took the bread out. Fortunately, it was done, almost overdone. *It's a good thing it didn't burn. It sounds like we are going to need that bread.* She was putting the fire out when she heard Katie close the front door.

They both grabbed baskets and made it outside to get the wash off the line.

"My, would you look at that sky! Dear Lord, you are the maker of wind and rain. Please protect all of this that has been dedicated to you. It's yours to do with as you feel is right; but, Lord, I don't understand destruction. Help me believe you will do what is best for us, but my request is that you will spare us any danger and keep all that you have given us safe under your everlasting wings as you have so many times in the past few months. In Jesus' name, amen."

"Katie, thank you for that prayer. Can you tell me what a twister is?" Willow asked as they hurriedly took the wash off the line.

"It's a mighty wind that turns in a very tight circle, and it moves sometimes in the air and sometimes on the ground. If it touches the ground, it can uproot trees or twist them right in half.

It can tear a house to shreds and take animals flying through the air. The best place to be is in a hole when that happens. The closest thing to a hole we have is the root cellar."

"Oh, I know what you are talking about. That is just not what we called it in the tribe."

"What did you call them?"

"Well, *nayaan*—"

"No, wait!" Katie interrupted. "Don't tell me, I wouldn't remember. Besides, I don't know what Josh and the boys are going to do with the animals. It's a good thing our cattle have already gone to market. We don't have that many to be threatened, if a twister comes our way. I'm a bit concerned about the goats. We just bought some more. We don't have time to get them to that ravine where Riley was shot. I don't know of any place closer that would do. I just have to leave all this in God's hands and trust Him to guide Josh. I wonder if all the men are here. I hope no one is out in the wide-open country. Maybe they can get to shelter in a canyon or cave or something."

"Now, what did you just say? You are going to leave all this in God's hands, right?"

"Yes, but—"

"No buts, God will take care of it all. We have to do what is in our hands to do and pray for the others. Let's include Brian and Todd and whoever is with them, okay?"

"Todd? Todd isn't here? What is he doing with Brian?"

"There was an incident in town, and Brian, Todd, and some of the other men went after those responsible. Michael's with them or else holding down the fort in town while Brian's gone."

"Michael isn't here either? How are the others going to manage shorthanded?"

"They have God's hand. It's pretty big!"

They finished taking down the wash and turned to go inside.

The wind began to whip their skirts as they walked back to the house. They looked at each other and quickened their pace to almost a run.

"I wonder if we should bring in some of that meat in the smokehouse just in case." Katie looked at Willow.

"I'll go out. I have on my leather. It doesn't get as wrapped around my legs as your gingham does. I don't want you to trip and fall."

With that, Willow left through the screen door, pulling the other one closed behind her. She reached the end of the porch, jumped down, and took off running to the smokehouse. Katie quickly started folding the laundry and putting it into stacks. She heard a thud on the back porch, then nothing. Shortly, she heard another thud, then nothing. Curiosity got the better of her. She looked out, and here came Willow running with a large chunk of meat in her arms. She got to the porch and pitched it. Katie laughed; there was that thud. Katie opened the door, went out, and began retrieving the meat, taking it inside and down to the root cellar. She took one of the clean blankets with her to spread out on one of the lower shelves and began to stack the meat on that. It was very cool down there and quite a relief from the heat and wind outside. As she climbed the steps from the root cellar, she heard another thud.

"What is she going to do…bring it all in?" Katie asked herself.

"I still haven't broken that habit of talking to myself," she said, shaking her head.

Katie retrieved another and another. Finally, Willow was bringing some in and met Katie on the steps to the root cellar. "Here, you take this one, and I'll get another one." She handed Katie the beef and left.

Soon, they had it all in there.

"I saved the best pieces. Now, if the smokehouse gets blown away, we will at least have really good meat!"

"I'm fervently praying for safety from this storm. We may not be in the cleft of a rock, but we are in His hands and under His wings. We will be safe, no matter what."

"I'm praying too. I'm also praying for Brian. We had a fight before we came out here together. I didn't even ask him for forgiveness. Sometimes, he makes me so mad, Katie. Why do men have to be so bossy?"

"Let's see…maybe it's because they feel responsible for us?"

"Well, he's not my dad, brother, husband, or anything else. He doesn't have to boss me around."

"Maybe he wants to be something else."

"Katie, he's ancient, and I'm probably eighteen now. I know he's at least thirty!"

"Willow, I'm twenty-one, and Josh is twenty-nine. It's not that bad, really. I feel very comfortable with an older man."

"Well, I'm going to do something with my life. I know I'm supposed to do something besides be a wife and a mother. I'm used to the open air and doing what I please. I want to be independent."

"Why don't you give that to the Lord as well? What does God want you to do? Have you asked him? Are you willing to sacrifice your will and allow him to lead you where you need to go?"

"Katie, I…I just have such mixed emotions. I really like Brian. I really do. I'm just not ready for marriage. I have been thinking about asking Doc if he would allow me to help him. I think

I would really like to be a nurse…or a doctor…now." She held up her hands in surrender at the look on Katie's face. "I know, I know. We don't have women doctors. Why not?"

"Where did all these thoughts come from?"

"Well, I have been in town, and I have seen how busy and needed Doc is. I love fixing medicines and taking care of the sick and hurt. I did that in the tribe. I learned so much from them.

Of course, it is a bit different from white man's medicine. I could learn that too. Then I would have great knowledge and be able to apply all I know to help more people."

"Does Mom know this?"

"No, you are the first I have told.

"Willow, we need to pray about all this. Too many things are coming at me at once. I'm not sure I know how to handle it all.

It's beginning to rain. We better get some water and bring it in.

We could put some blankets down in the root cellar to sit or lay down on. We probably should take a lantern down as well."

"I'll get the water. I don't mind getting a little wet," Willow said as she lifted the bucket to take out to the well. She was relieved not to have to talk or think about her feelings right now.

Katie came up from putting blankets and pillows down in the root cellar. She had taken a chair and a lantern down as well as her Bible.

Bang! The front door slammed against the wall.

"Hail!" Willow cried as she turned to look out the window as she heard the sound. She almost spilled the water in her hurry to reach the root cellar door.

No sooner had the front door closed than the back door opened. Josh hurried over to Katie and led her toward the root cellar.

"Get down there. Here, let me have that bucket. Good thinking!"

All three quickly descended the stairs and closed the door behind them. Josh and Katie snuggled closely to each other. He started whispering words of love and reassurance. A vivid picture of Katie's parents came to her mind. All of them sitting in the wagon on the way out to Texas, the rainstorm, lightning, Abigail and Katie scared to death and their brother, Benjamin, sound asleep. *Now, I've taken Mama's place. Now I know what she was feeling. Oh, I love you, Mama. I miss you.* She snuggled closer to Josh and closed her eyes.

The lamp cast an eerie glow off the objects encircled by dirt walls. The smoked meat smelled delicious. Yet the air was filled with a musty odor. Katie glanced at Willow. She was snuggled down on her blanket and hugging her pillow like it might fly away and she would not let go if it did.

"Josh, I have something I need to tell you."

"Yes, my love, I'm here, all for you."

"Well, according to Willow, that is, she told me, uh, well…"

"What are you trying to say?"

"Well, I don't know how to say it."

"Are you trying to tell me you are with child?"

Katie sat straight up. She looked Josh in the eye. "How did you know?"

"My dear, I am the oldest of my mother's children. I have seen every time she became pregnant. I know what it is when I see it.

You, on the other hand, seemed so blissfully innocent of the fact that you may be with child, I thought I would let you enjoy the wonder of finding out on your own."

"I wanted to surprise you." She pouted.

"Well, let's just say you did. You did surprise me by choosing a dark root cellar as the place of the announcement," he chuckled. Katie slapped his muscular upper arm. "So how did Willow know?"

"Same way you did. I didn't know she was here because I was sound asleep on the couch. I woke up to the smell of freshly baking bread and coffee. It smelled so good until I sat up. Then

I lost everything I had eaten, which wasn't much. I ran outside to the pecan tree and retched. She came out and helped me. I guess I can't hide all the noise I was making. Josh, I was so scared I was sick. I was afraid I was going to die or something, and

I didn't know how to tell you. After I had made a spectacle of myself, Willow told me I am with child and there is nothing to worry about."

"I guess her life in the tribe gave her quite the education. You can trust her in this, Katie; she probably knows more than either of us about it."

Willow sat up suddenly. "What is that noise?"

Josh got up and gingerly crept up the steps. He heard voices.

He pulled his gun and listened. Then, he heard someone call his name.

He cracked the door open. There stood Wulf and Clyde, looking like they had been dragged through the mud.

"What happened to you two?" Josh asked.

"We were running over here, and we both slipped and fell into a mud puddle. We wanted you to know we saw a twister, but it was up in the sky. Now, it's all calm out there, and we can see blue sky off to the southwest. We think we dodged a big one out there, by the grace of God." Clyde smiled and looked sideways at Wulf.

"So, what you are saying is that it's over?" Josh looked at the two with more behind the question than just what was on the surface.

Clyde elbowed Wulf. "Tell him." Wulf elbowed him back.

Josh was beginning to think the two of them had been around the twins too long and had picked up their main means of communication with each other.

"Well, boss. As you know, Clyde is powerful bothersome. He just won't let anything go, like someone scratchin' at a scab until it comes off an' then formin' a new scab and scratchin' that 'un off too. Well, he's been using every situation and opportunity to show me the love of Jesus and how Christians are just sinners saved by grace. None of us deserve salvation, he said. Well, with this twister business... well, it really got my attention and made me think about my own eternity. I decided to follow Jesus, right there in the middle of the storm. And Clyde said I had to tell you. So here I am."

Willow threw the door open, ran to Wulf, jumped up, and threw her arms around his neck. "Praise the Almighty God. He saved us all today, and especially you, Wulf. Do you know he may have brought that twister here for just this purpose? He has mighty big ways."

Josh stepped over to him and put his arm around his shoulders. "Dear Lord, how grateful we are today for the protection of your mighty wings in this potentially deadly storm, but instead of death, there's new life. We praise you for the gift of salvation for each of us and today for the fact that you have saved Wulf from an eternity filled with torment and pain. Give him the joy of your salvation each and every day of his life. May he never forget how he feels today and the reality of his salvation. In Jesus' name, amen."

Katie had come out too and stood just to Josh's side with tears running down her cheeks. "I remember my own day of salvation, Wulf. It is truly an awesome thing, such happiness and joy. He just keeps giving and giving. I pray you will see that in your own life."

Willow relinquished her place in Wulf's arms and stepped aside. He bent down and took Katie in his arms and gave her a gentle squeeze. "Unless I have missed my guess, there is more to be joyful about for you than your wedding and salvation."

Katie looked into Wulf's eyes. She looked at Clyde who was nodding. "Well, is there anyone who didn't know beside me?"

There was laughter all around. "There're just certain signs that are a sure give away, princess." Clyde took his turn hugging the new mother-to-be. Neither of the women minded the mud now on their clothes.

"Well, I want to be the first to tell Esther…if she doesn't know already. So you boys keep your mouths shut. Is that clear?" Katie shook her finger at each one like they were errant schoolboys.

They broke out into laughter and called for a toast to the new parents. Willow went out to the spring house and came back with a jar of apple cider from which she poured a small glass for each one there.

"Here's to the new parents. May the rest of their lives ring with the joy of many children's voices," Clyde said. "Hear, hear," rang with the clink of the glasses gracing each other with a slight touch.

After a little more conversation, Josh looked around. "Well, let's go have a look and see if there is any damage to be taken care of. Where are the twins?"

"Oh, as soon as it was clear, we sent them to ride out and check the stock. I trust the good Lord gave the cattle out there sense enough to get out of the hail, at least. I'm more worried about the hay and corn," Wulf said.

"Well, let's go see. Anything we can do for you ladies before we leave?" Josh asked.

"No, we can manage," Katie said, shooing them out the door.

"Wait! Yes, you can. Bring that bucket of water up from the root cellar, please. I don't feel like getting wet, again, and I don't want Katie to have to carry it up the steps," Willow said, looking at Katie.

"Your wish is my command," Wulf said. He quickly turned, walked down the steps, and effortlessly brought the heavy bucket back up.

"Just put it in the kitchen. Thanks, Wulf." Willow smiled her brightest smile.

"Katie may be Clyde's princess, but you are my little Indian princess," Wulf said as he beamed.

The men left to inspect the ranch. Katie looked at Willow.

"There must be a story there."

"Oh, there is. You see, he got his scar and lost his eye trying to protect his young Indian wife from some soldiers who came upon their camp. They killed her and left him the way he is. He thought he was going to die as well, but God saved him then and saved him again today. I am so happy! God is doing so much good. I wonder what good will come for Daisy." Willow looked wistfully out the window.

"Why, what's wrong with Daisy?" Katie asked.

"I shouldn't have said anything. I'll let Mom tell you. You'd better make sure you see them soon and tell them your good news! It can't be kept a secret long. You don't want them to find out from somebody else now, do you?"

"Oh no, I wouldn't want that to happen. When are you going back?"

"I was going to go tonight, but I think I'll wait until the morning or later in the day tomorrow. I want to be here to help you.

I'm pretty sure they can spare me at the hotel. I asked Brian to tell her I was staying. I just wanted them to know so they wouldn't be worried. They knew I might stay tonight. So, it won't be a problem."

"Oh, Willow, I'd be so glad to have you back home! I have been praying you would come. Of course, that was when I thought I might be dying."

Both girls burst out laughing again and gave each other hugs.

"Thank you for being my sister," they both said at the same time.

17

San Antonio, Texas, August 16

Oh my, this is not what I expected. The trip was better than I expected, but this 'city' is very rustic. There are so many buildings that look like they are made of mud or plaster or something. I think I will move on as quickly as possible. It's still early. I wonder where the next stage is headed."

Raven, now Erin, wandered around and stopped to get something to eat but couldn't wait to get out of San Antonio. The river wasn't even what she would consider a river compared to what she had seen back east, and it was a bit green. Then there was the odor. She couldn't quite put her finger on it—cows, maybe? Many of the women were cooking out of doors; all of these things were just too foreign to her. No, she would definitely move on, and the sooner the better.

"Excuse me, sir. Where does the next stagecoach go?"

"Well, little lady, the next one will make a stop in Crystal Springs and then go on to Kerrville and on up to Fredericksburg. Do ya wanna know beyond that?"

"No, I think I'll just head to Crystal Springs. Do they have a hotel there?"

"Oh yes, ma'am! Esther and Adam Schmitt run the best hotel anywhere near the Guadalupe."

Erin's brow wrinkled in consternation. "Guadalupe?"

The stationmaster grinned bigger than a man when he realizes, for the first time, he's looking at a beautiful woman. "Guadalupe

River. The prettiest river ya ever did see flowin' over limestone and sandstone, shinin' with that purdy turquoise water."

"Great! Then one ticket to Crystal Springs. When does the stage leave?"

"Oh, it's here already. The driver's changing horses and gettin' somethin' to eat."

"So, I'll just wait right here, if that's all right with you."

"Suit yerself. You should get to Crystal Springs by late afternoon. Here's your ticket. I'll take it when you board."

"Thank you so much." Erin sat down on a bench and decided to watch the people as they went about their daily tasks. Two women were headed her way carrying a carpetbag each and quite a few packages. They were in deep conversation and almost tripped over her feet as they approached the stage depot's door.

When they came out, they sat on the bench near her. *They must be traveling on the same stagecoach. I wonder if they're going to Crystal Springs as well.*

As Erin listened to them, she realized she couldn't understand a word they were saying. She listened closer trying not to be rude or noticeable but, still, couldn't seem to make out what they were saying.

"Excuse me, are you traveling to Crystal Springs?" she asked.

The women stopped talking and looked at her. The younger one smiled. "No, ve are traveling on to Fredericksburg. Ve are trying to decide if we should spend the night in Kerrville or vot?

The stage is a leetle late today. Ve don't even know if he is going to go on to Fredericksburg tonight."

"Forgive me, where are you from? You have a wonderful accent."

"Ve are German. Most everyone up there is German."

Erin began to think she had made another mistake. *Maybe I shouldn't go there. I can hardly understand what they are saying when they are speaking English.*

"Okay, ladies, let's get a move on. We need to make up for lost time," the stage driver urged.

Well, he seems to be in a hurry

"These yours?" He looked right at Erin.

"Yes, yes, they are." Erin watched as he bent down to load her luggage. She then headed toward the stagecoach, which was now situated right in front of her. The stationmaster hurried out the door and opened the door of the stage.

"Tickets, please," he said as if he didn't know they had tickets.

Erin handed him the ticket she had purchased from him just minutes before. "Strange little man," she muttered. This time, she had first choice of where to sit. She could ride facing forward, and so she did.

The other two women climbed into the coach and looked right at her. "You need to move, ve get sick riding backvards. Ve vould sit on that side."

Erin looked at them in amazement. She would have never said anything like that to anyone. She looked at them deeply and saw they really meant for her to move to the other side. She was not feeling very godly or charitable at the moment and had her heart set on riding facing forward. She had seen the scenery from a backward view the whole time she had been in a coach on this trip.

"Well"—she looked at the women and looked at her seat, then back at the women—"I believe the three of us can sit on this side if you don't mind being a bit bunched up. Suit yourself."

"Vell!" With that, the women sat down beside her and began to scowl.

The stage rocked as the men climbed aboard, and then it jerked forward as they started out of town.

Within the first couple of miles, the two women began to "adjust" in their seats squeezing closer and closer to Erin. She realized it was going to be a miserable trip if she didn't do something.

She looked out the window at the magnificent countryside. *How beautiful! Not at all flat and barren as I thought it would be. I have so much to learn about this part of the country.* She sat for a short while, then bowed her head.

Lord, what do you want me to do?

Immediately, verses came into her head. Whosoever shall compel thee to go a mile, go with him twain. Give to him that asketh thee, and from him that would borrow of thee turn not thou away.

Erin sat for a few more minutes taking in the wonderful rolling hills with their intermittent white rock, then red rock, and then white again, and the wispy looking trees with feathery leaves. Yes, and beyond were more rolling hills. Occasionally she saw deep ravines with a stream running through it. *This is wide, open beautiful country so hard and graceful at the same time.* The ladies beside her had quit moving, but they weren't talking either. A few minutes later, Erin decided she must move to the other side.

"Ladies, I fear I have made you uncomfortable. Since traveling backward does not seem to make me ill, I will move over to this side, and we can all have a window." *And share the dust!* "Perhaps it will be cooler for each of us."

The women nodded but did not say a word for the entire trip to Crystal Springs. *Maybe traveling with men would be better.*

About the time Erin thought she would die from hunger, she heard the driver holler, "Crystal Springs" and felt the stage slow its pace. She turned a bit to look out the window at the town she had randomly decided would be home. *Wooden structures, wonderful!* She settled back to wait for the stagecoach to stop, and stop it did, with a jerk that nearly threw her head off her shoulders.

The driver opened the door, and Erin began to rise to exit the stage. She was all but pushed back down into her seat by the two women who only wanted to stretch their legs. "Oh, well. I'll be leaving them to continue the journey. I hope they are in here alone for the rest of their trip so they can enjoy it," Erin muttered to herself.

When the coast was clear, Erin descended from the stage. She took a deep breath and looked around. *No foul odor. Everything looks very normal.* The hotel, an all-wooden structure with the typical two stories raised above street level with four steps leading up to the boardwalk in front of the door, held an inviting allure for her. Deep in her heart she felt she had come home.

The noises of the men changing out the teams of horses were the only loud sounds she heard. Her eyes drank in every aspect of the charming town. She turned just a bit to her right where she saw the saloon seeming to loom over her. She felt her stomach twist.

"Here's your luggage, miss. Enjoy your stay."

"Oh…uhm…thank you.'

"Board! Leaving for Kerrville, Fredericksburg, and points beyond!"

The shotgun ran over to the coach with a canteen in his hand.

"Got 'er filled. Barkeep was happy to 'blige us. It'll be better than hot water."

The driver just spat. He closed the door with the two ladies inside—one facing forward and the other facing back. *So, they get sick riding backwards, do they? Lord, help me be gracious.*

Just as the stage pulled away, Erin turned to look at the hotel again. She sighed and felt a tug at her skirt. She looked down and saw the most angelic face she had ever seen.

"Hey, lady, I'm Tad!" He stuck his hand out as if to shake hands. Erin smiled and took his hand in hers.

"Hello, Tad, I'm Miss Erin Kerr."

"I am happy to make your ac-quain-tance," Tad said very deliberately.

"And I am happy to make yours! My, someone has been working on their manners." Erin smiled at him.

"Yeah, if I don't practice, I won't ever get it right. That's what Mom says, and so does Mr. Riley. If they say it, it has to be true."

"I would love to meet them. Tad, I would like to stay at the hotel. Do you know if there is anyone there who can carry my luggage in?"

"Sure! My dad!" With that, Tad ran up the four steps to the boardwalk in front of the hotel and through the doors. "Dad!"

She heard, and then all was quiet.

She started to climb the steps, not quite deciding to leave her luggage sitting in the dirt road. With one foot on one step and the other foot on the lower step, she stopped and looked back at her luggage. The door to the hotel opened, and a very handsome man walked right down the steps, nodding at her. "Afternoon, miss." And he picked up her carpetbag and one end of the trunk.

Tad followed him out and picked the other end of the trunk up with two hands. "Now, son, I was just going to put it on my back."

"No, I can help, Pa, really."

"Listen, son. What I really need you to do is to go and ask Mr. Riley to come over to eat. We promised him we would share a meal on the first day of school. Now, go do that for me, please.

I can get these."

"All right! I get to see Mr. Riley again! Yay!" Off ran Tad toward the south end of the street. His father just shook his head and started climbing the steps. Erin moved quickly up the steps and held the door for him.

"Why, thank you, miss. You are very kind."

"Not at all, it is the least I can do for you since you are so gracious to carry these in for me."

"Let me get you checked in, and we can move them upstairs for you."

"Thank you so much."

"Just sign the book." Adam looked at the signature. "Now, Miss Erin Kerr, how long will you be staying with us?"

"I would like to find a permanent place to stay. I want to rent a room or find a building in which I can start my own business, which may have a dwelling above."

"Oh great! What business are you planning to start?"

"Well, I am a seamstress. I can also cook or clean. I can do almost anything to keep body and soul together."

"Well, I tell you what. Why don't you join us for dinner and we can discuss some of the possibilities? It will be my wife, Esther; Mr. Riley, who is the schoolmaster; and of course, Tad, our son. Let me take you to your room. I have a very nice corner room, which will give you a good view of the street. It's a little larger than the rooms most people use who are just passing through."

"Thank you, Mr.…I'm sorry, I don't remember your name."

"I don't believe I told it to you; it's Schmitt, Adam Schmitt."

"Oh yes. The stationmaster in San Antonio told me that. I had just forgotten. My mind must have been preoccupied."

"Charlie is a strange character, but a friend. I'll have to thank him the next time we're in San Antonio. Let's get you settled."

Early evening, August 16

"Mr. Riley! Mr. Riley! Chenowhat? You aren't gonna…oh!" Tad stomped his foot and hit his thigh with his hand. "I mean, going to believe it!"

Riley had just stepped out his door to pick some of the roses near his home to take to Esther and Adam in thanks for the dinner tonight. He turned at the very familiar voice and almost laughed. "Chenowhat?" Riley laughed out loud.

He enjoyed watching the energy and joy Tad exhibited toward learning and life in general. He had never really seen that boy sad. The time his mom and dad told him he couldn't have a pet constituted the only time he'd come close.

"Believe what, young man?"

"The prettiest lady just got off the stage, and she's stayin' in the hotel!"

"Yes, and did she ask for me?"

"Naw, she just wanted a room."

"Well then, I guess your folks checked her in."

"Yeah, Pa was carrying her trunk in when he told me to come over and remind you of dinner tonight. He said they promised 'cause of the first day of school. Mr. Riley, I loved it! You are the best teacher in the world!"

"That remains to be seen. Tell your pa I had not forgotten about our repast and am excessively anxious to join them for our scheduled dinner party. I shall be over in just a little while, once I cut some flowers for the table. Just look at these roses."

"They sure are beauties. I'll tell Ma to have a vase ready."

Riley laughed and waved at Tad as he took off back up the street. He turned to resume his task of cutting the roses, but his eye caught sight of the church that stood very close to the schoolhouse he had taken over and added on to with the reward money he had gotten.

"Lord, when will we get a preacher to come and live here? It's not that I don't appreciate the circuit-riding preachers who come in every now and then or the few men who take on the task of sharing the word of God with the rest of us each Sunday. We just need someone who cares about the community and knows our sorrows and joys. Not my will but thine be done. In Jesus' name, amen."

As Riley cut the red roses, he thought of Jesus. His blood, shed for me, the crown of thorns, the green of eternal life. What an illustration. I will have to use this with my students.

Riley went back into the house he could truly call his own. He wanted to make it a home, but he needed to get some curtains made and some more furniture. A bed, dresser, mirror, washstand, and table and chairs didn't exactly complete what was needed for making a place seem warm and comforting. He needed a rocker, at least, beside the fireplace.

I'll have to ask Marta about making me some curtains. I wonder what kind of fabric to use. I don't really know about all that. I'll put that on my list of things to do. I'll go by one day after school. With that thought firmly in place, he washed up and shaved again. He felt his late-in-the-day growth was a bit too noticeable for an evening out. When he finished getting ready, he carefully picked up the roses and headed out toward the hotel.

The day had begun to cool a bit from the mid-August heat and humidity from the brief shower earlier, and the sky had turned that deep purple he loved. As he walked past Doc McConnell's office, he noticed the buggy was gone, and no lights were lit inside. *I wonder who sent for his services. Father, Great Physician, be with Doc and whomever he attends tonight as your servant. Thank you, God. You are faithful to answer our prayers. It's in your son's name I pray. Amen.*

Next, he passed Marta's seamstress shop. Darkness ruled in her domain as well. He glanced toward the other end of the street to see if either the livery or the blacksmith shop showed any signs of life. No, nothing.

The light sure shines brightly down at the saloon. The faint sound of noise and laughter floated on the slight breeze across his face. Riley shook his head. *Don't let me get trapped in that world ever again, Lord, I beg you. Keep me far from sin. I just want to live for You, You alone.* After he walked by the closed doors of Breland's General Store, he started to cross into the light pooling out on the street. He stopped, then looked back at Marta's and Breland's now-empty stores. He offered a simple short prayer for Marta's and Breland's salvation and the peace of God they could have with it. There was a dim light in the upper rooms of Breland's store. *I wonder if that's where he lives. I'll need to ask.*

On the corner just across the street, the lights of the hotel created a warm glow to the ambiance of the area surrounding the

Inn of Happiness as he had begun to call it. His steps quickened, and he offered a brief prayer for the Schmitts and all who rested and availed themselves of repast under their roof.

Riley lightly stepped up the four steps to the boardwalk at the end of the hotel. The door stood open since Adam had installed the newfangled screen doors. It made the lobby much cooler since he put them on the back door as well, creating a cross-breeze. *What will they think of next?* Riley thought as he heard the door behind him slap against the wooden door frame.

"Riley! Oh, we are so glad to have you eat…um, dine… with us this glorious evening!" Esther smiled broadly. "How did I do? Is my vocabulary improving?"

"Esther, there was nothing wrong with your vocabulary in the first place." Riley bowed slightly to her and handed her the roses.

"For the table, from my garden. Who planted those roses? Have they been there long?"

She took the roses and his arm and led him toward the dining room. "I have no idea who planted them, and they have been there as long as I remember.

As they entered the room, she stopped and turned toward him.

"Riley, Adam and I have been talking about adding on to the hotel dining room. We thought we could put a sort of smallish private dining room in that space beside the back of the dining room and the end of the kosher kitchen. That would make the building completely straight on all sides. What do you think?"

"I think that would be a good idea. We could meet here for a men's Bible study and have breakfast during that time as well. I can think of quite a few uses for a private dining room. In fact, I'm excited about the possibility. The ladies of the town could even use it for a literary society meeting and Bible study also.

It would mean a little extra income for you and Adam. People would have to reserve it ahead of time. People with visitors or family coming to visit could have a special supper here. Yes, I like the idea very much!"

She led him to the round table in the back corner.

They were almost to the table when Riley grabbed Esther's arm, which was draped through his. "Speaking of liking very much, who is that?"

"Oh. Come on, Riley, I'll introduce you." Esther smiled as she squeezed his arm, feeling the tight muscle underneath his jacket. "Relax, Riley. She's just a female."

"I can see that, Esther. I can see that! A vision of loveliness just adds to our already-amazing day."

They reached the table, and Riley helped Esther to her seat.

"Thank you, Riley. Riley, I'd like to introduce Miss Erin Kerr to you. Miss Kerr, this is Mr. J. R. Riley, our schoolmaster and sometimes preacher."

"Pleased to make your acquaintance, Miss Kerr," Riley said as he lightly shook her hand.

"The pleasure is all mine, Mr. Riley."

Erin felt her neck heat up. *What's wrong with me? I've met many men in the past, and it has never caused me to react in this way.*

About that time, Adam and Tad came in and found their seats. Esther motioned to Mary Elizabeth, who had agreed to come and help out in the dining room since Willow had gone out to the ranch and Daisy, thankfully, was upstairs recovering from her injuries, which were not as life-threatening as first suspected, still extensive.

"Please put these in the vase I have set aside and bring them back to the table. Thank you, Mary Elizabeth."

The conversation at the table turned to school and how the first day went. Tad was so enthusiastic and expressive about all that went on at school, everyone laughed until they almost cried.

During dessert, Esther left the table and soon returned carrying a serving tray with tea brewing and a small pile of lemon drops on the side.

"I thought this would add the finishing touch to our delightful meal. Tea, anyone? I even included lemon drops for those who want. It is a wonderful addition we have gotten in the habit of since our precious daughter-in-love, Katie, needed that remedy after being strangled by a man bent on killing her. Fortunately, Michael, her foreman, came to the rescue. Her voice, although pretty hoarse for a time, is now back to normal, thanks to Doc's prescription for tea, preferably ginger if we could get it, and lemon drops. We all have taken up the habit of sucking on lemon drops. Preventive medicine, you know." Esther raised her eyebrows in humor as everyone agreed.

Everyone at the table knew the story of the lemon drops except for Erin. She looked confused at first but then relieved when everyone seemed to take a lemon drop. Some popped it right in their mouth, but Esther put hers on her saucer. "I save mine for the end," she explained. Tad joined in with, "I can't wait. I want mine right away!"

Erin laughed. She looked at each person then said, "I believe I will wait until I finish my tea." She smiled as she looked at each face and saw nothing unusual reflected there. She felt very relaxed and at home with this family. *Yes, I will stay here, at least to learn more about this town,* she thought as she sipped her tea and continued looking at each face, trying to read what each person was thinking.

Esther looked around the table as well, her eyes resting on Riley. "I believe we have covered everything there is to cover about the first day of school at your wonderful academy, Riley. How about we learn more about Erin?" She turned her head and looked into Erin's eyes and smiled.

Erin appeared calm and collected, but in reality, on the inside, her stomach was doing some wild twists and turns, not unlike the ship in that one storm they had encountered during her trip to New Orleans. She smoothed the skirt of her dress Sarah had so lovingly made. She thought of her new friend and missed her. She raised her eyes and took in the scene before her.

"I don't have a very interesting life. I lived back east. Both of my parents are dead. My father, who was a ship's captain, was lost at sea. Not many years later my mother died suddenly of a fever. She was a seamstress, and I learned to sew from her. I quit going to school when my dad died to help my mom with her business. A good friend, Captain Patrick McBride, was kind enough to provide me passage by ship to New Orleans, and then I took the stage to Houston, and on to San Antonio. I wasn't happy with either place although I made a very good friend in Houston. At any rate, I wanted to go farther west, so I got on the stage to Crystal Springs because I liked the name, I think. I really don't know why. I know I was thankful not to have to continue the ride with the two women who were also on board. They were miserable characters, very much like the stepsisters in *Cinderella* by Jacob and Wilhelm Grimm. Have you ever read that story?" She had skillfully changed the subject. She looked at each one at the table. Riley looked back at her intently.

"Did you read it in German?" Riley asked.

"No. One Christmas, my father gave me a *Grimm's Fairy Tales* translated into English. I have always loved to read." She took another sip of tea and savored each swallow. How good that tasted. She couldn't wait to try the lemon drop. If it helped her throat, she would be more excited than she ever was on Christmas morning.

"Do you know what you will want to do if you do stay here?" Esther asked.

"I would very much like to sew. However, I will do anything to be able to provide for myself. I can clean or cook as well. I wouldn't mind helping someone with their children if there was a need."

"My, you are from back east. There is no need, especially here in Crystal Springs, for a nanny or a housekeeper. I may have an idea, though. We have a seamstress here in town. She wants to increase her, how shall I say this? I guess her fashion choices. She wants to do more with leather. There seems to be quite an interest in leather riding skirts and the like. She taught herself how to work with it and does an exceptional job. Perhaps, she could use some help with the other sewing so she can focus on her leather work. We will go by and see her tomorrow, if you like, and I will introduce you."

"Oh, Mrs. Schmitt, you are so kind. I would love that."

"And where are you staying?" Riley asked. When Erin opened her mouth to respond, they said at the same time, "In the hotel, of course." Laughter rang like church bells on a wedding day.

Riley blushed a bright red. "How stupid of me! Esther, you and Adam will wonder if the new schoolmaster has qualifications to teach. I am beginning to wonder myself."

Erin answered, her eyes dark and deep with meaning,

"Nonsense, Mr. Riley, even a schoolmaster cannot be expected to know everything, especially when there may be other options available like...maybe...a boardinghouse?"

"Well, one of the widows in town, Mrs. Beunerkemper, did take in Daisy, but I don't think she intended to open a boardinghouse. We do have several buildings, which have upstairs space that is empty. Of course, they may be full of detritus," Riley explained.

"Full of what? That sounds ominous. I don't believe I've heard that word before," Erin replied with wonder although hoarsely.

She lifted the last of her tea and drank it.

"*Detritus.* It is a French word meaning basically 'odds and ends,' like boxes the owner may have stored in the upstairs, or things not needed at the time, that might be wanted later. I think it came from the term used for all the rubble left after a landslide."

"Fascinating, Mr. Riley! I believe I would like very much to attend your school. I missed so much in my later school years... working." Erin lifted the lemon drop and began sucking on it.

The tangy, soothing juice produced was delightful as well as helpful. She just found it very awkward to try to carry on a conversation with something in her mouth, yet she was quite unwilling to take the sweet and yet sour treat out of her mouth or to chew it up to hurry the process. She wanted to savor every last drop of the sweetened saliva she was swallowing.

"Umm!" She did not dare say a word for fear of being extremely rude.

Esther popped one in her mouth and began talking around it. "Erin, have you ever had a lemon drop before?"

Erin simply shook her head no.

"Do you like it?" Esther tried again to help the girl realize they were all friends, and everyone felt free to talk with a lemon drop in his mouth.

Erin nodded an enthusiastic nod.

Riley put his in his mouth. "Oh, Esther, what a delightful finish to the best meal and company I have had in weeks!" He also tried to make Erin feel comfortable by joining in the conversation.

"Adam, do we have any more of these around?" Esther asked her husband.

"I'm sure we do unless someone has been helping themselves to our stash of drops." He pointedly looked at Tad and ruffled his hair.

They all laughed again. "If any are missing, it was not me! You might have to check with the 'other son.' He seems to go straight there when he comes through the door."

"Now, Tad, you know he is not here that often. He deserves a treat when he comes to see us. I know he stops by Breland's store and picks up a bag for Katie before he leaves to go back to the ranch," his mother said to him. "Would you like some pie instead, Tad? Adam? Anyone?"

"No," everyone said at once, even Erin.

Erin smiled broadly, placed her napkin on the table, and began to rise. "If you will excuse me, I am bone weary from the trip today. I think I'll go ahead and turn in. I do want to thank you so much for inviting me to dinner and introducing me to lemon drops. Perhaps I will have to share a recipe I picked up in Houston for *lemonada*. It's a delicious drink."

Riley looked with hopeful anticipation at the words "introducing me to" and then just as deflated with the continuation of her sentence, "lemon drops."

Erin turned and looked directly to Riley. "Oh, and a new word, Mr. Riley."

"Well, it was the least I could do."

He seemed a bit distracted she thought as she gathered her skirt to try to escape the confines of the corner in which she had been sitting. Now was not the time to trip.

Realizing the hour had gotten late, Riley rose from his seat.

"I fear I must be on my way as well, Esther, Adam." He briefly bowed at the waist and lifted Esther's hand and gave it a brushing kiss. "My dear lady, you have certainly made my evening brighter by including this lovely woman in our dinner party this evening. It has been a memorable day. I never thought I would have the opportunity to open my own academy; and, with that dream come true, I look for the fulfillment of other dreams."

He turned and looked directly at Erin who was now free from the confines of the corner. "May I have the privilege of seeing you to your room? I wouldn't want any of the lobby ruffians to accost you as you cross the way."

Erin's heart began to beat so wildly it felt like wild horses were running in her chest. She stared at him, trying to get her emotions under control and not show her terror in her face.

"Why, Riley, what a sweet thing to offer. I'm sure Erin would not mind being escorted to her room, but you must not go in. What would people think? Mind your manners, young man."

"Esther! I would never think of compromising a woman's virtue, and I want to make sure she is protected from anyone who might see a woman alone and get the wrong idea," Riley protested, almost too loudly. He took control of his voice and manner and then turned to Erin. "I sincerely apologize if for one minute you thought I was being forward or inappropriate in my behavior."

"Thank you, Mr. Riley. I confess I was not sure what you meant. However, I know your intentions must be honorable since you are such good friends with the Schmitts. So I will accept your company to my door. I am rather tired and would like to get to my door without too much difficulty."

Riley looked at Esther with a "see there" look and offered his arm to Erin as they left the dining room.

"What did you mean by that comment, my dear?" Adam looked at his wife with almost a shocked expression painted across his face.

"Well, Adam, I could feel the discomfort radiating off Erin when Riley spoke. I don't think she knew exactly what he meant by his request. I just wanted to give him the opportunity to make it quite clear to her that he was not one of those men who would take advantage of a woman. She does not know him like we do, and I don't think he would have seen the look of terror I saw in her eyes."

"I didn't see it. How do you see things like that?"

"Every day now, I ask God to open my eyes to the needs of others. I think I was so much blinded to others before Katie came into our lives. Adam, I don't ever want to be like that again." Tears began to pool in Esther's eyes as she thought about the loneliness and horrors Katie had endured after her parents died so close together, and no one even knew she was alone out on their ranch.

Thoughtfully, Adam looked into his lovely wife's eyes.

"Perhaps I should start praying that prayer. I think I am beginning to become distant again and thinking everyone's condition in life is very much like mine. I think, sometimes, I must be the most inconsiderate man alive. Esther, will you forgive me?"

"For what, my dear?"

"For being less than I should be as a husband and father."

"In my eyes, Adam, you are just right. Now, if God is working on you, then perhaps, you ought to ask him for forgiveness and help. I know he will forgive you and give you the guidance you need to be the person he wants you to be."

"Do you think we can go out to the ranch tomorrow?" Adam was looking into the lobby as he asked. He watched Riley and Erin ascend the stairs arm in arm. He smiled.

"Darling, you can go out the ranch anytime you want to go. You know that. I will need to stay here with Daisy in such a bad way. And since Willow went out there for a visit, I really am needed right here. I don't have anyone to help Rose, except for Mary Elizabeth, who will fill in when someone is sick or indisposed, but not permanently. I really need to go ahead and wait on some tables now. Really, dear, if you want to go, go! I don't mind. I'd love to see Joshua, Katie, and Willow, but I don't think I can do it tomorrow."

"I understand. I think I will go. I want to see Joshua and the girls, of course! I need to go over and see Michael. I'll take him some food. I haven't seen much of him today since he has been covering the deputy duties while Brian and the rest took off early this afternoon."

Esther laughed, and Adam joined her.

"Thank you so much, Mr. Riley, for escorting me to my room. I hope it was not an inconvenience for you."

"Not at all, Miss Kerr. I hope you find what you are looking for here. Crystal Springs is a delightful place. We have our share of unsavory characters, but what a dull place it would be without them. They give life its color, and for those of us chosen of God to serve him, they provide us with a mission."

"Thank you again, Mr. Riley. Good night."

"Uh, Miss Kerr, would it be presumptuous of me to ask you…"

Erin's heart began its wild beating again. Fear was written all over her face.

"If we could pray together?" he continued without even noticing the change in her expression.

"Oh, Mr. Riley," Erin sighed with relief, "that would be a first for me, but one I would willingly accept."

"You have never prayed before?"

"No, I mean yes, I have prayed before, but, no, that is not what I meant. I have never had a man ask me to pray with him other than my father and Captain McBride. You are a first, in that you are not a family member or close friend of the family."

"Well then, let us proceed." Riley bowed his head and began, "Oh, mighty God, we certainly aren't worthy to come into your most holy presence. Yet we humbly come before you with hearts full of love for you and thankfulness for your grace, mercy, peace, provision, strength, wisdom, and a plethora of other things. The list goes on into infinity. You fill me with awe. How I thank you for allowing me to be a teacher. How I love filling young minds with your wisdom and truth while I teach them the basics and some of the more advanced academics they will need to become what you would have them be and accomplish the plan you have for each life. I thank you for the opportunity to meet and begin to get to know Raven, oh, I mean Miss Kerr. I pray you will comfort her and give her guidance on what she is to do here. Provide her with the work she seeks and give her a hope for her future, which is in your hands. I thank you for Esther, Adam, and Tad. Lord, that boy is so very special. How I long to see what a difference he will make wherever you send him in the ministry you lay out before him. I thank you for the opportunity to give him as much of the knowledge you have bestowed on me as your will dictates. We thank you for the fellowship we had tonight and only ask that you will continue your watch-care over us and give us a peaceful sleep. In Jesus' name, amen."

"Amen." Erin stood looking directly at Riley, her mouth agape, her eyes wide with a mixture of fear and wonder.

Riley slowly lifted his head and looked at her. He quirked his brows and tilted his head. "What?"

Erin swallowed to moisten her very dry mouth. "Why did you call me Raven?" she asked with a slight quiver in her voice.

"I am so sorry. Really! Usually, I am very good with names and have some insight into the person. I apologize. I know very well your name is Erin, but I have had a dream on my mind. In this dream, I was beside a stream and a raven kept bringing me food and drink, just like Elijah, yet different. I have been pondering the dream off and on all day. I had it this morning. Today, while teaching some of the children how to recognize various kinds of birds, using Audubon's book of bird illustrations, *Birds of America*. I called a robin a raven. All the children loved that, and we all had a good laugh about it. I know you are not a bird, but a beautiful woman with intelligence and a good sense of humor. Very fine qualities, I might add. I do apologize again for having called you Raven."

"Truly, I'm not offended, just amazed. You see my middle name *is* Raven. I go by either, but I like Erin. It is what my parents called me." Erin shyly smiled as she saw something new in Riley's eyes.

"Well, Miss Kerr, Erin, if I may, this has been a most delightful evening and one I will long remember. I trust you will have a most restful night and rise in the morning to a new beginning."

Riley bowed at the waist, smiled brightly, and turned to go back downstairs. He wanted to talk to Michael as soon as possible but did not want to appear rude. He was having trouble holding himself back.

"Good night, Mr. Riley." Erin began to insert her key but watched as he turned back to her.

"I apologize. I called you Erin just now without your permission. I don't know what came over me. My name is J. R. Riley, but my friends, and I would like for you to be one of them, call me Riley, just Riley. If you prefer, I will call you Miss Kerr. I trust that one day you will get to know me well enough to give me permission to call you Erin." *I prefer to think of you as my Raven. Only God knows.* Riley looked at her with fear and expectation of either rebuff, permission, or a conciliatory "Miss Kerr."

"Mr. Riley, I would be delighted to be your friend. Rarely have I found another with whom I am delighted to carry on a conversation. I would love to visit with you about some books I have read and hear what you think. I think I would like to be taught by you even though I am well beyond school age. I missed so much of my schooling after Daddy died. I am mostly self-taught. If I make errors, I wish for you to correct me. I feel my arithmetic is sadly lacking. Well, anyway, what I am trying to say, Riley, is that I would certainly not complain if you called me Erin. I know I have gone on and on just to get to that point. I tend to rattle on, it seems. I need to stop!" With that, Erin put her hand over her mouth and began to laugh. She could not believe she was talking that much without once feeling like she had to protect herself from a wrong impression. *Surely he would not think I am trying to flirt with him, would he?* She looked into Riley's eyes and began to realize he was laughing as well, not at her, but with her.

"Erin, you've made my day. I love to teach and would never pass up the opportunity to do so. I can give you some tutoring when you set the time and place. I trust you will find work shortly and perhaps a more permanent place to stay, a place you can call home. Just let me know. I have several friends who constantly tell me to 'speak plain English' because I use too many words to say what they can say in a few. I hope you will continue to speak as many words and words as you like whenever you are with me. I will thoroughly enjoy them. Now, I *will* say good night. I know you are weary from your travels today, indeed in the last week, coming all the way from New Orleans by stage. I must say my posterior extremity hurts just thinking about it. And with that delightful thought resting firmly in your mind, I'd best take my leave."

Erin laughed until she thought she would cry. "Thank you, Riley. It truly has been delightful! Good night." She turned her key, opened her door, and disappeared before Riley could make his feet move.

As he walked away, he first thought, *She is the answer to my dreams.* Then as he descended the stairs, his thoughts became, *I've got to see Michael. He is not going to believe this.* When he left the hotel, he looked around him and saw the stars shining brightly in the night sky. He suddenly realized, *I have school tomorrow! I can't talk to Michael. I can't be late to school. I'm the teacher! God, give me strength and self-control. I really need your help right now. And, God, I really do mean…right now!*

He walked reluctantly yet swiftly back toward his snug little home. Just the fact that he could will his feet to go in that direction reassured him God still gives strength to the weak. He turned toward his home and realized how dark it gets without a bright moon showing the way. He should have left a lamp burning in the window or out on the porch or something. He almost felt blind. *When did it get this dark?* He put his hands out to help him feel his way to his stairs. *We must have talked for hours!* Just then, a cloud moved and revealed a small sliver of a moon, but it gave enough light so Riley realized he was about two feet too far to the right of the stairs up to his home, and he was about to run right into the porch. "Thank you, Lord. May your light shine in me as you have shown through your light where I need to go.

Give me the opportunity to be that light for my students in the morning. You are so precious to me, dear Lord Jesus. Help me to be more like you."

Later, Riley rested his head on his pillow and closed his eyes.

He could still see her, and he smiled. He rolled to his left side and drifted into sleep hoping to see his Raven and obtain more understanding about his new Raven. The last words on his lips were, "Thank you, Lord."

Erin finished her preparations for bed, turned down the lamp, lowered her head to the pillow, and closed her eyes. She could still see him and hear his laughter and his voice; she smiled. She rolled to her right side and drifted into sleep hoping to see him again tomorrow and, with God's help, find a permanent place to live and work. The last words on her lips were, "Thank you, Lord."

18

The Cave, August 17

The first words out of Gruber's mouth as Brian rolled over and saw him tending the fire caused Brian to stop and stare at the man.

"We gotta get outta here and git these horses some water and grass!"

Brian had been so concerned for the men that he had not given the horses a thought. He was thoroughly ashamed of himself. He looked at Gruber and reevaluated his opinion of him. Yes, he was a simple man. Yes, he didn't use the kind of language every one of Brian's nearest friends used, but then neither did many other people. Perhaps, he had formed an opinion of the person tending the fire and food for the men on superficial qualities that didn't amount to a hill of beans.

Flopping back down on his bedroll, he looked at the ceiling of the cave, *Lord, forgive me. I have sinned and haven't even gotten my feet on the ground yet today. Help me to be attentive to your voice and your love today as we travel. I need to be sensitive to others and their needs and not be as selfish as I have been. If I was really honest with myself, I'd have to say pride is my biggest failing. Help me, dear Father. I am so weak! In Jesus' name, amen.*

Rolling over again, he threw back the cover, ran his hand through his hair, and slowly got to his feet. He still had his boots on. "Well, if I had died in my sleep last night, I would have died with my boots on," he said to no one in particular.

"I thunk we all would've," Gruber replied as he handed Brian a cup of coffee "I collected rainwater, yestaday."

"Good thinking. I hope we find water once we are down off this ledge."

"Ye,' sir, you, me, and the horses feel the same way. Don't know why, but I feel an urgency to leave," Gruber said, looking up with a crinkle in his brow.

"Okay. No breakfast, just coffee, if we have enough," Brian said.

"I used all but one canteen to make this. It'll hafta do." Gruber stared at the coffee pot looking like he half-expected it to talk back to him.

"All right, men. Let's get up and get movin'. It's light enough to move now, so let's do it. Get some coffee and we ride out. Let's pray we have a town to get back to." Brian shook Ruger with his boot, simply because he was the closest to him.

"I'm gettin'," Ruger groaned.

Leading their horses, it wasn't long before they made their way down a narrow "path" discovered by Todd and Ruger the evening before. Quickly, Brian mounted his horse, turned, and started toward the ravine God's sunset had pointed to the night before.

"Why'er we goin' ther'?" asked Gruber.

"It's called obedience. I just know that's where God wants me to go. I have to check it out," Brian replied.

"A'ight," Gruber said. There wasn't a hint of disapproval in his voice.

As they got closer, Todd pulled up alongside Brian. "Now, that is strange. The green trees were ripped right out of the ground and the dead one in that ravine is still standing. Maybe the twister didn't come this direction. But how could it miss?"

"It was a pretty wild time yesterday. I'm not sure I can tell you what direction it was really moving. Maybe it didn't stay on the ground. We can only thank God we had the shelter we had."

Brian spurred his horse and moved a little faster. He also felt an urgency he couldn't explain.

"Whoa." Brian looked down into the ravine. He blinked his eyes. He turned in his saddle and looked back at the men as they came closer. "We need to go that way and get down there."

With that, he veered off to the right. The men followed him.

They went about fifty yards and turned down onto a short path to the bottom.

"Will you look at this! Grass! Out here in the middle of nowhere and water! Amazing!" Ruger looked at Todd and shook his head. Brian turned, looked at them, and rode on. "That's not all."

The water seemed to be seeping out of the sandstone wall above them and collecting on the rocky creek bed in the middle of the ravine.

Brian reached the dead tree and practically jumped off his horse, which immediately turned to the water and grass. Brian, on the other hand, turned to the tree. Lying on the ground and hog-tied was a man in his late forties. Brian cut his hands and feet free.

"Water," the man whispered.

Brian reached for his canteen and shook it. "Empty!" He knelt beside his horse and filled the canteen with the fresh rainwater from the day before.

"Here ya go. Take it easy. Just a little at a time." Brian looked him over. He had some pretty bad bruises and some cuts. It looked like he had been beaten. His clothes were soaked, not surprising, since he had weathered the storm in the ravine.

"I can't believe you came. You must be an angel sent by God."

The man could hardly speak. Brian had to lean closely to hear him. Suddenly, Todd stood right beside them, and Brian had not even heard him walk up he was so intent on listening to the man.

"What does he need, Brian? Is there anything I can do?" Todd asked with tenderness in his voice.

"Get a blanket or two. I'll put one under his head, and we need one to cover him up." Todd started walking away. "Todd, thanks." Brian nodded his way. Todd just looked at him and waved his hand as if to say it was nothing.

"Mister, are you hurt anywhere besides the bruises and cuts?" "I don't think so. I just hurt all over. Hard to tell," he barely spoke more than a whisper.

Brian gave him another drink, and he took more this time.

"Do you feel like sitting up?"

Todd walked back with the blankets.

"The circulation's back in my hands. I can move them, at least. I'm not too sure about my legs. I think I'd like to sit up. They're tingling somethin' fierce."

Todd and Brian took either side of him and helped lean him up against the wall of the ravine right next to the tree. Todd draped one blanket behind him as Brian held him forward, making sure he didn't fall over.

"How's that? Do you feel light-headed?"

"No, this feels right good, compared to where I was a few minutes ago." His voice was stronger now.

"What happened?" Brian asked.

"I'm the stationmaster at a way station up near Austin. They killed my wife and my friend and his wife. They thought I was dead, but when they were moving the bodies into the station, I groaned. Their leader decided to use me as a bargaining chip if they needed one. So they tied me to a horse and took me with them as the station burned down. I couldn't decide if I wanted to die right there or kill them if I got the chance."

"How'd you get under this tree, if I can call it that?" Brian asked, looking up at the scraggly bleached silver dead wood.

"Well, the head man and his right-hand man decided to drop the rest of us off here and to take the horses and ride farther west in case anyone was following us. Ya, see, two of the men had grabbed a girl from a nearby town, and they did horrible things to her when they met up with us. Then they left her for dead. I didn't see how I was going to live through any of this. They're mean, wild men. They just aren't right in the head. The war, I reckon…" His voice trailed off as if he was remembering something from long ago. Brian and Todd just waited, giving him time.

"I reckon when the horses left, they decided to leave me too. Nobody wanted to carry me or drag me. I don't think they trusted me untied. I heard one of them say, 'If he's still alive when they come back to get us, we'll take him along." Another one said, 'If he ain't, no loss.' They have no respect for anyone. There's just something wrong with their heads. No decency about them at all." "Hey, boss. The horses're watered, and they have had a good bit of grass. The three of us think we should head on back to town if that's okay with you. Jakes said he would keep Pete behind him on his horse. If you need us here, we'll stay. Gruber is getting real antsy. You probably don't need him around." Ruger knew Gruber better than anyone else.

Brian nodded. "You fellas go on. We're going to take it easy.

One of us will have to ride double. Just drop Pete off at the jail.

Michael can put him in a cell. We'll take care of him later. He's in no rush."

"Once we get to town, if there is no need for me there, I can come back with a wagon and take this fella on in. Will that help?"

Ruger volunteered, pointing at the man on the ground.

"It would. But you do what's most urgent. If we're needed, then come and get him. If not, well, we'll get there eventually riding double," Brian said as he looked at Todd. Ruger nodded, got on his horse, and left.

"Did you say Pete?" the stationmaster asked.

"Yes, sir. Do you know which one he was?"

"Sure do. He's one of the sorriest people to walk the face of the earth. He lied out of both sides of his mouth. He said if I told him where we kept the money, no one would get hurt. We didn't have much at the station, certainly not enough to waste a life over. So I told them. It was all of twenty dollars. He got the money and came back outside and shot the three of them where they stood. Then he laughed and looked at me. I thought I was next. But he said, 'I'm not going to shoot you since there was twenty dollars.' Then he laughed so hard I thought he was going to fall down. Then he beat me to a pulp and left me for dead. He was one of the two that grabbed that girl in town and brought her back. I'll never forget the look on her face. She was so scared." He hung his head and began to cry. "I couldn't help her. I couldn't help her. I don't ever want to feel like that again."

"Well, he won't hurt anybody ever again." Todd helped the station master to stand up. "Now, Mr.....uh, what is your name? Mine is Todd, and that's Brian Daniels; he's the sheriff."

"Stevenson, Glenn Stevenson."

"Well, Mr. Stevenson, let's try to get the circulation going in those legs. Then we'll see about riding back to town. Take it easy, the ground's uneven, and there's water right in front of you. You don't want to slip and fall."

"Thank you, young man. Are you a doctor?"

Todd smiled. "No, sir. My pop is a doctor, though. I learned a good bit from him while I was growing up. I thought about becoming a nurse, but I just have always had a hankering to be a lawman. I have to try that first."

"A nurse?" Brian asked. "That explains some things."

"Like what?" Todd looked at him questioningly.

"Your compassion for one thing. It could be a really bad thing for someone who is facing a lying sidewinder. It could get you killed." Brian answered him with a little too much fire in his voice.

"Or someone else?" Todd asked.

"Well, that too."

"Don't worry, Brian. I'm sure you will let me know when I should be more cautious than compassionate. I promise I will listen to your voice of experience."

Brian looked over at Todd, expecting to see sarcasm written all over his face. All he saw was sincerity. He meant it. *Wow, I never thought I'd see the day when a young buck would be that humble. Maybe I need to learn a few things from him.*

"Come on, let's see if Glenn can stay seated behind you. Are you ready to take a ride, Glenn?" Brian looked over at Glenn who was managing to move on his own.

"I reckon I don't want to stay here any longer. It beats all why you fellas would come over to this ravine."

"God made it clear to me I needed to come here. I don't think it is a wise thing to go against God." With that, Brian mounted his horse.

"Come on, Glenn. I'll get on first, and then you put your foot in the stirrup and give me your left hand. I'll help pull you up if you need it. Will you be okay behind me?" Todd asked.

"I'll manage."

As they left the ravine and rode back toward town, not much was said. About halfway there, Glenn tapped Todd on the shoulder. "What'd he mean?"

"Who?" Todd asked.

"Sheriff Daniels. What did he mean God told him to go to the ravine? I've never heard of any such before."

"Well Brian, and I are, well, are Christians. We believe God leads us, and His way is made clear when we listen and pay attention to all things around us. Last night, Brian was praying for guidance on what to do because that twister tore everything up. We were going after those men who had kidnapped little Daisy to capture them. It just didn't turn out that way. God led us to a cave and the men at the same time the storm was coming. We were able to kill six of them. Pete was badly wounded. He died later. He was still alive when we got into the cave with our horses. Just shortly thereafter, the twister came knocking at the door. After the storm, nothing below the cave looked the same. Even the bodies of the men were gone. That's when Brian spent some real quiet time with God. When the sun went down, it looked like a finger pointed straight at that ravine. I saw it too. We both knew we needed to go there first thing in the morning. Horst Ruger and I had gone scouting and found a way down off the ledge. We all rode over to the ravine in the morning, and you know the rest."

"There were nine men. What happened to the others?"

"They had taken the horses on, as you know. We don't know what's happened to them. There are caves all over this area, and some are pretty large. Maybe they took shelter in one of them.

The storm destroyed any tracks they may have left. We need to get Jakes to the doctor, and we need to check on the town and surrounding area to see if anyone's hurt or in need of help. So we're headed back to town."

"Did you find that girl?"

"Daisy. We did. She was still alive when we left. I guess we will find out her condition when we get back."

Glenn looked up toward the sky and then off in the distance.

A tear slowly made its way down his cheek. He didn't even want to wipe it away or hide it. He was grief-stricken over his losses and hers. He couldn't believe they were both alive. Would they ever be truly whole again?

The sun was beginning to beat down on the riders as they crossed over the hill from which they could see the town.

"Glory be!" Gruber shouted. "Everything looks jest lak we left her."

As much as they wanted to gallop in, they looked over at Jakes. He needed to see Doc as soon as possible. His passenger was fine, but Jakes didn't need to ride hard or risk falling off his horse.

"Let's just ride easy." Ruger started toward town with a smile on his face and thanks in his heart.

"Gracious! You men look like you have been through hell and back. What happened?" Doc asked as they helped Jakes off his horse. "And who's that fella?"

"Doc, did you get a storm?" Ruger asked, looking around for damage.

"No, it rained a bit, but it was nothing. C'mon, Jakes, let's get you inside. What happened to you…?" Doc's voice trailed off as he helped Jakes into the office. Ruger took the reins and led the horse with Pete still draped over the back down to the sheriff's office. He looked back at Gruber. He was riding off toward his home.

"Can't blame him for that," Ruger said as he patted his horse's neck. He dismounted and headed toward the other horse. "C'mon, Pete, let's get you inside."

Ruger turned the door handle and kicked it open. Michael wasn't there, so he just proceeded to do as Brian had told him.

He put Pete in one of the jail cells on a cot, then left the jail, and headed for the cabinetmaker's place. *Shoulda locked the door! Naw, if someone wants that varmit, they can have him. That man doesn't even deserve a hole in the ground.*

As he entered the cabinet shop, Curtis looked up.

"Hey, Curtis! Got a man down in the jail who is going to need a box. Make it from the sorriest wood ya got. He doesn't need anything nice. He didn't do anything nice in his life, at least recently, anyway. We're better off without him."

"Who is it?"

"Name's Pete. Seems he is one of the ones who took Daisy."

"Why don't we just throw him on a burn pile and let the buzzards take what's left."

"I don't guess that would be very Christian of us."

"Who cares? I'm not worried about it. Never do have a preacher here except when they make it back around. You men who have been preachin' do a decent-enough job, but it's not like it's your job, ya know. Wonder when we'll have a real preacher."

"Don't know the answer to that one. For right now, we just do the best we can with who we have and those who come around. It was really nice that the preacher showed up just at the right time to marry Josh and Katie. I thought we were all going to have to go to San Antonio to find us a preacher to do it. Heck, we don't even have a judge or a lawyer here to do a civil ceremony. "

"Well, the town's growin'. Maybe a preacher, lawyer, or judge will come and take up residence permanent like." Curtis spit, missing the spittoon placed in the corner and contributing to the already wet dark spot on the floor.

"We can always pray."

"How big's this fella Pete?

"You can go measure him. He is in jail."

"Jail! It's a little late for that, ain't it?"

"Yep, but that's what Brian said to do. He's got his reasons."

"All right. Hey, Horst, I almost have your hutch done. You gonna surprise the missus with it?"

"Yep, our anniversary is comin' up, nearly twenty. It's about time she had somethin' for puttin' up with me."

"Ain't that the truth!" Curtis laughed as he grabbed a knotted string, and they both headed out walking toward the jail.

Todd tilted back his hat. "Doesn't look like it rained much here. That's strange."

"Twister storms can be like that. I just didn't think that one was. I thank God for sparing our town," Brian remarked.

"Let's go on in and get Mr. Stevenson here some help."

"I wonder if anyone has checked on the ranchers."

"It probably hasn't entered their minds since nothing bad happened here." Todd looked toward the north and then turned and looked toward the south. "I wonder which way it went."

"I tell you what, Todd, we'll get Mr. Stevenson situated with Doc, and I'll ride north and you ride south, and we will check on all the ranchers to see if they had any damage." With that, Brian kicked the sides of his horse, and they started toward town.

Todd caught up with him and looked his way. "Why do I have to go south?"

"I'm the sheriff, and I said so. Besides, if you're going to be a deputy of sorts, you need to get to know all the people around here. You know the ones north. I bet you don't know a soul south."

"Well, that is true enough."

"Besides, I have something I need to talk with Josh about, and I thought I would kill two birds with one stone."

"South it is."

A few minutes later, the men walked through the door to Doc's place. "Doc, you here?" Brian hollered out.

"Yep, just finishing up with Jakes. I'll be out in a minute."

"Here ya go, Mr. Stevenson. Just sit down right here. Doc will be out shortly. I'm just going to peek in and see Doc and Jakes for a minute, and then I'm riding out."

"What about Pete?" Todd asked.

"Oh, Pete. He had plum skipped my mind. We'll have to get Curtis down at the cabinet shop next to the lumberyard to see about making a coffin. I wish those Texas Rangers would get here. I'd like them to see him, before we plant him."

"How many ranches are south?"

"Let's see, I think the Rhineburg's ranch is vacant. They moved up to Dallas. So that would just be two that are close by.

Check those two and then come back. If everything is all right with them, ask one of them to send a rider to the other ranches down there, if anyone is still living in them. After that, you can get back here."

"Okay, why don't I stay and talk with Curtis, then go out. You can leave as soon as you have talked with Doc."

"That sounds good to me." Brian opened the door to the examining/surgery room. "Hey, Doc, Jakes, it sure is good to be home, isn't it?"

"Yep, you can say that again, Brian. I don't know if I'll be much good to you in the near future. I'm right-handed, and the varmint shot me in the right arm."

Brian walked all the way into the room and carefully closed the door behind him. "Well, hopefully, we won't be needin' any help again anytime soon. Doc, the man out there is the stationmaster from the way station that was burned. The bodies of the others, including his wife, who were there are burned in the building.

They took him as a hostage. I think he would have rather died with the others. He had to watch what they did to Daisy. I think it's really bothering him that he's still alive."

"Thanks for telling me that, Brian. I'll know better how to question him and how to measure his answers. I may need to put him up with Esther. She has Daisy over there. Daisy will be fine, physically. I had to take a few stitches here and there. She'll be sore for a while, but she will recover physically and, because of her age, rather quickly. I'm not too sure how she will do emotionally. Esther will do her best, and she will petition the Lord to intervene. Maybe I should start paying Esther. She makes a real good physical as well as emotional nurse."

"You sure are right on that account. I'm going out to check on the ranchers. We just barely escaped with our lives during a twister."

"Jakes was filling me in on that one. We never even thought of a twister. It was really dark to the northwest, though." Doc rubbed his chin.

"That would be northeast from where we were. I'd better go and check on all those folks. See ya later. Todd will be going south after he checks on some things around here."

19

The K & J Ranch

Katie, I've checked on everything around the house, and we are all set. Are you ready to go back to town with me? Is Josh going with us?" Willow asked as she came downstairs and saw Katie at work in the kitchen. Katie turned with tears in her eyes. "What's wrong?" Willow ran to her with open arms.

"I don't know. I just started crying. If I'm not sleepy or throwing up, for the third time this morning, I'm crying. Willow, are you sure I'm going to have a baby?" Katie began to sob.

"Yes, my dear sister. You are definitely going to have baby. This is just a phase. It will pass. Give it three months."

"Three months! I don't think I can do this."

"Well, you have at least one month behind you, so you only have two to go, maybe less, depending on when all this started.

Only you and Josh can figure that out. I'm not even going to ask."

Katie turned as red as a beet. "Oh my, what do you know about that?"

"My gracious, Katie. In the village, we lived in tepees. There was no privacy. Each family lived together. I lived with my adoptive parents and many times was wide awake when they…well, when they—"

"Spare me the details, please! I am beyond shock! I can't believe that. It is so personal; it is a very intimate spiritual communion between the husband and wife. I can't even imagine sharing it

162

with anyone to see. Oh my goodness. I can't get that picture out of my head. Well, I guess you won't need 'the talk' from Esther when the time comes for you to marry."

"Remember, Katie, I was pledged to be married to that horrible, abusive, murdering man in our tribe. That's why I ran away. I was only about fourteen at the time as close as I can figure, and I knew all about it by then. Of course, I wasn't too excited about it at that age. To tell the truth, I'm still not. I'll leave that up to you and all the rest of the married couples."

"I fear not all married couples are as blissfully happy as Adam and Esther or Josh and I. I have seen some who seemed completely miserable."

"Oh yes, shall we start with Marta and Oscar? Then we can move on to Mr. and Mrs. Breland. Wow! Now there's a couple! He spends more time upstairs in the saloon than he does at home."

"Now, Willow, how do you know that?" Katie looked at her in even more shock.

"Well, from my window at the hotel, I can see into some of the rooms on the second floor. They don't bother to close the curtains most of the time. I have seen him go into the saloon after he closes the store. Later, when I go upstairs to my room, I can see him and his lady of choice, seems to be the same one most of the time, go into the same room. I close my curtain so I don't have to see what is going on. Disgusting! Truthfully, I feel so sorry for those women. Some look about my age. They can't be happy doing what they are doing. What would drive a woman to do that? They would have to be desperate. Oh, Katie, let's put them on our prayer list. I wish there was some way I could reach them and tell them about the love of Christ. Do you think there is?"

"With God, all things are possible, Willow. I will promise to pray for them with you. We can also pray for God to provide a way for them to hear the Gospel, however he chooses."

"Katie, I want him to use me! I want to do something. Maybe I can volunteer my nursing skills somehow. I bet they never go to Doc."

"My dear, you don't officially have nursing skills. You better talk to Doc before you go rushing in. Remember, 'fools rush in where angels fear to tread.'"

"I've never heard that before. Is it in the Bible?"

"No, it is from a poem by Alexander Pope, 'An Essay on Criticism.'"

"I really need to go to school or get Riley to give me some suggested reading assignments. We could all read the same thing and then get together and discuss it. That would be fun."

"Well, to answer your very first question, yes."

"What was my very first question?"

"You asked if I was ready to go to town with you. You have certainly talked me out of my crying spell. I would love to go to town with you. Let's go get someone to hitch up the wagon."

"I was going to ride to town."

"I'm not sure Josh will let me ride. I think after I tell Esther and Adam about the baby, we will have all kinds of food or something to bring home. She will not let us out of town without a buckboard full of presents. You will also have anything you want to bring back. We should take the wagon to town."

"You're right. And since I'm coming back, I'll leave my horse here."

"I'll go ask Josh, or whoever is out in the barn today, to hitch up the wagon. Do you feel like driving it?"

"Uh, I can try, but I bet whoever is out in the barn will want to do that."

"Why?"

"Well, uh, why is there someone out in the yard or barn every day, staying close to the house?"

"Oh, I get your point. Yes, they are supposed to stay close to me. Josh just overreacts sometimes."

"I don't think so, Katie. Red isn't the only outlaw in the territory. We never know when someone may come riding in looking to cause trouble. We are even more vulnerable out on the road. I think it would be best if whoever is out there will at least ride their horse with us. I think I would feel more comfortable."

"Willow, weren't you just yesterday talking about being independent? You certainly are having some mood changes. What has come over you? Are you having second thoughts about Brian?"

"No, I like Brian. I think he's the nicest man I have ever known. But my knowledge of men is very limited, especially those of European descent. Indian men have a totally different mind-set about women. Their whole culture demands it. It has taken me some time to adjust to men treating me with respect and considering my preferences. Of course, that is also limited.

I know there are men of European background who are brutal, worse than those cultural differences found even between different tribes of Indians. Again, look at Oscar and how he treats Marta. It is more than shameful."

"How do you know about Oscar?"

"I've seen Marta's arms and neck all bruised. I have even seen her with a black eye. She said she ran into a door. I don't believe it for a minute, and neither does Esther. We just don't know what to do about it."

"What did Brian say when you told him?"

"I didn't tell him. Should I?"

"Yes, I believe you should. There must be some law against that sort of thing."

"If he doesn't know, I bet he could find out. He is very smart and loves researching the law." Willow smiled proudly as she said that. "I'm sure he will deal with Oscar."

"We can ask him when we get to town."

"If he's back."

"Back from where?"

"Remember, I told you he was out chasing some bad men."

"Oh yes, what was that about?"

"Oh look, it's Wulf!"

"Hey, Wulf! Katie and I need to go to town. She wants to see Esther, and I need to get my things and bring them out here. I'm moving back in so I can keep my eye on you." Willow teased and poked her finger in his chest. "I also want to talk to Doc. I have some questions for him. Could you hitch up the wagon for us, please? There's something sweet in it for you."

"Oh, I'll hitch up the wagon and get my horse. You ladies will not go riding into town alone. Not while I'm on watch. What kinda sweets?"

"I made cookies while Katie was doing her daily throwing up. She feels better now, so we can continue without incident, I hope."

"I'll get the horses hitched and mine saddled. You just march yourself back in the house and pack those cookies. I believe I feel a great hunger coming on that can only be satisfied by my sweet Indian princess's cookies."

Katie and Willow put on their most serious faces, turned, and went back into the house where they burst out laughing. "I didn't think I could hold that laugh that long. You better get those cookies packed up, or you are in a heap of trouble, little sis."

"I made a cute little drawstring bag out of some old denim pants Esther was going to throw away. I think they were Tad's that he outgrew. The denim is soft and well worn, so it was easy to work with. It was a simple thing to do. I will have to try my hand at something a little more demanding, like an apron. I know something about leather, but nothing about cloth. I really want to learn. Maybe Marta can teach me. I'll go get it from upstairs.

I thought I might need it for a little snack on the way home, so I stuck it in my jacket pocket just before I came out."

When she returned back downstairs, Katie had some cookies stacked and ready for packing. "Oh, how cute! You will have to make me one. I love it. It will be easy to turn inside out to wash all the crumbs out. You are very clever, you know that?"

Willow stuck her thumbs into her armpits and puffed out her chest. "Sure, I knew that. I'm surprised it took you so long to realize it, big sis." Again, they laughed.

"Oh, Willow, it feels so good to laugh. I have been so worried I haven't laughed in…well, a coon's age!"

"During hunting season or natural life span?"

"Silly!" Katie laughed again.

With the wagon waiting out front and Wulf on his horse waiting for them, they filled the bag and left, happily handing Wulf the treats. His smile stretched all the way across his face, a sight the girls had never seen before. He had smiled before, but not broadly. This smile reached all the way to his eye. He was truly happy, and it wasn't just the cookies.

"Let's not let grass grow under those wheels, girls, but we don't want to have a race to town either. Just go at a nice steady pace. We'll get there in no time," he reassured them.

Esther knocked softly on the door as she had done so often when Katie lay in the same bed. "Daisy? May I come in? I have something for you."

She heard a very small voice come from within. "Yes?"

Esther gently opened the door. She balanced a tray of tea and chicken broth as she entered the room. The very bruised and bloodied girl lay as if she were a corpse, her eyes nearly swollen shut. Angry cuts lashed crazily across her face, neck, and arms.

They couldn't be seen now, but they were also on her back and front. She had to be in agony.

"Darling, do you think you can sit up? I can fetch another pillow to put behind your head if you don't think you can sit up."

"No, it hurts to move. I can't, I can't." A tear formed in her left eye and slid down her cheek. Then one formed in the right eye and mirrored the path of the first tear. Soon, both eyes had tears running smoothly washing her cheeks and running into her ears. She didn't sob, but Esther could tell she wanted to do so.

"Well, that is perfectly all right. You do need some nourishment. It will help you heal. I brought some tea, which will help soothe your sorrow and will feel good on your throat. I have chicken broth that is always good medicine for whatever ails a body. I'd be happy to feed you if you'll let me."

Daisy barely nodded her head and slowly quit crying. Esther pulled a chair over to the table where she had placed the tray. She sat right next to the bed and took a spoon in which she lifted a little broth. She blew on it to cool it a bit and then placed it next to Daisy's lower lip. Daisy opened her mouth, and Esther let the liquid slowly slip into it.

Daisy swallowed the warm broth and tried to open her eyes more. "Good," she said.

"Would you like some more?" "Yes," she barely sighed.

This routine was repeated many times until all the broth was gone. The tea was the next thing to be served. Esther had put plenty of sugar in the tea. She remembered that when Daisy had first come to work for her, Daisy had really loved having anything sweet, almost like it was the first time she had ever had it. Was that another clue to her history? Esther thought she was beginning to put the pieces of the puzzle together.

When she was finished with the tea, Daisy turned her head just slightly toward Esther. "So good. Thank you."

"Daisy, sweet thing, I need to know if I am right about something. Will you please tell me the truth so I can help you even more?"

Daisy nodded slightly.

"Please tell me, are you an orphan?"

Daisy moaned, and tears began to fall. With great difficulty she said, "Please don't send me back, please, please, don't."

"I have no intention of sending you back. But now I know you have no one to notify of your misfortune. Now, I know you are mine to take care of with no one to interfere with my efforts. No one will come and take you away."

Daisy, again, tried to open her eyes to look at Esther's face and see if she meant what she said. All she could see were kindness and love.

"Now, dear, please tell me…how old are you, really?"

Daisy took a deep shuttering breath. She sighed and whispered, "Fifteen…almost."

Only fourteen. How horrible! Lord, what am I to do? I need help with this situation. I cannot even begin to understand what horrors she will be haunted by the rest of her life. Please give me guidance and direction. I must have help with helping her. I beg you, dear Father, Sovereign God, keep us all in the palm of Your hand and lead this little lost lamb to Your loving arms and saving grace.

"Does it hurt for me to smooth back your hair?"

"No," Daisy whispered through swollen lips. Places on her face and around her eyes showed where heavy fists and large hands had left ugly purple and red marks.

Lord, help her to heal quickly, please. She is so young.

"Do you ever pray, Daisy?"

"No, God doesn't listen."

"Yes, He listens. You would not be alive if He didn't listen. We were praying for you as soon as we found out you were missing. He answered our prayers. You are still alive when those men meant for you not to be."

Daisy began to cry.

"Now, listen to me. Daisy, it was not your fault. You did nothing wrong. In fact, you were trying to become better and doing something very right. No one thinks you are to blame, so please don't blame yourself. Please don't think anyone else is blaming you or is mad at you. In fact, quite the contrary."

Tears still ran down her cheeks. Esther opened a drawer in the bedside table and took out a handkerchief. "Here you go. Can you wipe your eyes and blow your nose?"

Daisy reached her hand and arm outside of the covers. The cuts were not too deep, but there was hardly a place on her arm that wasn't black and blue. *The animals! How can God allow them to live?* Esther handed the handkerchief to Daisy. "Now, if that is too painful, I can do it for you."

"No, I need to try. I need to move. I don't want to, but I will feel better if I do. I think."

"I think you would feel so much better if I arranged for a nice hot bath. Would you like that?"

"I don't know."

"The hot water would help to loosen up those tight muscles, and we can wash your hair. I know I always feel better with freshly washed hair."

"I guess."

"All right, I will arrange for the tub and hot water to be brought up here so you don't have to do anything but get out of bed and then back in. I will put clean sheets on while you bathe. I won't be gone long. You rest a bit. I'll take these dishes down. Do you want more to eat?"

"No, ma'am. Thank you."

Esther rose, took the tray with one hand, and, with the other, opened the door. She quietly closed it and walked down the hall, her heart heavy with grief for the young girl and all she had had to face. She began to cry and almost missed the first step on the stairs.

Get yourself together, Esther. You need to be strong, she thought as she waited until her tears stopped and then proceeded down the stairs. *How unusual! No one is in the lobby. Where is everyone?* she wondered.

She took the dishes to the kitchen. "Rose, I need enough hot water for a bath. Will you fix that for me, please?"

"Already done it."

Esther looked at her with surprise. "Really and truly, it's ready?"

"Yes, ma'am. I knowed you was gonna need it once you took her somethin' to eat. So, I jest went right on and fixed it fo' you and Miss Daisy. Is that little gal all right?"

"She ate. So all I need is the tub brought in from the back."

"Done."

"What?"

"Well, if 'n I was fixin' water, I knowed you was gonna need somethin' to put it in. So, I ask Mr. Adam to bring it in and take it up to her room."

"Well, Rose, you make my life so much easier. I believe some lavender soap and rose water will do just the trick to make her feel luxurious. I think I'll let her use mine."

"I hope you forgive me, but I also ask Mr. Adam to take those to her room."

"Rose, you amaze me."

"No, ma'am. That shouldn' be. I been 'round you many a year now, and I knows how yous thinks."

"As long as they are good thoughts, I don't mind you reading my mind. But don't listen when I am having bad thoughts."

"Now, Mrs. Esther, you knowed you don't have bad thoughts."

"Rose, I certainly do. I would hate for you to know what I was thinking about the men who did what they did to Daisy. How will she ever heal inside?"

"Now, Mrs. Esther, you knowed better than that. You can't do God's work. You gots ta leave that up ta him."

"Thank you, Rose. I better get up there and have Adam come get the water."

"I hear him coming down the stairs now."

Esther turned and left the kitchen and almost ran right into Adam as she turned the corner to enter the lobby. "Rose has the water ready. Is the tub in Daisy's room or out in the hall?"

"It is safely ensconced in the room, my dear."

"Good, then you can go ahead and bring up the water. You are such a dear. Thank you for taking care of that for me, and I didn't even have to ask." She smiled so sweetly at him, he wanted to kiss her, but she turned to the side and raced up the stairs.

"Maybe later, I'll get a proper thank-you." With that, he smiled and went to the kitchen. "You have water for me, my lady?"

"Yes, sir, knave, get yourself over to da stove and take it upstairs without fail. Da queen awaits."

This game had been going on for years between the two of them. Rose loved it as much as Adam did.

Adam made it to the room spilling only a little on his right leg. "Yes, the water is still hot," he said as he entered the room.

"I'll be back. I think there is another pail and if you need it, one to cool it down to a bearable state."

Esther saw the wet pants leg and giggled. "You speak like the voice of experience, sire."

"Your Highness is very observant. I shall return shortly since I am not of great height."

Esther and Daisy laughed at that. Daisy didn't have a big laugh, but a laugh nonetheless. That was a good sign. Esther thanked God as she lifted the large pail and proceeded to pour the steaming water into the tub. She added the rose water, and the fragrance filled the room. She then went to get fresh sheets and some towels.

20

rian opened the door to the jail. Michael sat behind the desk filling it and the chair. "Any trouble while I was gone?"

"Not much, besides having a dead man in one cell. I suppose you know about that.

"Yeah, that's Pete."

"I have Oscar and Rufus locked up, drunk and disorderly and being a public nuisance. They were at the saloon, got drunk, and started fighting again. This time they both wanted the same girl to pay attention to them. I was concerned they would start taking it out on the girl. As a result here they are. They both spent the night here. I hope Marta had a quiet night. I let her know I had him locked up. I didn't ride out to the Dalkes to let them know Rufus was here. They'll find out soon enough."

"If I had known, I could have told Todd to let them know.

He's on his way to see how the ranchers south of town fared during the storm."

"What storm, Brian?"

"We were west of town when we ran into the vermin who attacked Daisy, and we ran into a twister almost at the same time.

I'll have to tell you about it later. I need to go out to your ranch and see how everyone there is."

Michael looked up at him with very kind and knowing eyes.

"It's not my ranch, Brian, and everybody is fine. But you go and check. Look into how the Konrads managed. I bet they rarely have anyone drop by. I run into some of their hands when I'm out on the range scouting out there for potential trouble. We almost never see the mister and missus. I think his first name is Hans, and her name is Marlene."

"I'll do it. No time like the present when I have two men helping me keep the peace around here. You know, Michael, Todd's an amazing young man. I was so wrong about him. I want to get to know him better. You were right about me. I owe you an apology." "I knew you would see his good side, eventually. You know your attitude toward Todd hurt no one really but yourself. Take a lesson from Clyde—observe, analyze, and then make a decision. Clyde is a wise man, Brian, and Todd will be a really good help to you in the future."

"Thanks, Michael. I'll be back. Do you mind staying? I appreciate your help more than you know."

"You're welcome, Brian. Now, you best be going. I'll hold down the fort. There is a new lady here in town I have yet to meet. I need to do that."

"Really? What's her name?"

"Well, I haven't met her yet, but talk is her name is Miss Erin Kerr."

"An Anglo-Saxon rather than a German! Is she blonde like Willow and me or a redhead? Please don't tell me she is another dark-haired girl."

"I hear she has raven-black hair."

"Oh well, we certainly aren't gaining on the hair color side. I've never seen so many dark-haired people in one place. Maybe I should move to Sweden. I hear they're blond." Brian laughed as he left the jailhouse, waving toward Michael as he did.

Brian mounted his horse and headed out to the K & J Ranch. As he rode that way, his heart became burdened for his town and for all the lost souls who needed to be introduced to the love of Jesus. "Lord, I know I have burdens and cares for those I am in fellowship with and for those who believe like I do, but, Lord, I am realizing more and more that I haven't been caring for the Oscars and Martas of this world and all those who frequent the saloon. They don't even realize how sinful they are being by taking advantage of the women there. Help me to be more compassionate like Todd, yet keep me aware of the dangers lurking in the hearts and minds of those who would harm the good and innocent of this world. I want to be more like you, Jesus. Yes, make me more like you."

"Brian, where are you headed?"

Brian didn't even realize he was riding along with his eyes shut with his head looking up. He jerked his head in the direction of that, oh, so familiar voice.

"Willow, Katie, Wulf, goin' to town?"

Willow smiled shyly. "Why, yes, Sheriff. We are going in to see the family and to get my things. I'm going to move back out to the ranch. Katie needs my help, and I miss being there."

Brian raised his eyebrows. "I guess it is time to start jelly-making and canning the vegetables. It's always good to have someone to help with all that, I suppose. Maybe with you gone from town, I won't have so much to do to maintain the peace." He grinned.

Both the girls laughed.

Willow gave him a sassy look. "I'm glad I can be so accommodating. I didn't realize it was me disturbing your peace. I thought that was you yourself."

Brian didn't want to respond to that, so he tipped his hat and just said, "I'll see you ladies later. Wulf, keep a sharp eye out." He then thought to himself, *Maybe I just chose the wrong words. I hope I didn't offend him.* But he rode off and didn't look back. "If I don't make anything of it, maybe he won't take offense," Brian spoke aloud.

There was a time when that would have bothered me. Thank you, God, for giving me this incredible peace and understanding. What a difference you have made in my heart. Wulf turned and looked back at Brian and then turned back to pay attention to the road and surrounding area.

As they found themselves entering town, Wulf felt himself relax. He had not realized how tense he had gotten. "I believe I'll go with you to the hotel. I want to get some coffee and one of those sweet cinnamon things your mom makes, Katie."

"If there are any left. They seem to fly off the tray. We're going in there first. I think that's where we'll find our folks." Katie smiled in anticipation. She couldn't wait to tell them the news.

In just a few minutes, the girls were bounding up the steps and entering the hotel. They headed straight for the dining room.

A few people were still there. Mary Elizabeth was tending the front, and Rose was in the kitchen. "Where's Mama, Rose?" Katie asked.

"Chile, she jest went up to help Daisy tak a bath."

"Daisy? Is Daisy ill?"

Rose looked at Katie and glanced at Willow. Willow discreetly shook her head. Rose nodded.

"Yes, baby doll, she is feeling under the weather. She's up in your old room. Your mama will be back down in just a few minutes. You princesses go have a seat, and I'll have Mary Elizabeth bring you a treat."

"Where's Daddy?"

"Mr. Adam, he tuk da tub up to yo mama so Daisy can have a bath. Den he was gonna leave to go to your ranch for a visit. I guess you jest missed him. It hasn't been two minutes since I heard da back do' slam shut. I reckon dat was him."

Katie slumped a bit, then straightened her back. "All right, we will wait unless, Willow, you want to go up to your room and pack."

"No, I wouldn't want to miss out on my treat! I'll stay down here. It won't take me long to pack."

They chose seats where they could see through the doors and could be seen as well. Katie didn't want to miss their mom. She smiled as she remembered how quickly Esther adopted, unofficially of course, the two girls as her daughters. She didn't realize at the time that Katie and Josh, Esther and Adam's oldest son, would be married in the not-too-distant future.

As they sat and waited, a beautiful raven-haired woman entered the dining room and looked around tentatively. Willow jumped up from her seat, seeing Mary Elizabeth busy with some customers.

"Are you looking for someone, or are you alone? Perhaps I could help you." Willow smiled her most beautiful smile.

Erin smiled back at her. "No, I am alone. I was just wondering where to sit. I just came down for some tea and maybe a pancake."

Willow noticed Erin's voice was hoarse. Willow thought about Katie's description of how her voice sounded when Red had choked her. It must have been very much like this.

"I tell you what, why don't you sit with us? We are getting ready to have some refreshment as well and would enjoy talking with you. That is, if you don't mind the company."

"That would be lovely. Thank you so much."

Willow led the way to their table and introduced Katie. "I'm sorry. I don't believe I know your name."

"I apologize too. I should have introduced myself to you. I'm Erin Kerr."

"It is a pleasure to know you, Erin. Please join us." Katie gave her a warm and inviting smile. "We are just waiting for Esther to come down. You see, I married her son, and she has adopted both Willow and me as her daughters."

"She is the most delightful, loving woman I have met in well, I don't know when. Since my mother died, I guess." Erin looked around and didn't see anyone she had seen before, except Mary Elizabeth.

Willow jumped up again. "Did you say tea and a pancake? I'll go and get it for you. Mary Elizabeth is rather busy with that group over there." Erin nodded and watched Willow practically skip across the floor to the kitchen. It was not long before she came back carrying a tray with tea, coffee, and lemon drops.

As she set it down and began to empty the tray and place things on the table, she smiled. "Our food will be ready in just a bit. I thought we might want to get started on the lemon drops beforehand."

Katie looked at Willow. "None for me this morning. Thanks." Willow looked pointedly at her with a question in her eyes.

"I just wouldn't want to waste them. I think you know what I mean."

Willow nodded. "Well, perhaps Erin will share them with me." This time, she looked Erin in the eye with just a slight question shining in her blue, blue eyes.

"Oh yes! I had dinner with your parents, little brother, and the schoolmaster last night. They were so sweet to share your secret after-dinner treat with me. I am officially addicted to lemon drops. I will have to find where you purchase them and keep them in my room or even carry them with me in my reticule.

I don't think I will ever be without them again. Who would have known how soothing they would be on a hoarse throat?"

Katie lifted her eyes as she set her cup back in the saucer. "They were a lifesaver to me when my throat was injured by someone trying to choke me. Now, with the help of ginger tea and lemon drops, my voice is back to normal."

"I am glad to hear that. Perhaps, I will have the same fortune.

I pray so. Although my injury, similar to yours, happened almost a year ago. I pray God will grant healing even at this late date."

Erin quickly looked down and feared what she might see on the faces of the two girls.

"I am sorry you had to suffer. I still have nightmares about what happened to me. I will join your prayer for healing. Getting my voice back has helped me get over the emotional distress I feel—that and the love of Josh, Esther, Adam, Willow, and so many more, but mostly the love of God. He spared me for a reason, and now, I am seeing that more and more." Katie gently put her hand on her stomach.

Just then, Rose brought out three plates. One had a pancake as big as the plate, and the other two were crowned with the biggest cinnamon rolls the girls had ever seen.

"Oh, Rose!" Katie exclaimed. "How will we ever eat all of this?"

"You'll find a way, I's sure!" Rose chuckled all the way to the kitchen.

As they were taking the first bite, they stopped. "Oh, we forgot to pray! We should be grateful for this bountiful snack." Willow smiled broadly and took Katie's hand. She automatically reached for Erin's. Erin looked at Willow and Katie and extended her hands to both women. Willow asked God to bless the food set before them and to bless the work of their hands and to keep their thoughts pure throughout the day. She was about to say amen when she said, "Oh, and dear Father, since you are the Great Physician, please heal Erin's hoarseness and any emotional wounds she may have. We also ask your healing for Daisy. In Jesus' precious name. Amen."

Katie squeezed Erin's hand and smiled at her. "If there is ever anything I can do for you, just ask. If you just need to talk to someone who has been through a similar situation, it may help us both to talk about it and know the one we are talking to knows how we feel better than others who have not been through it."

Erin couldn't believe how absolutely loving these people were. Surely, God had brought her here to stay and make a living among these believing people who live what they believe. She had seen many churchgoing men come into her room. They claimed to be Christians but then didn't act or live like she thought Christians should. How could she say anything? She had been trapped in that life of sin for eight years. She wasn't living a Christian life either. How could God forgive her? What was she supposed to do? She had seen what William ordered done to the girls who tried to run away. She had prayed harder and harder that God would show her the way out. She just prayed William never found her.

"Did I upset you, Erin?" Katie asked, concerned.

"Oh no. I'm sorry. What you said made me go to my past and some very dark thoughts. I would very much like to talk with you. I think it would do us both some good." Erin took another bite of her pancake. "Oh, this is so good! The cinnamon rolls look delicious. My, what a great place to eat!"

"You can say that again." A low, deep voice said from behind Erin. Her cup stopped in midair, her throat constricted. *William?*

Before she could say anything, Willow jumped up with so much energy she almost upset the table.

"Wulf, where have you been? I thought you were hungry!"

He chuckled. "Now, I had some things to take care of. Men don't have the same privileges women do. You know, sit around and talk and suck on lemon drops. Men have to work so you ladies can enjoy these dainties."

Erin began to breathe again when she heard Willow call him Wulf. He sounded so much like William. She just held her breath.

"May I join you?"

Every fiber of Erin's body screamed no! It was not her place to refuse. She would just hurry and finish and excuse herself.

"Of course, you can join us! I'll just go ask Rose if she has another one of these cinnamon rolls. If not, you can share mine."

Willow gave the man a sweet smile.

Erin knew there couldn't be anything wrong with him.

Wulf sat down in the chair next to Erin. "Oh, I'm sorry, I didn't realize I didn't know you," Wulf said as he looked at Erin.

She glanced his way and almost coughed on the tea she had just taken a drink of when she saw the eye patch and scar marring his face. She swallowed it with difficulty and replied, "No, no, that's all right. I'm just meeting some new friends, I hope. You see, I'm new in town and am delighted to meet so many of the nice people here. My name is Miss Erin Kerr. I take it you are Wulf?"

"Yes, Wulfgang Shurtz. Wulf to my friends. I work at the K & J Ranch. So this lady right here"—he reached over and patted Katie's hand—"is my boss."

Katie laughed. "Not anymore. Josh has masterfully taken over those duties. I rarely have anything to do with the ranching now.

And to tell the truth, from the time that Michael came, I haven't.

Now, if I were completely honest, I would confess that I never did have control of the ranch. It and I were a wreck when Michael came. That reminds me I'll have to try and see him while I'm here. I miss him when he is gone."

"Your wish is my command," Michael said as he overheard what she said just as he entered the dining room of the hotel.

Willow was just coming back into the dining room when she saw Michael pull up a chair and squeeze in at the table. She whirled around and went back into the kitchen and came back out shortly with two mugs and a coffeepot.

"Coffee, gents?" She looked at them and grinned in a saucy way.

"Fill'er up, princess." Wulf reached for a cup.

"I think I'll have some of the tea this morning…with lemon drops, please."

"Comin' right up," Willow said as she turned and went back into the kitchen.

"Katie, who is your friend?" Michael asked while he was looking directly at Erin.

"Michael, this is Miss Erin Kerr. She's new in town. She and I have much in common. Erin, this is Michael. I call him my personal angel. He saved me from despair and helped to point me to Jesus who really and truly saved me. I don't know what I would do without Michael."

"Now, Katie, you would do just fine. You have Josh and so many others who are now looking out for you. You don't even really need me anymore."

"Michael! I will always need you. Don't even say that."

"Now, Katie, my dear sweet Katie, don't let me replace Jesus in your heart. Please, don't make an idol out of me. I am just a messenger and servant of God." Michael's eyes shone with a glow yet seemed a bit sad to Katie when he said that.

Wulf looked at Katie. "Katie, remember what Clyde says, 'If you let anything take the place of God in your life, he will take it away or allow you to be taken into captivity just like the Israelites.' I think, since he is obviously such a wise man, we can heed his warning. Clyde is speaking from experience, you know.

I have listened to him, and his wisdom and constant nagging made me realize I had to make a change in my life. I made the right decision."

"I know. Thank you for reminding me. I'm just so emotional right now."

"And why is that?" Esther said as she came to the table to give hugs all around.

"We may need to move to a big round table if Riley or Brian or both come in," Katie said, looking at the group gathering.

"No, Riley is teaching. School started yesterday, so he won't be here," Esther said as Michael gave her his chair and reached for another one. "Besides, look how cozy it is at this little table," Esther added and nodded her thanks to Michael.

"Brian was riding out to your ranch to check on all of you and then on out to Konrad's ranch to check on them."

"Oh, that's right! We saw him on the way in. What is wrong with my brain? I just am not myself."

"And how long has this been going on?" Esther asked with a knowing look.

Katie looked at her and then down at her lap. She swallowed back tears. She looked up again, and everyone was staring at her.

"Well, for a little while now. I'd remember more if I could stay awake and would quit throwing up." She laughed at the look on Esther's face.

"Oh, Katie! Katie! Praise the Lord! Does Josh know?"

"Of course. He knew before I did. Willow had to tell me."

"I had to tell you what?" Willow asked as she brought a platter full of cinnamon rolls and a tray of tea and coffee and the ever-present lemon drops.

"That I'm going to have a baby! I just can't get over saying it and knowing it's true."

"It's the most natural thing in the world. Almost every woman's dream," Esther said with tears of joy running down her face.

"I wish Adam was here to hear the news. Oh, we will have to go shopping."

Willow laughed out loud, and Katie joined her. "What?" Esther asked.

"We brought the wagon because we knew that would be your reaction," Katie said between laughs.

"Well, I guess it is. We will have to go see Marta and see if she can make you some clothes for an expanding waist line. Oh, and Erin, you must come with us. I can introduce you to Marta and see if she can use your help. What a great day this is becoming!"

"Are you sure?" Adam asked as Josh told him and Brian the good news.

"Yes, I'm as sure as I'm standing here. I've known longer than she has. She thought she was sick and going to die. She was afraid to tell me she was throwing up and really tired. She must think I'm deaf. You could hear her retching all the way to the big arroyo."

"Now, son, you may laugh now, but don't you ever let her know you are making fun of her misery. A woman's anger is never a pretty sight. You are to love her just as Christ loves his church.

You are to want the best for her and be willing to die for her."

"I know that. I just thought it was funny she thought she was keeping it a secret."

"Well, you know their brains do not work on logical things, especially when they are with child. I think every brain cell becomes occupied with creating that new life within them. Your Katie can't think of much else even though she doesn't know that, so be patient and understanding. Oh, and I'm sure your mother is going to be filling up your house with all kinds of—what was that word Riley used at dinner?—oh yes, *detritus*. I'm not sure it's an appropriate term for baby things, but I took it to mean something like clutter. I think maybe it is more in line with unwanted clutter. I just wanted to use my new word."

"*Detritus*...I'll have to store that one away and use it at the proper time."

"You and me both," Brian said as he turned to look at Josh.

"Josh, I need to go and meet the Konrads and check on them. Do you want to go with me? Adam, you can come too, if you want."

"I'd love to go," Josh said. "Let me go tell Clyde he has charge of the twins and the ranch while I'm gone. I don't know that I have ever met the Konrads. How do you know them?"

"I don't, Josh. It's a shame a twister had to bring me out here to meet them. I promised myself and God that I would do better.

Maybe that twister was meant to remind me. It did a pretty good job of getting rid of that trash, maybe I should say *detritus*, lying round on the rocks. We didn't have time to bring in the dead. So, God took care of them. I have no idea where to look for them."

Adam shook his head and looked around. "Well, men, I was going to say I needed to get back to town, but listening to you chastise yourselves for being slack in our promise to get to know the neighbors of town and check on them made me realize I've been doing the same thing. You know, I have gotten such good help with the hotel. I'm not really needed there as much. I could be the one to organize a visitation committee of sorts in town, and we could really get this thing going. So, I'll go with you and make them the first on my list to visit."

21

arta, are you here?" Esther called. The door was unlocked, so she had to be here. "You girls have a seat over there, and I'll check the back room.

Sometimes she's back there and doesn't hear the bell. She may need help with something."

Erin walked over to a dress form with a very stylish gingham dress on it. She lifted the hem and looked at the needlework. She looked closely at the details and the little extra care taken with the seams. "You are very fortunate to have such a fine seamstress here. I hope she will allow me to work with her."

Erin turned and took a seat with the other two on the love seat against the wall.

"Girls, Marta is back here trying to lift some boxes. Willow, could you come help, please?"

"Of course! I'd love to help."

"I could help too," Erin said as she started to rise.

"No, no. It's too crowded back here. There wouldn't be room. Just stay there and visit with Katie. You can keep her company and…remind her where she is every now and then." With that, Esther laughed and winked. Katie was laughing as well. Erin looked a little sad but had a seat next to Katie.

"What's wrong, Erin? I hope Mom poking fun at me didn't hurt your feelings."

"Not at all. I just, well, I don't want to talk about it right now. This isn't the time or the place. Maybe we will have a chance to talk later. I need to find work and a place to live first. That's my priority."

"There! We finished that little job. Now, Marta, any time you need some help lifting or just holding the ladder, you don't hesitate to call on me over at the hotel or send someone with a message. Okay?" Esther had her arm around Marta's shoulders and smiled encouragement.

"Esther, I could have gotten it done eventually."

Esther stopped and turned Marta to face her. She lowered her voice so it was just between the two of them. "You could have fallen and broken your head wide open too."

"Well, then my misery would be over." Marta's voice was almost a whisper.

"Marta, remember what I said about trusting in the Lord for your salvation?"

"Yes," she replied, frowning.

"Have you done that yet?"

"No, now don't nag me about it."

"Well, you know you will have more misery after death than you'll have during life if you don't. Yes, this misery will end, but that one goes on for eternity. So, please, don't wish for death."

There was no chastisement or berating tone to what Esther said. She felt nothing but love for this woman who so needed a friend and a savior.

"Here, I have a new friend I want you to meet." Esther quickly changed the subject and the level of her voice.

Marta looked to the love seat. Willow had joined the girls. She also saw Katie. Her eyes rested on the beautiful young woman about Katie's age sitting beside Katie.

"Marta, I would like for you to meet Miss Erin Kerr. Erin, this is Mrs. Marta Tucker."

"Pleased to meet you, Mrs. Tucker." Erin stood and offered Marta her hand.

"Likewise, Miss Kerr." The two women shook hands. "Are you visiting or what?"

"Well, I am looking to plant my roots. I would like to make this town my home if the people here will have me. I have made some very sweet friends, and I have only been here a day, almost. I arrived on the stage yesterday evening."

"Oh, I see. By yourself ?"

"Yes, ma'am. I am an orphan. There was nothing for me but bad memories back east. I decided to try the west and make new memories, good ones. Friends helped me get here. I liked the name of Crystal Springs and decided to take the stage here from San Antonio and see if I could call this home."

"What do you plan to do? Ain't much for young single women to do out here in the west unless you teach school or are you a saloon gal?"

"Marta! How dare you talk that way to this young lady? She happens to be a seamstress. Her mother was one and taught her how to sew. They made a living together after her father, who was a ship captain, drowned in a storm when his ship sank. Erin had to quit school to help her mother. I can't believe you talked like that. I have known you for a long time and have never seen you be that cruel."

"I'm sorry. I married a man who frequents that place, and he doesn't mind telling me so and telling me all about what he does. He loves to hurt me, and, I guess, I'm catching his meanness. So you sew?"

"Yes, ma'am. I was admiring your work on this gingham dress. You do very fine work. I was hoping you might need some help. Esther said you have started working in leather and would like to do more of that. I don't know how to do leather. I can certainly work with the fabrics so you will have more time for the leather. Or, if you would prefer, you could teach me what you do with leather, and I could learn that. Then you could work in the fabric, or we could share the chores. I am willing to do whatever you need, even lift heavy boxes." Erin lifted an eyebrow, smiled, and waited.

"Well, I am getting a mite busy. With two of us, we could get twice as much done. I have some orders I don't know how I am going to get to before Christmas! I had two people tell me yesterday they were coming in this week to order some shirts for their husbands. So, I guess we can give it a try. I don't know what to pay you. What were you expecting?"

"Well, what we could do is, if you are willing and no one lives upstairs, I could make the upstairs an apartment for me. I could just let you decide, after you see my work, what you think it's worth to you. I need enough to buy food. I don't have many expenses. I don't have any furniture, but perhaps there is some up there already."

"No, just dust and a bunch of boxes. I haven't finished unpacking. I just go up there and see what's in there. Maybe you could help me get more organized. I'd like for my customers to see what fabrics I have; then they could choose what they want. Some don't see what they want here; so they go over to Breland's place and pick something out. He buys the cheapest fabrics and then sells them like they are fine fabric. Most women can't tell the difference, but I bet you can. I certainly can. So, I do need to make some sort of display in here."

"I'd be happy to help with that. It sounds like fun actually!"

"Young uns always full of energy and excitement about new experiences. Well, I guess we have a deal. Just stay away from my husband! He ain't much, but he is mine. I don't feel like sharing the misery he causes me."

"Believe me, Mrs. Tucker, I am not interested in any men at this time. I want to find out who I am and what I can do."

They seemed to have forgotten the other three women were standing there and could hear every word.

"Erin, I have bedroom furniture you can use or have. I need to get a room cleaned out and ready for our new addition," Katie said shyly. We won't need it for a while, but you can have it as soon as you need it since we aren't using it now, anyway."

"Katie, couldn't the hands build a small table and chairs pretty quickly? I bet they wouldn't mind," Willow said. "I could make them cookies or pies as an extra incentive." She laughed.

Tears gathered in Erin's eyes. "God just keeps blessing and blessing! I am overwhelmed."

"Katie, we can spare one of those small square tables in the dining room and the chairs to go with it. We are going to start construction on the addition to the dining room, and I need to move some tables around. I was going to store some in the space under the hotel. Erin's using it would be a blessing to us. It won't get dirty up there."

"Well, it's dirty enough as it is! We're going to have to get a cleaning crew up there to take care of all that mess. I need to make room in the back for all those boxes," Marta caught the enthusiasm inspired by the conversation. She had not felt this good in years.

"I bet if I let Helga Ruger know about what we need as far as cleaning up, she would jump at taking charge. She really is the most organized person and can get people to do whatever needs to be done. They just seem to do what she says without another thought," Esther said, thinking out loud.

"I really hadn't ever given that any thought. That's the way she is when she comes in here. I just do whatever she says without even thinking about it," Marta agreed.

"I think I'll go see her now. Marta, Katie needs some things made that will expand as she does. I'm going to be a grand-mother! Hallelujah! I never thought I would see that day! Talk about God's blessings. We have so much to be thankful for."

"I'll be back. You girls take it easy and see what she has. Order whatever and how ever many you need, Katie." Esther shut the door, causing the little bell to ring happily in the room.

"Marta, is there something I can work on for you while you take her measurements and pick out fabric?" Erin asked.

"My, what a luxury! Why don't you go in the back and see what can be moved where in there. If you want the key upstairs, it is next to the staircase at the back of the store hanging on a nail. I had them build the staircase inside because I didn't want any of my fabric to get wet either going up or coming down. The locking door is at the bottom. That way I could go up and down without having to balance boxes or fabric on the landing and lock that door up there. I could leave that one open if I wanted to, but the door at the bottom is the one that locks. We could change it if you want to." Marta talked the whole time she was getting her tape measure and other things out to get Katie's measurements. "Just to look at you, don't look like you've gained an ounce since the weddin', so the measurements should be the same. Let's just check them. I have your paper right here."

Erin wandered to the back room and looked around, getting her bearings. She came back in the store. "Marta, do you have a lantern I can use? It's very dark back there."

"Sure, sure. It's on the little shelf right next to the door."

Erin turned and looked inside the room then turned back out. "I don't see it there."

"It should be there…wait a minute. I was working behind the door on something. I may have put it there. Look on the floor behind that big box. See if I left it there."

"It's here," Erin yelled from the back room. Marta nodded. It didn't matter if Erin couldn't see her.

Erin found a tinderbox on the shelf and lit the lamp with the flint and steel she found inside. "Oh my, what a mess! My goodness, this will take awhile. I'm going to have sore muscles, I can tell. But it is honest work," she whispered. "I think I'll see what's upstairs."

She found the door and the key. The door creaked eerily as she opened it. *I think those hinges need oil.* Each step she took creaked as well. *Maybe we need to renail these stairs.* The door at the top was standing open. *Well, all the noise sure would let me know when someone was coming up. That is almost as good as a watchdog barking. Maybe I should leave it alone.* Holding the lamp high, she looked around the large open space. There was a wall at the front of the store with a door in it as well. Erin raised her eyebrows and shrugged her shoulders. She made her way through the various boxes scattered in no particular order around the floor to the door in the wall. She had no idea what to expect. She opened the door. It was a small totally empty room, except for three boxes stacked pyramid style in front of each of the two windows. *I wonder what the intended purpose of this room is. I wouldn't want to sleep here with these large windows looking right on to the street. It may be a good place to sit in a rocker and sew and watch the world go by. I could put my table in here and eat while I look out as well. It is an unusual design. I wonder if the privy is out back.* She turned and closed the door to the room with windows on the world. She looked around to see what could be done with all the boxes. "I certainly will have plenty of space, nothing like my little prison back in Baltimore. My cabin on the ship was larger than that! I will have to take inventory up here and down there. I wonder if Marta knows what she has," Erin said to herself.

With that thought, Erin started down, the stairs creaking as she went. *Besides hearing people come up, I wouldn't be able to sneak out of the store. I'm going to give this some thought. I wouldn't want to get trapped up there.*

She found some paper and a pencil and began cataloging what she found in boxes. Mostly it seemed like a jumbled mess. The back room was filled with a series of shelves floor to ceiling all holding boxes. *It seems the boxes on the very top are empty. I could use those to sort the types and colors of fabric. I'd like to put some hanging lanterns in here so we wouldn't have to hold the lamp when we climb the ladder to the upper shelves. I bet Adam could do that. I'll ask Esther the next time I see her.* She heard the bell jingle and went to peek to see if it was Esther. Otherwise, she would keep exploring.

"Marta, do you have those dresses I ordered ready yet? I need them this weekend."

Erin didn't recognize the voice or the woman. She crept to the door and peeked out anyway.

"Well, I have this one gingham dress ready. I only have to finish sewing on the buttons, and the other one is in process. So I should have them ready this weekend, yes."

The gingham dress is clearly too small for the woman standing there. Maybe there is another gingham dress, or, maybe, it's a gift for her daughter, if she has one, or someone else, Erin thought.

Erin came out of the back room smoothing her skirts. "Marta, if you will direct me to the buttons and dress, I'll be happy to finish that for you while you check the measurements for Katie."

The woman's head whipped around and stared at Erin. "Who are you?"

"My name is Miss Erin Kerr, and I am working for Mrs. Tucker.

I have moved here from back east and was a seamstress there."

The woman made no remark; neither did she offer her name.

"Erin, this is Roselinde Gruber. Her husband is the barber here. Roselinde, this is Erin Kerr, my new *partner.*"

Erin looked at Marta in amazement and shock. She had not even hinted at being a partner. Katie looked at her as well with a questioning look.

Roselinde harrumphed and said, "I'll be back in an hour to pick up the two dresses. They better be ready." With that comment, she all but slammed the door behind her.

"That woman gets my goat every time she comes in here. Erin, just call me Marta."

"Very well, Marta, why did you say I was your partner to her? You know we never even spoke about such a thing."

"Well, I've been thinking as I have been measuring. If I make you a partner, then Oscar can't have my store when I die. It will be yours. We will have to make it legal and agree to a partnership thing or whatever you call it. We will need to get a lawyer, or maybe the banker Mr. Thomkins can make it legal-like for us. Otherwise, we may need to go to Kerrville and get us a lawyer. I think that's what I want to do, though. Is that all right with you?"

"Well, I am in shock right now. Let me think about all the possibilities and complications, but my immediate reaction tells me I'd be very happy with that arrangement. Marta, just let me pray about it, okay?"

"I'll pray too!" Katie said with wide-eyed wonder.

"Well, clock's ticking. Where are the dress and buttons?" Erin asked.

"The dress is right over against the back wall on that table. The buttons are in a little sack lying on top of it."

Erin went to the back wall and found everything just as Marta had said. She held up the dress and looked again at Marta. "Marta, this won't fit the woman who was just in here. Who is it for?"

"It's for her. She thinks that's her size. Then she takes it home and can't get it on. She comes back in all a rage. So, I 'remake the dress,' and she's happy. If I make it to fit the first time, she hates it. She is a real peculiar thing. All the big dresses are ready, I'm just not quite finished with the small ones. If you will just sew the buttons on that one, I'll finish with Katie and get going on finishing up the third one. These are the size of Willow. I know Esther has already asked I make a gingham one like the one on the dress form. I just couldn't sell it to her that day because Roselinde hadn't brought it back yet."

The women laughed. "Marta, you are something else. You know that?"

"What am I then?"

"I don't know, but it isn't like anyone I have ever known before." Katie laughed some more.

"Hold still, I have work to do!"

That only made Katie laugh even more. Tears started coming to her eyes. Finally, Marta was finished. "Now, Erin and I will pick out some very special fabric for you and get these things made for you. Do you trust us?"

Katie stopped laughing. "I guess so. I don't even know what I'm going to need. I think you know more about that than I do, Marta. Esther may have some things or fabric she has her heart set on. So, if she wants something, just do what she wants."

Katie was dabbing tears from her eyes when Esther came back. "What's wrong?"

"Nothing, we were just laughing so hard it made me cry. What did Helga say?"

"Oh, she jumped on that like a chicken on a June bug. I saw her eyes light up, and I could almost hear her brain yelling, 'A project'! Yes, she shooed me out of the house because she had to go and talk with some of the other ladies. I don't think we have to worry about the cleanup. Now, to find all the furniture and dishes and things you will need."

"Esther, while you're planning and such, talk this little missy into being my partner. I don't want Oscar to get it all, and I want to make it all legal like so he can't. She said she wants to pray about it, but I think you can probably see how good this would be for her."

Esther was in shock. "I will certainly talk to her about it. I will also talk to Adam about it. I don't know what needs to be done legally, but I'm sure someone here will know."

"I don't want Oscar to get wind of it. I'm sure Roselinde will spread the word as soon as can be. Please, don't take too long. He may kill me when he hears it."

Erin looked up and stuck her finger with the needle at the same time. "Ouch!" She put her finger in her mouth, keeping her from saying anything more.

"Marta." Esther cupped Marta's face in her hands and looked her in the eye. "If ever, and I mean ever, you feel like you are not safe, you run to the hotel, and you run as fast as you can run. If you don't feel safe there, we will escort you over to the jail and lock you in a cell where he can't get his hands on you. Don't you dare let him beat you to death! I mean that from my heart. If you are at the hotel, he will have to come through Adam and me to get to you. I think Adam can take him down. He's a good shot. He won't kill him, but he will stop him."

"I'll try." Marta's eyes brimmed with tears. Esther let go of her. "I'd better get back to the hotel. Katie, Willow, are you finished here?"

"Yes, ma'am," they said in unison.

"Erin, plan on eating dinner with us again tonight, please?"

"Thank you, Esther, I will be happy to join you tonight. What time do you close, Marta?"

"Usually around six. That gives the ranchers a little extra time to get here. Some of them wait until later in the day to come to town, and then they have a treat and eat at the hotel. Since school has started, they are doing that more. They will get used to the routine and let their kids ride in by themselves soon, I reckon."

"All right, then I will plan to be back over around six."

"Aren't you going to take a lunch break?"

"We have so much to do here, and I need to talk with Marta about some ideas I have. I don't think I'll have time to stop and eat."

Esther raised her eyebrows and cocked her head. "We'll see," was all she said, fully intending on bringing lunch over, then turned, and left the shop with Katie and Willow closing the door behind. Just before Katie closed the door, she stuck her head back in and blew Erin a kiss and gave her a wink.

"That's one special lady," Katie said as she caught up with Willow. Esther was already climbing the steps to the boardwalk in front of the hotel. Her skirts swaying to the rhythm of her pace indicated haste. "Mom's on a mission. I wonder what's going through her mind. She certainly has had quite a bit thrown at her today."

"I'd say," was all Willow said in response. She looked around for Wulf. She didn't see him, so they entered the hotel half-expecting him to be sitting in the lobby twirling his hat. No Wulf. They checked in the dining room. No Wulf. There were no customers, and Mary Elizabeth had taken some time to run home and check on things there. Rose was busy and hadn't seen Wulf. "Well, we can just go into the lobby and sit," Willow suggested.

"I think I would rather sit out front and do some people watching. I haven't done that since Clyde took me for a walk while I was here recuperating. I wonder if I can remember what he told me to look for."

"Sounds interesting. Let's do it." Willow grabbed Katie's hand and half-pulled her to the boardwalk out front. There were some rockers available, so they sat down and began to watch.

After a little while, Willow began to lean forward and squint. "Something's going on in the sheriff's office."

"How can you tell?"

"I see some violent movement through the window."

"Should we go over there?"

"No! Josh would have a fit if you were, in any way, put in danger. Michael's acting deputy while Brian's away. I think he can handle it."

The door to the jailhouse opened with a jerk. Oscar stormed out spewing profanities as he left slamming the door. He stomped down the street toward his blacksmith shop.

Pretty soon, Rufus opened the door and came out looking for his horse. He didn't see it anywhere, so he turned around and went into the jailhouse again.

The girls were fascinated with the spectacle. Katie nudged Willow. "Look!" She was pointing down at the livery. Oscar brought a horse out, pointed it south, and hit it on the rear. The horse took off at a trot with no rider.

The door to the jail opened again, and out stepped Rufus in time to see his horse approaching. He took off running to intercept the horse. He stopped and whistled, and the horse looked his way, slowed, and came up to him. He started to mount the horse but checked the chinches just in case. He led the horse over to a hitching post and tied him. He then proceeded to tighten the chinches and checked the bridle as well. He checked all of the hardware on his gear and then took the reins and mounted his horse. The last they saw of him was his back headed south.

"I hope he still has a job. He's pretty smart to check his gear since the horse came from Oscar's livery," Katie absently said as she looked at his back.

"You can say that again. Oscar isn't real careful. Did you know Rufus's been trying to court Dorothea Gruber? But her mom won't have any of that," Willow volunteered.

"I can't blame her. I wouldn't want my daughter being courted by a cowboy who frequents the saloon and takes advantage of the delights provided there. Men! Where *is* their sense? Why would they want to lower people's opinion of them by doing that?"

"Well, let's count the number of women out here and how many men there are. It is far from equal. I would guess that some of the men, especially cowboys, get lonely, and there aren't enough girls to go around, so they choose the ones who will take more than one and who will make each one of the men feel special."

"Is that the way it was in the tribe?"

"No, there were more women than men. Some men took more than one wife."

"Then how do you know about what goes on in the minds of men when there are a few women and more men?"

"I just know."

"Well then."

"Oh look! There's Doc McConnell. I want to talk with him. I thought he would never come back. His buggy has been gone all morning." Willow looked up to the sky. "It's almost lunchtime. Maybe that's why he is back. C'mon, let's go see him."

"Oh all right. I guess I should let him know I'm going to have a baby. He needs to know, I think."

The two slowly walked over to Doc's to allow him some time to give the horses a drink and get himself one as well. When they judged the time was right, they opened the door and went in.

"Ladies, how are you this lovely day?"

"We are just grand!" Katie went to him and gave him a hug. "I have a question for you, and so does Willow."

"Shoot."

Katie smiled and looked him right in the eye. "Doc, how would you like to deliver my baby?"

Doc's eyes roamed over Katie's body and looked her in the eye. "I don't think I'll do it today. When do you want to have that written on my calendar?"

"Oh, I don't know, I think around March sometime?"

"Katie, I'm so happy for you and Josh! When did you discover this?"

"Yesterday."

"Well, I hope you told Esther before you did me."

She laughed. "Of course!"

"Are you feeling well?"

"No, I keep throwing up and falling asleep. Except today, we've been so busy, I just haven't had time to stop and fall asleep."

"Well, when you need to sleep, it is best to do so. Your body is telling you something, and you don't want to argue with it."

"What is it telling me when I throw up?"

"That there are changes taking place in your body. Your chemistry is changing because you have another human growing inside of you. Your body has to take care of both of you, so it's adjusting. You'll get over it."

"Doc, everything is so new. I had no idea when I was brought to your office last March that all of this would happen in the next six months. It's just amazing!"

"Yes, it is. I wish my Dorothy was here to enjoy all of the excitement. She would love it."

"I wish I had known her."

Looking at Willow, Doc said, "Well then, young lady, what is your question? Not the same one, I hope."

Willow gave him a look of utter shock. "Oh no! Me? Never!"

"Never say never, Willow. That's like giving God a go-ahead sign."

Trying not to let the comment bother her, she looked right at Doc McConnell. "Doc, I was wondering if you would mind my helping you out some. I know quite a bit of Indian medicine. I can make medicine out of different plants, and I know some things about birthing babies." She elbowed Katie as she said that. "I was thinking that I might like to be a nurse."

"Well, let me think on that for a bit. I'll have to talk with Esther and Adam as well and get their opinion and permission. They are your parents, after all, even if it isn't really official; you needed them, and they needed you."

"I understand. I just wanted to let you know I was thinking about it. I have even thought about going to school. I read that Oberlin College in Ohio is allowing women to enter their scientific studies."

"Yes, they have begun that. I received a notice to that effect. I just don't know if you should leave home just yet. You have had quite a few major changes in your life, and I'm not sure Esther will be willing for you to go that far. I'll talk with them and let you know what I decide."

"Thanks for not just coming right out and saying no, Doc. At least you will consider it. I'll respect your decision."

"Run along now. I need to get some things done. I'll let you know."

22

don't think I've ever been out to this ranch. It's kinda stuck out here almost in the middle of nowhere and far from the main road," Brian observed.

"Well, it has plenty of space," Adam added.

The three men sat on their horses at the top of a rise and looked down on the ranch. "We should ride on in. They may start wondering what we're doing up here. I don't see any damage to any of the buildings. Maybe they're okay," Josh said.

The men nudged their horses and started down the rise to the ranch house. "It's almost as if this place was planted right out in the middle of a field. There are no trees for shade even near the house. I don't think any of the women I know would like that much," Adam commented and waited for the others to agree. No one said anything; it was like the others were very alert. Adam began to feel antsy. "Is something wrong?" he finally asked.

Brian glanced his way. "Something just doesn't feel right. It's just too quiet."

When they reached the ranch house, Brian called out, "Mr. Konrad, is everything all right here? I'm Brian Daniels, sheriff of Crystal Springs. We came out to check on how you folks fared during the twister."

"Maybe we should go out to the barn and check there," Josh suggested.

"Be careful!" Adam warned.

Just as Josh was turning his horse to go to the barn, a child's head popped up and looked out the window. Brian dismounted and walked up onto the porch. Josh stayed where he was as did Adam.

Brian knocked on the door. "Is anyone home? Do you need any help?"

He could hear the sound of feet running here and there. Then there was no noise, and then the sound of feet could be heard again. He leaned into the door to get a better idea of what was happening inside when he heard the sound of the bar being lifted from the door. He stepped back a step and waited. Mumbled talk could be heard behind the door. Then the door began to open very slowly. A girl about ten years old looked out at the three men.

"Hello," Brian said. "I'm Brian Daniels, the sheriff of Crystal Springs. This is Adam Schmitt and his son, Josh. Josh owns the ranch between you and Crystal Springs. He saw a twister yesterday going in this direction. Do you need any help?"

The girl nodded her head. She opened the door wider and said, "Mama's sick." She pointed to the door of a room on the other side of the house.

"Would you like for me to take a look at her?" Brian asked.

The girl nodded again, and tears began to pool in her eyes.

He took a step into the house and looked behind the front door. There were two little boys about four and five years old sitting on the floor staring up at him. Brian cautiously walked across the floor to the door indicated by the girl. Josh and Adam had dismounted and had come up on the porch by that time. "I'll stay with the children," Adam said. "Josh is going to keep watch out on the porch."

Brian knocked on the door. "Mrs. Konrad, it's Sheriff Daniels. May I come in?" He heard nothing. He carefully opened the door and looked in. Another girl about eight had a wet cloth on her mother's forehead. The mother looked almost as white as the sheet she lay under.

"Mama's sick."

"I see that. Let me see now." Brian felt the woman's face for sign of fever. She was very hot to the touch. "Has your mama been throwing up?"

The little girl nodded. "She's cold, and then she's hot. She's not going to die, is she?"

"No, not unless God wills it. Is there a wagon out in the barn?"

"Yes. Are you going to take her away?"

"Where is your daddy?" Clearly, this girl was more willing to talk than the older one or the two boys.

"He and his hands are taking care of the cattle up that way." She pointed west.

"Is he very far?"

"I don't know." She shrugged.

"Josh, can you hear me?" Brian said loudly but not yelling.

"Sure can. There's nothing moving out here."

"Go and see if there's a wagon in the barn, will ya? We have a very sick lady here we need to get to Doc. There are also four children, so far..."

"I'll do it." Josh's steps could be heard leaving the porch.

"Adam, do you see any food in the house?"

"I'll check." Adam made a quick check of the kitchen area. "Nope. Nothing much."

"Well, we are going to take the mom and the kids with us. They don't need to be here alone, and they look mighty hungry."

"I'll take care of getting them ready." Adam turned to the oldest girl. "We're going to take your mother to the doctor in town. I want you to find me some blankets to put in the back of the wagon to make a bed for her. You also need to gather some things for you and your brothers and sister to take with you in case you have to stay overnight. Your mother may not be able to come back home right away."

The girl nodded and started toward a trunk over by the wall next to the fireplace. As she picked out blankets, Adam tried to get the boys to talk, but they just wouldn't. *Boys this age just are not this quiet. They need to get out and run and play. We'll see what Tad can do with them.*

"Brian, Josh is here with the wagon."

"Thanks, Adam. If you'll fix a bed, I'll carry her out."

As Brian lifted her, she let out a moan and grabbed her side with her hands. He got her placed in the wagon, and the children loaded in with their few things and hopped on the wagon. "Adam, bring my horse, will ya?" He snapped the reins and started out down the ranch road toward the road leading to town.

"Sure thing, Brian, not that you can hear me," Adam muttered.

"That horse was the only animal I saw in the barn. What kind of ranch is this? What kind of man would leave his sick wife and children alone and go off somewhere? Dad, that just doesn't make sense to me," Josh vented.

"I know, son, but people are not all the same. We have to understand our differences and live as best we can together."

Brian drove straight to Doc's when he entered town. He really was driving the wagon too fast for in town, but he needed to get her to Doc quickly.

"Whoa!" Before the wagon was completely stopped, Brian had jumped out and had run around to the back of the wagon.

"C'mon, little lady. Let's get you to Doc." Brian looked at the children and said, "Let's move aside so I can get your ma out of the wagon." The eight-year-old shuffled aside and watched Brian pick her mom up like she weighed about five pounds. Josh was off his horse and opening the door to Doc's, helping Brian carry her in. Adam stayed with the children and tried to calm their fears.

Doc heard the racket and opened the door to the surgery room.

"What's going on out here?"

"Hurry, Doc, Mrs. Konrad is very ill. I think she is hurting inside over here. When I moved her, she groaned and grabbed that side of her stomach. She passed out sometime during the ride. Her kids are out in the wagon, and Adam is watching them, I think."

"Josh, go see if you can find Willow. This would be a good time for her to see what nursing is all about, and I could use the extra hands."

Josh turned and left as quickly as possible. He hurried into the hotel where he found them in the dining room chatting and drinking tea. "Willow, come quickly! Doc needs you!"

She jumped up and didn't say a word. She just rushed over to Doc's, holding her skirt up so she could run faster. Many a head turned to watch the spectacle.

"Doc, what do you need me to do?"

That was the last thing Brian heard as the door to the surgery closed right behind her. He stood up, shaking his head. "If I had that much energy, I would probably blow up like a cannonball."

He stepped out and immediately saw the four children, Adam very patiently telling them a story as they all sat on the back of the wagon. Josh was nowhere to be seen. *He must have stayed at the hotel.* He looked toward the hotel and back at Adam. "C'mon, let's go get something to drink. I think Doc will be awhile, and the kids are probably hungry."

Adam helped the boys down, and Brian helped the girls. They all held hands as they walked down the boardwalk toward the hotel. They climbed the steps and entered the lobby. The eyes of the children were almost bugging out of their heads as they looked around at the beautiful interior of the hotel. They had never seen anything so grand.

Adam looked at them. "Come this way. Let's get something to drink and maybe even a little snack. Oh look! There's our daughter-in-love and our son. Shall we join them?" He gently led the children over to the table where Katie and Josh were seated. Katie quickly got up and went to the kitchen. In about two seconds, or so it seemed, she was back with Rose right behind her, who looked at the situation and returned to the kitchen. The boys were wiggling in their chairs, but the girls were sitting quietly.

The eight-year-old looked at Adam and asked, "What are they going to do with my mama?"

"I don't rightly know, sweetheart. She's in good hands with Doc. If anything can be done, he will do it. Let's pray." He bowed his head and prayed for the safety and healing of their mother. He prayed for the Great Physician to guide Doc's hands and his decisions. He prayed for peace and comfort for the children. When he finished, Rose was there ready to place a plate of cake slices and glasses of milk for the children. She brought Adam some coffee and Josh a glass of water.

"You remembered," Josh almost whispered as he gave her his best smile.

"Yes, suh, I shore did. Did you ever think I would forget you and your love of water?"

"No. I do love it even more so now since I was in the cavalry. It is hotter than a flat skillet over a blue flame and dryer than a ten-year-old cow patty out there in the plains. Rose, I sure do appreciate your remembering. It means so much."

"Child, how could I ever forget my Joshua? You sho' is special to my heart." Rose turned and started walking back to the kitchen. She found she had to bring the corner of her apron up to her eye. "Musta got some dirt in this 'un and tother 'un too. I gots to be mo' car'ful," she mumbled to herself.

Josh looked at the children happily eating their cake and drinking their milk. They were becoming more animated. "Children, what are your names?" Josh asked.

The ten-year-old had just taken a bite of cake and just looked at him while she chewed it slowly. The eight-year-old looked at him and smiled. "She's Gretel; I'm Katrine." Pointing at the two boys, the oldest first, she said, "He's Hans Jr., and the least one is Klaus."

"Well, Katrine, was your mother sick when your pa and the men rode out this morning?"

"Oh no. She was fine. Pa asked her if she was feeling all right, and she said yes and to get out there and see about the cattle. She almost pushed him out the door and closed it behind him."

"When did she get sick?"

"Well, she stood and watched through the window as Pa and the others rode out. Then she went into the kitchen and started to work. She picked up a heavy kettle and let out a loud groan, and then she said, 'Oh, oh,' and was holding her side."

Katrine was now standing and acting out the scene with great emphasis and exaggerated gestures.

"She looked at us and said, 'Gretel, you are the oldest. You keep everyone safe. Mama has to go back to bed now. I have a sharp pain in my side. Don't go outside!'" Katrine shook her finger at Gretel still acting out what happened. "Mama almost yelled that. Mama closed her door. We were all scared. It wasn't long 'til you rode in because me and the boys had just begun to play a game, and Gretel went in to help mama." Katrine sat back down but continued.

"She was real hot, so Gretel came out and got a basin of water and a cloth to wash Mama's face. She had just gone back in the bedroom when you knocked on the door. That scared us even more. I traded places with her so she could answer the door and not leave Mama alone. Thank you for coming. I hope Mama gets better. The cake's really good." With that, she took another bite as if to save it from being eaten by any of her siblings.

"You are welcome, Katrine. We'll see if we can get you children some lunch shortly." Josh looked at his father as he said that.

Adam nodded his head.

The children looked at them as if they just might be Santa Claus right before their very eyes.

Brian leaned over and softly spoke to Adam, "I need to go out there and tell Mr. Konrad about his wife. I hope I can find him. Pray for me." He stood and looked at the children and Josh. "Excuse me, I need to run an errand. I'll be gone awhile."

Brian walked back over to his office, opened the door, and leaned in. He told Michael where he was going. Michael said, "I've got everything in hand. You need to find him."

"Michael, I forgot about Pete in here. Do you want to get in touch with Curtis and let him know?"

"Brian, he has been down here and taken measurements already. I just didn't know if you wanted him moved yet. I believe he's getting a little ripe."

"I wanted to look through the wanted posters and see if there is a price on his head."

"I'll do that. You go on."

Brian closed the door, got his horse, and left quickly riding back north out of town. No sooner had the dust settled than Todd came riding back in and went directly to the sheriff's office.

He was surprised to see Michael still there. Michael explained what had been happening and where Brian had gone.

Todd shook his head. "Things sure have been busy around here. I'm wondering about the two men who got away with the horses. What are we going to do about them? How are we even going to know if they are still alive?"

"I'm pretty sure they made it to shelter. I think we should leave those two in the hands of the Texas Rangers. They should be here today," remarked Michael.

"I wish we could have gotten those men and just been able to hand them over to the Rangers when they got here." Todd looked west out the window and then back at Michael. "Maybe I should—"

"No." Michael stood and looked Todd in the eye. "That would be a fool's errand. You need to get back to the ranch. I need you out there. There is work to be done. I sent Wulf back already. You need to get out there and help with all that needs to be done there. We cannot neglect our first calling."

"Well, what about you?"

"Todd, you know better than that. I don't have to explain anything to you. I'm the foreman. God has led me here for a short time, and this is what he wants me to do right now to free Brian up to accomplish something he needs to do. Now, you need to accomplish what God has appointed for you to do today."

"Yes, sir. I'm sorry, Michael. You're right. I was getting carried away. I'll start right now, and I'll try to be more obedient in the future. I apologize."

"Apology accepted." Michael walked with Todd to the door.

They were just about to open the door when they heard horses riding in at a pretty good clip. Michael opened the door and stepped out with Todd right behind him. Four Texas Rangers looked down at them from where they sat on their horses.

"Sheriff Brian Daniels?" one of them asked.

"No, I'm his deputy. The sheriff had to ride out to a ranch a little while ago.

"We need to know everything he knows about the riders who came through here. We've been trailing them from the way station, and they came very near here."

"Yes, sir, they did. Won't you come inside? Todd here can fill you in on all he knows. Then Brian can tell you exactly what he knows beyond that when he gets back."

"All right." All four dismounted and walked in to the office right behind Michael and Todd, each slapping his hat against his thigh.

"First, I want to show you someone."

Michael led them over to the cell where Pete was laying. "Here is one of the men from that gang."

The head Ranger, Dan Stewart, walked over to the body. "Kinda dead, ain't he?"

"Yep."

"Ole Pete won't be much help," Dan said.

"So, you recognize him?"

"Yep. At least now we know who we are dealing with. Good riddance to this one."

Todd stood back a little from the scene, but he couldn't help but add, "Good riddance to most of them."

The Rangers turned and looked at him. "Tell us what you know," Dan said.

Todd filled them in on what had happened to Daisy, the shoot-out in the rain, the twister, and finding Mr. Stevenson.

He also told them the twister probably wiped out any tracks the other two may have left.

"It may take awhile, but we *will* find them. You say the other two took the horses?"

"Yes, they left these fellas on foot. That's also why they left Stevenson in the ravine, hog-tied. Those other two will have plenty of fresh horse flesh to just keep riding if they need to do it. Unless, of course, God took care of them."

"Well, there are plenty of caves out that way, and some are big enough to get horses and men in." Dan shook his head. "I don't think God took care of them. I think we'll find them. They may not be as brave with the rest of their men gone. Of course, they won't know that, will they?"

"No, sir."

"Well, you've been a big help, son. I thank you."

"Dan, why don't you and your men go over to the hotel and eat a hot meal before you set out again? It will do you good and give you a brief but much-needed rest," Michael suggested.

Hopeful looks from the other three honed in on Dan. Dan looked their way. "Might not be a bad idea," Dan said as he looked back at them.

Michael nodded. "Best food in town! Unless you're around for one of our 'eatin' on the grounds' after church one Sunday."

"Well then, let's get to it." The four men turned and walked out and headed for the hotel.

Michael grinned as if he knew something they didn't know, but they were about to find out. "Yep," was all he said. He turned and looked at Todd. "You need to get back to the ranch now. You have done very well today. I know you have worked hard. Did you get to talk with the Dalkes?"

"Well, yes and no. Mr. and Mrs. weren't there. I talked to their daughter. They didn't even have rain."

"Lenore? Is that who you talked to?"

"Yes, I guess. She didn't tell me her name. She's about fourteen, fifteen, pretty girl. Actually, now that I think about it, she's a really pretty girl, very nice too."

"Yep, that's Lenore. She's almost sixteen. Lenore has a very special heart and is very compassionate and loving. Yes, she's a very good girl and will be a woman of excellent quality."

"Well, I'll get back to the ranch then. See you later, Michael."

"I'll be back in a while."

23

arta?" Erin stuck her head out of the back room. Her hair was covered with dust and cobwebs.

"Yes?" Marta looked around at Erin and smiled. "Do you care how I arrange things back here? I don't want to mess up your, uh, system of organization."

"Don't have a system. I just put things where I can fit them in. Do what you want. If I can't find something, I'll ask you. Sure is nice to have someone to talk with. I appreciate you coming in and being willing to work with an old lady like me."

"Marta, you are not old. How old are you, thirty?"

"I'm thirty-six. The twins were born when I was nineteen. I lost some babies after them. I don't know why they lived and the others didn't. Those boys were so tiny. We had to keep them in a box by the fireplace to keep them warm. They's real tough inside.

I just hope they don't turn out like their pa. I'm glad they's out at the ranch. It will do them a heap a good. I'm sad I don't get to see them much, but maybe I can get out there sometime and see them."

"Well, now that I'm here, perhaps you can take some time and just do that. I know they would love to see you! We will have to plan a time for you to go."

"I don't have any way to get there, so it's best not to dream."

"Why not just hire a buggy?"

"'Cause, I'd have to get it from my husband, Oscar. He runs the livery, and he's the blacksmith."

"Well then, perhaps, I'll hire a buggy to go out and visit. We can both go and just close the store or do it after hours."

"You would do that? No, I can't go after hours. Oscar would come home and wonder where I was, and then there would be hell to pay."

"Then how about if I hire the buggy and bring it to the back of the store. You take it to the ranch, and I'll just stay here and work. That way the store stays open, we don't get behind, and you get to see your boys."

"I don't know. I'd have to take the road right by the blacksmith shop. He'd see me sure as you're standing there."

"Then we will just have to pray God gives us an opportunity to get you there. We will leave it in His hands. He knows best how to arrange things. How about some lunch?"

"Don't eat lunch."

"Oh well, I do." Erin walked out into the room far enough that the sunlight coming through the front windows caught her in its light. "Oh dear! I am covered in dust and dirt. What in the world! I could never be seen in public looking like this!" She grabbed a brush and started brushing the dust and cobwebs off the skirt of her dress.

The door opened, and the little bell jangled. "Good morn—no...afternoon, ladies!"

"Riley, What are you doing here? School isn't out."

"Nope, it's lunchtime. I got in a little late last night to get things lined up for today, so instead of letting that go, I just didn't make a lunch this morning. So I'm headed to the hotel. Would you like to go? I'll escort you ladies."

"Don't eat lunch," Marta said without lifting her eyes to either one of them.

"I'm covered in dirt. I've been cleaning the back room and had decided not to stop. I am hungry, though. I just don't think I should be seen in public."

"Okay, I'll just order lunch and bring it back here. What is your favorite, chicken or steak?"

"I believe I'd prefer chicken."

"You've got it. See you soon." "Riley! Thank you."

He smiled and left, gently closing the door behind him. "Marta, is there a well outside?"

"Nope. I never needed one. I hadn't thought of that. Well, HB next door, he probably has one, but it's probably out front where that big water trough is."

"Well, I'll just quickly go and fill a bucket with water and wash my face and hands a bit. I don't want to touch any fabric and get it dirty." She smiled as she grabbed a bucket she found in the back and went out the front, the bell tinkling behind her.

Shortly, Riley was back with two lunches and three pieces of apple pie. He brought forks, knives, and some napkins. Erin had fixed up a place to sit and eat. They laughed and talked all during lunch; even Marta accepted the piece of pie. "I haven't had pie in a coon's age. I wish I had time to do all those things, but I just have to keep up with all these orders."

"Speaking of that, I need some curtains and some sheets and pillowcases, maybe some towels. Do you do that kind of sewing? Riley asked, looking directly at Marta.

"I don't usually, but I could. Maybe Erin could do it. I don't like that kind of thing. Erin, do you do that kind of sewing?"

"I do all kinds of sewing. Riley, I will need to see the windows and get some measurements. When would be a good time to come down and look at what you have in mind?" Erin sounded all business, but in her heart, she knew she would love to see more of this very gentle gentleman. She enjoyed being with him, and it seemed they never ran out of things to talk about.

"How about today after school is out. I'll ask Tad to come and get you and bring you back to my place. Then he can stay while we conduct business. I don't want to give anyone cause for uncalled-for remarks."

"Why, thank you, Riley. That is very considerate. I had not even thought of that possibility. Everyone is very kind here."

"Not everyone, but most everyone. It only takes one rumor to start, and it's like wildfire even among kind people. I don't want that to happen."

"Thank you, again."

Marta looked up and smiled. "You're a smart one, ain't you, Riley?" With that she laughed, shook her head, and went back to work.

"I'd better get going, or I'll be late for school! He laughed as he gathered up the dishes and things and hurried back to the hotel and then waved through the window as he went back to school. Children were arriving back from their lunch break. Tad had invited the students to come to the back of the hotel where they had a table with benches. They loved eating their lunch there.

Esther didn't mind. She loved seeing the children there. "We may need more tables and benches," she said as she watched them.

Two men rode slowly into town and went directly to the livery.

Oscar looked them over. He didn't like what he saw. If their money was good, he'd deal with them. "What can I do for you?"

"We just need to put these horses in your corral while we go get a bite to eat, if that's okay with you?"

"I don't mind. That'll be $3."

"*Three dollars!* That's highway robbery."

"Well, this is the only place to keep them, and they will be eating my hay, and you have a mess of them. So, if you want to do something else, go ahead."

The two looked at each other and expressed their disapproval with a string of profanities, but they got off their horses and paid him the three dollars.

"I'll take care of them."

"See that you do, mister, or you *will* pay."

The two left and headed to the hotel. They were tired, hungry, and in a foul mood.

Michael watched as they walked up the steps to the hotel boardwalk and entered the lobby. He strapped on his gun and headed that way.

When he went in the lobby, he headed over to the desk and spoke with Adam. He had taken the Konrad children upstairs for naps after lunch. Esther was upstairs with Daisy. Mary Elizabeth was in the dining room waiting on the tables, and Rose was in the kitchen. Yes, the Rangers were still in there just finishing up with their pie. Other than them and the two that just arrived, the dining room was empty.

I'd better be very subtle about this. I need to disarm them as soon as can be. He walked slowly into the dining room. The men had taken a table over by the window. "Mary Elizabeth, Esther needs your help upstairs, please."

"Sure thing, Michael." She left and started up the stairs.

"Hey, Rose, how are you today?"

"I's just as happy as a tick on a hound dog."

"That's good. Say, do you have any of those *really big chicken fried steaks hanging out back?*"

Rose looked at him like he was crazy. She almost said something and then caught the look in his face. He mouthed to her,

"Leave."

She made a little chuckle and said, "I don't kno', Michael, I's has'ta go see's."

"Take your time. I can wait." He nodded. Rose turned and disappeared into the kitchen and out the back door.

The Rangers were watching him and wondering what was going on. Michael sat down at the table nearest the entrance into the dining room. The two men by the window were watching him as well. He was a really big man and would catch anyone's attention. They were talking in low tones. One was eyeing the board on the wall that listed what was available to eat.

Dan got up from his seat and walked over to Michael's table and sat down with his back to the kitchen. "How are you, Michael?"

"Cautious," he whispered. Then in a normal tone, he added, "I have been better. I'm as hungry as a wolverine after a long winter."

"I'll recommend this place. They have great food. It tastes like what my mom would make." Dan answered in a casual tone and looked at Michael. "I'd ask you to join us, but we were about ready to leave."

"Don't be in a hurry, Dan. You can always go huntin'. Did you finish your pie?"

"Almost."

"Why don't you bring it over, if those brothers of yours didn't eat it all. I have something I want to discuss with you."

"Sure."

Dan got up and went back, retrieved his pie, and brought it over to the table.

"Dan, you know you were telling me about that huntin' trip, and I've been really thinking about it. I just don't think this is a good time to go huntin'. I don't think you will find what you're looking for way out there." Michael flung his hand out toward the windows. Dan followed the direction of his hand. He then realized what Michael was trying to get across to him.

"I think it would be best to stay closer to home. You never know what the cat will drag in. I'm just giving you some advice. Take it or leave it. My lumbago is telling me that it's not a good time to go huntin'. You know what they say about my lumbago. It's just never wrong." Michael laughed, and Dan laughed with him.

"Dan, if I were you, I'd leave Indian style."

Dan nodded and took the last bite of his pie. "Thanks, Michael. I'll talk it over with the brothers."

He left his plate and went back over to the table with the other Rangers. He was talking with them and pointing at Michael.

One of the men laughed, and another one made a show of looking disappointed shaking his head. They got up and walked away from the table in a straight line. As soon as they were stretched out through the room, they pulled their guns and pointed them at the two men by the windows. "Hold it right there. Keep your hands where I can see them," Dan said. The two by the window were taken by surprise and didn't have a chance to even flinch.

"What is the meaning of this?" the older of the two asked.

"I'm arresting you two for the murder of three people at the way station and attempted murder of two others."

"What? Well, we never—"

"Didn't ask you. Get their guns, Sam, and anything else they might have on them."

Sam, the last one in the line, walked up behind the closest one and took his guns, knives, and a derringer he had up his sleeve.

He then tied his hands behind him and tied him to the chair so he could go to the other man. Dan had moved behind him and kept his gun on the man's head while Sam had searched the first man. They got them tied together and began leading them to the jail. Dan turned toward Michael, but he was gone.

They led the men out into the street. The door to the jail opened. "I have their accommodations ready, gents. If you want to bring them right in here, we can go and get our witness… or two, if she will come. That way, you can be sure you have the right men."

Dan nodded and moved on toward the jail. The others followed with the two men tied firmly and roped together with a Ranger holding each end. They weren't going anywhere.

After getting the prisoners ensconced in one cell and enjoying their surprise at seeing Pete lying on one of the cots, Dan and Michael sat down and had a chat. The other three Rangers decided to go back and get some more pie and coffee since they didn't have to go "huntin'."

A short time later, Brian came riding back in with Mr. Konrad.

They rode directly to the Doc's office and hurried in. No one was in the waiting room. They could hear subdued talking in the surgery. Brian knocked at the door. "Don't come in!" Doc yelled.

Brian looked at Hans. "I guess we'll just have to wait right here. I can go and get you something to eat or some coffee, anything?"

"No, I couldn't eat a thing. Where are the children?"

"In good hands. The owner of the hotel has taken charge of them. They are probably over there eating lunch, or they have eaten and gone to play or to sleep. Shoot, Esther or Adam may be reading them a story. Not much happens around here; they're fine, Hans. Don't worry. Just pray for your wife. I know I need a cup of coffee. I'll bring you one as well."

Brian left him sitting there and made his way over to the hotel.

Rose met him at the counter, her eyes wild and wide. "Where you been?"

"I went out to fetch Hans Konrad and tell him about his wife. Why?"

"Ooh! I just thought I was a dead woman! Two outlaws come in her', but Mr. Michael and da four Rangers dey takes care of dem. Dey over at da jailhouse now."

Brian cocked his head and looked hard at her. "I'll check with Michael. But for this moment, I need a cup of coffee for me and one to take to Mr. Konrad."

"Yes, suh. I gets it."

"Thanks, Rose, you're the best."

"Sho' is!" She laughed all the way to the stove and retrieved the cups and coffee, her hands shaking a bit.

"Thanks again, Rose. Here, keep the change!" He put a dollar on the counter and left with the two cups.

"Maybe dis day ain't too bad afta all."

When Brian walked in Doc's office, Hans wasn't in the room.

Brian just sat down and decided he would drink both cups if Konrad didn't come back soon. He had most of a half of a cup gone when the surgery door opened, and Hans came out.

Brian put the cup down near the other one and walked over to him. "Hans?"

"She's going to be fine if there is no infection. Her appendix had to be taken out. Doc said it was close, but she didn't lose the baby. I didn't even know she was going to have another one. If you hadn't gotten her here when you did, she probably would have died. How can I thank you? You saved my precious wife."

"No thanks necessary. I'm just glad I could find you."

"I think I'll take that coffee now. I'm feelin' a bit shaky."

"It's right here."

"Thanks."

The men sat and didn't say a word for many minutes. Hans put his cup between his hands, rolling it like he was making clay snakes. "I was thinking, Brian, maybe we should get to know people a little better. It's good to have neighbors, especially in time of trouble."

"It is a good thing, and you couldn't ask for better neighbors than the Schmitts. They really and truly are the salt of the earth.

Get to know them. Their parents are the owners of the hotel. We are very blessed to have them here."

"I'll do it." He finished his coffee and rose. "I need to see my children. You know, Sheriff, I asked her if she was feeling all right this morning. She just didn't look right to me. She said she was fine and for me and the boys to go on. We didn't know what we would find up in the hills. We had seen that twister hit the ground, or at least it looked like it did from our vantage point.

We didn't know if we had any cattle left or not. I was torn about going, but she said she was fine. I guess she just knew it was important to find the cattle, and she didn't think it was anything except maybe she was with child. I am so thankful for Doc. He says she will have a scar, and it will take awhile to heal, but she should be back to normal in a few months, maybe a little more.

Do you think we can find my kids?"

"Right this way," Brian said as he finished his coffee, picked up Hans's empty cup, and then led the way to the hotel.

"Hello, Adam, this is Hans Konrad. Hans, this is Adam Schmitt." The two shook hands. "Hans would like to see his children."

"Oh. Well, after lunch, I sent the older ones back to school with Tad, and the two little ones are upstairs taking a nap. School will be out around three o'clock. We could go and get them if you would like."

"No, I'll just go see the little ones. Just checking. I know you did a good job. I just need to see them. We have a school?"

"Yes, Mr. J. R. Riley is the schoolmaster. He built a house right next to the school and enlarged the school building this summer and decided to start school the middle of August, so the students could be home at harvest if they were needed. He will do special classes during that time if any of the students are able to come for an intense study of just one subject. Then after the harvest, the regular school course of study will continue," Adam explained.

"I don't know why we didn't know. We will send the girls. I think we will wait until next year to send little Hans."

"Here, I'll take you to the room where the boys are sleeping."

"Adam, I'm headed over to the office. Thanks for everything."

"You're welcome, Brian. Glad you are back."

"Oh, Adam, is Esther with Daisy?"

"Yes, Daisy was taking a bath, but I see the tub out in the hall, so she's finished. Esther should be down in a few minutes," Adam said from the top of the stairs.

"I needed to talk with Daisy. Maybe I should just go on to the office now and check back in a little bit."

It didn't take him long to cross the street and enter his office.

Michael stood. "I'm glad you're back. We had a delivery of a couple of surprise packages. Brian, this is Dan; Dan, Brian. These are the four Texas Rangers who were looking into that way station murder and burning. Is Mr. Stevenson going to stay at the hotel?"

"I'm pretty sure he is. I doubt he will want to go back to the way station if they rebuild, but maybe he will. He was pretty roughed up. I'm telling you that hotel is turning into a hospital. They have those back east. I saw one once," Brian said, suddenly feeling like he had revealed too much about himself.

"I know Adam and Esther don't mind. They see it as a ministry, I'm sure."

"This is a really nice town. I wouldn't mind moving my wife and daughter here to live. I'd feel better about leaving them when I have to ride out on a mission," Dan said. "Everyone seems to get along."

"Most everyone gets along. Every town has their grumpy men and sour women. We have our fair share, but we are praying for them."

"Oh, that's why y'all get along. This is a prayin' town? Who's your minister?"

"We don't have one. We have a circuit-riding preacher who comes through irregularly at best, but when he does, it is a real treat. In the meantime, we take turns sharing scripture and leading worship. Usually, we get together in groups and share meals.

It's a good way to get to know one another and those who come in from out on the ranches don't have to hurry back. They get to fellowship with us and contribute to the common meal, so they feel more of a part of the community.

"More people from the outlying ranches have started talking about building Sunday houses in town. That way they could come in on Saturday and stay in their Sunday house for the whole weekend. Then they could deliver the kids to school on Monday and go on home. Our schoolmaster has room for boarding some students if they live too far away to come and go each day. We are fortunate to have him."

"I'm going to talk with my wife and my bosses up in Waco.

We need more coverage in this part of the territory, and that would put me closer to home, if they agree."

"We'd be grateful to have you. We'll pray God works it out for you to come," Brian added.

The door opened, and Curtis stuck his head in. "Sorry, am I interrupting something?"

"No, Curtis, are you here to pick up Pete?" Michael asked.

"Yes, sir, if you're finished with him."

"Yes. We are. Mr. Stevenson and these hombres here in the cells identified him a little while ago. Have you got a wagon outside?"

"Yes, sir."

"We'll help you carry him."

"I could bring the box in and put him in it first, and then it might be easier to carry him out."

"If you want to do it that way, that's fine."

They carried the box in the cell, placed it on two chairs, and lifted Pete's body into it. Curtis put the lid on and nailed it shut.

They picked up the box and navigated back out to the wagon.

"That went well. Thanks, Curtis. We were beginning to think we smelled something, but it was probably nothing." Brian gave Curtis a pat on the back.

"Probably not yet, but it would've been soon. You want me to bury him out in the cemetery just anywhere?" Curtis asked as he climbed up on the seat of the wagon.

"Put him on the far side up on the hill apiece. If people want to bury family members near their loved ones, they will be able to do that without having a stranger separating them," Brian instructed. He and Dan watched him drive away.

"Brian," Dan said. "There is a reward for the capture of these men. Since you brought Pete in and killed the others with the exception of these two snakes inside, perhaps you would want the money to go to the victims. What do you think?"

"Well, I know Mr. Stevenson has lost everything. He might appreciate it. Daisy certainly should have something, but perhaps a trust of some sort could be set up for her. She is very young.

You met Mr. Stevenson when he identified the two in there. You haven't met Daisy. I'm not surprised she couldn't come downstairs. What do you think?"

"I can see what I can do. Thanks, Brian. I really appreciate your help. Oh, and Michael's too! He is quite the man, isn't he?"

"You've got that right."

"Is that the school bell? My goodness! Marta, how has the day flown by so fast? Are we finished with those little dresses? Or do we need to sew the buttons on the last one?"

"We're finished. Erin, I don't think I realized how lonely I've been. I'm glad you're here with me."

The door opened, and in walked about six women carrying brooms, mops, buckets, and rags. Erin blinked and stared.

"Well, it didn't take you long to find some helpers. That's a mighty good thing you're doing, Helga. We appreciate it so very much. This is Miss Erin Kerr. She's a seamstress and a mighty good one too. So it won't matter which of us works on your things; you won't be able to tell them apart."

Helga made a curt nod toward Erin. "Nice to meet ya." She turned toward the rest, clearly focused on what she was doing, and said, "Well, ladies, let's go see what needs to be done."

Ding-a-ling. The bell over the door signaled another customer. Everyone stopped and turned to see Tad walk through the doorway. A questioning look came over each face.

"Oh, Tad, I almost forgot. Let me get my tape measure and some paper and a pencil to write with. We can go immediately. Thank you for coming to escort me." Erin smiled her sweetest smile at him, then picked up the things she needed.

Marta escorted the other ladies to the back of the store and showed them the stairs to the apartment above. Erin left with Tad.

"Mr. Riley said to go ahead to his house. He has some things to do at school, but he wanted you to go ahead and get started.

He'll come on over in a little bit."

"That sounds fine. Are you going to be my helper?" "If you need me, I'll help ya."

Erin giggled and gave Tad a very quick side hug. "Thank you, Tad. I certainly do need a helper."

They entered the house without so much as knocking. Erin's eyes wandered around the very spacious but sparsely furnished room. "Well, this is a project. Let's start with this front window." She pulled two chairs over and had Tad stand on one chair while she stood on the other with the tape measure stretched between them. They measured from one outside edge of the window frame to the other. She wrote down her numbers.

"Now, Tad, I need you to get down. I'll hold my end up here, and you hold the very end of the tape at the bottom of the windowsill. That's right, just like that." She wrote those figures down.

"I imagine all the windows are the same, but it is best to measure each one to make sure. So, let's do that, okay?"

They finished three windows, and they all had the same measurements. They were about to go into the next room to see what was needed there when the door opened.

"Ah, you are both hard at work. May I help in any way?"

"Are all the windows identical?" Erin asked.

"Yes, indeed they are. I like sunshine and moonshine. I like watching nature, so where many people limit the number of windows in their homes, I didn't. The only window that is a different size is the one I had put in this washroom."

"Washroom?" Erin questioned.

"Yes, you see, I have read about how the Babylonians and even castles of the Middle Ages had rooms in which one could take care of their necessary toilette. We still have the outhouse outside, but I have a place for a tub and washbasin and a potbellied stove so the hot water will be right there. I even had a hand pump put in the kitchen sink. That way, I don't have to go out to a well to bring up a bucket of water. Anyway, I put in just a small window so there wouldn't be a window on the world during my very private times." Riley blushed. "Sorry, I didn't mean to be so explicit. Forgive me."

Erin laughed. "Riley, if you only knew! I have to have a talk with you one of these days very soon. I have grown to trust you, and I've only known you a whole twenty-four hours. I think I'd better get to know you a little better before I start talking in depth about myself."

"I would like to get to know you better too. If you would like to wait to tell me, that just means we have to see more of each other."

Erin blushed a little and smiled. "Do you have colors or fabrics in mind when you see your curtains hanging in the big room, your bedroom, or this washroom?" Erin asked, evading the implications of his comment so she didn't have to voice one of her own.

"No."

"No?"

"No."

"Well, what is your favorite color?"

"I like them all. Well, I don't want black curtains. I think any other color would be fine."

"Do you want a solid color or some kind of print, gingham, or something?"

"I can't make those choices. I'm confused already. I tell you what. Why don't I leave it in Marta's and your hands? Just make what you like. Make the color and style, plain or prints, whatever you like, make them to please yourselves. I will like it since it doesn't matter to me. I just want to be able to close them for privacy, and I want them clean. I want to cheer this place up and make it home. I also need a tablecloth and some napkins. I want some dishtowels and towels for drying after I've had my bath. I need all the linens. I have one set of sheets, so I need more. I can't wash them and put them right back on the bed."

"Carte Blanche, monsieur?"

"Pour vous, mademoiselle, oui."

They both laughed. "You have heard almost the extent of my French, sir. I beg you speak English from this point on."

"Well, my French is not much better. I fear I know a smattering of several languages. I keep picking up a little more all the time. I enjoy them. I hear a bit of German around here frequently. Maybe that one will be next." Riley blushed again as he said that.

"I'm sure you are a very good teacher. One who wants to learn has a passion for learning and teaching others the same. I will pick out some fabrics for your approval."

"No, no, just make the curtains the way you would want them. I'm sure they will suit my exquisite taste in all things 'material.'"

Again, they laughed at his pun.

Tad looked at them like they were crazy and went to sit over by the window in the front room. "Are we finished yet?" he asked more to the window than to either of the others in the room.

"Oh, Tad, I'm so sorry. Yes, almost. I need to get the measurements for the window in the washroom. Do you want to help me?"

"No, Mr. Riley can do it. I'll just sit here and watch the trees and things."

They looked at him and then at each other. They shrugged their shoulders at the same time and went in to measure the smaller window.

As soon as they were finished, Erin turned and looked Riley in the eye. "I must go now, Mr. Riley. I'm sure Tad would like to play. The ladies came to clean the apartment above the shop just as I was leaving. I would like to get there and help, if I can. I will start on your curtains tomorrow." Leaving the washroom, she turned to look at Tad "Come, Tad, let's get back to the shop and you can go see your folks."

Tad hopped off the chair and moved it back to the table where they had gotten it. "Yes, ma'am, let's go. Bye, Mr. Riley."

"Bye, Tad, my man. Be careful with Miss Kerr now. You go straight home after you drop her off at the shop."

"Yes, sir."

24

Now, Daisy, you need to get out of bed more. You will be really sore if you don't. You need to move those muscles and loosen them up." Esther put her arm around Daisy and assisted her to a standing position. She gently held her until she was sure she was steady on her feet.

"I'm not sure I can move. I'm scared, ma'am."

"You have to give it a try. Just getting in and out of the tub hasn't been too bad. Has it?"

"No, ma'am."

"Then try to walk to the door and back. I'm right here. I'll help you if you need it." Esther encouraged her to do her best.

"I'll try."

Daisy began on shaky legs, but by the time she reached the door of the room, she was more steady and sure of her footing.

She turned and reached for the wall. "Oh, I'm dizzy!"

"I think you turned too fast. Just stand there a minute and then come back."

"Okay. I mean, Yes, ma'am."

Esther shook her head slightly. *She's trying so hard to be respectful and change from whatever she learned growing up. What a sweet girl. I need to work harder with her.*

"I made it! I want to try again. Would that be all right?"

"Absolutely. The more you walk, the better you will feel."

"I feel better already." Daisy kept walking back and forth between the bed and the door. She turned and walked by the window and glanced out. "I had grown so used to these walls I forgot there is a world out there. I don't know if I can go out there."

"Well, how about we bring a little of that world in here first?" Esther ventured a suggestion. "I want to bring Marta or Erin up here to get your measurements. You are going to need some new clothes."

"I can't afford any new clothes. I have one dress left." Daisy flopped down on the bed. "Ouch! I guess I shouldn't a done that!"

"No, you shouldn't have in any case. A lady does not flop down; she sits down, gracefully. We will have to practice that as well. It's a good thing you are young. You will heal faster."

"Will these cuts leave bad scars?"

"I don't know, Daisy. I'll ask Doc."

"I hope not. I don't want to be all scarred up!"

"I know, dear. You rest now, and I'll go and see what I can find out. If you feel up to walking more, you may, but don't leave the room. You are not properly dressed."

"Yes, ma'am."

Esther left the room and descended the stairs faster than a lady should. *I'm glad Daisy didn't see that. I'm sure I looked like a horse clomping down those stairs! Well, Doc McConnell's first, then Marta's place, and maybe one of them can come back with me.* She hurried out the door and ran right into Willow.

"Oh, Willow, what are you doing here?"

"Well, I rode in with Katie and one thing led to another, and I just got finished helping Doc with surgery. Oh, Esther, that was the most exhilarating experience I've had in just forever! I want to be a nurse. What do you think?"

"Well, I was just on my way over to Doc's to ask if there was anything that would help heal cuts and such so they don't leave a bad scar. So, I'll talk to him about nursing. I know you have quite a bit of knowledge from the tribe on healing herbs and plants, I think it might be a good thing for you to know more."

"Oh, Esther, just use aloe vera on those. I'll find it for you."

"Really?"

"Yes, aloe vera leaves have a gooey substance in them with great healing powers. The Indians used it all the time for burns, cuts, bites, many things. I'll get it." Willow didn't wait for a response; she turned, ran down the steps, and out toward the countryside behind the hotel and the rest of town.

Esther shook her head and walked over to Doc's office. *I'll have to talk to Doc about all this. I don't want her getting in over her head. She has more energy and drive and independence than should be in a girl.*

"Doc, are you here?"

"Be right there."

Esther sat in one of the chairs in the sitting area of Doc's office and home. The two-storied building had the office downstairs and home upstairs. *I have told him time and time again, he should have that staircase outside covered so people who need him in the middle of the night or in the snow or rain wouldn't have to stand outside in the weather to get to him. They might even slip and fall getting hurt while trying to get help for someone else. Has he listened to me or any woman? No! What man does?* The more she sat and waited, the more put out she became with men.

The door opened to the surgery, and out came a man she didn't recognize.

"I shouldn't have listened to her, Doc. I should have stayed close. I knew she didn't look good, and I was worried, but she insisted that I go on. I need to not pay so much attention to what she says anymore and go with my gut feeling. Thanks for letting me see her again, Doc. I just had to make sure she was still okay before I left."

Esther's eyes almost bugged out of her head. *Not listen to her? What is he thinking?*

"She could have died!"

Doc nodded. "Yes, it is a very good thing Brian, Adam, and Josh came when they did. It was close, Hans. I won't tell you different. You are a blessed man to still have your wife. But listen, Hans. Don't be too hard on her. She knew you were worried about your cattle, and she didn't want to be a bother to you. She didn't know she was that sick. She probably thought she was just feeling queasy from carrying another baby."

"I know. I just don't know what the children and I would do without her. I don't think I could live."

"God would give you the strength if it had been His will. Fortunately, it wasn't. She is still with us."

Esther bowed her head. *Thank you, Lord, for the lesson you just gave me. I'm so sorry I was so prideful and Eve-like. I should be content to be in the position of wife that you have given me. I need to focus on performing your will within the life you have chosen for me and not on trying to control everyone else's life. Please forgive me. I am yours. In Jesus' name, amen.*

"Let us know what we can do to help, Hans."

"I'm going out to the ranch and then coming back with some overnight things for me and the children. We'll check into the hotel for the night and be close by. I'll have my foreman take care of the ranch. Can I check on Marlene when I get back?"

"Of course, you can. I live upstairs. If you don't see a light on here, then come up there. I'll see you later." Doc looked at Esther whose head was bowed. "Can I help you with something, Esther?"

Esther wanted to make a suggestion about the stairs again but decided not to say a word. "Doc, Daisy has some nasty cuts, as you know. Do you know of anything that would help heal those so as to not leave much of a scar?"

"Not really, and it's a shame too, such needless punishment for a young girl."

"Willow suggested aloe vera. She said the Indians use it for any number of things and that was one of them along with burns. Do you think I should try that?"

"Well now, you know Willow helped me with the surgery I just performed on Marlene Konrad. She had appendicitis. If it had not been for Willow's help, I don't think we would have had the success we had. She's a natural at medicine. She could be a doctor, if anyone would let her. I'd really like to have her work for me as my nurse. I thought I'd better check with you first, though."

"Doc, you and I know how independent she is. I can't fault her. She was raised by the Indians after her family was killed by them, and she lived on her own in a cave when she ran away from the tribe. God has made her who she is, a strange mixture of a lady and, dare I say, savage? I won't stand in her way. I don't think I could."

"I was hoping you would say that. What about Adam?"

"He would never stand in her way, either. She really does have a will of her own."

"She knows more about plants and some healing mixtures than I do. If she says aloe will help, then why not try it? Where is she?"

"She went out to find some aloe. Doc, do you need me to take Mrs. Konrad to the hotel?"

"No, Esther, I don't want to move her. I'm going to let her stay here for a bit."

"Do you have a place where she can stay? I don't think I would want her sleeping on that table back there."

"I do have a small room back there that has a small bed in it.

Her husband helped me move her to that room just now. So, I will stay up with her for a good bit, probably most of the night. I've slept in a chair many times. It won't hurt me to do it again."

"We could take turns if you would like to get some rest. I don't want anything to happen to her or you." Esther's face showed great concern for the doctor. He was not as young as he used to be.

"We'll see how she's doing in a little while. She's asleep right now. She doesn't have any fever now for which I am tremendously thankful. God, the Great Physician, is good, and I am counting on His help with this case."

"Amen. I'm sure Adam has Mr. Konrad and his children all settled in a room or, maybe, two." She smiled at Doc, and he smiled back at her. He understood her meaning.

"Doc, do you want me to tell Willow she is now your nurse?"

"That will be fine if you can get her to stop long enough to tell her."

Esther laughed. "If you need anything, you will let me know, won't you?"

"As always."

Esther left, stopped by Marta's, and returned to the hotel. She found Josh and Katie ready to leave, but Willow was nowhere to be seen. "Where's Willow?" she asked them.

"We have no idea. She went running out into the wilderness and hasn't returned that we know of."

"I'd better check on Daisy. Don't leave yet; I have some things for you. I won't be long."

Katie and Josh settled themselves on the rockers on the front porch. He took her hand and began to thank God for her and their child who was on the way. He thanked God that Brian, Adam, and he had found Mrs. Konrad and gotten her to Doc in time. Then he began to thank God for all their blessings of late and found he had an overwhelming amount for which to be thankful. Katie, whose eyes were closed, was thanking God in her heart as well. When Josh spoke to her, she jumped and found she had fallen asleep while praying. She silently chastised herself but then felt it was probably very normal given her condition. She looked at Josh and smiled. He seemed to be staring at something directly across from them. She looked but didn't see anything out of the ordinary.

"What are you thinking?" she asked.

Josh looked at her and smiled. "Nothing."

"Oh, come on now, Josh. You were so deep in thought I thought you were going to bore holes in the bank over there. What was it?"

"No, really, I wasn't thinking about anything."

"Men! You know sometimes you are just like my father. I remember him telling mother the same thing when she would ask that question. Well, if you don't want to tell me, that is just fine with me."

"Really, Katie. I wasn't thinking about anything. I don't even think I was really looking at the bank. I was just resting my brain."

"Well, I'm glad you can do that. My brain doesn't seem to stop!"

"What's going on? You aren't arguing, are you?" Esther asked when she came back out.

"No, Josh was thinking and says he wasn't and won't tell me what he was thinking."

"Katie, all men seem to do that. I don't know where they go in that head of theirs, but it isn't here. Maybe their brains just stop functioning for a little bit. Mine certainly doesn't! Adam does that all the time. Speaking of Adam, he's on his way down with a trunk I want you to take out to the ranch. It has all the baby things I had for Josh and Tad. That should give you a good start.

Willow was with Daisy and was spreading aloe on her wounds. She says it will help heal them."

"Daisy? What happened to Daisy?"

"You don't know?" Esther asked, surprised. Josh looked at her with a painful look and a little warning as well.

Adam came out with the trunk and put it in the back of the wagon along with the load of potatoes and squash he had put there earlier.

"What happened? Well, there is no time to relate the *whole* story. Suffice it to say, she got hurt and ended up with some cuts that we were afraid would scar, but Willow went out and found some aloe and is using the jelly part inside the leaves to put on the cuts to help them heal. Oh look! Here comes Willow now. Maybe you won't be too late getting home."

"Poor girl. I hope she isn't too hurt. I'll pray for her." Kate smiled at her mom and then beamed at Willow as she bounded down the stairs and out the door.

"All right, let's make tracks for home!" she said as she practically jumped into the wagon.

"Willow, dear, you must really start behaving more like a lady than a school girl. I know that will be very difficult since you have so much energy, but you can at least try when you are in public, please."

"Yes, ma'am. I'm sorry. I just have so much in my head I need to do and don't want to miss a minute in which to accomplish it all."

"Well, Doc said to tell you he would love to have you help him and be his nurse. I'm not sure how that will work with you out at the ranch, now."

"Yippee! Katie and I will talk about it tomorrow, and we can figure out a plan. I am bringing back a few things to the ranch.

Katie, I'm thankful you didn't give Abigail's clothes to anyone after she died. With them still out there, I can wear those. So, I left many of my new things here. I'll just have to get used to living in two places."

"Bye, now. Take care. We love you." Adam and Esther waved them on their way.

The three of them rode out of town and headed back to the ranch with Josh's horse tied to the back of the wagon.

25

I don't care what you say, Michael. She has no business becoming a nurse." Brian was speaking louder than he should. He knew it, yet he just couldn't seem to help himself.

"Brian, why do you feel you can control what happens in Willow's life?"

"I don't. I just feel like it is wrong for a woman to be a nurse."

"You didn't seem to mind when Doc called on Esther to come and help him."

"Well, that's different. Esther is Esther, and Willow is Willow."

"That made a whole heap of sense. What did you mean by that?"

"I don't know...Esther is a woman. Willow's just a kid."

"With the experiences in life Willow has undergone, seems to me she has had more maturing experiences than many grown men I have known. She's going to surprise you, Brian. You need to look at who the person is inside and not their age or looks in order to determine if they are mature or not."

"Well"—Brian rubbed his chin, then his whole face, and then pinched the bridge of his nose—"I just worry about her. She is just so, so sudden. Do you get my meaning?" He started pacing. "She isn't just fixin' to do something. She just up and does it! She just about drives me crazy."

"It drives you crazy because you care a little more about her well-being than you do for anyone else's in the community?"

"No, yes, well, maybe. I don't know, Michael. Like earlier. She went running out to find some aloe when those outlaws could have been out there ready to grab their next victim."

"But they were in the hands of Dan and the others. There was no danger."

"But she didn't know that!" Brian threw his hands in the air above his head then let them fall back and slap his thighs.

"Maybe she did. In any case, I admire the man who tries to lasso that little gal. She would give a rattlesnake something to think about. She certainly will keep life interesting. Have you seen the way she handles a knife? She has one hidden on her at all times."

"Really?" Brian stopped pacing and looked dumbfounded at Michael.

"Remember, Brian, she was raised by the Indians. She has seen so much bad done to them and by them, she knows how to handle it. Evil is not new to her, peace is, and she is so happy to have it. Don't deny her that happiness. You need to look for your own and embrace it."

"Where is my happiness? Not back east. I love it out west, but I am getting pretty weary of this job."

"What is it you want to do, Brian?"

"I'd like to go to law school and be a lawyer."

Michael didn't seem surprised. "Why don't you look into it? We have Todd who will make a great lawman, and Dan is moving his family here and will continue to be a Ranger. This town is growin', and if you want to come back and open a law practice, I'm sure there will be plenty of business for you here, if this has become your home."

"Michael, that would be a dream come true. I don't even know where to start."

"It will come to you when it's time. I'd better get back to the ranch. I've been away quite a while now. I'll see you later."

"Take care. You will probably catch up with Josh and the girls.

I can't imagine him taking it anything but slowly with Katie being with child. He'll be much more cautious now. Willow will be wishing she had ridden her horse," he said, laughing.

"You are so right, Brian. You are so right."

26

Mid-September

O h, how wonderful these last few weeks have been!" Erin was in awe of where she was and how wonderful God had been to her. She came down the stairs to the shop. Her home upstairs had been fully equipped by just about everyone. She had written thank-you notes to everyone she knew had donated things and done the cleaning. She was getting to know Marta better and better. She entered the shop and found Marta excitedly unpacking another crate. "Marta, what have you ordered now?"

"Oh, Erin, you are not going to believe this. I've been wantin' one for ever so long, and with the two of us working, I could afford to order one, and it came in last evening. Just wait 'til you see it."

"What is it?"

"Just wait a minute. Here, hold this and I'll get this lid off."

Marta handed Erin the crowbar and hammer. She began to throw the packing material all around the storage room.

I'll have to clean this again. Erin thought, *I hope I'm as excited as she is.*

"Oh look, look! Help me get it out!"

"A sewing machine? Marta! This will help so much with getting all that sewing done we have on order. Do you know how to use it?"

"I can learn. It can't be too hard. Do you?"

"Yes, my mother had one. I learned from her how to use it. I can teach you."

"Now, where'll we put it?" Marta asked, eyes gleaming with excitement!

"I don't think I would put it right in front of a window, but close enough to get good light. It helps if we can see really well to thread the needle and locate the seam allowance. Oh, Marta, I just can't believe this! We need to put the top on the bottom so it will stand up. It's in two pieces. Maybe we should get Mr. Jakes to come over and put the parts together."

"You think he can do it?"

"He should. He runs the hardware store. I bet all those farming tools and such don't come shipped in one piece."

"Maybe…okay, go and get him. I…I can't wait."

Erin quickly left the shop and ran up to the hardware store located between the hotel and the livery.

"Oh, Mr. Jakes."

"Why, mornin', Miss Erin. What can I do for you?"

"Well, Marta and I have a piece of equipment that needs to be put together. Do you think you could help us?"

"Certainly. Let me put my sign up that says I am out and will be back shortly, and I'll be right there. Do you know what tools I'll need?"

"I don't have the slightest idea. Perhaps a screwdriver?"

"What are you putting together?"

"A sewing machine!" Erin revealed her excitement.

"Can't say as I've seen one in person. I'll bring my tool apron and hope I have the right things. If not, I'll come back and get what I need. I sure am glad my arm has healed up right nice."

"I heard about your adventure when I came to town. I am thankful to God for his healing powers and the blessings he has showered down on everyone here in this wonderful town. You are a very brave man, Mr. Jakes."

"Aw, shucks, it weren't nothin'."

After the exciting morning of getting the sewing machine up and running, Erin decided to try again with Marta.

"I can't believe how I cried during the church service the last two Sundays. Then I realized it is because I had not been in a church in so very long, and I was truly worshiping for the first time in such a long time. Riley does such a good job preaching. He has preached these last two Sundays, and I was so moved by what he had to say about forgiveness and giving all our hurts and sorrows to God. I have needed to do that."

"I can't go to church. If I did, Oscar would beat me nearly to death. I see what you and Esther have, and I wish I could get it, but I can't."

"Marta, you don't have to go to church to *get it*. All you have to do is pray to God to give you his free gift of salvation. Church is where we go to grow in our faith. I understand not wanting to get another beating. I really do."

"When have you ever had a beating?"

"My voice is the way it is because of a beating I received at the hands of a man I hardly knew. He wanted to kill me. He beat me and choked me until I passed out. If it had not been for another man coming to my rescue, he would have killed me. Yes, I understand your fear."

"I had no idea. That's kinda like Daisy. She was beaten and done worse to by men she didn't know. I don't know if she is going to be able to get back in the public. She is afraid of what they are goin' to say about her. That's why I hide the bruises my Oscar gives me."

"Have you told the sheriff about what Oscar does?"

"Wouldn't make any difference. Women have very few rights in this world and none when it comes to how their husbands treat them."

"That isn't right. What can be done?"

"Well, nothin', I reckon. I just have to be careful around Oscar.

Sometimes, that doesn't even help. He's just mean. I'm glad the boys aren't livin' at home anymore. They's better off out at the ranch, but I miss 'em."

"Marta, if there is ever anything I can do for you, will you let me know?"

"Just pray for me."

"I do that every day, more than once a day."

"Really? Why, thank ya."

"Marta, you can pray too."

"God don't listen to the likes of me."

"He listens. Oh yes, he listens."

"I don't know how to pray."

"You know how to talk with me, don't you?" Erin put her arm around Marta's shoulders and gave her a squeeze.

"Why sure. You're standing right there and you're no different than me. God, well, God is God, ya know."

"He's right here too. All you have to do is tell him things just like you tell me. Just talk to him. He's waiting to hear your words of saying you are sorry for all the sins, bad things, you have done. We all sin daily. So we need to ask for forgiveness daily. But we only need to ask once for salvation from hell and eternal pain and suffering out of his presence. He will give that salvation to us when we ask Jesus to come into our heart to live with us forever."

As Erin talked, she became more and more excited about the truth of the gospel. Her words were spoken with heartfelt intensity and joy. Suddenly, she just started praying out loud for Marta's salvation and realization that God loved her with an everlasting love.

Marta stood beside the sewing machine and watched Erin become lost in her own relationship with God. She was in awe of how moved Erin was just talking to God on her behalf. She began to cry and left for the back room. Erin was totally unaware of her leaving. She didn't stop praying for some time. When she did, she didn't see Marta anywhere. She moved toward the back room. When she got to the door, she heard crying in the direction of the back corner. She walked that way.

"Marta, I'm so sorry if I upset you. Please, please, forgive me. I would never do anything to hurt you. Please, say you will. Please?"

"You didn't do nothin' to hurt me. You just made me know God cares. And you care. I just haven't ever had that. I do, Erin, I do want what you and Esther have. Show me how to get it. Please?"

Erin knelt beside Marta, and she shared Bible verses. When she came to John 3:16, "For God so loved the world that he gave his only begotten Son, that whosoever believeth in Him should not perish, but have everlasting life," Marta began to weep again.

"I want to pray, Erin. Help me say the right things."

"Just pray like you're talking to me. Just tell God what you want to do and what you want Him to do. Tell Him you are sorry for your wrongdoings and wrong thoughts, and that you want Jesus, His only Son, to save you from your sins and come into your heart to stay."

"God, I know I'm not the best person in the world, so I have plenty of sins, more than I can count. So, if'n you don't mind, I'd really appreciate it if you would forgive me. I need to be forgiven really bad. I want to be like Erin and Esther. I want the love they have. They say it's the love of Jesus shinin' through them, and if that's so, then I want Jesus to come into my heart too. Would you make that possible, please?"

Marta began to really sob at that point. She could not say another word. Erin just put her arm around Marta's shoulders and hugged her. "Lord, hear this simple and sincere prayer by this beautiful woman. She truly does have a heart seeking after you. I pray she will feel your love and comfort even now. In Jesus' name, amen."

"Amen."

Erin continued to hold Marta.

Marta calmed down and looked at Erin in the dim light filtering through the door from the showroom. "Erin, I feel it. It is overwhelming. Thank you for caring enough to help me. You are my angel of mercy. I will never forget you."

"I'm going to go into the other room in case we have anyone drop in. You stay back here as long as you need to. If you want to go upstairs, I have some water up there. You can make yourself some tea and even take a little nap, if you feel like it. Make my little home yours, Marta."

"I think I might go and wash my face, but I'll be fine. I'll be back in a minute."

"Do you mind if I use the sewing machine?"

"Not at all, go right ahead. I'll be down quicker than a frog snatchin' a fly outta the air."

"I love you, Marta."

"I love you too, Erin. Oh, and, Erin, I contacted a lawyer in Kerrville. He said he will bring the papers down for us to sign.

He doesn't usually do that, but he needs to answer some questions Brian has. He'll be here tomorrow."

"That's fine. Thank you, Marta."

With that, the two women went their separate ways, but their hearts remained together, right in the hand of God.

"Riley, what are you doing here? Why aren't you in school?" "Now, you sound like a mother hen. Young lady, I am on my lunch break. I brought you lunch, and I brought Marta a slice of pie."

"Why did you do all this again?"

"Because the two of you are miracle workers. I can't believe the transformation in my humble abode. It looks like a palace.

I love the fabrics you used for the curtains. The tablecloth complements them. The whole ambiance of the simple dwelling has been transformed from cold and sterile to warm and inviting. You aren't even finished and the whole place feels different. How can I thank you? Perhaps with…lunch and pie? Of course, I will pay you as soon as I receive the bill."

Marta looked bewildered. "Erin, what is he talking about?" "He does go on, doesn't he? He is simply saying thank you for a job well done. He brought us a gift, lunch for me and pie for you since you don't eat lunch."

"Well, I never! I believe you are the best customer I've ever had. Where's my pie?"

They all joined in a laugh.

"You two go upstairs and eat at the table. I don't want any food on my sewing. I'll just stay here so the shop won't be closed."

"Now, Marta. It would not be proper for Riley to be in my room without a chaperone. You just flip the sign to Closed and lock the door and come up with us. We can all three share the table." Erin hoped to get Marta to relax some.

"I guess I could use a break." She got up and moved to lock the door and flip the sign. "Riley, do you think you could come over some afternoon after school and give Erin and me some Bible learnin' while we sew? I can't come to church, so I'm missin' out."

Riley looked at Erin with a shocked expression and then quickly schooled his face. "Why, yes, of course, Marta. I would be happy to do that. What would you like for me to teach you?"

"I want to know more about Jesus. You see, today, just a little bit ago, I asked him into my heart to live. If he is going to be livin' in there, I s'pose I should know him, don't you think?"

"Yes, I think you are exactly right. What day would be best?"

"Any day you can make it. I know sometimes you have to do other things so we will let you surprise us. We can listen and sew at the same time."

"You might want to have your Bible with you so you can read the scriptures along with me."

"Don't have one."

"I can fix that. I'll do that today…after school." "A'right. See ya after school today. Now, let's eat."

The three quickly moved up the stairs and into Erin's apartment. "Why, Miss Kerr, this is charming! Who would have thought you could make one big room look so homey?

"Well, through that door, I have curtains over the windows facing the street, and I have a rocker in there. I like to sit and sew or knit. Sometimes, I read my Bible in there, especially in the mornings. This has been a wonderful place for me to live. Marta has become a dear, dear friend. I'm so glad I came here to live."

Riley looked at her and smiled. "I am too. You have made a difference in at least one life already."

27

Early October

I t's finished, Josh. You want to go see?"

"No, Wulf, I think I'll just take Katie out there and enjoy it with her. I'd like to see it through her eyes. I know you men have done a superb job with it."

"You know what's best. When do you want to go? Ya see, we would kinda like to be there too, if you get my meanin'?"

"I certainly do, and I wouldn't want you to miss it." Josh looked up to the sky. "Let's see, it's still early. And it's Saturday. We could get in touch with everyone else. They know to be ready. Why not go today? If you'll hitch up the wagon, I'll take her out there in that and go real slow. You fellas go ahead and ride out when you want to and get things going out there. Willow's supposed to ride to town and let everyone else know. I'll wake Katie up if she's sleeping. She doesn't want to miss this!"

"Right you are. We'll get 'er done right away. You want the wagon near the back door?"

"That would be great! Thanks, Wulf. You, Clyde, and the twins have become quite a team. How are things out in the bunkhouse?"

"Great! We're teachin' them young'uns a thing or two. We are even reading the Bible together. I think those boys just may come around sooner than I did, that's for sure!" He walked away laughing and shaking his head. Soon, he disappeared into the barn, and Josh could still hear the echoes of his laugh bouncing off the inside walls of the big building.

Smiling, he said, "What a difference God has made in that man's life. Thank you, Jesus!" With that, he turned toward the house to see if he could get Katie to go for a ride with him.

The fragrance of pie baking in the oven met him before he even got on the back porch. "Maybe I won't have to wake her up."

He came in the door and let the screen door slap shut behind him. No one was in the kitchen, and he stood there a minute to let his eyes adjust to the darker surroundings.

There was Katie, fast asleep on the couch. Her head resting, of course, on the pillow Mrs. Gruber made for them for a wedding present. He smiled. It had been her constant companion and a permanent head rest whenever she took a nap.

He sat there, looking at her sleep. He just couldn't bring himself to wake her up. He heard the men bring the wagon to the back. *I'll have to wake her sometime.* He sat in the rocker near the fireplace watching her sleep and waited a little longer.

"Katie, darling? Katie. Wake up, my love. I have a surprise for you. Katie?"

"Hmmm?"

He started to lift her. "Come on. We're gonna take a little ride. I think you need some fresh air and sunshine. Let's go."

"What?"

"Never mind. Do you trust me?"

"Yes."

"We're going to take a little ride and get some fresh air and sunshine. Maybe we'll go take a ride out to the camp and take a walk in the woods. Would you like that?"

"Yes."

"Katie, are you awake?"

"Yes."

"I may have to put you down because I think I need to record this date in our family Bible. I don't believe you have ever been at a lack of words before. This has to be a day of remembrance for us, our children, and grandchildren. The day Katie Schmitt could only say yes. You are very agreeable."

"Yes, I am."

"Do the pies need to be taken out?"

"Don't worry about those. I'll take care of it," Willow said from behind them.

Josh was almost to the door with his arms full of Katie. He turned around so quickly he almost lost her. "Willow! I had forgotten you are here. I'm so sorry. I have been a bit preoccupied."

He gave Katie a little smile and then bounced her up in his arms like he was trying not to drop her and get a better grip.

Willow, dressed in her riding outfit, laughed at the spectacle.

"You two go on and leave me here. I'm going to be busy with all the housework this big sister of mine seems to be able to sleep through for some strange reason." She winked at him and jerked her head toward the front of the house to send a special message.

Josh kicked the back door open, and there was the wagon waiting just like Wulf said it would be. He even had a canteen of water and a blanket tucked inside the back right behind the seat.

"Up you go, Mrs. Schmitt. Careful now. Make room for me, please?"

"Oh, you are so picky. You want to sit up here too? Well then, you have to drive the team."

"Yes, ma'am. Your wish is my command."

"Well then, drive. I want to see the scenery. Where are we going? Wait! I need to use the privy!"

Josh laughed, climbed down, and helped her down. She practically ran to the outhouse. Willow poked her head out the back and indicated she was leaving. When Katie came back, she walked much more sedately and a little more awake than she had been."

"I thought you might want to go out to the camp and maybe take a walk in the woods to the spring pond." He helped her back into the wagon.

"That would be lovely!" She adjusted her skirts and patted her hair.

It wasn't too long, and they were playing a game. Josh had Katie close her eyes and tell him what she could see in her mind. "Where are we, Katie?"

"Well, we are passing the clump of trees just beyond the bunkhouse."

"You are right. Are you peeking?"

"No, I'm not peeking. I am shocked you would even suggest a thing like that."

This went on for quite some time. Josh finally took his bandana from around his neck. "Okay, I'm going to make sure you aren't peeking. Tie this around your eyes, and then I'm going to wait a little bit and ask you where we are. Is that fair?"

"You are such a doubting Thomas. You know what?" she asked as she tied the bandana around her head to cover her eyes.

"What?"

"I have heard that expression for years and never knew it referred to Thomas, Jesus' disciple. It makes so much sense now."

"Yes, it is amazing how many sayings we have in our language that refer back to things in the Bible. Some are direct quotes.

For instance, we say, 'Do unto others as you would have them do unto you.'"

"Yes, the golden rule."

"It's a direct quote from Jesus."

"Really?" Katie suddenly lurched sideways. "Josh! Be careful, what do you think you are doing?" She reached to take the blindfold off. Josh reached over and gently placed his hand on hers.

"Oh no you don't. No peeking allowed."

"But you almost killed me." She pouted.

"I was just trying to get you closer to me on the seat."

"Oh, you romantic. All you have to do is ask."

"Okay, well, where are we? No peeking!"

"Umm, almost to the area near the ravine that is just beyond the woods just after the bunkhouse."

"Nope, close, but that isn't right. Try again."

Josh deliberately led the horses in a circle broad enough to be a gradual one.

"Oh, we are turning, so then it must be at the fallen tree on the way to the big arroyo."

"Oh, you are good. But that is not it."

They then went up a rise and continued straight. Josh turned left in a gentle circle, hardly noticeable.

"Josh, I'm getting confused. We must have been closer to the little arroyo and are now headed toward the big arroyo."

Josh pulled the horses to a stop. "Well, you are better than I thought. You can take your blindfold off now."

Katie reached up to take the blindfold off when she felt his lips touch hers and her arms reached for him and encircled his neck instead. He pulled her closer and deepened their kiss. Katie didn't care where they were; she was enjoying where she was right then.

Josh slowly pulled away and held her in his arms. He whispered in her ear, "Do you know how much I love you?"

"As much as I love you?" she asked.

"I know I would die for you. Let me help you down before you take off your blindfold, okay?"

"Sure, why not?"

She waited patiently, reliving that kiss in her head and heart.

She felt his hands reach for her waist, stood, and turned. He firmly gripped her and lifted her down from the wagon.

"Okay now, let's get this blindfold off and see where we are."

She reached to untie the blindfold and loosened it enough so he could just slip it off her head. He was standing directly in front of her blocking her view. He had her facing back the way they had come. Josh moved out of the way.

"Well, this is near where we made the camp for the roundup. Isn't it?"

Josh slowly turned her around.

Katie gasped. "Oh, Josh! I can't believe it! A house? I didn't even know you were working on it. This is right where we were going to put the line shack."

"This is the line shack or whatever you want to call it."

"I want to call it Rettunghaus, or Rettungsturm. This is where I found Jesus, my salvation, the true Messiah. Oh, Josh, this is the best surprise ever. You can blindfold me anytime you want to, especially if I get this kind of surprise. Thank you so much. Can I go in?"

"Absolutely! There are more surprises waiting."

Katie laughed that tinkling, adorable laugh of hers. As she raised her foot to climb the steps to the porch, she could smell food. She turned to Josh with a questioning look.

"After you, my lady."

She walked on up and entered the house. There they were, all the men. Now she understood why people called the table a "groaning board." They had so much food on the table it had to be groaning under the weight of it. They all looked at her in expectation, even the twins were quiet.

"Oh my, I don't know if I can stand all this happiness. You men have worked so hard and have kept this secret so well. I never even guessed. The thought never entered my mind. I did think, someday...but I never thought today! I can't wait to see all of it. There are more doors, not just one room? Oh, this is so fun!

And you have even managed to build the furniture too. Oh, I am so happy. Thank you, thank you all!"

Suddenly, Katie began to cry. Josh just put his arms around her and allowed her to thoroughly soak the front of his shirt. He kept rubbing the back of her head or her back. When she stopped,

Clyde jumped to his feet.

"Let's eat! Food's gettin' cold!" Everyone laughed and stood.

Clyde reached for a plate and handed it to Katie. "Now, princess, this may not measure up to what you put before us out here, but we did our best. At least it isn't just beans and biscuits!"

Katie managed a laugh and headed for the table completely loaded with food. "We built a campfire out back, even if it isn't dark, if you want to sit out there to eat," Clyde added.

"It will be just like old times. I'd love that," Katie almost whispered.

"After we eat, we will show you around. I think you will be very surprised."

They heard a horse galloping up out front. Wulf looked out. "She's here."

In about two seconds, the door opened, and in walked Willow. "You started before I could get here?"

"We knew you'd make it. Katie is just starting. You're next," Josh laughed.

Wulf handed Willow a plate and made a sweeping bow. "Now, this is truly a family! I just love all of you. Thank you for including me in the party."

"Someone is missing." Katie turned and surveyed the group.

"Not for long. He'll be here. I left to let him know as soon as you two were riding out. Yes, Josh, I took the pies out! Oh yeah, he said he might bring a friend if that was okay. I told him sure."

Katie wondered if that friend would be Tad. She was so hungry; she feared she'd need another plate. She and Willow finished and headed out the back door to the campfire. "Oh look, they have dug a pit and lined it with stones. This will be more permanent."

"It's just like the Indians do it." Willow smiled. "It brings back some good memories. They weren't all bad."

The girls chose log seats out of the smoke. The men began to file out with plates piled high. Before they were all out, two more wagons arrived. Adam, Esther, and Tad were in one, and Riley and Erin were in the other. They quickly got down and came into the house. Michael turned and smiled at them. "Grab a plate and join the party. We've all moved outside to the campfire. If you want to stay in here, you can."

Riley looked at Erin. "No, we'll be out as soon as we can satisfy the hunger in our eyes with the feast on our plates. As soon as we join the happy throng out back, we will proceed to fill our stomachs with this hardy repast"

"Oh, okay. We will wait for you to get out here before we ask God to bless our food and fellowship," Michael added.

"Then we best move quickly through this smorgasbord."

They each filled their plates and moved to join the others.

As each one reached their stopping place, they just remained in happy contentment on their log bench, too full to move.

Esther grabbed a bucket and proceeded to gather the dirty blue speckled plates and cups of those who were finished. "I'll just take these inside."

"We'll take them to the spring later to wash them," Katie said.

"Why, Katie, dear, did you not see the pump in the kitchen? You have a hand pump for water right inside the kitchen. It's the newest thing! I'm going to get one in the kitchen at the hotel. How convenient it is. That was probably the hardest thing the men had to do when building the house, but it will be worth all their effort," Esther said enthusiastically.

"Oh my. I'll have to see that, but right now, I don't think I can move." Katie laughed.

Riley looked at Esther. "Esther, when you get back from inside. I believe this is the right time and place for me to share my story." He turned and looked around at the group. "Almost everyone I care about is here, and I did promise to tell it under the proper circumstances. Well, this is the best time I've seen yet and definitely the right place. So, with your indulgence, I will tell my story." *I'll just have to tell Brian later.*

"Ooh, I'll hurry. I don't want to miss a word."

"I will be succinct."

"That will be the day." Josh laughed. They all joined him, and the twins elbowed each other and laughed even though they didn't really know what he meant.

"I don't know anything really about my beginnings, my parents, when or where I was born. All I know is that my name is Riley. I was found by an elderly couple who came upon our still smoldering-covered wagon. My parents were dead. They evidently had arrows sticking out of them. The old man proceeded to bury them, while the old woman began looking through the things that weren't completely burned to try to find a name they could put on the grave marker when he finished with the burying, perhaps, even the name of some relative they could inform of my parents' deaths. All she found was a mostly burned Bible. The only legible name that remained was Riley. Dear Mr. and Mrs. Spreckels were about to finish up when they heard me cry. She said I howled. I believe she exaggerated. Nevertheless, if I had not cried, they would have left me there unnoticed. I had been covered up and was lying under the wagon. Miraculously, the blanket over me didn't catch fire, and the Indians who attacked our wagon didn't notice me."

Riley paused a moment, took a deep breath, then continued,

"Mrs. Spreckels quickly gathered me into her arms and found what little she could to comfort me. They had water, which I greedily drank. She thinks I was about ten months old. They took me to their home and raised me until I was about four. She said they were too old, and I needed someone younger to take care of me. They called me Riley, J. R. Riley. I was adopted by the new schoolteacher, Miss Lydia Helms. She was absolutely wonderful!"

Riley smiled and looked at the sky. He looked at the group. "I was able to see the Spreckels, and they became grandparents to me. Gram Spreckels would make the most wonderful cookies. When I was a little older, I asked what the J. R. stood for. I wanted to know my name. Gram Spreckels lovingly sat me beside her and put her arm around me. She kissed the top of my head, smiled, and said in the kindest tone of voice I have ever heard, 'God knows your name, pumpkin. We called you J. R. because all we knew was Riley. The *J. R.* stands for "Just Riley." We couldn't tell if that was a first name or a last name. We did know it was a name connected to you. We didn't want to call you Just Riley Riley, so we called you J. R. Riley. We love you no matter what your name is, and you will always be Just Riley to us.'

"I was too young to understand all the implications of what she was saying. I just wanted a name. I decided I'd rather go by J. R. than Just Riley, and I have kept it that way ever since."

Riley rubbed his hands together. "Now, Miss Helms raised me as her sort of son. I was not to call her mother. I could call her Aunt Lydia if we were outside of school, but I couldn't in any way insinuate that she was my mother. Obviously, if she was my mother and not married, she wouldn't be able to work. So, it was better that she became my guardian. I lived with her twelve years.

She was my teacher in school and out of school. She taught me everything. I learned Latin and Greek from her. I learned all my math, science, and history from her. We had wonderful discussions on philosophy. She was truly a highly intelligent woman, especially for her age. She was only eighteen when she took me in.

She was new to town, and she loved children. There was another couple who were interested in having a child they could use to help work the farm. She couldn't bear to see a child of such great potential lose the chance to grow in that intelligence, as she put it. Instead, she decided to take me in. She begged the Spreckels to let her take me rather than having my mind neglected. She would teach me, and I could become someone great! Well, they knew I was teachable, and being in town, they would be able to see me more often.

"When I was about fourteen, she began to be courted by the new minister in town. He was very taken with her and her intellect and became very serious about her. It seems none of the other eligible bachelors in town measured up to her standards, or they didn't like the idea of her already having a child to rear, even if I wasn't hers. As a result, she had never married." Riley shifted and seemed to tense. "But the new minister, after two years of courtship, finally asked her to marry him. She accepted. That was when he told her that I would have to go. He would not be sharing her with a sixteen-year-old young man. It was time I made it out in the world on my own. She didn't know I had overheard that conversation. She asked him if he was giving her an ultimatum, him or me. Essentially, he said that yes if that was how she wanted to look at it. She asked him if she could pray about that. I think he was surprised she had to. He thought the choice was obvious. I knew I had to do something to relieve her of that burden. I couldn't just come right out and say I heard what he said. I needed to use psychology on her."

Riley rubbed his face and looked again at the fire and the group. Each one seemed to be sitting on the edge of their seat.

"I took the atlas and slipped into my room. I lit an oil lamp and began looking at the different places in the United States. The war had been over for five years at that time, so I was looking at the places west of the Mississippi. I was not interested in going east.

Besides, my parents had been traveling west, I assume, because there was more promise for them west of the Mississippi. I heard the door close, and I heard her soft footfalls on the floor. I could picture her turning out lanterns and probably wondering where I was. She evidently saw the light under my door, for I heard a soft knock. I told her to come in. When she opened the door, I could see the weight of the world full of worry, and perhaps some fear, etched on her mind and reflected on her face.

"I smiled. She walked over and sat on the edge of the bed.

'What are you doing?' she asked, truly interested. I told her I was looking at all the places I had never been and thinking I would really like to take an adventure. I wanted to go and see things and experience things that were not available in Macon or anywhere else in Missouri. I told her I had been bitten by wanderlust. Her eyes were sad. She said, 'I had hoped you would go to college.' I told her she had given me more than any college could. She smiled and then said, 'No, J. R., your curiosity and thirst for knowledge have driven me to learn right along with you. You have taught me more than I knew when you came home with me. You are so much more to me than a son. You are my true friend.

"Tears glistened on the edge of her lashes. 'Tell me, when were you thinking of making this adventure?' I told her I didn't know, but I thought I would go before school started again. I had already finished all the subjects I needed for a diploma, in fact, more than enough. I had grown so much the last two years that I was the same height then as I am now though I have filled out a bit." Riley patted his stomach.

With that, everyone laughed. Katie was crying, but she laughed as well. Erin's dark eyes were riveted on his. She was peering deep into his soul. Suddenly, she said, "There is more, isn't there? You need to tell it all."

Riley looked deeply at her and nodded.

He took a deep breath. "Yes, yes, there is more. I left the day of her wedding. I had promised I would stay for that. I didn't stay for the reception that followed. I had told her I wouldn't. She understood. I was the one to give her away. After the service, I went up to Reverend Davenport and said to him, 'I have given her to you to cherish, to protect, and to love as Christ loves the church. I expect you to die for her if it comes to that. If I ever find out you did any less, I'll come back.' I didn't wait for a retort. I just got on my horse and left. I rode for Oklahoma, then Texas. I worked at being a cowboy." He glanced around.

"I became despondent, however, and found myself being lured by new experiences into which I should have never allowed myself to experience. I began to drink and gamble. Of course, when Satan sets a trap and a believer steps into that trap, Satan won't set him free again. It takes the mighty hand of God to free us from Satan's trap. I knew better, but I stepped into that trap anyway. I had quit reading my Bible. I had quit praying. Reverend Davenport had made me mad at God and at the church. I had decided I didn't want anything to do with them. However, God never lets go. We might let go of Him, but He never lets go of us." Riley scrubbed his hand across his face, swallowed hard, looked around at each face, took a deep breath, and then continued, "One payday I allowed myself to be talked into joining some of the cowboys in their revelries in town. I fear I became excessively impaired in my judgment by the alcohol I consumed. I won some money, more than I had when I entered the saloon, and used some of it to pay for some pleasures I had yet to experience. The young woman was my first teacher in the ways of carnal sin. I will spare you the details or much of that information, but I became a regular visitor. I had a wild idea that I would save her from that place. But I found out she didn't want to be saved from that. I still can't figure that out. I just don't understand. And yet, why would she believe that I wanted her to come and be my wife? She was probably wiser than I. Perhaps, she could see what I felt was lust and not love."

Riley looked around and saw each one leaning forward, silently urging him on. "God's Spirit was at work within me though. Eventually, I came to the realization that I was just as bad, no, probably worse off than she was because I knew the truth and had turned my back on all I believed. She wouldn't have that job if there were no men like me. I am eternally sorry for those sins. I don't know how I will ever be able to make that up to her. I will never be able to find her, but maybe I can help someone else who is in need. It may be some young man headed for destruction in one of those places. Maybe it will be a woman who needs help, or someone who found herself doing the only thing she can do. If I can pass on what God has given me, whether it is material goods, or more importantly spiritual truth, then maybe I can make up for what I did to that young woman and the witness I destroyed with the cowboys who were with me. I became the hypocrite. I should have never been anything less than what God had appointed me to be." Riley looked directly at each one's eyes. "I ask your forgiveness for my failings. I should have done this long ago, before you entrusted the education of the townfolks' children into my hands. If you find me unworthy, then please let me know. As much as I would hate to leave, I would. It would break my heart, but I would go."

For a moment there was silence. Adam rose to his feet.

"Ladies, gentlemen, before us we see a contrite heart. This is what God is looking for in each of us, repentance. What is God's reaction to Riley at this moment? Search your hearts and respond as God would."

The twins elbowed each other and shrugged their shoulders.

Their eyes were intent on each face around the fire. The shades of night were gathering. Stars twinkled above, and the moon was rising. Not a soul spoke; each one was searching his heart. Finally, Josh stood.

"He who is without sin cast the first stone." He walked over to Riley, pulled him to his feet, and gave him a strong and sincere hug. "I love you, Riley. I couldn't ask for a better friend. I trust you will still be here when our little one starts school. I trust you to not only prepare our child, hopefully, children, through their education, but I also trust you to prepare them spiritually. I know you will incorporate the Word of God thoroughly studied into their lessons in school. I also trust you to live what you teach. I have seen you have learned much from life, even if you are younger than I."

"Thank you, Josh. I don't deserve your love or friendship, but I am humbled by it. You have been a wonderful example to me of what a Christian should be. I hope we will remain friends, even when I have to discipline your children."

"Oh, Riley," Willow said as she wiped tears from her eyes. "We are both orphans. You may not realize how very precious that is to me. I feel like someone understands the questions and sense of loss experienced by me and any of those of us who didn't have the opportunity to experience the normal home life like so many others have. It is a mystery to us. I at least remember my name. I can't fathom not knowing even though I don't go by that name. Riley, I promise to be a better friend. I hope we will have more opportunities to talk." She then said something in Comanche.

Riley looked at her with questioning eyes. "What does that mean?"

"Brother of my being." She smiled. I'm adopting you as my big brother. I may ask you to teach me Latin. Can you do that?"

"Certainly! Why do you want to learn Latin?"

"I'm going to be a nurse. I've been helping Doc, and I want to go to college and then bring back what I have learned and work with him contributing that knowledge and skill. But I don't have a formal education. I think I could learn quickly, though."

"Yes, I believe you could. You already know two languages. A third shouldn't be too difficult. Also, you seem to remember everything you see or read."

Each one around the circle spoke to Riley. They spoke words of encouragement and love. It was a healing time for them and each grew closer in fellowship with each other and with God. The only one who hadn't moved or spoken was Erin. She would save her comments for the ride home.

28

The washed dishes filled the shelves. The food packed away in baskets was placed snuggly in the wagons to take back to the house and hotel. Each wagon and rider held a lantern to help navigate back to the ranch house in the now-growing dark.

Josh and Katie stood on the porch waving good-bye to each guest. Their horses had been put under a lean-to as a temporary stall for them. The wagon was at the north end of the house and the tack was hanging over the rail on the back porch.

"Well, Mrs. Schmitt, are you ready to go to bed or do you want to stay up for a little while?"

"I can't believe we're staying here for the night. This must be a dream. What a wonderful cozy little place we have here. I'll be able to come to the roundup even with a baby. Two bedrooms!

Josh, you were listening to my thoughts. I just didn't know you were starting on this project so soon. I was planning on asking you if we could have two bedrooms. I love you. You are so aware of me. I don't know how to say it. You *know* me."

"Yes, I do, and I couldn't be happier."

"Josh, do you think Riley will be all right? I don't want him to think his past means any of us don't like him anymore. He did believe us, didn't he?"

"I think Riley will be just fine. In fact, he will be more than fine. I believe he is in the center of God's Will. What better place to be?"

"You're right. I wish my family could have been here. I wish they had known the truth. Oh, why, Josh? Why did they have to die? I can't seem to get that thought out of my head. I know there's nothing I can do to change it, but I wish we had known the truth and accepted it before they died."

"We'll ask God to give you peace. He is the only one who can. Trust him, my love, just trust him to have everything under control. He is sovereign. I think you are very tired right now and need to rest. So let's go to bed."

"You are being very quiet, Erin. Are you upset with me?" Riley looked at Erin as he pulled from the lane out onto the road back into town.

Erin's head jerked up and she looked over at him. The lantern light caused shadows to race across his face as it swung with the sway of the wagon.

"No, Riley, I'm not upset with you. I am merely pensive. I have so much to say and don't know how to say it. You have bared your soul to these people, and they have embraced you. You have a history with them. They *know* you. You felt comfortable telling them all that you told them. I'm new. Each of us has a story. None of us has the same story. They may be similar stories, but not the same. Willow, for instance, feels a new connection with you because you have similar stories, but they are still different. It's almost like 'walk a mile in my shoes.' Well, in a way, you have walked a mile in my shoes.

Riley opened his mouth to say something. Erin turned and placed her gloved finger tips on his lips. "No, please, let me speak."

Riley looked at her and nodded. As soon as she touched him, he felt the Spirit of the Lord fill his being and was afraid to speak.

"I am that girl, Riley. I am her in so many ways." She lowered her eyes and began to relate her story, not leaving out any of the details of her trials. She began by telling of her salvation, her love of God, and how her parents died. She told of her kidnapping.

She told of her humiliation at the hands of William, who wanted the privilege, as he put it, of 'breaking her in,' as if she was a bucking bronco that needed to be broken. She told of the horrors of the punishments given to any girl who tried to run away. She told of the loss of her baby at the hands of a doctor who owed William favors in exchange for money and favors from the girls. She told him how she didn't know if she could even have children now. She told him of the near-death beating she received from the hands of one of the patrons, and how it had ruined her voice. She told him how God had supplied a way to escape. She told of the kind sea captain and the family connection there. She told of Sarah and of Mr. LeFleur. She told of the Martinez family and their goodness to her. How God had been leading her all the way to Crystal Springs and how she now was soon to be legally in partnership with Marta, thanks to their meetings with the lawyer.

She told of Marta's fear of Oscar. A fear Erin knew. She had tasted its bitterness. She told him of how she lives in constant fear of being found by William and having no way to oppose him. She then related that according to the lawyer, Marta has no rights when it comes to her husband, that she herself has no real rights, and how she feels so utterly alone. She told him of her trust in God, knowing he would look out for her, but still continually battles the fear Satan keeps putting in her mind. She told of the nightmares she has had almost every night.

She stopped, and as she was pouring out her heart out to him, her eyes also began pouring out tears of sorrow and fear. She began to sob and to cry out to God for relief.

Riley stood, lifted his hands to heaven, and began to pray. He had stopped the wagon. Long before that, Adam and his family were far ahead of them, maybe even back in town. Riley's prayer for comfort and for joy to fill Erin's heart felt to her like showers of blessing upon her head and shoulders. His words were not aimed at her, but he was talking directly to God as if he was looking the Almighty One in the face. Riley was standing right beside her, yet he hadn't touched her. She had been so afraid he would. When she began to cry, she feared he would try to comfort her. She dreaded she would let him. She was terrified they would both again fall into temptation. On the other hand, she was afraid he wouldn't try to comfort her.

Will he reject me and ridicule me or just walk away? She felt the anxiety of never seeing him again. But he didn't do any of those things; he prayed for her. She looked up at him in awe. *Here is a man who is so close to God he can be completely caught up in interceding for me, a filthy and vile creature, that he is altogether lost to the fact of my presence.*

She slid to her knees on the floor of the wagon in front of the seat, leaning on it, and she poured her heart out to God. As she did, she felt a peace and a light come into her heart the likes of which she had never felt before. She continued to pray until her soul was as quiet as a snowy winter night. She slowly lifted her eyes and saw Riley sitting on the seat next to her, his head bowed and his hands clasped. She raised herself up and sat on the bench seat of the wagon. He turned his head and smiled at her, then spoke.

"Wow! I have never experienced anything like that before. I am speechless."

"Yes, I am in awe. I feel so much peace. Riley, is there anything I can do for you? I feel you have done so much for me, and I have shown you nothing except suspicion and doubt. Oh, I know how to talk with men and make them feel comfortable, but I also know how to hide my true feelings from them. I am a master liar. I had to be. I was in such bondage."

"Yes, you can do something for me."

A twinge of fear skittered through Erin's heart.

"I want to tell you about my dream. Will you hear it?"

"Yes, I will listen and I will hear it."

"I was lying beside the part of the Crystal Springs River, which is farther from town. I need to take you there so you can see it.

Anyway, I was there, and an old raven flew down and brought me food and drink. She looked very old. Then she flew away. Later she came back with more food and drink, but she looked younger, much younger. She flew away again and again, but my raven kept coming back. This time, she didn't have food or drink with her, but I could see into her, and she was so wounded, not on the outside but on the inside. There were wounds and scars all over her insides. God impressed on me that I was to take care of this raven and be His hands to heal her. Raven, I believe you are that raven. I have felt the presence of God tonight. I know He has a plan for us. I know this is sudden, and you are not in the emotional state in which to realistically look at this, but do you think there may be a future for us together? I truly feel a connection between us."

"You're right, Riley, when you said I am not in the emotional state in which to realistically look at this. I think God is dealing with both of us. We have not known each other for very long, although it has been several weeks, enjoyable weeks, a month, perhaps a little more. I think I need to talk with Captain McBride. I will write him a letter. I have no idea when he will receive it. I will also write to Sarah, for she may know his schedule. In the meantime, I will be happy to spend time with you and get to know you better. I don't know how much more there is to know. We have both bared our souls tonight. I have nothing left hidden to share with you. You know everything there is to know about me, all the good and all the bad. Yes, I am wounded. There is much to heal. I don't know if I will ever get over them killing the child I was carrying. I have no way of knowing who the father was, but it was *my* baby. Oh, how that hurt. Riley, will I ever get over that sorrow?"

Riley reached over and then withdrew his arm. "I started to hug you, but I fear that would offend you. I don't want you ever to think I am treating you inappropriately or that I'm trying to get you to do something inappropriate. I respect you, Erin, and I promise I do not think less of you because of the things through which you have come. Where you are headed is much more important to me. I promise not to touch you without your permission."

"Thank you, Riley. I think right now we need to get back into town, or we will have a scandal on our hands."

"Then we would have to get married!" he said with a bit of a laugh. "I wouldn't want to start that way. I want us to make that decision on our own, with God's help."

"Riley, please, be my friend, a true friend. Please, don't ignore me tomorrow. I don't think I could bear it. You know, Marta is hurting as well. She is terribly abused by her husband, Oscar. I'm very worried about her. She is impressed with your friendship. She is very thankful for your business as well. You have helped her self-confidence and helped her financially. I don't think Oscar knows how well she is doing. Her parents gave her that shop. I don't think they liked Oscar, and he was courting her at the time. She said she was stubborn, and they couldn't tell her anything about him that would change her mind.

"Her parents said she could have the store as long as he didn't know it was hers. For all Oscar knows, she's working for them.

They moved a few years back, and they made it clear to her in front of Oscar that she needed to pay them each month for their part of the business. He also thinks she's renting the building from them."

Erin turned to face Riley a little better. "She went to visit them about two years ago in Abilene. He made her go alone because he needed the boys around to help him with the blacksmithing. She was actually going to visit their graves. She had gotten word they had both been killed in a wagon accident, and she had inherited their home and belongings. She went up to sell everything and bring back a few precious mementos. Oscar doesn't know. He thinks they are still alive. She's afraid of what he will do to her if he ever finds out."

Riley shook his head. "How sad for her. She has not had an easy time of it. The law would be on his side if she tries to have something done about the abuse. Women don't have a plethora of rights, not even a miniscule amount when it comes to husband-

and-wife disputes, I'm afraid. Some men misinterpret submission. I fear Oscar is one of those. Does she have a plan?"

"Well, sort of. There was a lawyer in town about a week and a half ago, maybe a little more. He came to see Brian. Anyway, while he was here, he came over and talked with her. She's paying him to draw up partnership papers for us. If anything happens to her, the whole business and building will go to me and vice versa.

She thinks more likely it will go to me rather than to her. The lawyer said he would be back down soon to see Brian again and bring those documents with him. He will file them in Kerrville.

"We have also made a makeshift plan if Oscar beats her up again. Everything isn't settled yet. I know if she runs away, he will look upstairs first. So she can't come to me. Next, he will look at the hotel. So we were thinking maybe out at Josh and Katie's place. That was Esther's idea. We just don't know how to get her past the blacksmith's place without him seeing her. I would have to rent a wagon from him. We are really at a loss as to how to go about that. Do you have any ideas?"

"Well, I do have a small plan in mind. Let me ponder it and I'll get back with you."

"Thank you, Riley. I really fear for her life. She is such a new Christian. I pray God will deliver her as He has me from the shackles of bondage."

"Well, here we are, and it looks like the lamps were left on for you. What a kind thought."

Riley got down from the wagon and helped Erin down. He then escorted her to the door. She took out a key but the door wasn't locked. She looked at Riley, "I'm afraid."

"Would you like for me to go in and see if everything is all right?"

"I don't want to be out here by myself either."

"Let's go in together. You live upstairs. Surely, it would all right for me to escort you to your door."

"Well, all right. That sounds reasonable."

Together, they stepped into the large room filled with fabric and dresses. The smell of cotton and the burning oil lanterns filled the room.

"Marta? Are you here?" Erin called. There was no answer. They had just entered the back room when they heard the bell over the front door jingle. Erin's wide eyes jerked toward Riley.

"Get behind me and stay there."

Riley stepped out into the room. Brian stood just inside the door.

With relief, Riley looked at him. "Brian, you actually caused our hearts to beat at a greater velocity than normal. In fact, you scared us. The door was unlocked and the lamps were burning. Is something going on?"

"No, Marta came over when she was headed home. She said you all had gone out to Josh and Katie's for a 'big to-do,' as she put it, and asked me to keep an eye on the shop. She was going to leave it open and the lamps on so Erin wouldn't come back to a 'dark, scary place,' her words exactly. She wanted me to come over and make sure you made it in all right."

Relief was written all over Erin's face. "Oh, Brian, I was so afraid something had happened to her." Tears pooled in her eyes. She tried to blink them back and failed miserably.

"Why?"

"Oh, Sheriff, surely you know how Oscar beats her!" Erin almost wailed.

Riley wanted to put his arm around her so desperately. Instead, he offered her his handkerchief. Brian stared at them.

"Now, I talked with him about that, and he said he knew it was wrong, and he wouldn't do it anymore."

"Was that today?" Erin asked sarcastically.

Brian looked at her. "No, actually it was a couple of months ago.

"Well, Sheriff Daniels, she came in this morning with fresh bruises and a busted lip. I'd say he hasn't let up any since this is a normal occurrence. Almost as soon as the bruises and cuts heal, he gives her new ones. I don't think he was listening while you were talking." Erin's ire was obviously kindled. "You would have as much success talking to a drunk about not drinking and a...a...man who visits the upstairs of the saloon to give up his lusts. Do you think you would have much success? Well, do you? Did you even ask her about her lip?"

Both men stared at her in shocked silence. They had never seen a woman be so bold and brassy. Erin suddenly realized she had lost control and felt her face turn a very heated red. She covered her face with Riley's handkerchief, turned, and literally ran to the stairs leading to her apartment. They could hear the squeak of the stairs as she ascended.

"Well, I guess I've been told. What brought that on?"

"We have all had an emotional night. I guess she was just overwrought."

"What went on out at the Schmitts' ranch?"

"Well, Josh surprised Katie with a line shack out where the campsite for roundup was."

"That's emotional?"

"Well, this line shack could be classified as a small house. It has two bedrooms, a big room, a kitchen with a real water pump, stove and a fireplace, and then, a porch that goes around the house. He even built a bench out by the spring pond. She was beyond overjoyed."

The men turned out lamps and closed the door. "How are we going to lock this door?" Riley asked.

"I'll go by the Tuckers' place and let Marta know the door is unlocked. I'll word it so Oscar won't get upset, I hope. Maybe she will just give me the key, and I'll lock up and then take it back to her."

"Whatever you think is best, Brian. And, Brian, please don't hold any offense against Erin. She has been through so much.

She just knows talking doesn't do anything to stop the kind of abuse Marta is experiencing. I have a feeling Daisy is in much the same state. I don't think she will ever see the world as a kind place unless Jesus gets her in his hands and redeems her soul. Even then, she will still have those scars inside and out to remind her of the cruelty she suffered at the hands of men."

"I just don't understand what gets into men to cause them to do such horrible things to another human being. We are seeing way too much of that these days. It must be a result of the war."

"No, Brian, I just think we are more aware of it. I believe it has gone on since the beginning of time. Sin is sin. Cruelty to other humans began when Cain killed Abel. It didn't stop there. It just got worse."

"Riley, I'm going back to law school. I am going to become a lawyer. Maybe I can help in that way. I can't do much as a sheriff.

I have applied to the law school in Cincinnati, Ohio, and written for Johns Hopkins to send my records to them."

Riley sat down on one of the chairs outside of Marta's shop, his mouth agape. "When did you decide all that?"

"I've been praying about it. My friend who is a lawyer in

Kerrville came down, and we had a long talk. He said he would write a reference letter for me, if I needed it. This town needs a lawyer, Riley. We're growing, and I want to come back here and give more to the community than I can as a lawman. Todd will make a fine lawman, and Dan just moved his family here this week. The Rangers are going to let him make his home here and patrol this area. He will be able to cover more of the western territory from here than he could with his home in Waco. God's moving in a mighty way. I already have three years of school finished. I just need to finish up, pass the bar, and get myself back here."

"I don't know what to say. How does Willow feel about all this?"

"What does Willow have to do with it?"

"Brian, you cannot continue to deny the two of you are at least drawn to each other. She is the perfect woman for you."

"She is barely a woman if she is that."

"What are you saying? She's too young for you? In years, maybe it would be an unusual match, but her life experience and independence are just what you need. She is much older in common sense than anyone else with her years."

"Well, I need to see about that key." With that, Brian turned his back on Riley and started walking toward the Tucker place.

Riley bowed his head and prayed for Brian and Willow as well as Erin, Marta, and Oscar. The Lord had laid a heavy burden on his heart for this whole town. Again, the noise and tinny music from the saloon drifted down the street, and he began to pray for the lost souls inside. It didn't seem long before he heard footsteps on the boardwalk. Looking up, he saw Brian coming back alone.

"She gave me the key." He locked the door and started to leave. Riley just sat with his head bowed, praying for Brian. Brian stopped. He turned and slowly walked back to Riley. "Riley, I'm sorry. You're right, about so many things. I'll talk with her. I'll tell her my plans, soon. I promise."

Riley stood, walked out into the street, and looked up into the dark windows of Erin's apartment. He watched Brian's back as he made his way back to the Tuckers, and then he walked home. He would need all the sleep he could get. He felt completely drained.

29

October 1880

he brisk breeze fluttered through Willow's hair as she ran across the street with the letter clutched in her hand. Her heart beat with excitement as she let the screen door bang behind her.

"Esther! Adam!"

The lunch crowd had dissipated so she found them in the dining room drinking coffee and looking at some options for paint to use in the new small dining room. They were excited it was almost complete. Daisy came in and placed two slices of pie in front of them. The scars on her face were hardly noticeable now, and she continued to use the aloe on them as well as the others.

Her face beamed as she saw Willow come in.

"Miss Willow, would you like a piece of pie and some coffee?"

"No, thank you, Daisy. I'm too excited to eat anything. I received a letter today from Oberlin, and I haven't even opened it yet. I wanted Esther and Adam to be with me."

"Can I stay?" Daisy quietly asked.

"Of course, you can stay! Come, sit next to me." Willow smiled at the tenderhearted girl.

"Well, open it!" Adam said as he reached for her hand and squeezed it. He prayed a quick prayer, the one that never fails, "Thy will be done."

Everyone said, "Amen."

Willow tore open the envelope and began reading the contents aloud. When she got to the part that said, "You have been accepted to Oberlin School of Scientific Studies," hurrahs and congratulations echoed from the walls of the dining room. Rose came in to see what they were yelling about, and Daisy jumped up and down. Suddenly, she stopped jumping, and she blushed. She mumbled her apologies. "I'm sorry. I shouldn't have acted like a little girl. I'm trying to be more ladylike."

"You are doing just fine, Daisy. You have improved so much from when you first arrived. I am very proud of you," Esther said as she rose and hugged the young lady. "We are all excited and would have loved to feel free to jump up and down as well. We just feel too constrained by society's expectations, I fear."

Willow looked up at Daisy's smiling face. "How are the sewing lessons coming? I hear you are doing very well."

"Yes, ma'am, Miss Willow. I'm enjoying them very much, and Miss Erin is so patient with me. She even said maybe when I'm a bit older, I could learn to do the sewing machine. Mrs. Tucker just laughed. I'm not so sure she'll let me. I sure do enjoy the Bible studies Mr. Riley has with them after school on Wednesdays and Fridays. I didn't know the Bible had that much in it." Daisy looked around at the others staring at her. "Well, I guess I'd better get upstairs and do something to help. Can I change the linens in the family rooms or something? I need to earn my wages."

"Sweetheart, you are earning your wages. I tell you what. Our rooms do need to be dusted. Why don't you do that? When you are finished, you can go on over and learn some more sewing."

"Thank you, ma'am." Daisy even did a little curtsey before she turned and left the room.

"Now, where did she learn that? I have never told her to curtsey. Adam, remind me to ask her."

"Ask her what, Esther?"

"Weren't you listening? Oh, never mind."

"Of course, I was listening. Never mind what?"

"Oh, Adam. I think I like the light yellow for that room."

Although it does have windows on the south and west sides so maybe blue would be better," Esther said, looking pointedly at him.

Suddenly, Willow stood. "I have to go and tell Doc the news! I'll see you two later. Bye, Rose!"

"Bye, chile, don't get run over by some cowboy riding too fast through town. You're too excited to be payin' attention to what is goin' on 'round you."

"Love you too, Rose!"

They all laughed as she ran out the door.

She opened the door and ran right into Brian. He grabbed her upper arms and steadied the both of them hoping to prevent a fall. She felt like she had run into a brick wall.

"Oh, Brian. I am so sorry! I'm just so excited!"

"No harm done. Are you all right?"

"Yes."

"I've just received a letter of acceptance to Oberlin...Law School," they said at the same time.

"What?" again, they talked over each other.

"Ladies first." Brian indicated a seat on the bench outside on the boardwalk. They both sat down.

"I said I just received a letter of acceptance to Oberlin. I'm going to their School of Scientific Studies. I leave in June for entrance testing to see if I will be placed in the classical school or preparatory program."

Brian's shocked expression confused Willow.

"What's wrong, Brian? Are you not glad for me?"

"I'm very glad for you. I'm just astonished. I've received a letter of acceptance to the law school at the College of Cincinnati, as well. I am going to finish my law degree. They have accepted my courses from Johns Hopkins. I had been studying to be a lawyer prior to coming here. I had a falling out with my father and felt I needed to leave, to get away for a while. He wanted me to be a doctor and didn't understand why I 'persisted in the ridiculous profession of law.' He said I should be 'more interested in helping people than just making money.' He just couldn't see how being a lawyer could help anyone. Anyway, I could also leave in June. I would be happy to be your traveling companion and protector on the trip and while we are in Ohio. Even if we aren't in the same place, I will always be there for you, Willow."

"Brian, I just...I don't...why didn't you tell me before?"

"I didn't know if I would be accepted. I didn't want anyone thinking that I'd be leaving and then never leave. I wanted to be sure it was God's will before I announced the change."

"Who will keep the peace around here? What will Crystal Springs do without you?"

"I plan to talk with Todd about that. I think he will make an excellent lawman. He has something special about him. I'm pretty sure he plans to stay around here. He has been riding through town and heading south every chance he gets, these days."

"What do you mean?"

"Well, I think there's more than just scenery on the south road that has gotten his attention. I'd hate to say anything more. Just pay close attention when he comes to town or when he attends church. In fact, watch him this weekend at church. Riley's preaching again. I really love it when he preaches. He gets me right between the eyes every time. I will miss that while I'm away. I hope I can find a good church up there, within walking distance. It will be really cold there in the winter."

"Oh, I hadn't thought about that yet. I'll need some heavier winter clothes. I'll have to talk with Mom, I mean Esther, about that."

"It's okay to call her mom with me. I understand."

"Thank you. She has been more than a mother to Katie and me. I'm afraid I will get really homesick. Brian, I'm really glad you will be there. It will seem like we aren't so far from home if we are there together every now and then."

"How long is your course of study?"

"Four years if I'm placed in the classical program. Longer if I am in the preparatory program. Yours?"

"Well, I already have some under my belt, and they have accepted all of them. I will finish in a year and a half if I do well in the rest. Then I will stay and study for the bar exam. I'll take that, and if I pass, I will be a sure enough lawyer."

"So, you are from the East?"

"Yes, my family lives in Baltimore, Maryland. My father is a doctor. He treats the upper society and has a partnership in a hospital there. I'm his only son. I have three sisters. Needless to say, I'm a great disappointment to him."

"Brian, in a way, you are also an orphan. I had no idea. I'm so sorry. Do you ever hear from your sisters?"

"No, no one knows where I am."

"Where will you go after you become a lawyer?"

"Right back here. I will open an office right here in Crystal Springs. We need a lawyer here, and I may even become a judge one day. I think I would like that."

"I want to come back and be Doc's nurse. He has done so much for me. I even know Latin now, thanks, in part, to my lessons with Riley. We are working on writing it and more translation. In addition, he has also been teaching me Greek! That is one hard language to learn. Do you know about declensions? There are declensions for every word! Well, don't get me started on that. It makes my brain hurt!"

Brian laughed. He looked at Willow and saw in her a true maturity he had refused to see before. Not knowing he would be going to Ohio, she was willing to travel away from "home" and everything and everyone she knew in order to become a nurse. *In order to help others, she would willingly suffer loneliness. She certainly exhibits the selfless qualities I admire most in people. God certainly has coordinated these plans for our lives to coincide with each other. Perhaps, she is the one God has planned for me. I need to pray more diligently about that, especially now.*

"Well," Brian said as he slapped both hands against his thighs, "I want to tell Adam and Esther. You need to run on and tell Doc. His buggy's still down there, so he's in."

"Oh yes! I can't wait to let him know. Thank you, Brian. I am not nearly as apprehensive about going now that I know you will be going with me. Thank you so much."

"Don't thank me, thank God. He is the one who made all these arrangements. We will be studying some distance away from each other, but the train goes between the two, so it won't be too hard to visit. I'll come there. You don't need to be traveling alone."

"Yes, yes, you are right. Only God could work all this out. I'll see you later." With those words hanging in the air, she quickened her pace down the south steps and across the street to the next row of buildings, briskly walking past the general store and Marta's dress shop. She waved at Erin and Marta as she passed their window. They were busy, one measuring fabric and the other using the sewing machine. They both glanced up at the sound of hurried steps on the wooden walk and waved back.

Willow rushed into the office to find Doc McConnell to give him the good news.

Right after school, Riley hurried to the dress shop with books in hand. When he opened the door, he found Marta looking better than ever and Erin radiant serving tea to Marta and Daisy. He realized it was more than a break; it was a lesson in etiquette. He approached with a gentlemanly stride, bowed at the waist. "I beg your pardon, ladies. I don't mean to be rude, but would it be possible for me to join you in a cup of tea?"

"Why, certainly, sir. I shall go and bring another cup. In the meantime, let me pour you this one, and please, help yourself to the scones."

"No, no, I shall wait for you to return."

Erin gracefully hurried out of the room, her heart pounding like runaway horses in the wild. She was just fine until he entered the store. *Lord, why does he affect me in such a way?* She ascended the stairs to her apartment, retrieved the cup and saucer from the cabinet, and quickly, but carefully, went back down to the sitting area in the shop.

"Here we are. Now, Daisy, place the napkin on your lap this way. Hold the saucer in your left hand and lift the cup…no, no, by the little handle. That's right. Now, sip, don't gulp. Good!"

"Will I ever learn to be more ladylike?" Daisy asked forlornly.

"Where there is a will, there is a way. With God, all things are possible."

"Please, pass the scones," Riley said as he quickly lifted and lowered his eyebrows three times. All three ladies giggled. Daisy lifted the tray and held it out toward him. He picked one up and placed it on the little plate he had been given. Daisy began to place the plate of scones back on the table.

"Oh, wait, I believe I'll take just one more. You know, to save you the trouble of having to lift that terribly heavy thing again for me." That time, they all laughed. The lesson continued until they were quite satisfied with their afternoon tea. Erin was in her element. When she was a young girl, they always had afternoon tea whether her father was home or not. Her mother had taken great pains to teach her manners and proper etiquette. Those lessons had served her well in her survival in *the house*. She had been in demand by the more refined customers. Only that once had she suffered from the more brutal of the men who frequented that establishment. God had saved her from her bondage, and now she was passing on what she had learned from her mother to these two more unfortunate women, older and younger than she.

She felt blessed by God for the privilege of doing so.

The bell over the door jingled, and Mrs. Gruber began to walk in. She looked at the group gathered.

"Oh," she said as she pointedly looked at Daisy. "I'll come back some other time."

Erin quickly got up and excused herself. She reached the door before it closed completely behind Mrs. Gruber and stepped out, closing it behind herself. "Mrs. Gruber, wait. Please, do not be like this."

"Why…I don't know…what you mean."

"Mrs. Gruber, you made it more than evident that you did not want to be in the same room with Daisy. Your look told the story you couldn't hide. You felt soiled somehow being there with her."

"Well, you know what she did!"

"Yes, Mrs. Gruber, she walked to work."

"No, you know. She allowed those men to…well, you know… to—"

"Mrs. Gruber, there was no way she could have helped what happened to her. She had no control over that situation."

"My daughter would never have allowed that to happen to her!"

"Your daughter, although several years older than Daisy, is a scant inch taller than she and only about five pounds heavier. There is no way your daughter could have overpowered two grown, war-trained men intent on kidnapping her. How would she have ever gotten away from nine men intent on doing her harm? Daisy has been through so much in her life already. God would have us ease some of her grief. Your daughter still has both her parents, she still has a home, she has a very handsome male paying her some attention. Mrs. Gruber, please, be the Christian woman I know you are and please, please, come back inside and have some tea with us. How would you want others to treat your daughter if this situation involved her rather than Daisy?"

"My husband rode out with the posse and came back alive. I am thankful for that. He talked about how evil they were. I am so sorry, Erin, I don't think I ever even stopped to think about all of that. I think I'd just die if it really did happen to my beautiful Dorothea."

"Daisy has enough scars without anyone adding to them. She has physical scars and emotional scars. She is just now getting out in public. Let's not make her future cause her to wish she had died. God saved her life for a reason. Please come back in for tea.

When you look at her, I hope you will see your daughter and treat Daisy like you would want Dorothea treated."

"Oh yes, of course. I just don't know if I can do it. I'm just not sure."

"Well, Mrs. Gruber, why don't we just pray about it right now, right here?" With that, Erin took Mrs. Gruber's hand and began to pray. Mrs. Gruber stared at Erin and then lowered her eyes and began to feel tears form in her eyes.

After Erin's amen, Mrs. Gruber opened her eyes and stared at her again. "I don't think I have ever heard a woman pray like that. Where did you learn to talk with God like he…he's standing right here?"

"My mother prayed like that, and so did my dear daddy. I thought that was how everyone prayed."

"No, dear, not everyone prays like that. Most of the women I know, if they are asked to pray, they want to know ahead of time so they can write one out."

"There isn't anything wrong with writing out prayers, Mrs. Gruber. I just wish everyone could feel what I feel when I just talk to Jesus and our Father with the freedom to know they love me and just want me to talk with them. It doesn't have to be perfect, just sincere."

"I'm going to have to try that. And, Erin, please, just call me Roselinde."

"Are you sure, Mrs. Gruber? You are a very dear customer, and I feel I should show you more respect."

"Well, I appreciate your respect, but I would prefer your friendship."

"You certainly have that. If you would like to be Roselinde, then Roselinde it is."

Erin turned to go inside. She cracked the door and put one foot on the threshold and turned toward her new friend. "Coming, Roselinde?"

"Oh, I feel so embarrassed!"

"No need. Just be the noble woman I know you are. If you feel you need to apologize, then I would say God is directing you to do so. It is better not to put him off."

"Well, I guess you are right there. All right, I'll come in. Stay close to me, at least for a little bit, please. I need your strength."

"No, Roselinde, you need God's strength. Don't look to my strength to get you through. I will disappoint you. God is the only one we can depend on to be consistent, always there, always keeping his Word."

Roselinde took a deep breath and let it out. "Let's go then."

The two women walked into the shop. All eyes turned toward them with the exception of Daisy's. Daisy bowed her head and started taking fistfuls of her dress fabric and squeezing wrinkles into the skirt of her dress. Mrs. Gruber took one look, and her heart broke. She had caused this young woman pain, excruciating emotional pain. She could see her daughter standing there and would not want her to feel like that.

"I'm so sorry, Daisy. I am thoroughly ashamed of myself. Will you please forgive me? I would like to be your friend, please?"

Riley's eyes filled with tears. He never thought "the old battle axe," as some called her, would ever be this tender and sincerely repentant. He closed his eyes and said a quick prayer. Marta stood and put her arm around Daisy. She then looked at Mrs. Gruber.

"Mrs. Gruber, it was a terrible, mean thing you did. I can see you are truly sorry for doing it. It took a lotta guts to come back in here and say yer sorry. I would very much like to be your friend or were you just talkin' to Daisy?"

"Oh no, I meant you too, Marta." Roselinde was shocked at the change in Marta. She had always thought very little of Marta because everyone knew her husband beat her, so there had to be something wrong with her. Now, she saw a wonderful change. "How about it, Daisy? Will you forgive me? It was mean of me to leave and look at you, well, glare, if truth be told."

Daisy slowly raised her head. She looked at Mrs. Gruber through unshed tears. She tried to smile, but it was more of a quivering of lips rather than a smile. She turned her head just a bit to look at Erin. Erin nodded her head and smiled at Daisy in encouragement.

"I'm not sure what to say," Daisy almost whispered. "I reckon I forgive you. And I'd be pleased to get to know you better, and then we can see about the 'friend' part. You might change your mind."

"Well, I understand that, and I agree to your terms. I would like you to meet my daughter, Dorothea. Would you like that?"

"I don't know. I'm not so pretty now, never was. She probably would feel ashamed to be seen with me and laugh about me behind my back. I don't know her, but I understand she is just a little older than me."

"I think you would find her heart softer than mine. She hasn't had a chance to see much of the world and remains untouched by much of its meanness. I have seen too much, and it has rubbed off on me. I am so sorry. Please, please, forgive me."

"Already said I would."

"But I don't feel like you are feeling it from your heart; you just know that is what Marta and Erin would like to hear you say. I am willing to accept it as it is though and pray you will feel it in your heart someday."

Erin looked at them both and then at Marta. "Well, ladies, shall we have a little more tea? Riley, you may stay and have another scone." She laughed. Her laughter had the effect of new fallen snow on a hard, crusty ground. Soon, the blanket of camaraderie covered the room, and all were in good humor. The scar across Daisy's left cheek and down her chin and neck turned pink as she flushed from all the emotion. No one even seemed to notice, and for the first time, she felt like she just might be normal. Orphans rarely feel that way.

Riley stayed for a short while longer watching and admiring Erin from a distance. She was amazing. She had handled a very bad situation with the grace and kindness of a seasoned Christian. Had the years spent in bondage caused her to be drawn closer to God? He saw no self-pity in her.

"Ladies, I must run on about my business. I appreciate being included in your 'tea party' and would very much enjoy coming again should the time arise for such an occasion. If you will excuse me, I shall make my departure with sheer joy pouring from my bosom." Riley rose from his seat and made a quick bow from the waist, turned, and headed toward the door.

"Oh, Miss Kerr, if I may have a word with you, please?"

Erin stepped toward the door as he opened it, and he escorted her out to the walk in front of the store.

"I hope you don't mind me calling you out here like this. I just wanted to tell you how ardently I admire you. You showed such love in what could have been a terrible situation. You were kind and graceful to all involved. I would like to talk with you further on this if we could spend time, perhaps at supper, and talk?"

"Mr. Riley." She smiled her most genuine smile. "I would be delighted to take our next repast together...shall I cook or shall you?"

"Why don't we cook?"

"I am not opposed to sharing the duty, my place or yours?"

"I would very much like to eat at your place. That way we would be more in the public eye and not secreted away at my more remote dwelling."

"Oh, Riley! You are so funny. I accept your gracious offer and will expect you to bring the...what...for the meal?"

"I will bring my appetite!"

They both laughed. Erin looked at him, tilted her head as if in question. "About six?"

"Six it is!"

He turned and walked toward his home, and Erin reentered the shop.

Marta looked at her with a wrinkled brow. "Now, what did he want?"

"Oh, he just wanted to talk over some theological ideas we have been discussing, and he invited himself to supper."

Everyone laughed.

"We will be having supper upstairs around six, so help me out. What shall I prepare? I don't have a clue what he likes or even what I should serve. Mrs. Gru—I mean, Roselinde, what do you suggest?"

Roselinde looked at the watch she had hanging on a chain around her neck. "Well, missy, you don't have much time, perhaps some chicken would be best. You could fry up some and have some green beans to go with that and, of course, mashed potatoes. You probably have bread made."

"Well, no, I don't."

"Then make biscuits."

"I'll have to go to Breland's to get some chicken, I guess."

Roselinde waved her hand in the air. "No, you don't need a whole chicken. Just go over to the hotel and ask Esther. She will probably give you the pieces you need since she knows Riley better than we do. If you don't know how to fix it, ask her how."

"You don't think she would think I was being presumptuous, do you? I will offer to pay her for everything."

"She won't take it, but you can ask." Roselinde got up to leave.

"Ladies, this has been the best afternoon I have spent in many years. I hope I can come again."

"You are always welcome, Roselinde." Marta walked with her to the door.

Erin couldn't believe Esther! She had told Erin to come back later, and she would have everything she needed ready to take back. She had no idea Esther would have prepared food ready. Riley would be over in about thirty minutes. She would keep everything warm in the warming oven and get the table set. She paused for a moment and thanked God for the peace she felt about having Riley come to her home.

How strange since being kidnapped, I have not had the fear of being forced into having intimacy with a man gone from the very forefront of my mind. Yet tonight, I hadn't thought of it until just now, and not because of fear, but because of the peace I feel. I know for a certainty Riley would never force himself on me. Thank you, God, for healing some of my wounds. Thank you for bringing healing to Daisy. If it be your will, Lord, take the scars away or, at least, make them less noticeable. I thank you for the improvement in my voice. You are good, dear God. You are all I need.

The knock on her door made her jerk her head up. "Ouch! Why did I do that?" Erin rubbed her neck where a sharp pain shot up her head. She felt the tight knot and rubbed it as she made her way to the door.

"Who is it?" she asked as she put her hand on the knob.

"It's Riley, Raven. I mean Erin. Sorry."

She opened the door to the most beautiful single rose she had ever seen.

"I only had one left. I knew I had to share it." Riley looked at her. Her hand still rubbed her neck. "What's wrong?"

"Oh, Riley, I'm speechless, the rose is just beautiful. Please, come in. Nothing is wrong. I jerked my head up and caused a muscle knot to form. It will lessen shortly. Here, finish setting the table while I put this lovely gift in water."

Riley could see what else needed to be done. Erin placed the rose in a shallow bowl and put it in the center of the table. She then went to get the food out of the warming oven. The table was set; the food was on the table. Riley looked pleased; Erin's heart was soaring.

"Allow me to help you be seated," Riley said as he pulled out a chair. "This looks delicious!"

"I'm sure it is, um, since Esther and Rose cooked it." Erin lowered her eyes and smiled.

"But your hands placed it on the table. So I consider this as you serving me my supper."

Erin laughed merrily. "You say the nicest things, Riley, always willing to give more credit than what is due. Thank you for making me feel so good."

"Your voice seems to be less hoarse. Do you think the lemon drops are helping?"

"I don't know, I think it must be mostly God, but I am not willing to give them up yet. I may never do so!"

The conversation remained light while they ate. Erin served a final cup of coffee and asked, "Riley, do you think Dorothea will befriend Daisy?"

"I believe that Mrs. Gruber will encourage her to do so. The change in such a short time in Mrs. Gruber this afternoon was, should I say, shocking? She has been a busybody ever since she came. It is amazing her daughter isn't the same."

"Perhaps, she is of a different temperament. I have only seen her at church and briefly around town, always with her mother. I wonder, do you think she is lonely for someone of her own age?"

"That could very well be. Perhaps, this will turn into a friendship that will be beneficial to both parties."

The loud bang downstairs had them both on their feet in seconds.

"What was that?" Erin looked worried, her eyes large with fright.

"You stay here. I'll go down and look."

"Oh, do be careful, Riley. I couldn't bear for anything to happen to you."

"I'll be fine. You stay put. I'll protect you."

Erin had never had anyone say such a kind thing to her. She had been told she would be guarded, but never protected.

Riley cautiously walked down the stairs. Erin knew exactly where he was when she heard the step creak. Her heart pounding, she prayed for his safety.

"Erin! Come here quickly!"

She found it hard to move. Fright had her nailed in place, just as the nails held Jesus to the cross. He sacrificed for her. Surely, she could sacrifice for Riley.

"Erin!"

"Coming! I'm coming," she said as she hurried down the stairs.

30

O h no. Please, God, no! Riley, run get Doc. I'll sit right here with her."

Riley moved like lightning out the back door that now hung crazily, the doorjamb splintered and the lock broken.

Marta lay still as stone, her chest barely moving up and down.

Erin prayed without ceasing as she knelt beside her dear partner, so broken and bruised. Blood now marred the memory of the happy expressions on Marta's face from earlier in the day.

"Marta, it's Erin. Can you hear me? Please, please hold on.

Doc is on the way, and I'm sure God will keep you safe. Just trust him. He promised never to leave you or forsake you. He is the Great Physician. He can heal all our wounds. He even heals our hidden ones. I promise. I know it is true. He's healing mine."

"What happened here?" Doc's voice registered before Erin was even aware he was standing there.

"I don't know. Someone has kicked in the door, and here Marta lies. Whoever did it must have thrown her in here. We heard a noise, and Riley came down to investigate. I was too afraid. What can I do to help?"

"Pray! Someone go over to the hotel and get Willow. She is staying over there tonight, thank God. Hurry!"

"I'll go," Riley said as he started running down the back alley in the opposite direction from Doc's place.

"Who could have done this?" Erin asked even when, in her heart, she felt she knew the answer.

"I think there's only one person who would do this. Perhaps you should go and get Brian although there is no law against a man beating his wife."

"My heart is breaking. I'll go. I just hate to leave her. I wish I could exchange places with her and take at least some of her pain."

"I need help getting her to my office. That and prayer will help her most now."

"I'll go."

Erin left the lighted lamp with Doc and made her way to the other lamp across the storage room. Her hands trembled so much she wasn't sure she would be able to light it. She managed at last! Hurrying to the front door, she bumped into the corner of the cutting table. "Ouch!" *I'll have a nice bruise myself.* As she unlocked the front door, she heard voices in the back. She fought the urge to return as she opened the door and practically ran to Brian's office. The light was on, and the door was ajar.

"Sheriff, are you here?" she asked as she rushed into the office.

"I'm back here. Just a minute."

"Doc, needs you quickly."

Brianimmergedfromthebackcarryingablanket.

"What's happened?"

"It's Marta. She's in a bad way. He needs to get her to his office and needs help."

Brian dropped the blanket and scowled in the direction of the cells. "Well, Oscar can do without a blanket for right now."

He walked briskly toward her, took her arm, and led her out of the office, closing the door behind him. He practically pulled her with him.

"It's a good thing I'm tall," she mumbled under her breath.

"What did you say?" asked Brian

"Nothing."

At the front door of the shop, Brian took the lamp from her, led the way in, and quickly disappeared into the storage room.

"Ouch! Well, I'll have a matching set of bruises. Marta, I pray this will take some of your pain away. I said I wanted some of it," she said to herself.

Before she could get to the back, Brian was back with the light. "Where are they?"

"They were here when Doc sent me to get you. As I opened the front door, I heard voices. He had sent for Willow. Maybe Adam and Esther came as well."

"Let's go to his office. I want to know more about this."

"Well, whoever did this kicked in the back door, and it looked like just threw her in."

"Lord, keep me from killing him."

"Do you think it was Oscar?"

"I know it was. I have him locked up right now. He may never get that blanket."

"What did he do? Turn himself in?"

"No, he almost killed one of the girls down at the saloon.

He already had blood on him when he went in there. She didn't want to go with him, but her boss made her. I won't go into the details. Some of the men at the saloon heard her screams and went up to help. They were going to take her to Doc. He will have a busy night."

"God, help Oscar. He needs you so much. Open his eyes."

"I find it harder and harder to pray for some of my prisoners.

I'm afraid I'm becoming calloused. Maybe the next sheriff will be better at not letting all this evil eat away at his soul. I have to pray constantly for the love of Christ to flow through me."

"Here we are. It does look busy." Erin looked in and saw only one empty seat.

"Here, ma'am. You can sit here."

The man sounded innocent enough, but his eyes told an entirely different story.

"Thank you, I'll just see if Doc needs me," she responded.

Brian knocked on the door. Adam opened it.

"Thank goodness you're here. Come in both of you." Brian and Erin entered Doc's examining room.

"Esther and I need to get back over to the hotel. Things are really hopping over there tonight. You'd think it was mating time in a rabbit warren. Daisy is doing better, but she still doesn't feel comfortable waiting tables, and Willow is needed here. So we need to get back."

He and Esther made their way out of Doc's, the sound of their steps diminishing down the boardwalk.

"Erin, go back into the recovery, please, and sit with Sarah Jane. She needs a woman's understanding right now. I need Willow here to help with Marta's injuries."

"Will Marta be all right? Doc, I need to know, please?"

"It will depend on her. I think she will make a full recovery if she wants to. One of her arms is broken. The other was dislocated.

She won't be sewing for a good while."

"I'll manage that, but she can't stay at home. She needs someone to care for her."

"We'll figure that out later."

"Thank you for telling me. Please direct me to your recovery room."

"I'll show you," Riley said.

"Oh, Riley, I'm so sorry I didn't even acknowledge your presence." Erin smiled.

"Thank you," Doc said with a quick nod.

"This way."

Before they entered the room, Riley turned to her. "Erin, God has sent you here for this very purpose. You are the only one who can reach this girl. She needs you, and I do mean *you*, right now.

Let God lead you in what you say, but you may have to tell your story. Her injuries aren't as severe as Marta's, but this one may not have the will to live, if you can't reach her."

"Oh, Riley, is she one of the saloon girls? I guess I wasn't really listening when Brian was talking to me about Oscar. Now, it all makes sense to me. Pray with me before I go in."

The two bowed their heads, and Riley led in prayer for God to lead, direct, and use Erin in this very difficult situation. "Lord, please give her the strength she is going to need to face her own demons. Satan, right now, is laughing, thinking he has a victory here. Help us in our weakness to be strong and overcome the evil one. Help us to show these broken hearts they can be healed through your love and your healing power. In Jesus' name, amen."

"Thank you, Riley." Erin took a deep breath, lightly tapped on the door. She opened it, stepped into the room, and then closed the door behind her.

A young woman lay on the bed, the once-white sheets now stained with red. Erin caught her breath and exhaled slowly and quietly walked over to the bed. "Hello, Sarah Jane. I'm Erin. I thought you might like some company while you had to wait for the doctor to finish with his first patient. Are you in quite a bit of pain? Is there anything I can get for you or help you with?"

"What are you, some sort of do-gooder? You wouldn't even come through the door if you really knew who I am."

"You are Sarah Jane. You are a prostitute. And Sarah Jane, that makes no difference to me because, you see, I was where you are before I escaped the evil that held me. I'm here because I believe God has sent me to you in your time of great need. He wants to show His love for you just as He did for me. Will you allow me to help you? I have an idea of what Oscar did to you. It was done to me. The man, the customer who brutalized me, was intent on killing me. He choked me and damaged my vocal cords, so I sound hoarse even to this day."

Sarah Jane opened her eyes and turned her head to look at Erin. "Ain't you that sewin' woman?"

"Yes, I am."

"If you're tellin' the truth, how come all those people still come to your shop?"

"I didn't work here. You see, I was kidnapped and forced into prostitution when I was sixteen. I worked for eight years and finally was able to escape. So far, my former 'employer' hasn't found me."

"When he does, there'll be hell to pay. You'll never be able to get completely away."

"I believe I will. I believe you can too. Do you want to go back?"

"What? To that mess? Smell whiskey breath, sweat, and all the rest? No, but I don't know anything else. I woulda done somethin' else…if I had known how. My pa was a mean 'un. He was the first to do me. Then my brothers took over. They used to brag about it to the rest of the men folk, so then my uncle got in the act. I got tired of it, and Ma wouldn't do nothin'. She said there was nothin' she could do, so she told me to run away. I did." Sarah Jane moved painfully in the bed. "Now, I just do it with anybody who can pay the price. 'Course, I don't get the money. That rat that runs the saloon takes all of it. He says he feeds us and gives us a bedroom all our own. We don't even have to share with anyone else, except the customer. Now, ain't that a fine thing? He didn't even come up there tonight to help me. If some of the other men hadna come, I probably would be dead. Oscar worked me over pretty good. I think he was tired, though. He had been in a fight or somethin'. He had blood all over his clothes."

"Yes, he came there after beating his wife nearly to death. She is the one the Doc is working on right now. Do you really want to go back to that?"

"Hell no! But what am I supposed to do? I don't have any money! All I have is my body. 'Sides no self-respecting person would hire me even to clean the slop jars."

"I would. And I know someone else who would. In fact, I know several people who would do that. Tell me, what is it you would like to do?"

"Besides doin' nothin', I guess I need to learn to cook, clean, and sew. I don't think I have a prayer without those."

"Do you know Esther Schmitt?"

"I don't believe I've had the pleasure." Sarah's tone was mocking.

"Are you in pain? Could I get you some water? Perhaps, another blanket? Truly, you don't seem to be yourself."

"Are you making fun of me?"

"No, but I do know you have learned to be polite to people and talk sweet talk. So, I know you must be in pain to let your tone slip like that."

"Oh, maybe you was a 'lady of the night.' You know Oscar was kinda a regular of mine, but I had never seen him like this. He came in all bloody and walked right up to me, grabbed me around the waist, and pulled me so tight against him I almost lost my breath. Then he grabbed my jaw and forced a really hard kiss on me. I might have fainted for lack of breath if the boss hadna told him to take it upstairs. Well, he picked me up and started up the stairs. The boss hollered at me to start taking my dress off so he wouldn't rip it. He said if he did it would come out of my pay, and he laughed. Well, I knew what that meant...he is my pay. None of the girls want to go to his bed, believe me. Well, Oscar took that as permission to rip the dress. So as soon as he put me down, he started pullin' on it. Look what he did to me."

Sarah Jane threw back the covers and showed Erin her many bite and scratch wounds. Bruises were everywhere.

"He slapped me once, busted my lip, then I guess he thought twice about that. The boss don't want his girls looks messed with, so he quit."

"We need to get some aloe on those bites and scratches."

"Why are you so nice to me? Most women wouldn't want to even talk to me. They'd look at this and tell me it was what I deserved."

"Like I said, I've been there. No one was there for me except for God. You see, I believed in Him as a child and growing up I read and studied God's Word, the Bible. I knew he would never leave me or forsake me. It was through his strength I made it through my bondage and into freedom."

"Yeah, well, I ain't ever known him so he don't care a bit about me."

"Sarah Jane, 'For God so loved the world that he gave his only begotten son, that whosoever believeth in him should not perish but have everlasting life.' That is in John, a book in the Bible. It is divided into chapters and verses. That verse can be found in John, the third chapter, and it's the sixteenth verse. You see, we are all sinners. None of us is perfect. God doesn't care how *bad* our sin is. He is more interested in the condition of our heart. If he calls us to come to him, we must respond. For me, it was irresistible grace. How could I turn away from a love so strong and so big that it provided a way for my sins to be covered over? The penalty for that sin, which is death, was paid by God's perfect son, Jesus.

He took my place on the cross, suffering cruelty worse than you or I have suffered, and he died in my place. He died in your place as well.

"Sarah Jane, think about this. If someone walked into that saloon and paid the boss far more than you are worth just to take you with Him, would you go? If He told you he loved you and wanted you to be his bride? Would you go? If he wanted to get you out of that horrible bondage you are in and set you free, would you go? If He promised to dress you in white robes, not those horrible immodest red things we've been given to wear, would you go? If He never asked you to do anything for these things, it was all a free gift, would you go?"

"H...heck yeah! A gal would be stupid not to go."

"That is what that verse means. He is asking you to become his bride, take the free gift of salvation, and be cleansed from all your sin, washed whiter than snow through the blood sacrificed by His only son, Jesus. All you need to say is yes. Pray to Him to give you that gift, and He will do it. You don't have to pay him anything for it. If you did, then it wouldn't be a gift."

"How do you talk to someone who ain't even here?"

"Oh, but He is here, right here in this room. He is waiting to come into your heart. He is already in mine, and He wants to be in yours too. He won't come to you uninvited. He never forces himself on anyone. It's just like opening your door and seeing someone standing there. You have two choices. You can say, 'C'mon in,' or say, 'Go away. I don't want you here.'"

Erin sat down on a chair she pulled close to the bed and leaned forward. "Listen closely, Sarah Jane. When Jesus knocks and you open that door, your eyes behold the one who loves you, even in all of your sin, more than anyone ever could. In fact, He loves you so much He died for you, then came back to life, desiring to live with you forever. Who could turn down that promise?"

"I ain't never prayed before. I don't even know how. So, I guess I'm outta luck. How do ya do that?"

"Have you been talking with me?"

"Yeah." Sarah Jane looked at Erin with the look of stupid question in her eyes.

"You do the same thing with him. Talk to Him just like he is sitting on the end of your bed."

Sarah Jane quickly pulled the covers back over her. She looked shocked.

"You reckon He saw me?"

"He has seen everything you have ever done and heard everything you have ever said. He has even heard what you have thought. He knows how many hairs you have on your head. And, Sarah Jane, He *loves* you."

"Ain't nobody ever loved me. Not even my ma."

"God does. He is waiting to hear your answer. Do you want me to leave the room? Would that be better?"

"No! Don't leave me alone with Him."

Erin almost laughed. "Sarah Jane, yes, He is the righteous and just God, but He is also the loving and caring God. You have nothing to fear."

"Just thinking He's here scares the h—oops, sorry—dickens outta me. Do you think He knows what I was gonna say?"

"Yes, He knows. He loves you, Sarah Jane. Can you even begin to believe that? I know you say no one has ever loved you, but God has loved you even before you were born. He knew you and loved you then. Will you talk to him?"

"I want to. I's scared to. I don't want to wait, but I don't want to start neither."

"Sarah Jane, every ending is a new beginning. That is my gift to you. I promise He will make the old things pass away and make everything new. Your heart will be changed if you want it to be. If you want to become a new creature, you will. Remember,

I had to leave the old life behind. I'm not looking back. I won't go back there. I have a new life. God has blessed me so much. I want you to meet a dear friend of mine. He is like an uncle to me."

"I know all about uncles."

"Not that kind. He has taken care of me and provided for me like I was his daughter. He was my father's very close friend. My father was a ship captain and was lost at sea. My mother died of a fever, and on that very day, I was kidnapped and forced to work in a house of prostitution. God's Word kept me going. I knew he would deliver me one day. It took eight years, but it did happen.

Now, that day for you may be today. Will you take it?"

"Let me think on it."

"That's fine. Would you like some tea? I'll go and make some."

"That does sound good. Could you check and see how soon the doc can get to me. I don't want the boss to come lookin' for me to come back to work."

"I'll check," Erin said, biting her lip, trying not to laugh at the idea of her going back to work in her condition. Clearly, Oscar had forced himself on her.

She stepped into the hall and saw no one. Voices could be heard coming from the surgery so they were no longer in the examining room. The door had a sign Do Not Enter on it. Erin turned the other way to see if she could find a kitchen or something. She found a stove that was hot with a pot of water simmering on the top. A kettle was nearby.

I wonder where the well is. I don't want to use their hot water if they need it for the surgery. Maybe I should just run over to the hotel and get some tea and, maybe, some sandwiches or something. She went back to the waiting room, which was now empty. *That's a relief.* She saw her lamp still lit and sitting on a table near the front door. *Thank you, Lord.* She stepped out into the night. *Oh my, it has gotten chilly. I should have gotten a wrap. Well, never mind now. Wait, I pass right by the shop. I can grab one.* She entered the shop, which was still unlocked. *That was careless of me.* She grabbed a shawl that was draped over the back of the settee. *I don't even remember what I did with the key.* She touched the doorknob to go back out and felt the key still in the keyhole. She gave a sigh of relief. *Thank you, Lord. Take care of everything, please. I'm not thinking straight and am in such an emotional mess right now, I need your help.* She went back outside and locked the door and then quickly made her way to the hotel.

She entered the lobby, greeting Adam who stood behind the desk.

"What do you need, Erin?"

"Well, I don't know where anything is at Doc's, and Sarah Jane could use a cup of tea. I thought maybe a few sandwiches would be in order too. I don't know. In time of stress, we either get hungry or lose our appetites. What do you think, Adam?"

"Well, I'd say, everyone could use a cup of tea or some coffee.

Doc's coffee isn't the best, but it's not the worst, either. I doubt he has any made or has time right now to make it. Let me see what we still have in the kitchen. The dining room is almost empty. Just one man is still in there."

"I'll wait right here." "Right."

Erin sat down in one of the red velvet chairs next to a lovely table. On it, she saw Adam had placed a Bible. *How wonderful!* She lifted it and began reading the Psalms.

"Erin? Is that you?"

Erin looked up and jumped from her seat. She ran, threw her arms around Captain McBride, and began to sob into his chest.

"What's wrong? What is going on?"

"Nothing. Nothing. It is just so good to see you! Why didn't you tell me you were coming? I thought you were going to be here in November." Erin tried to dry her eyes, but the tears just kept coming.

"But, my dear, it is November, November 1, as a matter of fact."

"Oh, you!" Erin playfully swatted his chest. She stepped back and looked up into his very kind and loving eyes. "Oh, how I have missed you. I have had a very trying and emotional night, Captain. I could use your very helpful advice. We need to talk. I fear it will have to wait until tomorrow since I am on a mission right now."

"In God's time. We'll wait on his direction. I talked with Sarah. She loves you so and has enjoyed your letters. She wanted to come, but it just wasn't the right time. She could use some help, I believe, if you ever decide to change your scenery. In the interim she had me bring this." He held up the cane.

"Oh! My cane!" Erin dabbed at her eyes. "No, my dear Captain, I fear I have lost my heart to Crystal Springs. God clearly has me here for a reason."

"Oh, I didn't know you two knew each other," Adam said, a little bit of concern in his voice.

"Oh, Adam! This is a dear family friend, Captain McBride.

He is like an uncle to me. Captain McBride, I'd like to introduce Adam Schmitt, the owner of this wonderful establishment and a brother in Christ."

"Yes, we met when he registered, but that was about it. You are most welcome, Captain McBride. May I ask what you are a captain of?"

"I'm a ship's captain. Erin's father and I were close friends. He had his own ship as well. I tried to find her after her parents died, but God did not allow that until eight years after her mother went home to glory. I helped Erin journey here and promised to come and visit. So, here I am."

"Again, sir, you are very welcome here, and I hope you will stay as long as you can. Here are some things you asked for, Erin. I hope you won't think I'm being too bold, but I sent for Curtis to board up your back door. You won't be able to get in that way, but at least, it isn't wide open."

Captain McBride's brow wrinkled with his frown. "I believe I will walk with you. Where are you going?"

"I'm taking these things to Doc's. I believe they will be needed."

Erin turned and picked up the lamp she still had. Captain McBride took the tray from Adam, and they walked on down the steps to the road. "It's just down this way a bit." Erin talked incessantly, giving McBride a rundown on every character behind every door they passed and trying to tell him about what had happened earlier in the evening. The more she talked, the more an idea began to form in his mind. They entered Doc's. Riley sat alone in the waiting room.

"Riley, I would love to introduce you to my uncle of sorts, Captain McBride," she said as she took the tray from McBride.

Riley jumped up. "Sir, you do not know what a pleasure it is to finally meet you." Riley grabbed McBride's hand and began to pump it like it was the handle to a pump that needed priming.

"Erin has told me all about you. I want to thank you from the bottom of my heart for being an instrument of God and willing to do his will, protecting Erin and seeing to her needs. I thank God for you every night in my prayers. Now, I am able to thank you in person. What a blessing!"

Suddenly, Riley let go of McBride's hand, clasped his hands together, bowed his head, and began praying. "Thank you, Lord, for the many blessings you have poured down upon us in this one night, a night so full of terror and hardship. You are the Almighty God, Prince of Peace, and Savior to all. You are our Provider, Protector, and Planner of our lives. May we be found faithful. In your Son's name we pray, amen."

Erin smiled and headed toward the room with the stove. "I'll just put these back here. I'll be back in a moment."

"So, are you the minister?"

"No, no, or yes, no. You see, we don't have a minister. A circuit-riding preacher comes through infrequently. I am the schoolmaster. I have established an academy here. The men, who are willing to, take turns preaching on Sundays. It seems I get more than my fair share of the privilege, and I find myself counseling and praying with, as well as for, people here and there throughout our quaint little village although now it is more of a bustling town. I am having more and more call me to come and see someone who is sick and, even on two occasions, to pray with someone who was dying. Then I held the service for their burial. So, it seems I am kind of their minister, just not officially. Perhaps we will be able to hire someone in the not-too-distant future. We have just acquired a new family from up near Austin, a Texas Ranger and his wife and daughter. He's gone much of the time, so this makes a nice place for his family. Little by little, we are growing. In fact, I know a certain young lady who would love to have you closer and see you more often."

McBride laughed a hardy laugh. "I see now why you are the one they call on to preach. You have plenty of words! I'm not complaining. I'm just amazed! You seemed so quiet and subdued when I first walked in."

"Usually when I am sitting in that posture, it is because I am praying, which I was doing, when you walked in."

"I see. So you are a man who prays continually, it appears."

"Yes, sir, I seem to do that. Even while I am teaching my students, I shoot 'arrow prayers,' as I call them, to *my* Rabbi. We are all in need of instruction, are we not?"

"It would seem so. Where do you live, Mr. Riley? I believe I would very much like to visit with you while I am here."

"I live at the end of this boardwalk and a little beyond it. You can't miss it. The church is near my school. I have a rather large yard. I wanted to provide plenty of play area for my students. I have a small dormitory behind the school, but none of my present students stay over. They all come and go from home. I'm hoping to have boarding students soon. Word we have a place for children to stay needs to spread to the ranchers who live farther out. Perhaps even some of the students from communities that don't have a school will take advantage of the situation here. I believe God has called me to provide this opportunity for the children of the Hill Country."

"I see. Well, I will have to allow plenty of time for our visit. We may still not have time to finish our conversation."

"What conversation? What are you two cooking up?" Erin asked as she heard the last of what McBride had said.

"Oh, now, I was just poking fun at Mr. Riley here. It seems he has a gift of language and conversation," McBride said laughingly.

"Oh yes, isn't it grand! We have had the best of times just talking. I don't think we could ever tire of visiting with one another.

We took a picnic out to Crystal Springs River and didn't stop talking the whole time. It is a lovely area. You should go and see it. Riley must tell you his dream about that place. It in itself has a healing quality."

McBride looked at Erin, studying her expression, and he realized she was not looking at him but directly at Mr. Riley and he, at her. He suddenly realized there was much more going on here than just friendship. *Oh yes, Mr. Riley, I certainly will be visiting you!*

31

hree days had passed. Everything was set. Michael came in for supplies and left. Not a soul realized that part of what he had loaded on his wagon was Marta. Even Mr. Breland didn't realize it.

Sarah Jane had also disappeared. She had left one night after Katie and Josh had come to town to visit with Esther and Adam.

Curtis had completely repaired the back door of Erin's shop as people called it. She had decided to find a name for it so that would stop. She would ask Marta about that. Since she couldn't see Marta soon, she would let people call it what they wanted.

Captain McBride walked past the shop and decided to stop in. Erin was in the middle of another etiquette lesson with Daisy.

"Oh, please, stay and have tea and scones with us. Daisy is becoming quite the little hostess. Daisy, I would like to introduce my uncle, Captain McBride. Captain McBride, this is Daisy Schmitt." Daisy looked at her with wide eyes.

"Oh no, ma'am. I'm not a Schmitt.

"Well, what is your last name then?"

"I don't know. They didn't give any of us one at the orphanage. I don't know who my folks were. I guess I don't have a last name."

"Well, then for today, it is Schmitt."

"Do you take sugar in your tea, sir?" Daisy asked tentatively yet with a slight smile. *I have a last name, at least for today.* Her heart felt a tad less broken and bruised.

"Aye, I do. Make it three lumps, if you please."

"We don't have lumps, Captain, just teaspoons," Erin said with a bright smile and a little laugh.

"Well then, three teaspoons!"

"That will be syrup!" Erin laughed in earnest.

"I like it like that."

"Very well, three teaspoons, Daisy. And now, Captain, where were you headed? I saw you pass, then change direction, and come back. Did you forget where the shop is?"

"No, I was headed to have another very nice chat with Mr. Riley. Since it is still a little early though, I thought I would stop in and see you, my dear, and then move on to his humble abode, which is quite nice, by the way. I especially like the curtains and other linens he can't stop talking about."

Erin giggled. "How you do go on? I know he doesn't talk about those curtains."

"I beg your pardon, but upon my very first visit with him, I got the tour of all your handiwork. I even had to feel them. I must say I was impressed. You did a lovely job on them, and I am very impressed with this little shop."

"It is Marta's and, well, mine too. All right, enough of that talk. Let's have a conversation in which Daisy may have a fair share."

McBride sat in the rocker on the front porch of Riley's house. He watched the children run from the school. *Not many children here.*

"Mr. Riley, where are all the children?"

"Oh, McBride, good to see you. This is our harvest break. I have only a few students here during this time. We are doing an intense six-week study while the other children help with the harvest and postharvest duties at home. Instead of letting the others who don't live on farms lose time at school, I have developed a special course that fits right into six weeks. We are only studying one thing during this time and are spending the whole time on it."

"So, what are you studying?"

"Greek."

"Greek! Why, whatever for?"

"Truthfully, because it helps me remember it. I am taking classes to become an ordained minister so I can perform marriages and baptize those who come to Christ and also so we can have communion more than every so often when the circuit rider comes through. We don't even know when he will be here. He hasn't been here in quite some time. He just shows up. As it is, if someone wants to get married, they have to be ready at the drop of a hat when he rides in."

"Speaking of marriage, I believe there is something you want to talk to me about. Am I wrong?" McBride asked.

"No, sir, you are not wrong. I feel I must tell you about myself. Erin knows…as do our closest friends."

As evening darkened, Riley opened his heart to Captain McBride. He told him the whole story just as he had to the group gathered at the line shack. McBride rocked and listened. As he finished, Riley told of his dream the morning of the day Erin arrived. He told the older man about the ride back from the party and how Erin had poured out her heart and soul to him and revealed her story.

"She is the daughter of my heart. You realize that, don't you?"

"Yes, sir, I do indeed. I believe you have become a father figure to her as well. Sir, I love her with an everlasting love that cannot be overcome. She is my Raven. She is healing my hunger and thirst for loving Christian companionship and I, in turn, am being used by God to heal those hidden wounds within her. I would be so thankful if you would grant me permission at the right time to ask Erin Raven Kerr to be my wife."

"Riley, I don't think I could part with her to anyone who did not love her for who she is rather than for her beauty. For beauty fades, and age makes life richer. The longer two people love and cherish each other, the better their relationship is and truly the more beautiful they become inside. I remember my dearest Catherine. She was the most beautiful woman in the world. God took her from me, but I will see her again. I am blessed to have Erin. Even though she isn't my own daughter, she is like one to me. Catherine and I never had any children. I don't know why. That was in God's plan, and that is all I need to know. If you can love Erin, knowing all she has been through and leaving it behind, starting fresh, then you are truly a man of God. I would trust her to your care. So help me if I ever hear of any meanness toward her from you, like bringing up her past and using it against her, I'll have you keelhauled! With that said, I give you my blessing because, Mr. Riley, I don't believe you would ever do such a thing."

"Sir, do you want to talk with Erin and see how she feels about all of this?"

"I might, but I don't think it's necessary. I've seen the way she looks at you. I've seen how she lights up when you walk in, how she delights in your every word…and there are plenty of them. No, I think her heart is yours. Just don't break it."

"I know she'll want you to be at the wedding. When do you have to leave? How long can you stay?"

"Well, now, that is something I need to think on. I may need to borrow her for a week or so. I want to take her to Houston and then we can come back. Can you do without her for a little while?"

"I won't like it. What's more important is can the shop do without her? With Marta gone, and Christmas coming, she's very busy right now."

"You do have a point. Well, let's see. I'll give it some more thought and talk with you again. Right now, I need to go get something to eat and visit with Erin. I believe I'll take her to eat at the hotel. Would you like to join us, Riley?"

"Yes, sir!"

"Well, come along then!"

32

At the K & J line shack

Ma, how're you doin'?" Wade asked as he helped her sit up in bed.

"I can at least talk now. I thought there fer a while, I'd have to learn sign language. I don't know if I could get used ta doing those funny little signs."

"Cade's got some good smellin' soup cookin' out in the kitchen. Do you feel like gettin' up?"

"I don't rightly know 'til I try. I'm pretty sore. It would prob'ly do me good ta try."

"Well, let's give her a try then. Here, I'll hep ya."

"Ooh my goodness, that hurts. I made it tho'."

"You're a tough one, Ma."

"It does feel good to be on my two feet. Hold on to my left arm. It feels better every day. I guess your pa thought he'd broken it, too. I thank God it was just out of joint. It looked broken, I guess. At least I can use it. Too bad I'm right-handed."

"Ma, sometimes I just want to kill Pa. I hate what he does to you and what he used to do to us."

"Now, Wade, and you too, Cade, we have to pray for your pa's soul. He needs to get right with God. I tried to tell him that, and that's what got me this beatin'. Just think of what Jesus suffered at the hands of those who hated him. What else can I expect?

Yer pa doesn't know Jesus, and he says he can't stand to hear that name. He wasn't striking out at me as much as he was at Jesus. I can bear the pain when I realize how much Jesus bore for me. Ya see? He was trying to kill Jesus all over again. It jest can't be done. Now, you boys need to git right with God. You never have asked him into yer heart. Ya gotta do it. It makes all the dif'rence in tha world." With that, Marta sat down in the chair by the table. "Whoa, that tuckered me right out."

"You shouldna talked so much, Ma," Cade said with sincere concern.

"Twern't the talkin', 'twas the walkin' that tuckered me out. I done gone lost some of my strength."

"Gettin' beat up will sure do it." Wade said. Cade elbowed him in the ribs. "Quit it out, Cade."

"Then don't be so stupid!"

Wade turned and glared at his brother. Marta just shook her head.

"You boys better listen to what I say. It's the best thing I ever done."

They heard a wagon coming up to the shack. Cade walked to the front door and looked out. "It's Mrs. Katie. She's got someone with her." He opened the door and watched from behind the screen door.

"Hello, Cade. How are you? Is everything fine here?" Katie said as she walked up the steps.

"Yes, ma'am. You sure are welcome to come in."

With that, he swung the screen door open. "Wow, it's gotten colder out. Best hurry in."

"Cade, I want you to meet Daisy Schmitt. She is another orphan adopted by Esther and Adam, so she's a new sister. Daisy, this is Cade, and his twin is Wade."

The two women slipped into the cabin. "Oh, Marta, you're up! How wonderful!"

Marta slowly rose from the chair. "It is pure pleasure to see you, Katie. That dress looks right nice on you. And, Daisy, you look so good too. I am so thankful to see you."

Katie looked around and smiled. "Oh, that soup smells so good. You have a nice fire going here in the fireplace too. It's so cozy. I hope you feel at home here."

"Yes, ma'am. We sure do appreciate you allowing us to stay here with Ma."

"Mrs. Katie, do you hear any news from town? Ma's wonderin' about the shop."

Katie helped Marta sit back down.

"Well, things are going well at the shop. In fact, Daisy's been helping out some with sewing on buttons and such. Haven't you, Daisy?"

Katie looked at Daisy who was standing near the fire looking straight at Wade. Katie looked at Wade. He was staring back at Daisy.

"Daisy?" Katie said a little louder.

"Um, sorry, what did you say?"

"I was telling them about you helping at the shop."

"Oh yes. I'm really liking learning to sew. It's a fine thing to do. I brought some dresses out for Sarah Jane. I think she will like them."

"Sarah Jane? Who's Sarah Jane?" Cade asked.

"She's living with Josh and me while she recovers from the beating your pa gave her the same night he beat up your ma."

"Why would he do that? Has Pa gone crazy in the head?" the boys said together. Marta shook her head.

"I reckon she's a workin' gal. He frequented the saloon. He was so keyed up he didn't get it out of his system before he went over there. I'm sorry she received the end of my beating."

"Some of the men customers came to her aid. The owner didn't even lift a finger to help," Katie said as she shook her head. "Why is the world so mean? There is no call for it to be like that." Tears began to pool in her eyes.

"What's Pa doing now?"

"I'm sorry, but he's in jail. Sarah Jane has pressed charges against him. It seems that a woman not married to a man has more rights than the man's wife. I'm sorry, Marta, but it seems the only way Oscar can be held accountable for what he did to you is if he had killed you. That doesn't make any sense to me."

"You won't ever have to worry about that with your husband. He worships the ground you walk on." Marta took Katie's hand and patted it and smiled up at her. "Your marriage is what a marriage is supposed to be like.

"Why didn't you bring her out here with you? I'd like to meet her," Marta said.

"Well, Marta, I think she felt like maybe you wouldn't want to ever see her since she was...oh, how can I say this? I don't know what to call her. She is such a sweet girl and has been through so much. She had been mistreated all her life, and she is just trying to adjust to being left alone for the first time in her life.

When Erin comes out to visit, you would think an angel had walked in. Sarah Jane asks her a million questions and relates things to her that I would never think of bringing up, much less have answers for. Erin just seems to know what to say and when. She's a marvel!"

"Please tell Sarah Jane I don't hold nothin' agin' her. I'd love to have her company. Lord knows I would have hated her before, but not now. I have Jesus to thank for that. All I feel for her is compassion and a hope she will come to know Jesus as her savior just as I have."

"She prayed with Erin while Doc was working on you. She has come to know Jesus, personally, just like you."

"Well then, there's even more reason for her to come and visit.

She's my sister in Christ, just like you are and Erin is. Praise the Lord!"

"I'm going out to cut some wood," Cade said. Something was troubling his heart, and he just needed to be alone.

"Need some help?" Wade asked.

"Nope, just don't let the soup burn. You might need to get the cornbread going."

"I can do that, Wade, if you'll show me where things are," Daisy said as she smiled at him.

"Sure, come on in her'."

Katie and Marta looked at each other.

"Marta, when did the boys get interested in girls?"

"Just now, I reckon."

Both women laughed, and Katie pulled out a chair, sat down, and starting rubbing her rounded stomach. "My, I feel like I've been liftin' a bundle of bricks today. I need to get a load off my feet."

"Well, you are carrying a mighty precious load there now, aren't you?"

"You're so right. This little one is mighty active. He just kicks all the time!"

"I sure know how that feels! Try carrying two!"

"One's enough, thanks."

"Truthfully, Katie, how is the shop goin'?"

"Now, Marta, you know Erin probably better than anyone. She is a very capable seamstress and an extremely good businessperson. She has quite a few Christmas orders and is always stitching on something everywhere she goes. She made the most beautiful hand-stitched handkerchiefs while we visited the last time she came out."

"Now, I wonder who that is," Marta said, cocking her head when she heard a horse gallop up. "Wade, someone's here. Go see who it is, please."

Wade nodded and went to the door. Just as he got to it, someone soundly knocked on the door. "Who is it?" Wade asked.

"Brian Daniels."

Wade opened the door, putting his gun back in his holster as he did so. "Sheriff, what's happened? You look 'most sick."

"Is your mother here?"

314

"Yes, sir, she is."

"I need to speak with her. May I?"

"Of course, com' in."

Marta had turned and was looking at the door. Katie was right there with her hand gently resting on Marta's shoulder.

Brian took off his hat and nodded at Katie. "Katie." She could see his eyes had turned a dark blue and seemed filled with deep emotion.

"Mrs. Tucker, I'm so sorry to have to tell you this— Oscar's dead."

"Dead? How?" Tears were brimming in her eyes. Katie gasped and covered her mouth.

Wade put his hand on Brian's arm. "Wait. Let me get Cade in here."

He walked to the back door, opened it, and hollered, "Cade, c'mere, quick! Hurry!" And then, he shut the door. "It's blasted cold out there. Are we goin' ta have snow, ya reckon?"

"I don't know. It is cold though," Brian answered just as the back door opened and Cade walked in.

"What's happened?"

"Pa's dead."

"What? How?"

Brian looked each one in the face. Daisy had come out of the kitchen and was standing behind Wade. "There is no gentle way of saying this. He hanged himself in his jail cell. I left to go get his meal from the hotel, and when I got back, he was hanging in his cell. He used a torn-up sheet. He had braided it, so it wasn't something done on the spur of the moment. He had to have been planning this. I'm so sorry. I just feel awful that I didn't say more to him about Jesus."

"He wouldna listened. I tried to tell him about Jesus and his forgiveness, but look what it got me." Marta's sad eyes looked Brian in the eye. Somehow, she conveyed to him that he was not to blame himself. "Oscar was a grown man, an' he's the only one responsible for his decisions. Tain't lak he never'd heard about Jesus. He just couldn't stand the name, much less the man. I'm sorry he will be sufferin' for eternity, but that was his choice."

"Least ways he won't beat ya no more, Ma," Cade said.

"He won't beat none a us'uns," Wade added.

"No, no, that he won't." One single tear slowly ran down Marta's cheek. "But he had been a better man before. I jest don' know what came over him. My ma and pa didn't trust him and didn't want me to marry him, but I wouldna listen to 'em. Shoulda."

"Marta, what do you want us to do? We will take care of all the details for you. You don't need to go back to town yet. We can take you for the funeral."

"Won't be no funeral. He didn't believe in God. We might as well just bury him. Maybe Riley can say a prayer over the casket for anyone who is there to not go the same way, but I don't think we need anything else."

"Ma, you don't need to go. It's too cold, and we don't want anything to happen to you. With Pa dead, maybe Daisy or Sarah Jane can stay here with you while we go to the buryin'. Don't seem right, none a us showin' up."

"I'll pay for the pine box. Either one a you boys want the smithy or livery?" Marta asked. She was very calm.

Brian looked at her in wonder at how calm she was. That one tear proved to be the only testament to her grief. She had loved him at one time, but his cruelty, especially of late, had driven from her heart what remained of that love.

"No, ma'am, I don't want neither of 'em," Cade said with an edge of bitterness in his voice.

"I'd like to think on it fer a bit, Ma. I know I don't want the smithy, but I might be interested in the livery. I really like messin' with horses, but I love ranchin' too! Let me think on it, a'right?"

"Sure, son, think on it all you want. I'll go ahead and see if'n anyone wants to be the blacksmith. We need one."

Brian looked at her. "Mrs. Tucker, we will have to see what bills Oscar had and pay those off first."

"That's fine, Sheriff. If you will compile those fer me since I'm sure not goin' into town anytime soon, I would appreciate it. I'll take care of his bills. Now, if you would inquire into who might be interested in being our blacksmith, I'd appreciate that as well." Brian and Kate looked at her doubtfully. "Now, Marta, Oscar may have run up some considerable bills at the saloon."

"I know it. With Breland too probably. I'll cover what he can't with what's left of what he has in the bank, under the bed, or wherever he kept his money recently. He didn't trust me, so he moved it frequently. But who was it that cleaned that house? Me! I found it eventually. He would give me a little grocery money, and I made do on that. But you forget, Sheriff, Katie, I do have my own business. I guess he thought I wasn't makin' anything on it. Well, I did, and there is plenty to cover his indiscretions. I don't know if I'll ever be able to sew anymore; only God knows that. I'm not worried, though, 'cause Erin has it covered. She's a marvel! God sent her to me just in time. I guess he knew I'd need her. She's the one who really introduced me to Jesus. Esther kept tellin' me, but I wouldn't listen. It took Erin livin' him right in front of my eyes. Now, that girl has a story to tell. I don't know who all is ready to hear it, but it's powerful."

"Excuse me," Daisy quietly said. "The corn bread and soup are ready. I set another place for you, Sheriff. I figured you were as hungry as the rest of us. I'll put it on the table while everyone gets seated."

For a slight moment, there was shocked silence. It seemed everyone else had forgotten about Daisy. Katie got up and moved her chair closer to the table. That prompted Brian to help Marta and the rest began to move into the places set.

33

ut you can't leave! It seems like you just got here." Erin had tears brimming in her eyes threatening to spill over the edge like a waterfall.

"I won't be gone long. I have some important business to take care of in Houston, and I'll be back by Thanksgiving, before if things go as I plan. Believe me, I'll be back! Please don't cry. Just trust me, trust God. This is for the best."

"Can't you tell me why you're going?"

"Stage leaving! Get on board!" the driver yelled.

"I have to go. I'll send you a telegram."

With that, Captain McBride stepped up into the stage, and in a breath, it rolled away.

Erin rested one hand over her heart and the other clutched a handkerchief over her mouth. She would not cause a scene in the street, but as soon as she could get back to her little home over the shop, she was going to cry like a baby. That was her plan, and she would not be deterred.

"What is wrong, Erin?"

"Oh, Riley!" Erin threw herself into his arms and began to cry right there on Main Street where the entire world could see. His arms gently encircled her, and he began to pat her back. "I think my heart is going to break!"

"Please, Erin, tell me what has happened?" He was completely surprised by her physical touch. He almost became breathless.

Never had he imagined the feel of her to be so thrilling. He needed to get her somewhere where he could release her or he would begin kissing her right there in front of everyone watching. He opened his eyes and could see several of the women of Crystal Springs stood with their mouths agape. He released his hold on Erin, not suddenly, but caringly. He put both hands on her upper arms, looked her in the eye, and smiled.

"I think I'd better get you back to your shop. Then we can talk about this in private. Do you think you can walk without assistance?"

Erin's eyes bulged. She put her handkerchief up to her mouth and nodded her head.

Riley offered her his arm. She looked at it and then around them and then back at him and shook her head. She slowly put her arm through his and with a slight stumble began walking back to her shop.

Once inside, she all but fell onto the small love seat in the sitting area.

"Oh, Riley, what am I going to do? He left me and didn't even explain why!"

"Are you talking about Captain McBride?" Riley asked and couldn't keep the relief out of his voice.

"Yes. Why would he do that? He just suddenly left."

"He is coming back, isn't he?"

"Well, he said he was, before Thanksgiving, if everything went as he planned."

"Then why are you so upset? He just needed to go and take care of something that came up, I suppose. Things like that happen all the time."

"But not to me!"

"May I?" Riley asked, indicating the seat next to her.

"Certainly. I'm so sorry. How rude of me."

"Thank you. Raven, I mean Erin. Please listen to me. You are upset. You have had just over a week to visit with him, and some pretty haughty people have been demanding you finish their holiday dresses and other sewn gifts before even the Advent weeks are upon us. You have felt compelled to work on things, and you don't have Marta to help. Daisy has been of some assistance but not so much as she would if she had had more training. There just has not been time. A few women in this town just need to know the love of Jesus, then they would be more understanding." Riley hadn't even realized he had put his arm around her shoulders as he sat next to her.

Erin turned, patting her eyes and cheeks. "You are right. I just was taken by surprise. If I had known ahead of time he was leaving, we could have had a farewell dinner last night. Instead, we had a quick supper in the hotel.

"I know. Remember, I was there."

"Oh yes. Sorry." Erin's cheeks turned a brighter shade of pink when she realized she had forgotten all about Riley. "How about I fix some tea?"

"That, my dear, would be lovely."

Erin disappeared and was gone a little while. The bell over the door jingled. Riley stood and faced Mrs. Jakes as she came in.

"Oh, Mr. Riley. I didn't expect to see you here. Where is Erin?"

"She went to fix some tea, Mrs. Jakes. Would you care for some? I believe there are plenty of cups and things here for a whole gaggle, I mean group, of ladies to have tea."

"Is Erin upset about something? I've never seen her cry before."

"Her dearest friend in the world, an uncle who took her in when she needed help, had to suddenly leave. She was not ready for him to go, and it upset her to have to say good-bye so soon after his arrival for a visit. Please, stay and have some tea. I think she feels very lonely right now and could use the company." *And we, or I, could use a chaperone.*

"No, thank you. I believe I have another appointment in just a few minutes."

"Before you go, Mrs. Jakes. How is your husband getting along after his close encounter with death? That in itself can be a very trying time on you all. God was very good to him that day. It doesn't seem like it was three months ago. Is he doing all right?"

"Oh, my husband, right. Well, he is doing just fine…working…and uh, all uh."

"You are very fortunate to still have him. Think how lonely you would be if he had not come back."

"Well, yes, I see what you mean."

"God bless you, Mrs. Jakes. I trust you thank God every day for his great provision for you through allowing your husband to live. You are greatly blessed, and it is good to always pass on the blessings to others. Good day to you, Mrs. Jakes."

"Good day, Pastor…I mean Mr. Riley."

He heard the bell jingle as she left. He sat down and bowed his head, then began to pray.

"Who came in?"

Erin's voice drew him from his meditation. "Mrs. Jakes. She just wanted to know what your problem was, to tell you the honest truth, so she could report back to her group of friends. "

"That sounds about right. What did you tell her?"

"The truth. Your uncle left unexpectedly, and you were upset because you wanted him to stay."

"That satisfied her?"

"Yes, after I reminded her how close she came to losing her own husband in August."

"Riley, you didn't!"

"I did. You know, I think that is what God wanted me to do. Something seemed to click with her."

Erin set the tea things down and began serving. As she reached for another cup, Riley took her hand and knelt in front of her.

"I know this may be the wrong time, but I can't wait another second. Erin, I love you with all my heart and I can't bear the thought of living without you beside me. If you feel it is God's will for your life to love me and be my wife, I would be so honored to have you as my partner in life until death do us part."

"Riley." Tears began to pool in her eyes once again. "Riley, I would be so honored to be your wife. I have never felt so complete with anyone else, not even Captain McBride. You make me whole, and I love you so much. I was afraid to love you. I was afraid of what you would say when you found out what I was, but you didn't shun me, you prayed. Oh, how that touched me. You have never physically touched me until today. I have never felt such respect given me. Riley, please touch me, now. I really need a hug."

Riley was more than happy to grant that request.

34

Ten days later, November 17

You are back! Praise God. Did you get my letter? I sent it to Sarah." Erin's eyes sparkled with unspeakable joy.

"Yes, my dear, I certainly did get your note. I brought a gift for you." Captain McBride turned and opened the door to Erin's shop. "I had to get some help with it."

Erin walked toward the door just as Sarah came through it carrying a rather large box. Erin squealed and all but ran to her. McBride quickly took the box so the women could hug one another. Tears were flowing from both sets of eyes; and, to tell the truth, McBride's eyes were a little moist as well.

"Sarah, Sarah, I can't believe it! Oh, I am so happy! My joy overflows my soul."

McBride put the box on the nearby table and turned to stand next to Sarah. "Erin, I would like to introduce you to Mrs. Patrick McBride. Sarah has been kind enough to finally say yes to my many pleas for her hand. She has been in my heart for a couple of years now and has finally seen the wisdom of marrying me."

"Oh, I am so happy for you both. Can the day get any better?"

Sarah smiled and looked up into Patrick's eyes. "Yes, I think maybe it can. Open your present."

"Oh, my present! The two of you are the best present ever."

Erin turned and opened the box and pulled back the paper covering the most beautiful wedding dress she had ever seen. "But how did you know? I, I don't think I told you Riley proposed. I wanted to tell you myself."

"Riley asked for my permission before I left. I knew that man could not wait long to ask you. I went back to Houston to see if one more plea would get her to say yes. She did. God was making the way for the rest of my plan. Sarah said she was making a wedding dress for someone who broke off her engagement after which the young man tragically was killed in a carriage accident. She wished she could give it to you because it would fit you perfectly. I suggested she do just that. Oh, there is someone else I want you to meet."

Captain McBride went back to the door and opened it. In walked a short balding man dressed all in black. "Erin, I would like for you to meet the Reverend Mr. Humphries. He has come from Houston to perform your wedding...tomorrow. Riley, you can come in now!"

Riley walked through the open door straight to Erin. He knelt in front of her once again. "Erin, when I asked before if you would be my wife, I came to you empty-handed. I would now like to ask you once again, in front of these witnesses, possessing neither riches nor fame, just a simple man asking if you will consent to be my wife."

"Riley, once again, I am happy to accept your offer regardless of how little you possess."

"Then I offer you this, a gift to me from dear Captain McBride, which I pass on to you to wear with pride and joy. It was the ring of his many long years of marriage to his beloved Catherine, who lent you her name in your escape."

"Oh! I will gladly wear it."

Riley slipped the ring onto Erin's finger. Captain McBride winked at the couple and squeezed Sarah closer to him.

Epilogue

On Friday, November 18, 1880, Riley and Erin became man and wife. The church was filled with happy people and even Marta made her way up front with both boys.

Captain McBride gave Erin away while Sarah sat as mother of the bride.

Sarah Jane, along with Daisy, came in and sat with Marta.

Adam and Esther held the reception in the hotel, and joy filled the room.

"I'm getting to be an old hand at this. I'm glad Riley gave us a few days advanced notice. It was more than Erin had. Isn't she lovely, Adam?" Esther asked when they had a moment to stop and chat.

"Yes, she is extremely lovely. Riley will be a very happy man."

"Daisy and Sarah Jane are moving into Erin's apartment.

Sarah Jane will be staying out at Katie and Josh's off and on.

Willow is excited about being here so she can help Doc with delivering Katie's baby. Since Willow and Brian are both leaving to go to school in June, Sarah Jane will move out there to help with the baby, and Todd will be the new sheriff."

"Yes, things seem to be working out. Marta has sold the smithy to Jarvis Smith, a dear friend of Rose and Julius, who has just moved here with his family. He's a kind man. Have you met him yet, my dear?"

"No, but I'm sure I will."

"I am glad Brian and Willow can travel together although they do tend to argue frequently. We will have to pray earnestly for them. They will have quite an adjustment up there in Ohio.

It's a shame they couldn't go to the same school. God knows best. Brian plans on visiting Oberlin frequently."

"Yes, they will have quite an adjustment to the weather if nothing else. Did you hear? The McBrides are taking their honeymoon on his ship with Erin and Riley in tow! About two months ago, he had the quarters changed to include two larger private rooms, and the crew's quarters are also better, how fortuitous!"

"Well, they will have a grand time together. In fact, everyone will be happy on that trip. They leave tomorrow for Houston and then will set sail on Thanksgiving. Katie wants us to have Thanksgiving out at their place and has invited the Konrads to join them. It will be an early afternoon meal and then they have activities planned for everyone. I think they have some goat chasing planned for the children. That should be fun to watch. Oh, and Brian is invited too. Now, imagine that!" Esther and Adam laughed then gave each other a hug and a quick kiss.

The next morning the stage pulled away headed toward San Antonio and then Houston. Both couples chatted until Captain McBride was breathing deeply. Sarah's head rested against his broad shoulder as she *rested* her eyes.

"I can't believe how I escaped from William. He used to call me Raven because of my black hair. Raven is my middle name but I never told him that. I hated he called me that. I don't mind you calling me that, though. You have a very biblical reason for doing so. Riley, you have truly helped me heal. The nightmares I used to have about the house in Baltimore, the men who would frequent that place, and especially William and his henchmen have ceased to wake me in the night. That is a miracle. I hope they are out of my life forever!"

Riley whispered in Erin's ear, "You have always been my

Raven. I think of Elijah and how God provided for him through the ravens. God's word tells us in 1 Kings 17:4–6.

'And it shall be, that thou shalt drink of the brook; and I have commanded the ravens to feed thee there. So, he went and did according unto the word of the Lord; for he went and dwelt by the brook Cherith, that is before Jordan. And the ravens brought him bread and flesh in the morning, and bread and flesh in the evening; and he drank from the brook.'

"You have nothing to fear. I will protect you, God will protect you, and his angels will protect you," Riley said as he leaned over and gave her a sweet, promising kiss.

Several hours later, in the late afternoon, another stage pulled up in front of the Crystal Springs Hotel.

"LeFleur, she better be here. I'm tired of lookin' through every nothin' town in Texas. I want to get back to New Orleans or even back to Baltimore." The man spit, dusted his clothes off with his hat, and scowled at the town in general.

"Shut up your complaining, John. If I had realized it was her when we were on the stage, she'd have never gotten off in Houston. Who would have thought that old lady was actually a bird escapin' the cage? You and your contacts were supposed to keep an eye on every hotel."

"We did. I told you I thought that was her voice the night she checked in. How was I to know he gave her a different room?"

"Well, we better find her soon. William will kill us if we don't!"

As the men looked up, a dog growled at them from under the raised boardwalk in front of the hotel.

Author's Thoughts

It seems domestic violence is on the increase. Perhaps there is more media coverage as high-profile men face charges of domestic violence and rape. Demonstrations on campuses tell of the long-existing problem of drugged rape and gang rape with accusations of Administration turning a blind eye and even at times being accused of making the girl or girls feel it was their fault the rape occurred.

The national government did not pass a law against violence toward women and sexual harassment in the workplace until 1978. In the 1800s and later, some states had tried to pass legislation protecting women, but the laws were found to be unconstitutional. Even now, a woman can have a judge give her a restraining order, yet nothing seems to be done until the man actually does something to her to violate that order. Too many times, the "thing" done is murder. Then we find, for that woman, it was too late. Many of the men who are the ones being restrained say that it only makes them madder at the woman. They end up planning more violence rather than leaving her alone.

The violence starts at a young age. I have seen girls in elementary through high school have to suffer incestuous relationships, sexual bullying from both sexes at school and through social media, and even rape sometimes as they are walking home from school. Many of the pregnancies were from forced relations. By the time the girl is in high school, she has the mind-set of not being liked if she doesn't go all the way with the boy she likes that week. So many times I have been told by the pregnant girl that she is going to keep her baby because she wants someone to love her. They just don't realize how very selfish babies are. The demands put on the mother by the needs of that child so often keep a teen mother from finishing school. There are many childless couples who would love to adopt a child, and yet, it is harder and harder for them to find a child in the United States. As a result, they look in foreign countries for a child they can love and nurture.

Jesus treated women with respect and actually set a new standard for women during the time he walked the earth. Today, women who grew up in Christian homes and married men who hold to biblical truth understand the love and comfort of their savior, Jesus. Many women are protected from the violence by the presence of the Holy Spirit in their lives. However, like Erin, they go through horrific circumstances. I pray they, like Erin, find they are able to use their experiences to reach unsaved women—like Marta, Daisy, and Sarah Jane, who have suffered the same things. They need the Lord in their lives just as we do. Many times, I and others have said, "There but by the grace of God go I." We need to reach out to these women and help them.

I pray we will.